How do you choose between what's right and revenge?

"You'll let them live," I whispered hoarsely. "They've slaughtered and tortured and enslaved us, and you'll just let them live."

"No," she answered quietly. "I'll *make* them live."

"And what's the difference?" I sneered.

"Terms and conditions," she answered. "I told you I was tortured? The man who ordered that is still alive, and he's going to stay that way. In fact, he's immortal now. He's living in a comfortable pair of rooms in the middle of his home city, and he'll live there forever, nice and cozy. He can't go outside. He can't talk with another human being face-to-face. He can't even go comfortably insane. He's alive and stable, and we're going to keep him that way. He never gets away from what he's done, never gets to a better life or another life. He never meets his Maker or sees his Heaven. He gets to watch while the kingdom he built fades from the historical record and the city he ruined is rebuilt by his enemies and opened up wide, because all the people he tried to lead to his brutal salvation like his enemies' way better.

"He's ours. He's *mine*, in his two-room cell, forever and ever.

"Do you want revenge for you and yours? Help me make the Blood Family live with what they've done."

My hand [...] drum against my thigh. "I[...]

BITTER ANGELS

C. L. ANDERSON

BALLANTINE BOOKS
NEW YORK

A Spectra Mass Market Original

Copyright © 2009 by Sarah Zettel

Published in the United States by Spectra, an imprint of The Random
House Publishing Group, a division of Random House, Inc., New York.

SPECTRA and the portrayal of a boxed "s" are trademarks
of Random House, Inc.

ISBN: 978-0-553-59217-7

Cover design by Jamie S. Warren
Cover illustration by Chris McGrath

Printed in the United States of America

www.ballantinebooks.com

9 8 7 6 5 4 3 2 1

This book is dedicated to my husband, Tim.

ACKNOWLEDGMENTS

The author would like to thank Juliet Ulman and David Pomerico for all their help bringing this book into existence, and, as always, the Untitled and Excelsior writers' groups who patiently sat through many drafts.

PROLOGUE

DONNELLY

Nikko Donnelly stood beside the sealed, arched air lock, his attention fixed on the screen in front of him. He did not even glance at the wonders in the black sky outside. He spent far too much time staring out at them as it was. Instead, he watched the ship finishing its approach to Habitat 3. It was a badly thought-out and desperately maintained collection of tubes and spheres, only capable of lumbering between thin atmosphere and no atmosphere.

Donnelly was wizened, grizzled, and tired; tired of himself, tired of his world, tired of more things than he could name. His people called him "Old Donnelly" behind his back and "Sir" to his face, because whatever else he was, he remained the commander of Habitat 3 in the Erasmus System.

The Erasmus System's first human colonists had tightly focused imaginations and never got around to naming their space stations, let alone any of the purely decorative worlds that could be seen from its windows. They all went about their orbits tagged with codes for use by pilots and the flight controllers; R3ES1, R3ES2, Habitat 1, Habitat 2, and so on.

Outside, the clumsy ship matched Habitat 3's spin and eased its docking bolts toward the port. The magnets seized tight. The red lights beside the air lock's polished-metal door blinked to green.

Donnelly could imagine the crew letting out sighs of relief. One more run completed, and once more, everything held. Unfeeling as he was, Donnelly had enough sympathy for the crew that he cycled quickly through the checks coming up on the ancient screen. Once this would have been done automatically, but it had proved too easy to hack the commands and let uninvited guests onto the habitats. Donnelly did not consider himself a slow learner.

When it came to machines, at any rate.

At last, Habitat 3 gave him permission to pressurize the air locks and cargo bay. He laid his palm on the door's access pad, and the metal door shuddered as it rose.

The cargo bay was a cavernous, meticulously clean place. Shining white composite coated its deck and curving walls. Red lines on the floor marked off unloading bays. Blank black screens and access pads dotted the walls behind the bays.

Once, six or seven ships a day had docked here. Now, the chamber echoed to the sound of Donnelly's footsteps as he stumped across the deck. A single line of half-rusted pallet carts waited beside the outer air lock. All the rest of the equipment was in storage, and no one, least of all Donnelly, expected it to be brought out again.

Donnelly palmed the next access pad and the sleek white inner door lifted away to reveal the outer air lock and the incoming ship's battered, soot-streaked door. That door hissed loudly as it slid open.

The first person to step into Donnelly's empty cargo bay was a little man with neatly curled black hair. He came from a world where brilliant color was the fashion, but he himself wore sparkling black and gleaming white: black coat, white trousers, polished black boots, white gloves. Donnelly, in his battered boots and heavy work jacket, shunted his jaw back and forth a few times to keep from sneering.

"Good to see you again, Nikko," said the little man.

"Bloom." Donnelly nodded. "How's the run?"

Bloom shrugged in answer. "Too long, too cramped, and too cold, but we all do as we must. Are you ready for us?"

"Cleared out level five. Dare and his people were here a week ago, but they only filled it up by about a quarter."

"Good. They've warned you the runs are going to pick up tempo for a while?"

Donnelly nodded, more than a little annoyed that Bloom didn't think he knew his job. What was worse, however, was that this time Donnelly really *didn't* know what his job was. He'd been told to make sure the habitat was in top working order. He'd been told to start minimizing the internal supports and furnishings, and maximizing the holding capacity, but no one had told him why.

"Better get to it, then," Donnelly grunted.

"As you say," agreed Bloom blandly.

Behind Bloom, the ship's cargo doors slid back to reveal a solid wall of silver canisters, each one about the size of Bloom's torso. The ship's crew, a group as hardened as Donnelly—with even less use for Bloom than Donnelly had—began sliding out pallets full of the canisters and stacking them on the waiting carts.

The gravity was light, but inertia was in good working order, and the massive cargo took careful handling. Only once did a worker, a young man with a stubbly chin and one eye sealed half-shut by an old burn, look up at the mismatched set of supervisors.

"What are these things?" he asked, clipping a strap around a full load of pallets.

Bloom beat Donnelly to it. "They're your cargo, and your job is to shift them."

"Yeah, but . . ."

"Yeah, but, what?" Bloom expertly mocked his nasal young voice. "Are you getting paid to do your job or to stand around with your flap open?"

The crewman muttered under his breath and glanced at his captain. The man grimaced. An amethyst tooth flashed in the harsh light as he signaled for patience.

Bloom just turned away.

"You say these are to go to level five?" he asked Donnelly.

"Yeah." Donnelly nodded.

"I can take it from here. You can go back to your other duties."

Donnelly clenched his jaw, knowing that he had no real duties to return to, a fact that stung worse than his casual dismissal and even worse than being stuck in this echoing tin can, utterly and completely dependent on people he couldn't trust and who didn't give a good goddamn about him, blood ties or no.

"I don't suppose you're going to tell me what's going on either," he muttered to Bloom.

Bloom's smile was thin and mirthless. "No, I don't suppose I am."

"Do you actually know?"

This time, Bloom just shrugged. "I don't particularly care."

Donnelly knew he should let it go, but he couldn't. He was tired and he was cold. He knew things were coming to a head. He didn't know how or why, but he did know how deadly ignorance could be.

"The First Bloods are gonna fuck you over with the rest of us, do you know that much?"

"Oh, no," replied Bloom softly. "Not this time."

ONE

TERESE

"Bianca's dead. We need you to come back."

That was how it started for me. A few words, and Misao Smith's familiar voice.

Bianca's dead.

I stood there, staring at my handset while those words sank through brain and blood to tangle around my guts. Behind me, the noise from Allie's twenty-fifth-birthday dinner kept on. We were holding it on our glassed-in balcony. Outside, Lake Superior's turbulent waters were as iron grey as the low blanket of clouds overhead. Allie sat at the head of the confetti-littered table, laughing in that odd hiccoughing way she's had ever since she was four, while Jo and Dale gave each other shit about . . . something. Any second, David was going to tell the two of them to calm down. Then they'd start giving the old man shit for treating them like they were all still four.

I hadn't switched the screen on. I remember being vaguely grateful for the oversight. This way, my family wouldn't see who interrupted Allie's day.

Bianca's dead.

I hadn't seen Bianca for over three decades, but I hadn't forgotten her for a single day. She was my first mentor in the Guardians, and my best friend for my entire service.

"Terese?" asked Misao coolly.

"Yeah, yeah. I'm still here." Mostly. Part of me stood beside Bianca, seeing her toss her hair back over her shoulder, like she did when she was getting serious. Nothing could convince her to cut that hair, even though it constantly got in her way.

Bianca's dead.

"How . . . ?"

"I can't tell you on this set." Misao's voice was flat, final, and annoyed.

I pinched the bridge of my nose hard, trying to get the pain to focus me. My hand started to twitch. In another second I'd be shaking. The happy family noises all fell away. David and the kids had noticed something was wrong.

Misao let out a long sigh, the sound of strained patience. "Will you come in?"

The thousand things I could say flashed through my mind. *Misao, it's my kid's birthday, for God's sake! What happened? Tell me what happened! No! I'm done with this. I promised them all I was done!*

Silence behind me. Silence on the handset.

"Tomorrow," I said.

"There's no . . ."

But I switched it off and turned away. My whole family was staring at me.

My family. My life and heart distributed among four separate lives. Dark, intense Allie, home tonight for the family celebration and out tomorrow with her friends doing things I suspect I wouldn't want to know about. Jo, our middle child, had dyed herself white to stand out in our little crowd. Dale, my youngest, my son, the earth-brown image of his father with the same eyes set in his handsome young face.

His father, my husband, David stood up and walked around the table.

"What's happened? Who was that?"

I couldn't answer. I just held out the set, and he saw the name. He sucked in his breath sharply. Behind us, all the kids cast glances at each other. There gets to be a kind of telepathy in a family. There are words you stop needing to say. In ours they were "the Guardians."

"They want me to go in tomorrow," I said.

"Will you?"

I nodded.

"Terese . . ." He drew my name out into a warning.

I tried to dismiss it. "Misao won't let me alone until I hear them out, David. The sooner I do, the sooner I can tell him to . . . bugger off." My voice was far weaker than I wanted it to be, a fact that David did not miss.

"What else did he say?"

I met his gaze, oddly helpless. "Bianca."

He saw the tears at the corner of my eyes, and he knew the rest.

David folded me in his arms and rested his hand on the back of my head. I closed my eyes, breathing in his scent, willing myself to sink into his warmth and remain solidly in the safe, whole present. But my mind wouldn't let go. I kept seeing Bianca: dark, stout, stubborn Bianca, with her gleaming eyes. Smart, fast, ruthless, fearless. Canny in ways I couldn't begin to match. Where had she been deployed? I didn't know. I'd lost track.

When the hell did I start losing track?

"Come on." David kissed the top of my head. "We haven't cut the cake yet."

"Right. Right." I wiped at my eyes and attempted to smile at my children, none of whom smiled back. I sat down at our table and handed Allie the knife. But the party was really over, and we all knew it.

Four in the morning. I couldn't sleep and I was back in the dining room. We turned off the noise filters at night, so I could hear Lake Superior's waves rushing up to the shore. The late-November wind muttered out there, piling up the heavy clouds. The weight of the air told me snow rode on the back of that wind. The moon had gone down, and the windows were utterly black. I could see myself clearly; a faded ghost in a satin robe wavering in the depths of the black glass. I smiled grimly at the thought. By rights, I should have been a ghost by now.

I rubbed behind my ear; the very bottom of the curve between my skull and my neck. There was nothing but smooth skin there now, but I still carried the harsh memory of the wound and the pain, where they'd cut out my Companion.

The Companion is the tool and backup each field officer in the Guardians is given just in case they are captured in a war zone. The Companion is a friend, a reminder, a helper, and, if you're extremely unlucky, he or she is the witness to your death.

They are also one of the few secrets the Guardians actually keep. I should say kept. They're certainly not a secret anymore.

During the Redeemer Uprising four decades ago, I was captured. I was tossed in a dark cell and dragged out on occasion so I could be made to experience a lot of pain. My captors managed to detect my Companion and when they did, they cut it out of me, quickly and brutally. Then they tossed me back into the dark.

It was Bianca who rescued me. She pulled me out of that black hole.

She saved my life.

That was what made this so bad. Bianca was dead, and not only was I not there to save her, I hadn't even known she was in danger.

The sound of Dale's snoring cut through all my heavy thoughts, accompanied by the soft breathing of the heat pump. Something beeped in the kitchen. In the living room, something else pinged in answer.

Night noises. Home noises.

This wasn't the first place David and I lived together, or even the third. We'd bumped up against each other occasionally over the years before we got married in the middle of what you could call unsettled times in our lives. We were well into our third centuries then—that time when most people had officially launched from their second families and were starting to build their third. David had left his birth family and tried a marriage family, but it hadn't gone anywhere and he hadn't tried again. I was trying to create something I could call normality as fast as I could. He found me fascinating, in a wounded-bird kind of way. I found him wonderful, in a lifeline kind of way. It was mutual need that passed for love, and we got married.

Under those conditions, we moved around a lot. Bangkok. Moscow. San Francisco. We had an apartment up the Adas Apaba cable for a while, and then there was the year down in Marianas. It was there, we, or rather I, hit bottom literally as well as figuratively. David threatened to leave, which finally got me into the kind of treatment, both mental and physical, that I'd been refusing for years.

When I got out, we found this place in the middle of Lake Superior. Whitecap was a new, small town on a new, small island. We both craved peace and quiet, but we believed it was just for a little while.

Instead, that desire broadened and deepened. Against the odds, our tumult turned into real love, for this place and for each other. We built and added and accumulated and stored. We found out which restaurants we both liked and where the good doctors and stylists were. There were more exciting places to be, and some even more beautiful, but we were settled. Settled enough that the morning the house-doc put up the flag that I was carrying our first child, we did nothing but celebrate.

I heard a step on the bare floor and straightened, instantly alert. Some instincts do not go away. David's reflection moved to join mine in the black glass, getting closer, until I could feel his warmth against my skin.

"Do you think it's because of the Erasmus System?" His breath stirred my hair. Picking conversations back up, even after hours of silence, was something he'd always done.

"It's got to be. That's the only one I'm doing analysis on right now."

We were silent for a while. There was only one question in his solemn eyes, and I waited for him to ask it.

"Why are they calling you in? You could give them all your current analysis over the set."

"I don't know." What I didn't say was how much it scared me that Misao had called at all. If the Guardians were calling in thirty-year retirees, it meant one of the dozen hot spots I knew about, plus any new ones I might not, was close to exploding into actual war.

War. The ancient, perverse, pervasive nightmare we'd banished from the Solar System with the Pax Solaris, the Common Cause Covenant, and the Laws of Humanity. I'd dedicated my life to preventing its return as human beings spread themselves out into the galaxy. The effort nearly took my sanity and my life. I'd tried to retire, to enjoy the peace I'd helped to keep, but it seemed war had come down to find me. I looked up at the clouds and wondered what was behind them.

"You could refuse," said David. I didn't even have to respond to that. David's mouth twisted up. Distaste, or just frustration? I couldn't tell, and that bothered me.

"I'm sorry, David." Sorry for being what I was. Sorry for not having worked harder to crush that last little stone in my heart that still had the word DUTY carved on it. It hurt, that stone, and I wanted it gone.

I faced David, putting my back to the darkness outside the house and inside my own thoughts. I had to tilt my head far back to look into his eyes and my chest constricted.

"Maybe it was always borrowed time anyway," I murmured. "Maybe we should just be grateful for what we've had."

"Don't say that," he whispered fiercely. "We did not borrow our life together. We earned it. We fought for it."

He wrapped me in his arms and I leaned against him so my ear pressed against his heart. It beat in a soft, steady counterpoint to the rhythm of the waves outside.

"Come back to bed," he breathed in my ear.

"If I haven't slept by now, I'm not going to."

"So we won't sleep. Come back to bed."

I let him steer me back to our room, past the sounds of our sleeping offspring. I let him thumb the privacy screen into place, turning the threshold opaque and soundproof, and come to me. I let him peel my robe slowly off my shoulders and send it whispering down to the floor so we could be skin to skin with the sound of the wind and the waves all around us. I let him stroke me and touch me until I didn't care what was waiting on the other side of night's darkness, as long as I had this moment and David's warmth beneath my hands.

And in the end, I did sleep.

TWO

AMERAND

It was Emiliya Varus who warned me Terese would become important in my life.

I was in bad shape when I arrived on Hospital, one of the Erasmus System's inhabited moons, named, like the others, after its purpose. Most of my fuel and ballast were gone, burned up during a run after water smugglers. Somewhere in the excitement, a safety belt broke, sending our third, Marko Keich, careening across the cockpit. He now had a gash in his head, another on his hand, and a vague look in his eyes that made me suspect major concussion.

We had to drift into port on inertia and minuscule readjustments. Emiliya was there waiting for us at the bottom of the elevator.

"Hello, Brother Amerand," she said as she shoved the gurney forward so Ceshame and I could lay Marko out on it.

"Hello, Sister Emiliya." Emiliya was no relation to me that either of us knows, but this was the polite greeting between Oblivion's children.

She bent over Marko, probing the scabbing wounds with her long, pale fingers. She had inherited pale skin, light hair, and blue eyes from her long-absent father, but her delicate frame was a consequence of our environment. Strength and fitness training were mandatory for medical personnel, as they were for the Security, but no matter how hard she worked, her build remained slender, almost attenuated.

Marko screamed as Emiliya's long, sharp fingers hit a

particularly sore spot. My second, Ceshame, rolled his eyes to Leda, who'd come out of the elevator behind us with the ship's official record in her hand. I took it from her, noted that the seal was intact, and passed it to one of the Clerks waiting behind Emiliya.

The First Bloods, the family who ran and owned the Erasmus System, did not like electronic networks. They were too easy to turn against those in power, so they developed something more in keeping with the Erasmus System in general, a network of dedicated bureaucratic spies with a truly banal name.

The Clerks came out of the military academy, just like the secops did. They were, in fact, what the majority of the cadets there turned into. Almost nobody actually wanted to be a Clerk. Almost nobody liked them. But then, how do you like the person whose job it is to hold you hostage?

"You will report for debriefing in four hours, Captain Jireu," the Clerk said. Her voice was thin and high, and poked uncomfortably at my ears. I bowed. She signaled to her colleague, who pushed past us and disappeared into the elevator. "You two can come with me now." She crooked her finger at Ceshame and Leda. My crew kept their faces strictly neutral as they followed after her around the corridor into the main hospital complex. Standard Operating Procedure; do not give us any more time to coordinate stories. Who knew? We might have somehow been in league with the smugglers whose ship we'd just hulled.

Emiliya was sponging the blood off Marko's face. He lay still on the gurney, eyes shut and face relaxed. I guessed she had given him a sedative. She lifted her eyes to meet mine.

"This is minor, Amerand," she told me. "Painful and inconvenient, but minor. We'll put the patches on and install him in observation, just to make sure everything takes. All right?"

"You'll do it?" Emiliya Varus and I grew up together. When I got put into the Security, she got put into the Medical. She not only survived the competition in that academy, she made it all the way through the university, not at the highest level, but she did reach the rank of General Physician. This qualified her to work on temporary and sudden conditions, things that didn't involve tinkering on the cellular level. Breaks and burns, cuts and tears, were specialties of hers, as were a whole host of things she called "inorganic alterations," which, as near as I could understand it, primarily involved people trying to smuggle contraband under their own skins.

As a result, she saw a lot of the Security, and we saw a lot of her. I didn't owe Marko much, but he was one of my people, and I wanted him in the hands of someone I trusted.

"I can. It won't take long." Emiliya considered. "How about I meet you up in Lounge 12?"

"All right," I agreed as she got behind the gurney and started pushing. "See you in a few." I made a half bow as she steered Marko around the corner, taking the left-hand branch. I took the right, moving into the pastel-and-silver complex that was Hospital.

With exceptions in a few dormitory areas reserved for paying patients, Hospital was not made to imitate a surface city. The shafts, train chutes, and pedestrian corridors all had an enclosed feel to them. There were few places you were permitted to go, and no arrangements made for relaxation or entertainment once you got there, unless you went up to the public port yards.

The floors Hospital and its committees reserved for the

Security were not top tier, but they were comfortable. We got private rooms for sleeping, sitting rooms wired for entertainment, and small, well-catered dining areas to ourselves. The light was full-spectrum and steady, fading and brightening to give us a full day and a solid night that were comforting in ways I only understood in the wordless bottom of my mind.

Lounge 12 was plain but serviceable, and at the moment empty, except for a fragile-looking man whom I thought I might recognize from other times. A fair number of Oblivion's children ended up permanently on Hospital. There were no gangs there, and plenty of food and water, which made it a good berth, even if you were only waiting on the medical personnel.

I took a corner booth. Because of our light gravity, we went in for fixed and solid furniture. The booths and tables, lounges and couches, were metal-framed with spring seats and thick cushions—all bolted to the floor. The man I half recognized hurried over with a teapot and a stoneware mug. He didn't meet my eyes as he set them down, and he hurried away quickly after fulfilling my request for a second mug. I let him go. He didn't want me to know him and I didn't have any reason to go against his wishes.

Except for that shy man and the softly humming service drones cleaning the carpets and walls, I had the place to myself. I poured myself a mug of tarry black tea powerful enough to strip paint. I had drunk about half when Emiliya finally walked through the door.

"Hello again, Sister Emiliya," I said. She slid into the booth beside me. I filled the other mug and pushed it toward her.

"Hello again, Brother Amerand. You're looking well." I suppose this was mostly true. I have enough hard work in my life that my bones are strong and my body in proportion with itself.

"And you," I answered politely. Actually, what struck me was that Emiliya looked halfway to wrecked. She wore the traditional white coat and trousers of her profession. Her gloves were spotless, but the rest of her uniform was rumpled. I'd have said it looked like she'd slept in it, but I was certain she hadn't been anywhere near her bed for at least twenty-four hours.

"So, what've they got you doing?" I asked casually.

"What haven't they got me doing?" she grumbled. Her sharp-boned face was drawn tight. Lines had etched themselves deep in her high forehead and between her brows. "There's a whole lot of screech and clash about this new bunch of saints coming out of the Pax Solaris."

"What, more charity workers?" *Why would there be any screech about Solaran charity workers?* But I didn't let that question make it past my eyes.

Emiliya shrugged her bony shoulders, irritated. "I suppose. But in addition to my regular shifts, I've been in half a dozen different conferences about the new precautions and procedures we're going to have for them. Orders from Fortress," she added softly.

What does Fortress care about the Solaris saints? Better question: What have the saints done to make Fortress care? But all I did was lift my eyebrows and take another sip of tea.

The only people of the Pax Solaris I knew directly were those who were permitted in to assist with humanitarian relief. We of Erasmus once were very rich, or rather, the free among us were relatively rich and the Blood Family was astoundingly rich. Since the invention of the internal drive for faster-than-light travel, however, there was much less wealth to go around and the Blood Family had become willing to let other people feed and care for those they could not make money from.

Emiliya took another drink and pulled a face. "They're shunting them all over to your lot on Dazzle . . ."

"Oh, joy."

"And I'm in charge of 'data acquisition.'" She softly smiled at me. "At least we'll be able to see something of each other."

"Data acquisition?" I said.

Emiliya nodded slowly. "Just bioscans and sample gathering, but it's all fairly high priority." Behind us, the cleaner drones hummed, gliding back and forth across the carpet, and back and forth across the walls. "It's a great opportunity," Emiliya added. "I'm really glad to have a chance to make the new program a success."

We sat silent for a moment. As a Security captain, my clearances were higher than hers. Theoretically, there was nothing she could tell me that I couldn't hear, but we both knew enough not to trust to that too much. The cleaner navigated the curve around our booth and drifted away, sliding under one of the empty tables, searching for crumbs.

Here's the thing about constant surveillance—the question you must ask yourself is not "Am I being overheard?" but "Is anybody *paying attention* to me?" Emiliya was involved in a change of routine. She had very good reason to suspect that the Clerks were paying attention. She had to be very careful, and I had to respect that.

"How's my mother?" Emiliya asked suddenly.

"She's well, and Parisch sends his love." I kept Emiliya's family on my patrol schedule, whether I needed to or not.

"Can you take a letter for me?"

"Anytime. I'm here for at least another six hours. You can

leave it at Port 9 for me to pick up." Screen calls home were expensive. The access fees would be added to what she owed Fortress, which—on top of the costs of her education, her housing, her board, her breathing—was quite a lot. Emiliya was grimly determined to pay her debt off. I wondered if this new duty might come with a bonus and if that was why she'd taken it on.

Emiliya nodded, gulped her tea, and looked toward the closed door for a long moment. The wall cleaner clicked across a seam and back again. The floor cleaner's hum dropped a little as it bumped over the floor vent.

We talked of this and that, old friends catching up, nothing more. Every now and then we tossed in something positive about our missions and assignments for form's sake, until finally Emiliya finished the last of her tea. "I'll see you out there," she said.

"We go where we're needed," I acknowledged.

I cleared the mugs and the teapot, handing them off to the kitchen man. Emiliya touched my arm in parting and gave me her softest smile. I covered her hand, a friendly gesture, nothing more.

Sometimes I wanted more from her, and sometimes, I thought, she wanted more from me. But those times had never seemed to synch up properly.

At least that was what I believed then. It was certainly easier.

We parted ways. She went to her duties, I went to my debriefing, which was no more unpleasant than those things ever were. The high-voiced Clerk played the record over for me, stopping at key points to ask questions, which I answered as briefly as I could.

In the end, she could find no reason to hold me and I

was released with permission to leave for Dazzle in nine hours.

Which left me with rather a lot of time to kill. I left a message for Emiliya and headed up to Port 9.

Port 9 was the biggest of the public ports on Hospital. It had an air lock at its entrance and orderlies who checked you through and scanned you thoroughly to make sure you were not walking off with any unauthorized cargo or walking in with unexpected microbial passengers.

I checked out clean and was allowed to enter. When the air-lock door wheezed open, a fog of odor and noise rolled out. In front of me spread a hive of motion and color packed into a cavern that was too big to take in with a single glance, but still felt too small to hold the crowd. The scent of hot oil wrapped the rapid clatter of conversation. Shouts of greeting or of winning gamblers rode waves of citrus and carbon grease. The black sky opened above the transparent ceiling. The gaudy spheres of the gas giants, and the gleaming white disk of Fortress, all ice and vigilance, looked down on us all.

I steeled myself against the black vacuum with its white eye and strode into the crowds.

Hospital was the one Erasmus moon that had never ceased to operate on a twenty-four-hour schedule, so the yard was crammed whenever you arrived. Its chaotic passthroughs were hemmed in by food and drink stalls or larger insulated structures where you could rent a bed for whatever you might need a bed for. There were entertainment stalls and cubicles, and screens for receiving news or sending messages, which, of course, recorded and stored everything that passed through them. There were even some legal gambling venues, always very popular. And as in any port, there was a sort of floating hiring fair going on for those ships lucky enough to have trading licenses.

Despite the constant traffic, the port arcade's carpets were immaculate. The polished walls gleamed from constant cleaning, but you couldn't hear the drones' hums and clicks over the rumble and rush of human activity. Which was part of the point. What with the food, games, and cheap drink, you were supposed to forget about them. I suppose it worked sometimes, because the Clerks kept the system rigidly in place.

I stopped at an information booth and my uniform got me instant access to a screen so I could check on the status of my ship and the whereabouts of my remaining crew. Leda and Ceshame had lost no time availing themselves of port privileges. As long as they turned up vertical and sober in six hours, I wasn't going to complain.

I rambled through the port, browsing the goods, eyeing my fellow visitors. My uniform was looked at with a nod by some and a suspicious squint by others. At that point I was not paying much attention to either. I was puzzling out what Emiliya had said about her new assignment and trying to fit it in with what I knew about the Blood Family's priorities, which were first, to survive, and second, to maintain their wealth.

I quickly tired of aimless rambling and turned my path toward a little stall near the center of the arcade. It had no sign, but everybody knew it as "Nana's." It was run in those days by a young woman who had grown up in the arcade and learned the secrets of cooking for its people from her mother, Nana, and her grandmother, Nana. The fish tacos and rice stew were the best you could get in the whole of Erasmus.

The spicy scents went straight to my stomach as I walked up to the stall, which was made from lashed-together decking and salvaged furniture struts. The current Nana flashed me a gap-toothed smile and loaded up a ceramic plate with tacos and doughnuts hot enough to burn my fingers. Grabbing the plate quickly, I moved aside, my first bite already on the way to my mouth.

The flash of medical whites caught my eye as I chewed, and as I looked up, the crowds shifted again, and I caught a glimpse of Emiliya. My spirits lifted . . . and then I saw who she was talking to.

I dropped my plate on Nana's counter and shoved my way through the crowd. Emiliya and the man both looked up, startled as I bore down.

We all stared at each other, and the man smiled, flashing an amethyst tooth in place of one of his canines.

"Hey, Brother Amerand."

"Kapa Lu," I whispered.

Emiliya yanked her arm out of his grip.

Kapa looked from me to Emiliya. "Well. This is timing."

Kapa, Emiliya, and I had run the tunnels together as children and tried to lay claim to the streets of Dazzle after the Breakout. Together, he and I made it through five years of the Security academy.

Then Kapa disappeared.

"At least now I know where you're getting your talk from," Kapa said to Emiliya.

"Think what you want," she muttered.

I finally found my voice. "How the hell did you get in here?"

Kapa rolled his eyes. "Like I was trying to tell *Dr. Varus* here"—he sneered her name and title—"I'm paid up. Clean and legal. Check my records if you don't believe me." He nodded toward the info stall across the aisle.

"How'd that happen?"

"I have seen the light, Brother. Crime doesn't pay and a heavy conscience is too high a lease for my life." Kapa grinned, flashing that lavender tooth again.

I'd seen that carved on the tunnel walls near the Oblivion gates too. At least, I'd seen parts of it. Defacing the old signs was a popular pastime.

"So, clean-legal-and-paid-up, what're you doing out here?"

Kapa looked to Emiliya, and Emiliya looked back, but only for a second before she turned her face away.

"I can't," she said, more to the crowd than to him.

Anger sparked in Kapa's hard eyes. "You used to trust me."

"Before you went into the shadows," she said.

"Is that what this is?" They'd both forgotten me. Kapa stepped toward her, his body making a plea to her, even as his voice grew hard. "I'm sorry, Emiliya. Sorry my escape made things tough for you . . ."

She stared at him, slack-jawed. "I was locked up with the Clerks for days, and my records are permanently dinged. You left me to this, Kapa. *This.*" She held up her empty, too-thin hands. "For ten years!"

"I am sorry, E," said Kapa softly. "You've got no idea what it took to get me in here even this soon."

"You shouldn't have come at all. I've got people paying attention to me now. I may have to explain this."

She turned and strode away into the crowds. Kapa swore and made to follow, but I stepped into his path. He lifted his hand, a casual gesture from someone used to brute force.

But he took a second look at my uniform coat and lowered it again.

"What're you really doing here?" I asked.

Emiliya wasn't the only one who'd suffered for being Kapa's friend. The morning after he vanished from the academy, I stood in the lineup and got grilled by the instructors and their Clerks. I told them he'd gone to join the shadows—the smugglers, thieves, and other chaos makers—because they already knew that. I didn't tell them I had a feeling it was coming and, thankfully, they didn't ask. I didn't ask, and they didn't tell me, if they'd found the last letter, the one from his parents, the one that told him they were going to commit suicide.

I never did find out how it had gotten smuggled in.

Kapa's eyes slid past me, following the path Emiliya had taken. Then he collected himself. He smiled the sly smile I remembered from when we were boys. It was a strange thing to see in his scarred man's face.

"What am I doin' here? A little of this, a little of that." He waggled his hand. "And you, Brother?"

"Little of this, little of that," I answered.

"Not in that uniform." He crossed his arms and eyed me. "You shoulda jumped with me."

"I had my reasons." I shrugged and glanced uneasily around. This was dangerous, and if Kapa didn't care, I had to. Just standing here with him was enough to get me hauled into a corruption investigation, but I wasn't about to let him go until I was sure Emiliya had enough time to get away.

"Your 'reasons' are going to get you killed," he said seriously.

"Not before yours do."

Kapa's eyes narrowed. "Maybe, maybe not. Maybe we're on the same team for a while."

"What're you talking about?"

The corner of his mouth curled up. He had me, and he knew it. "Take off the coat, and I'll tell you."

I snorted. "In uniform or out, I'm still in the Security."

He shrugged. "Maybe. Take off the coat, and I'll tell you."

"Oh for fuck's sake . . ." I stripped my coat off and slung it over my shoulder. It was rash, but I wanted to come out of this with the feeling that I'd actually learned something. I could use that as my excuse later if this was played back for me. I could say I was trying to get information from Kapa.

Kapa grinned and slapped my shoulder. "That's more like it, Brother Amerand."

He strolled away, following the curve of the wall until he stopped at a point between two bay doors. I would bet my payroll that he'd somehow managed to work out the pattern the cleaning drones followed and had brought us to a point that was acoustically dead, at least for the moment.

Kapa leaned his shoulder against the wall and looked me up and down. I made myself wait. Kapa loved to brag, and patience had never really been his strong point. He'd give it up before long.

"There's new money coming in, Amerand. New opportunities. Maybe you could talk Emiliya around for me."

"Is this about the new bunch of saints coming out of Solaris?"

That surprised him. "You heard already?" But within a few heartbeats he'd settled back down. "Yeah, I guess you would."

"Kapa," I said. "The Solarans are strict legals. They are not going to be dishing out anything to smugglers."

"I keep telling you, Brother, I'm legal now." Kapa's gaze roamed around the port, taking in the knots of spacers, the trade, and the talk. Someone at the dice game shouted. Cards and chits changed hands amid general laughter. "A lot of people think the new heads of the First Bloods are already shaking things up around here. And there's always cash for some smart player in a shakeup."

Which meant someone was paying him for something and that somebody had already laid out a great deal to clear his record.

Somebody had bought Kapa.

The idea made me sick. I couldn't understand why. I hated what he did—hated the smugglers and the chaos makers because they fed the gangs and the tunnel czars. I hated the way he could so casually suggest I give up my family to the Clerks and their executioners. But I'd always had a strange . . . respect for Kapa. Of all the people I knew, he was the only one who was really his own master.

"Kapa. Don't mess with this. Emiliya says Fortress is taking an interest."

"You'd better believe it."

I prodded him in the shoulder with my finger. The look he gave me was dangerous, but at least he was looking at me. "Do not mess with Fortress, Kapa. The new *Saeos* are not, I repeat, *not* like old Lou and Bea. They are diamond hard and twice as sharp."

He swatted at my hand, but I'd already pulled it back. "I know, Amerand. That's what I'm trying to tell you." He leaned close. He smelled of whiskey, smoke, and sweat, but his eyes were clear and steady. "What I tried to tell her."

A streak of cold shuddered across my shoulders. "You're not making sense."

"I'm making plenty of sense, you just don't want to believe what your clean little ears are hearing." He shrugged again, his sharp, restless gaze roaming across the port yard, cutting out whatever he thought he could use. "The *Saeos* themselves are setting up something special for Solaris, and it's all hands to help Erasmus and we all rise together."

My mouth went dry. "Kapa, you even think about pulling Emiliya into this and I will kill you with my bare hands."

"News for you, Brother." He prodded me in the shoulder, once. "She's already in it. I was here to get her out."

With that, he strolled away across the open port.

THREE
TERESE

When I woke up the morning after Misao's phone call, I'd managed to deal with the guilt and fear brought by the news of Bianca's death by becoming righteously angry. What the hell did Misao think he was doing, calling me up on my daughter's birthday? If he thought he could just interrupt my life anytime he felt like it, he'd learn different. He could just wait until I was damn good and ready to see him.

So I lingered with my family. David made his classic slow-recovery breakfast: waffles with butter and maple syrup, or ice cream if you wanted it, which the kids invariably did, except for Jo, who ate her waffles naked to prove one of her more esoteric points. Don't ask me which one. There was also bacon and stewed apples. Not even Jo turned those down. I drank a third cup of coffee while talking about nothing much with the kids.

I felt Bianca's eyes on me the whole time. Her dead gaze made a pressure that started right in the black hole beneath my skull. I ignored it as best I was able. If I wasn't successful, the kids didn't say anything. Neither did David.

Jo was leaving that day, returning to Hong Kong on the spaceplane. Allie and Dale were staying over. Jo and I would take the cable together to the Ashland 'port. I'd say good-bye to her there, then catch the bullet train down to Chicago. That would put me at the office at about five o'clock. If Misao wanted to badger me for an extra-long time, he'd have to go hungry to do it, and serve him right . . .

I'm a liar.

This is what was really going on:

I was scared. I was doing everything I could not to admit that. I was afraid of what would happen once I walked back into that building, of what I would think and feel once I heard what the emergency was and how Bianca had died. I didn't want to leave my family as we sat around the chipped, stained dining table, stuffing food that was going to mean an extra cholesterol-flush for me and David, and laughing at jokes that were over a decade old.

But there was that stone in my heart and Bianca's cold gaze on the back of my neck, and neither one would go away.

"Your eye's twitching."

I jerked my head around and stared at Jo, who pulled a face back at me. We stood on the transit platform, waiting for the cable bus with our small packs on our shoulders and Jo's luggage piled around us. The lake winds whipped outside the station's transparent shields, but in here, we were toasty warm and could safely watch the gale raging across Lake Superior. Jo and I had the platform to ourselves. The nervous wouldn't take the cable on a day like this, but I sort of liked the iron-grey sky and the waters dancing beneath the wind.

Wars had once been fought over the water in the Great Lakes. Nasty little wars, with smuggling and sabotaged pipelines, and starving locals and slave labor. Now my family lived peacefully on an artificial island in the middle of it, where the architects went in for tempered glass and molded wood, because you only lived out in the middle of Lake Superior for the view, so they wanted to make sure you got as much of it as possible.

The grey waters surged below us, but in the distance we could see the deep greens and reds of forested cliffs. Soon, they'd be white with snow, like a line of clouds caught between sky and water.

"So, are you going to tell me who Bianca is?" Jo folded her arms. Her long white hair was piled in elaborate red-tipped ringlets on top of her head. She'd eschewed a hat, and was muffled deep in a black coat, a stark contrast with her artificially ivory-colored skin. Slim red boots encased her legs and a red scarf did more to call attention to her slender throat than keep it warm. I wouldn't call the look beautiful, but it was arresting—like her words.

"Dad always told us never to ask, about the Guardians, about anything," Jo went on. "He told us to let you make your peace with it. That was your business. Making peace." She cocked her head. "How's that working out?"

"Jo . . ." I began, but the cable bus pulled in—a string of colorful, flexible cars hung on the white spiderweb that stretched from tower to tower over the choppy waters.

The doors slipped open and a few passengers climbed out. We stepped in, presenting our palms to the door monitors. I made my way to a spot by the window and took off my small pack, tucking it in the holder in front of me. Raindrops smacked against the window, showing minute ice crystals in each tiny puddle.

Ugly weather, settling in for the long haul. How metaphoric.

Jo plunked herself down beside me, resting her pack on her knees. "You were saying?"

The pain was starting up, a steady throb behind my right ear. "Never mind."

The car lurched slightly and started forward. In less than

a minute, we were gliding above the waters, heading swiftly and smoothly toward the shore.

"Never mind your never mind," Jo snapped. "Are you going to tell me who Bianca is?"

I sighed. Stubborn girl. Stubborn woman. How very like her mother, David would have said, *had said*, more than once.

"Bianca is . . . was . . . a data tracker."

"What, like an analyst?"

Annoyance pricked me. How could she not know this? Then I remembered. It was because I had consistently refused to talk about it with her or either of her siblings. And while the Guardians make a great show of not keeping any more secrets than is strictly necessary, we also don't go around advertising our ranks and specialties.

They don't. I meant they, not we.

"A data tracker is a kind of analyst," I said, lacing my fingers together. "Bianca looked at data flow, ephemeral or solid, in context. A whole world's worth of it, if she had access. Years of it, if necessary. When she was done, she could predict the critical decision points in real time: people, news sources, gossips, whatever. If you could control the points she identified, you'd cool down any hot spot within a few weeks. She was always right. Always."

"You didn't have an AI that could do that?"

"Not the way she could." I smiled a little, remembering the glint in Bianca's eyes and the sharp twist to her grin that came when she finally had the answer.

Got'cha, she'd whisper to the screen. *You're mine now.* "Bianca could practically feel the current of human thought. She knew who was taking their cues from their spouses, their lovers, their kids. Give her a week in a place where she knew the language, and she'd know which gossip influenced which listener, and how that line of listening tracked to the center of the power structure, no matter how deep the real power was hidden. It was spooky."

It took Jo a moment to digest this. She scrunched down into her coat and watched the evergreen-crowned coast getting closer. "Were you friends?" she asked at last.

I blinked. How did you explain your relationship with someone who had been under your command for more than two decades? How do you begin to untangle that web of duty and love?

How do you explain your relationship with someone who'd saved your life?

"Yes," I said, because it was easiest. "We were friends."

"Then I'm sorry you lost her."

"Thank you," I said with overly bland graciousness. I watched Jo jiggle her leg up and down, tapping her heel on the floor in uneasy rhythm. She wasn't done yet.

"Was that what you did? When you were in the Guardians? Were you a data tracker too?"

I sighed. I had no one to blame but myself for this interrogation. "No. I was a Field Commander."

"Dad never told us," she said pointedly.

"No," I agreed.

The red bootheel went rat-a-tat against the floor. My eye twitched. Another sound hovered on the edge of memory. I felt it grate against my eardrums and on the tip of my spine. Rat-a-tat. I smelled burning.

"It never went away, though," Jo was saying. "The Guardians. It just sort of hung in the air all the time, like when you can't figure out where that smell is coming from."

That smell. The burning. I knew where it came from—the past. *Stay here. Stay here with your daughter.* I sighed. "All right, Jo. You're right. We should have told you. I'm sorry."

She didn't believe me, but she went quiet, and for the moment that was all I wanted. I'd be sorry for this later. I was sorry for it at that moment. I should have gone alone. My family had no part of this.

The cable bus let us off at the Ashland International Transit Port. The 'port surged with people, robot carts, and security drones. The roar of the planes pressed down against the tidal rush of thousands of voices.

I hugged my daughter at the archway covering the space between the train platforms and the entrance to the plane gates. Jo hugged me back, pressing her face against my shoulder, and I felt the love surging out of her, warmth into my cold. I held her there for a long moment, and she let me.

Then she pulled back, holding me at arm's length. You could see the little girl who was still inside if you knew how to look behind the sophisticated shield in her pale blue eyes.

"You'll call, right?" she asked earnestly. "You won't go without calling?"

"I'm not going anywhere, Jo."

Her face twisted up in disbelief and I instantly wanted to take back my words. Jo turned away and waded into the crowd, finding her way confidently and not looking back once.

I stood where I was while all the warmth from her embrace turned to an extra layer of ice inside.

I could have turned back then. I could have said it wasn't worth it and gone home. I was retired. I was free. This war, if it was a war, was for other people. I was too old, too wounded, too long retired.

Instead, I stepped onto the bullet to Chicago. I found an empty seat by the curving window in the lounge and watched the green-and-grey blur of the world I'd already left streak by.

FOUR

TERESE

Chicago is the Second City, a fact that has never ceased to annoy it. Ever the younger sibling, it has exulted in being boisterous, unruly, and proud of itself even in defeat. During the Great Lakes wars, it neither walled itself off like Toronto, nor changed sides multiple times like Detroit. Chicago remained true to its own traditions and threw open its doors to all comers, turning into a free port where anything was allowed, with the possible exception of getting caught interfering with somebody else's business.

Now it is one of the tallest cities in the world, a place of laser-lit and solar-powered towers: marble white, sandstone red, granite pink, crystal, diamond, ruby, amber, emerald, and sapphire. Cable cars, elevated maglev trains, and pedestrian walkways with stained-glass windows lace those towers together. This shining urban web straddles the remains of the ground-level city with its ragged parklands and urban antiquities. Some of those old ground-level neighborhoods are living enclaves existing in the twilight of the new city, while others are quietly crumbling monuments to the old days, both good and bad. The crowds for the ghost tours on Halloween and St. Valentine's Day in Chicago rival the ones down in New Orleans on Katrina Day.

Among the most enduring of these ghosts is Union Station.

"Attention, passengers. Union Station is an active advertising zone. If you do not wish to input/download/receive personal advertisements, please turn off all information-input facilities."

I made sure my handset was switched off and gathered up my coat and gloves and slung my pack over my shoulder. Setting my jaw, I joined the river of my fellow passengers spilling out into the antique sandstone-and-marble hall.

I don't have eye or ear implants, so I had nothing to shield my senses from the riot. The onslaught of noise and color threatened to drag me under. A hundred billboards flashed images too fast for me to take in. Dozens of different songs blared in my ears. Artificial breezes wafted the scents of food and perfume at me, alternately making me salivate and tightening my stomach from the unpalatable combinations. The whole place seemed to be a hangout for the hyperchic, the exotic, and the truly bizarre, as paid actors and models tried to compete with the billboards for my attention.

I gulped air and found that, as thick as the artificial miasma was, I could still breathe. It took a moment, but I was able to narrow my focus down to the real and scan the crowds that waited for the disembarking passengers. No one came forward to meet me. Of course not. I had deliberately not told anyone when I was coming.

I strode across the main terminal, automatically adopting my "not a tourist" walk: eyes straight ahead, shoulders square, put on your coat as you walk, don't let the people or the ads catch your attention, and for the love of all that is sacred, don't let an ad-bot catch up with you.

In the express elevator, I endured two giggly, much-enhanced and tattooed actors talking enthusiastically about the new game they'd been playing the night before. It seemed to involve death, zombies, acrobatics, and a lot of VR sex.

I had to stop myself from sprinting down the walkway

toward the Dearborn Zone El train. I crossed out of the confines of Union Station accompanied by a fanfare of "come back soon" and "you've still got time to take advantage . . ." messages from various motion-sensitive billboards, and instantly relaxed.

At least until I saw Vijay Kochinski on the bench.

He was already in the act of taking off his glasses and tucking them into his jacket pocket as I threaded my way across the half-full platform. I stopped directly in front of him as he stood up.

"Hello, Terese." He said it with that extra weight people give an inadequate greeting that comes after a long absence.

"Hello, Vijay."

Vijay had been Optimized as a child. Some parents will do everything they can afford—and a few things they can't—to give their child an advantage, materially or genetically. It has long been known that people automatically respond more favorably to tall men, and to handsome men, and to men with blue eyes (which I've never understood, but there it is). So Vijay had been inspected, injected, and worked over until he had all that, and a bit more.

Like a lot of other Optimized children, Vijay had nearly killed himself with drugs and dangerous stunts, which degenerated into actual disfiguration gestures. Years of individual therapy and opto-support groups, combined with some remod surgery to take down the hyperhandsomeness, had straightened him out. But he'd kept the height. Liked the view, he said.

"Took your time," he remarked at last. He looked me up and down, taking in what had stayed the same and how much had changed. Vijay had let himself age, but not like I had. After I had the kids, I let myself go, happily and comfortably. I now was as round in the hip and midriff as I'd always been in the bosom and had streaks of grey in my curling black hair. Vijay's sleek green thermal jacket was tailored enough to show he was still in very good shape. His hair was salt-and-pepper, but still full and shining. His face was lined, and had that weathered quality that spoke of real sun and wind rather than cosmetic treatment.

"Yeah." I shoved my hands into my coat pockets. I couldn't help glancing around me. Our fellow travelers were paying about as much attention as city dwellers ever do to strangers' conversations, that is to say, none.

"How pissed is Misao?" I asked.

Vijay shook his head, very slowly, his lips pursed. "Not at all. This should worry you."

It did. A lot. I looked away and bit my lip.

The El was crowded. It always is. I grabbed a strap and swayed shoulder to shoulder with Vijay and a mix of sleep-deprived commuters, ebullient college students, bright-eyed tourists, and a hyperactive business wonk. But at least the smells of humanity were as natural as they ever get, and if anyone was trying to sell me something, they had to be quiet about it or the spy cameras would ban them from public transport for six months.

I could have sprung for a private car. I don't know why I was determined not to. Perhaps to prove I could handle crowds and the unexpected. There had been a time when I couldn't, but I was over that. I was a new woman. My own woman with my own good life. I had survived something no one else had. I could take whatever came on my own terms.

The El snaked through the landscape of sparkling towers, stark white light, and storm-grey sky. Drone-planes and sea-gulls skimmed past us. At last, we slowed and stopped, and the carefully designed, accentless, genderless, and inoffensive voice said, "Daley Tower, Number Four."

It took several seconds before I could make myself step out onto the platform. In the end, it was Vijay's patient and sympathetic look that stiffened my nerves. The doors whooshed right behind me and the train slipped soundlessly away, its breeze ruffling the curls on the back of my scalp.

Don't stop. Don't think about it. Just walk. I brushed past Vijay and let him fall into step behind me.

The entrance to the Special Forces HQ in Chicago is a pair of glass doors with plain metal handles that take your palm prints when you pull on them. The only permanent decoration is the message painted in black on the transparent surface.

UNITED WORLD GOVERNMENT FOR EARTH
DEPARTMENT OF PEACE AND SECURITY MAINTENANCE
SPECIAL FORCES DIVISION
CHICAGO BRANCH

The handle was cold beneath my now-identified palm. I hadn't been around in such a long time that the door monitor felt the need to flash the small print for me:

By entering these premises you have forfeited the rights of privacy and anonymity granted under UWG Common Cause Covenant 21:38:06. Personal background search and retrieval may be initiated at any time by any UWG-DPSM-SFD-CB employee or official designate, living or automated. Any word or action committed on the premises may be recorded and used in any official or legal proceedings initiated by or against the entrant.

"And you have a nice day," I muttered as I walked through the door. Behind me, Vijay snickered quietly. The door did not answer.

I don't know why I was surprised to see they'd redecorated the lobby. Somehow, you expect places you've left to freeze, like your memories of them have. It's egotistical, but no one really wants to believe the world goes on without them.

Reception was still a huge, curving wooden desk with the Chicago skyline carved in bas-relief on its face, but the carpets were now an antique Persian pattern instead of institutional beige. They'd put in groves of miniature orange and rose trees under full-spectrum lights. The chairs and sofas had embroidered cushions in wooden frames instead of overstuffed leather.

One of them was taken up by another familiar form.

"Siri." Surprise froze me in place for a moment.

"Field Commander." Siri Baijahn's voice was sour and her arms were folded. She was thinner than when I'd last seen her. She'd changed her hair to a glossy copper color but still wore it in the straight, short cut I remembered. Her skin was darker, either from dye or sun exposure, I couldn't tell yet. When not on assignment, Siri went in for brilliant-colored clothes, her answer to the dictum that we needed to keep ourselves within local norms when we were in the field. Today, she wore an orange-and-gold-thread wrap-around top with flowing sleeves, bright red slacks, and boots that reminded me a lot of the ones Jo had been wearing. Must be the latest thing.

"Welcome back," she said, and the bitterness in her voice was corrosive.

"I'm not back," I told her, told *them*, tried to tell myself. "I'm just going to hear Misao out."

She looked me up and down with eyes as acid bright as her tone had been. "Then why bother? You could have done that much on your set."

"I don't have the proper clearance anymore."

The way she turned her back on me said what she thought of this excuse. Siri had been furious when I decided to leave. Even knowing everything that had happened to me, I strongly suspected she still saw what I did as some kind of dereliction of duty. She had been Bianca's protégé for two decades by the time I left and had swallowed all of Bianca's lessons about service.

I looked up at Vijay, hoping for help, but he had closed himself off. He had to work with Siri, I reasoned.

"So why'd you come out to meet me?" I asked Siri. "Vijay could have walked me back."

That stopped her. She turned. "Because it's important and you've always been the best under pressure." She said it without rancor and without jealousy. "Because I was hoping for a minute to see my friend before you turned back into my ex-commander."

We locked gazes, each one waiting to see if the other would shift, back down, or be embarrassed.

"I'm sorry," I whispered.

"Yeah. Me too." Some of the acid bled away, but none of the wariness did. "Come on," she said. "The Little Big's waiting."

I handed off my coat and small pack for reception to inspect and keep, then followed Siri inside. Like the lobby, the halls had more colors than I remembered. They were peaceful, contrasting patterns with lots of jewel tones to offset the bone whites and greys that made up the frames and the trims. The screens on the walls alternated news-feeds with landscapes and music. There were more of them than I remembered, too, and they kept catching at my peripheral vision.

The people I passed, however, were exactly as I remembered: Serious, soberly dressed, and traditionally styled, they were absorbed in their own thoughts or conversations. If anyone glanced at me, it was fleeting. I was just another visitor to the office. Except for Vijay, Siri, and Misao, there might not be anybody left who remembered my face. The average life span might be three hundred years in these modern times, but the average career of a Guardian was less than a tenth of that.

Now that Siri was with us, the silence was much less comfortable. My back started to ache from the tension that seized my shoulders.

Vijay tried to break through with some light gossip. "You still with David?" he asked.

"Yeah."

Siri palmed us through an inner door and shot Vijay a scathing glance as we walked past, as if she couldn't believe he'd bring up such a subject. Vijay just raised his eyebrows at her. She shrugged irritably.

Families are not the only ones who can communicate without speaking.

"And David's still a Van Helsing?"

I put on an offended air. "Immortality Infractions Investigator, if you please."

This apparently confused Vijay. His forehead bunched up. "I.I.I. is better than Van Helsing?"

"Shut up, Vijay."

He chuckled. "Welcome home, Terese."

Misao had a garden office. At the moment, he had the shields up to keep in the heat and keep out the wind of the Chicago winter. The effect was that of walking into a peaceful, well-tended courtyard, with a large desk and several comfortable chairs in the middle. The branches of winter-naked maples made charcoal sketches against the grey-stone walls. Evergreens spread dark canopies for the scarlet-berried hollies. Even under the leaden sky, it looked festive.

As Vijay pushed open the door, Misao glanced up from his active desktop and touched the OFF command with a short, blunt finger. The desk went dark before I was two steps into his office space and my ex-commander stood up to acknowledge me.

Guardian Marshal-Steward Misao Smith had most emphatically not been optimized. He looked up to every one of his team, except me. This had earned him the nickname of "Little Big," of which he was perfectly aware. He still had the smooth, round face that belonged to a man on the threshold of his fifth decade and the fireplug build of someone who had kept himself fit all his life. His ruthlessly slicked-back hair was solid black and the awareness behind his green eyes still knife-sharp.

"Thank you, Agent Kochinski, Coordinator Baijahn." Misao sat back in his leather chair. Vijay nodded and looked to Siri. The look she shot back toward him was almost a challenge. But they had been dismissed, and they walked out, letting the door swing shut.

Misao, unperturbed and perfectly patient, looked me up and down just like Vijay had.

In an instant, I realized how futile my little attempt to

discomfort my former chief by making him wait was. I grew smaller as I settled into the visitor's chair, my defenses slipping from me like the flimsy constructs they were. Trying to reacquaint myself with my own backbone, I silently told Misao to go to hell in every language I knew.

This changed nothing. I hadn't said a word, and I had already blinked.

"How are you, Field Commander Drajeske?" Misao inquired as he reclaimed his own chair.

I matched his cool gaze and pulled out my best office manners. "Fine, thank you, Marshal-Steward Smith. And yourself?"

One finger on his right hand twitched. "I am terrible," he said. "And I expect to be worse in the very near future."

"I am sorry to hear that, Marshal-Steward."

Formality makes a kind of lacquer for the soul. It is beautifully slick and impossible to see through. Lacquer is also watertight. Nothing gets out, and nothing gets in.

I couldn't let *anything* else get in. It had been too easy to fall into the old talk with Vijay.

"Perhaps you would like to know why I have requested you share this very bad time with me."

I didn't answer him. Overhead, the clouds shifted. Shadows rippled over the stones ringing the holly beds.

"You're here because Bianca Fayette asked for you to replace her."

My lacquer shattered. I stared at Misao, and I knew my face had gone white. Misao, on the other hand, did not move.

It's one of the many unusual traditions in the Guardians. You can, if you want, name your own replacement. It's not official, and it's fairly easily overridden, but it can carry some weight. My replacement, Caesar, got my job on my say-so.

"She died in the field. Her body was recovered on Moonfour in the Erasmus System. Her Companion's record indicates that her last instructions included making sure that you personally came to Moonfour to take up the mission."

This was why he hadn't been impatient or angry. He knew that however I'd come in—whether red-hot or ice-cold—this would undo me.

I remembered the cell where I lay on harsh stone in that unending nightmare darkness. I remembered the beam of white light. I squinted in bewildered pain to see the neat, square hole getting bigger and bigger where the wall was methodically dismantled. I remembered how I shrank away from the silhouette that catapulted toward me, how I couldn't comprehend it could bring anything but more pain.

"Easy, Terese. Easy. It's me. I got you . . ."

Easy, Terese.

I licked my lips and I hated Misao with everything I had. But that flame burned itself out in a couple of heartbeats.

Easy, Terese.

"What . . . what was she doing in Erasmus?" Moonfour, that was the one called Dazzle. Once it had been a pleasure palace the size of Mars. Now it was the crumbling and violence-prone home for a jumbled and repressed population without options.

Misao's mouth straightened into a hard, thin line for a moment before he answered. "She was completing a grand tour with Captain Baijahn. Our ambassador in the system, Philippe Diego y Bern"—he paused, and I nodded, acknowledging I knew the man—"asked her to stay behind to help with what he felt was soon going to become a major refugee situation."

That wasn't too surprising. The situation on Erasmus had stabilized for the moment (as far as I knew), but for a lot of the people there, life was eked out on the barest margins.

"How . . . how did Bianca die?"

"It seems she found her own way out."

Tremors traveled up my right hand, little butterfly wings brushing against my bones.

"She was . . . captured?" Harsh, cold stone, the stink of my own blood, the hole, the black, silent hole brimming over with pain . . .

"Abducted at the very least."

"How?" I asked hoarsely. "Who did it?"

Anger flickered across Misao's tightly controlled features. "We don't know."

"But you retrieved her Companion . . ." The Companion should contain a complete record of her doings, whom she'd met with, where she'd gone. Everything since her last download.

"The Companion was damaged." Misao's words made me go cold. "Her body had been left to rot, Terese. We got back bones and putrefied flesh, and not a lot of that because the rats had been at it for at least a week."

Leaving no witness to the reasons that drove her to take her own life. No one to bring her justice or redemption. There wasn't enough anger in the world to adequately answer this.

I looked into Misao's tired, grieving face.

"Can I talk to it?"

"Are you coming back?"

I couldn't answer. The words dried up in my mind. His

question blocked off my thoughts. I had to clear my throat, shift my weight before I could jar some syllables into place. Misao, of course, missed none of that.

"Misao, you cannot possibly want me for this, for whatever it is. I've been gone thirty years!" I was pleading now, and I hated it, but I couldn't think of anything else to do. Bianca was watching me. I could feel her, right at my back. *Get me out of this, Misao. Please. Tell her I can't do this.*

"I don't want you," he said flatly. "But I have very little choice right now. If the current data is correct, we are probably one year away from the Erasmans launching a war on the Solar System, and the Guardians are stretched so thin across so many hot spots we are in danger of disintegrating. If I have to bring back every discharged officer who still has a pulse to prevent that, I will."

"*Erasmus* launching a war?" I could barely frame the thought, never mind the words. "You can't be serious. They're scrambling for survival right now. They haven't got the resources to launch any kind of attack . . ."

Misao's steady silence told me I was wrong. Dead wrong. I felt the blood drain slowly from my face, leaving me cold. "What have I missed?"

"Are you coming back?"

Fine. Fine. It's an out. Take it. Remember David. Remember you promised. Take your out and run!

I stood. I met those icy green eyes. I felt Bianca behind me. He knew she was there. He knew it and he was not going to give me one ounce of relief.

"I promised, Misao," I whispered. "Before we ever got married, I swore to David I was retired."

"Then you do not have the clearance to be briefed about the current situation on Erasmus. Good-bye, Mrs. Drajeske."

I couldn't breathe. If he'd punched me in the gut, I couldn't have been in more pain.

You son of a bitch. You cold, manipulative son of a bitch.

"Just tell me," I croaked. My throat was sore. How had that happened? I felt like I'd been shouting, but I hadn't raised my voice since I came here. "Did Bianca really say she wanted me out there?"

Misao laid his hand flat on the desk. "Come here, Jeri-miah."

The opaque shield that covered the door to the corridor cleared. The door behind it opened, and a young man seemed to walk up the hall and stand framed in the threshold. He was lanky, with copper-brown skin and coffee-brown eyes that drooped in the corners. His straight black hair flopped into his eyes so that he had to keep pushing it back. It made him look boyishly handsome. He probably had a mischievous smile when he wasn't looking so solemn.

Once our Companions are installed and established, we meet with an artist for several sessions to describe our impressions of our Companions. A VR portrait is made and stored with our files. This allows for interactive sessions in the real world to reinforce and refine the "relationship."

Many of us have good-looking Companions, or at least cute ones. I know one Guardian whose Companion was an eight-year-old girl, and another who had an angel, and yet another who'd had Coco the Wonder Dog. That your Companion appears as someone you'd want to love and protect is part of the point. It helps you fight to stay alive longer.

My own Companion, Dylan, was taller than I was and older than I was, with rich brown eyes that crinkled up in the corners when he smiled and cinnamon-brown hair he wore in a ponytail. He had a Celtic knotwork tattoo around

one biceps, and on his forearm was a set of plain black letters proclaiming ENTER HERE FOR FULL EXPLANATION. I had
been surprised at the ink. I never liked it. I'd asked him to
get rid of it once, and he just looked wounded. I chuckled
and let it go.

"Hello, Marshal-Steward. How can I help you?" Jerimiah's
voice was light, in keeping with his appearance. It didn't sound
quite right, somehow. The accent . . . something . . . it wasn't
what it should have been.

"Jerimiah, can you tell us how Field Coordinator Fayette
was captured?"

I thought Jerimiah hesitated a little as he looked toward
me, but I told myself that was my imagination. This was no
thinking creature. The mind behind it, Bianca's mind, was
dead. This was an illusion created by a delicate web of chips
and artificial neurons.

"I don't know how we were captured, not completely. I
am damaged." Jerimiah spread his hands. His fingernails
were chewed down to the quick. I guess a lifetime in Bianca's
head could make you nervous.

In front of me now, the Companion Jerimiah kicked at
the carpet. "We were . . . waiting for someone. There was an
appointment Bianca needed to keep, but not on Dazzle. We
were on Dazzle, waiting for someone to take us to see . . ."
He shook his head. "I am sorry. That's gone. But she was very
concerned about the refugee problem, or wanting to create
the refugee problem or . . ." His hands with their chewed-on
nails curled into fists. The artist had done a good job with
the detail and definition of Jerimiah's face. I could see the
sorrow in the drooping corners of his eyes. The mellow voice
hesitated just a little, a fine simulation of feeling. It made me
want to reach out to a hand that wasn't there.

I remembered what Misao had said about the rats and shuddered. Could a Companion feel pain, apart from the host's pain? I suddenly felt guilty about not knowing that.

When I woke up in my Redemption cell with the crusted bandage behind my ear and no Dylan in my head, I tried to kill myself. My captors had found the suicide switch too, but I kept trying.

I'd almost succeeded by the time Bianca took apart the cell wall and pulled me out. I hadn't, even then, stopped to think what Dylan felt in his last moments.

"Word had been spreading about the Pax Solaris's open-border policy," Jerimiah was saying. "Moonfive, Oblivion, attempted a large-scale diaspora once before."

"I know," I cut him off.

"Bianca was afraid they might try a diaspora again, to reach the Pax worlds, and that there might be a large number of deaths if that happened."

"Why were you in Erasmus?" I asked Jerimiah.

"We were finishing off the Grand Tour. Bianca wanted to make the rounds, to see if she still wanted to remain a Guardian."

A hundred years ago she'd done the same thing, with me.

"Was she the one who discovered Erasmus was a hot spot?" I asked.

Jerimiah nodded. This time he was looking at Misao. Misao looked back, closed-off and impassive as ever. "She believed it was going to blow soon."

"Did she have proof?"

Jerimiah shifted his weight, displaying a kind of uncertainty I had never seen in a Companion. Dylan had never acted like this. "She was looking for it."

"Did she find it?" I pressed, feeling guilty at pushing so much on a kid, but I was not going to stop.

Jerimiah bit down on his lower lip and shook his head hard. "I don't know. I was damaged. We went to Market. We went to Fortress. We went to Fortress a lot. We talked to the ambassador and to the Erasmus *Saeos*." The title was a corruption of the old corporate title, *CEO*, firmly marking Erasmus's origins as a for-profit colony. "She made friends with them. I have some records of this." He pressed his hand against the threshold and Misao's desk lit up to show the crosslooks. I could easily believe Bianca had made friends with the Blood Family. She could charm anybody if she really wanted to, and she was not above using that talent for work . . . or for play.

My gaze slid sideways to Misao. His finger was twitching, wanting to tap out some command on the tabletop. He'd spoken with certainty. A year away from a war, he'd said. But Jerimiah said she'd only been looking for the proof. Either he'd lied to me, or they'd learned something Misao hadn't told me yet.

Hadn't told me and wouldn't tell me until I took the oath again.

I turned back to Jerimiah. "Then what?" I asked.

"I don't know," Jerimiah muttered angrily. "I don't *know*. She died. She died with me in her mind, and I don't know how!"

Suspicion bloomed hot and horrendous inside me. "You said you had her last words!" I snapped at Misao. "You said she asked for me!"

"He had to play her last words for me too," said Jerimiah. "Some of my surviving nodes became disconnected, and I was not able to reintegrate them."

Misao never took his gaze off me. He moved a finger sideways and I heard Jerimiah's voice over my set.

"I'm ready, Bianca."

"Okay. Okay." That was Bianca's husky alto, instantly recognizable to me. But it wasn't the easy, laughing voice I knew so well. It was choking, raw and filled with tears.

"...Oh...Oh...it is my time. My time...I didn't believe this day would come...I'd only hoped...I'd prayed...But here it is. Finally, here it is. Oh, Jerimiah, you can tell them...Please tell them, Terese really is the one I want to replace me. It's true. I swear. Bring her in and it'll fall into place...I swear, I swear, I swear...No one else can make it work. Make sure they know, and make sure they know it was me who said it. They'll listen to you. Please, tell them."

I couldn't move. Sweat, or perhaps a tear, trickled down my cheek, and I still couldn't move. In the threshold, Jerimiah bowed his head.

"I'll tell them, Bianca. Don't worry. I'm here with you."

"Thank you, Jerimiah. Thank you. Oh, God, I'm shaking. I wanted so much...Well...Good-bye!"

"Good-bye, Bianca."

A snap, a shuffle of cloth, and a soft thump, and silence. Silence stretching out until it felt like pain.

"Thank you, Jerimiah," said Misao.

Jerimiah looked up, his face blank and bleak, and more than a little ashamed. "I'm sorry," he whispered again. Then he turned and walked away, and the shield darkened, becoming a blank covering for the door again.

I was shaking. I was as cold as if there were nothing between me and the winter outside. It was too hard, too much. Too many memories flooded me, drowning thought.

I could barely breathe. I was going to be sick in another minute.

"I can't," I whispered. "*I can't.*"

Misao pressed both palms against the desk. I don't know what he was going to say. I never found out. At that moment, a chime sounded on my set followed immediately by a voice.

"Terese? I'm in the lobby."

It was David.

FIVE

TERESE

Misao glanced at his desk, where there was, of course, a report on who'd just called. His eyes widened and his head jerked up. For one of the few times in my career, I saw Marshal-Steward Misao Smith at a loss.

I touched my set to acknowledge the call. "Excuse me," I said to Misao.

I walked out into the hall. The door closed after me.

I hate doors. I hate hearing them open and shut. I hate the drafts and the clanks, the rattles and the clicks. I hate them closing in front of me, or behind me. After all this time, after all the therapy and regrowth, I still hate doors.

Move. He can see you standing here.

I moved back through the busy labyrinth by instinct and memory rather than conscious thought. It wasn't until I had my hand on the palm reader which, on the near side, would verify that I had the legal right to walk out of this building that I even realized I'd made it back to the lobby.

And there stood David, and beside him, pale and defiant, stood Jo.

We stared at each other in silence for a long time. David's face creased up tight, trying to find some kind of expression that suited the clamor inside him. I stood in front of him, slump-shouldered and exhausted.

To make matters even more surreal, I noticed that we weren't alone. Vijay and Siri occupied one corner of the lobby. I don't know how those two got there ahead of me, but my old team and my family cast sideways glances at each other, neither side quite sure who that was over there.

I wanted to laugh. I wanted to cry. I couldn't do either. I couldn't even move.

David touched Jo's arm. "I'll talk to your mother alone. You've still got that plane to catch."

Jo tilted her chin up. "Not until I'm sure she's not going to do something stupid." She projected an air of righteousness that can only come from someone who hasn't even finished her third decade.

I felt Siri's eyes burning into the back of my neck.

"It'll be all right," said David softly to Jo. "I'll meet you there."

I didn't think Jo was going to listen at first. She stepped toward me. "See you back home," she said. Then she turned and walked out, tall and confident: confident that she had successfully removed my choices, confident she had saved me from myself.

Anger surfaced: a parent's strange, uncomfortable anger at a child who simply doesn't *understand*. It is an awful anger, because you're only getting angry at the reflections of your mistakes.

Siri walked up beside me. "Mother? Then this is . . ."

"David Drajeske." David held out his hand.

"Siri Baijahn." Siri shook his hand, because what else was she going to do? Her eyes were hard as she sized him up, and she flickered a glance at me to say, *This is what you left us for? This exhausted, aging, worried man?*

Family telepathy.

"Vijay Kochinski." David and Vijay shook hands. This time the glance went between Siri and Vijay and I felt the current of implied understanding, but of what I couldn't tell, and my anger redoubled.

Manipulative little Misao wannabes.

"Not here," I said to David. I walked past him and pushed open the doors. *Let Vijay and Siri take that back to the boss.*

David followed me in silence, and I let him keep following me. I'd be damned if I was going to talk to him where Misao, and Vijay, and Siri could listen in. I was not going to turn around and say, "What were you thinking!" "Why are you doing this?" or "What on *earth* made you bring Jo into this?" where they could hear me do it. More than that: I was not going to open my mouth until I had at least some idea what was going to come out.

The top of Daley Tower 4 has a living roof: a beautiful green and flowering formal garden, shielded from the harsh winds and winters. There is even a marble fountain carved in a very bad classical Greek-revival style.

I pushed open the door, gritting my teeth as the clean, conifer-scented air wafted over me. It was full dark, and there were only a few footlights on to show us the white-gravel pathways. The winter city, with its colored lights and veins of darkness, spread around us. The shields didn't filter out the noise, and I could hear Chicago's rushing, enervating cacophony.

I stalked down the central path. We had the place to ourselves. The fountain had been switched off for the night and its central faun was giving me a sarcastic look.

I sank down on a granite bench and looked out across the ledge.

"They got to you, didn't they?" David breathed. "You would have re-upped."

"How did you know?"

"I guessed. And I talked to Jo."

Of course. I could picture Jo pacing the boarding lounge at the 'port, trying to make up her mind. I could picture her face, the stern set of her jaw the moment her internal righteousness won out and she ordered her set to connect to her father, so she could tell him I was about to betray them even before I was sure myself.

But then, perhaps I was wrong. David was an experienced investigator, after all. He had lived with me for the same thirty-five years I'd lived with him. He might have been the one to call Jo.

"I'm sorry, David. Really." I was. Honestly, truly. Sorry about more things than I could count.

But David had never let me take the easy way out, and he wasn't about to now. When he walked into my line of sight, he was shaking. His big, competent hands trembled though he held them in tight fists at his side.

"That's all you've got to say?" he whispered. He wasn't a shouter, my David. The more angry he got, the more intense and passionate, the softer his voice grew. "You promised! You swore you were done!"

Anger, sluggish and bitter as old blood, dripped into the place where I kept my love for David. If you want to get a good fury going, there's nothing like guilt for fuel. I didn't want him here. He did not belong here. This was my other life, from before our family existed. I had traveled back in time. He had no right to follow me. Why couldn't he just go *away*?

"You say you trust me? How about trusting me enough to believe I'll come back!" *Go away, go home, don't BE here. This isn't your life. There's no room for you here!*

Disbelief slackened David's features. He rallied, but it

was a slow process. Like me, he was swimming against the current of the years. He walked to the low wall that circled the rooftop, to look at the restless sparks of city light. He spread his hands on the ledge, leaning all his weight on them as if testing the strength of the stone.

As if testing the strength of himself.

"How can you go back to the Guardians, Terese?" he said finally. "They broke you into pieces."

"They didn't break me. That was the Redeemers." The hands slick with my blood, and the pain and the filthy faces grinning and crooning about the will of God . . .

"The Guardians sent you."

"I volunteered. I knew the risks." Flash anger, hot and fresh, pulled me to my feet and clenched my fists. "Damn it, stop blaming the Guardians!"

"Why?" David swung around. "You've blamed them for years!"

I had. I did. My knees shook. "I might have been wrong," I whispered.

"*Now* you tell me."

I stared at him, my eyes stinging with exhaustion and emotion, and the sound that emerged from my open mouth was the last one I expected.

I started to laugh.

I dissolved into a torrent of giggles that buckled my knees so I had to drop back down onto the bench and press my hands against my face to catch the tears.

While I tried to get myself back under control, I felt David's warmth and smelled his distinct scent as he sat down beside me.

"I'm sorry," I said.

"It's all right," he said in that bland tone that meant all

that was right was my reaction to this moment. But at least it was a start.

I lifted my face, wiping my damp palms on my trousers. "I didn't lie to you," I said hoarsely. "Up until yesterday, I meant it. I never would have gone back. Up until three hours ago I meant it." It was the truth. "But . . . something has gone very wrong, David. Somehow, this little chunk of anarchy has become a threat at the worst possible time."

He made no reply to this, just scraped his shoes on the path as he shifted his weight. The sound reminded me of how Jerimiah had kicked at the carpet, and I remembered the suppressed anger vibrating through the whole of Misao's frame.

"They must be desperate," I whispered. "Why in the hell else would they want *me* back?"

David blew out a long breath. "Because you've survived what no one else has."

I lifted my eyes, rendered mute again. If his sorrow had undone me, watching slow, reluctant understanding take hold in him was enough to shatter me.

"Is it really war?" he asked.

"I think it could be. It's something bad. Misao is scared. I've never seen him scared before."

"But they haven't shown you any real evidence."

I thought again about how Misao had said it was a sure thing—but Jerimiah, who had been there, with Bianca— inside Bianca—said they'd found no proof. I tried very hard to squelch that memory, afraid David would read the doubt in my eyes.

"They can't show me the secured evidence until I'm under oath again."

"An oath you were ready to take just because Misao is scared and Bianca is dead."

"No!" I rubbed the spot behind my right ear. "Because the system I'm expert in is a hot spot and is about to explode. Because they *need* me."

Except he was right. I hadn't asked. I hadn't thought.

Oh, I was sure there was trouble. I believed something unprecedented was happening in Erasmus. But I hadn't demanded real proof. They had said it, and I had believed.

David did not look away. He blinked once, as if he were perfectly calm, but he read all this in my struggling expression. At last he sighed and stared out across the city, getting lost in the lights and motion for a moment.

"We live too long," he muttered.

I struggled to work out the connection and failed. "What?"

"We live too long," he said again. He shoved his hair back from his head with both hands. "Three hundred years, four hundred. We create one family, two, three . . . we sign contracts with the people we live with like it's possible to just shut off our feelings on a prearranged date." He snickered and my stomach sloshed, empty and queasy. *Go away*, I'd thought. *This is not your life.* "Did you hear, they're trying to develop a way to shut down memories of previous families so you can start your second, or third, without any . . . baggage. Of course, the lawyers'll also have to develop forms so you can notify your previous family that you've decided to forget them so they don't come looking for you. Except it won't work," he said. "I don't care what they do. It's all one life. Emotion gets piled on top of emotion, loyalty on top of loyalty, until we're answering to so many masters we can't do right by anybody."

I shivered as the cold in my heart leached through to my skin. "What are you going to do?"

He shifted around until he faced me fully, sad but calm. "What are *you* going to do?"

There are moments when you know the truth, and it is absolute. "I will not risk war in the Solar System. Not while our children live here."

He heard me. Finally. David had never seen even a small war, but he'd heard my stories. He'd seen what it had done to me.

Think about it. Think about what it's done to me. Think about your son, your daughters, called upon to take this kind of damage. To inflict this kind of damage.

Because that was part of the Common Cause. If we did go to war, if it did happen, the draft would be universal. No one who had entered their third decade would be spared. No business, no asset was exempt from conscription or confiscation. The effort would be total until the war was over. It would take Dale, Allie, Jo, him, me. All of us.

Slowly, David reached for me. He took both my hands in his. His hands were so cold. I folded my fingers around his, trying instinctively to warm them, before I realized I had no warmth left to give.

"They broke you, Terese," he whispered. "They took you and used you and broke you. How do I let you go back to that?"

I shook my head. The artificial breeze brought us the scent of earth, and allowed me to feel the dampness on my cheeks. "I don't know, David."

We sat there, awkward, all the weight of history between us, yet unable to let go of each other's hands. I remembered everything—all the times he'd pulled me out of the cellar of my despair, all the times I'd fought with him, cried, and demanded so much of him. And here I was, making another demand while I did the thing I swore I'd never do.

My reason was sound. My duty was absolute. That did not change the fact that I had sworn I would not go back to the Guardians. David had limits. There was only so much he was willing to take. Unlike some people, he was not a bottomless pit for punishment.

That was the problem. He'd die for the kids, and for me, but he would not suffer for us. Not for long anyway, and not without a reason he could fully comprehend.

Was that too much? Was that unfair? I'm pretty sure it was, but the thought kept ringing round my head in the heavy silence. Suddenly I missed Dylan. He would have known what to say right now. He would have held my hand and kept me from feeling so alone with my husband.

But Dylan was gone, gone even longer and farther than Bianca.

"Stay with me, David," I said abruptly. David was not part of the blood and the pain. David was the sunlight, the peace, and the freedom. I could have that for one last moment. Surely, that was not too much to ask.

He considered it, weighing whatever he was able to read in my eyes.

"I'll stay for tonight," he said.

"And tomorrow?"

"Tomorrow, you're returning to your old life, and even if there was room for me in there, there wouldn't be time. I'll go home."

It was honesty. It wasn't what I wanted, but it was all I had the right to ask for. I don't know which of us leaned toward the other first, but we wrapped our arms around each other and held on like that for a long, long time.

When I finally let go I said, "There's a couple of things I have to take care of first. I'll meet you at the Palmer House when I'm done, okay?"

He nodded. "The kids are angry. Not just Jo, either. She called Dale and Allie too. They are truly furious."

"I'm not surprised. They're probably in conference right now, trying to decide what they're going to do about Mother."

"You owe them an explanation."

"Yes."

He nodded once. "Okay, then. I'll go get Jo on her plane, and I'll tell her you'll be in touch before anything else happens."

"She won't want to go."

His smile was brief and bittersweet. "So what else is new?" His fingertips brushed my hand as he turned away.

I didn't sit and watch him leave. A kind of grim determination settled over me and I rose and walked toward a secondary stairway. I strode down the steps, through the doors, and back down the halls. My peripheral vision was gone. I could only see straight ahead. Nobody got in my way. Nothing shut down in front of me. Misao's door opened before I had to stretch out my hand.

He was still behind his desk. I swear he didn't even have to look up. He'd been waiting for me, the son of a bitch. What was more, he'd brought Vijay and Siri in to wait with him.

"I am a Grade 3 for pay and benefits, and it all goes into trust for my kids," I announced. "If I am hospitalized or killed, they get my pay, and they will keep getting it as long as they live, and it gets transferred down to the first-generation heirs if that takes a thousand years. You work it out with the bean counters and legal."

Misao nodded.

"And you are paying all my expenses while I'm evaluated and retrained. All of them. If I want grain-fed beef and caviar three times a day until we launch, you are paying for it."

He nodded once more and I drew in a ragged breath. "And there's one more thing."

"Yes?" Even now there was no impatience in Misao's tone.

"I won't have a Companion." My voice had found its steadiness again, and something of its strength. This was it. My ultimate condition. Not even Bianca's ghost could argue with this one. "If you require me to carry a Companion, I will not accept this commission."

How badly do you want me, Marshal-Steward? Bad enough to make an exception to the rules?

Vijay shifted his weight. I could feel how badly he wanted to protest. I wondered what his Companion was saying to him at that moment.

Misao just blinked at me. I think I prayed at that moment, but I could not for the life of me tell you what I prayed for.

"Very well. I will make sure your exception goes through."

The door in my mind sounded very loud as it slammed. It had been my last out, my last chance, and he wasn't even arguing.

Why in all the names of God isn't he even arguing?

Misao got to his feet. He touched a command on the desk and a red square lit up in front of where I stood. My palm itched. I laid it on the desk's smooth, cool surface. Red light filtered through skin and blood, making the edges of my fingers glow.

"Are you Terese Lynn Drajeske?" asked Misao.

"I am."

"Do you solemnly swear upon this life and all others to come that you will faithfully uphold and defend the laws and conventions of the United World Government of Earth?"

"I do swear."

The first time I took the oath, I was in my third decade. My palms were sweating and my uniform itched. The oath was being read off the desktop by Marshal-Steward Amelia Dan—a willowy, white-haired woman with a voice like an opera singer's. Maybe Jo would look like her one day.

"Do you solemnly swear that you will keep the secrets imparted to you by the Department of Peace and Security Maintenance or their duly appointed representatives in the course of your duty?"

"I do swear."

I was in my sixteenth decade, and my palms were sweating and my uniform collar itched. We were outdoors then, under a canopy, with a brass band waiting beside the stage. Misao, in his dress blues and white gloves, administered the oath he'd memorized so I could take up my new rank as Field Commander. I could feel Bianca grinning behind me then too, and Vijay, and Siri.

"What is the first precept?" asked Misao.

Response was automatic. The words welled up from my center. I could not have kept silent even if I'd wanted to. I was Terese Drajeske, here and now, with Misao, Siri, Vijay, and my own battered self. "Peace is my duty. Peace is what I am called to watch and expand. I hold close the knowledge that any death by my hand may start the war without end. Only peace creates life. Only life creates peace."

The light under my hand changed from red to green, and

it was done. I blinked and drew in a shaky breath. It was then I noticed the pain had stopped.

Oh, David.

I waited for either Siri or Vijay to welcome me back. Neither did. Misao touched another few commands. "Thank you, Field Commander."

I nodded curtly. Misao, my chief once more, bowed his head. We stood like that in silence for a moment. He was telling me he was sorry. Not for what he was doing, but that he could not pay the price himself. Vijay had tried to tell me the same thing, I think, but I hadn't been ready to feel it. Maybe taking the oath again had reopened the old channels. Maybe now that I'd actually reached the point of no return, I needed to grab hold of those around me so I would stop feeling so desperately alone.

At the time, I didn't know which of these was the truth.

I still don't.

SIX

AMERAND

"Welcome back, Captain Jireu."

My personal Clerk, Hamahd, was waiting for me as soon as I emerged into Dazzle's battered port yard. The dusty, open space was the polar opposite of Hospital's flashy arcade. Anything glamorous, valuable, or useful had been stripped away a long time ago. Bare stone and pitted, dirt-smeared concrete baked beneath the lighting panels.

"Thank you, Hamahd." I pressed my palm against the pad Hamahd held out, officially swearing that I had gone out with three crew and come back with two because of officially sanctioned and recorded actions taken in the line of duty. The cameras had already recorded my arrival, but Hamahd was particular. His eyes shone bright and beady as a snake's. He was watching and was not going to disguise the fact. It was one of the things I liked most about him. If I had to have a minder, I preferred that we were both up-front about it.

"Is there anything I should be aware of?" I asked.

"Commander Barclay has asked to see you." Hamahd tucked the pad under his arm. As always, his long black coat was immaculate. It hung in heavy folds over his prominent belly and brushed the top of his neat boots.

"Right away?"

"Yes."

I sighed. My head ached.

I wanted to go down to the base streets and the tunnels. I wanted noise and faces. I wanted to talk to people and hear them talk to me, about life and complaints and trivia. I wanted to see Father.

I wanted the Security to go away for a while. I had done next to nothing on the trip but sit in silence and think. The ship was hyperwired, and small. Leda and Ceshame and I got on all right, but if they saw an opportunity for advancement, they'd take it. It had not been safe to say one word about Emiliya, to pull her letter out of my pocket, or to seek out additional information about Kapa. All I could do was sit in my couch or my pilot's chair and turn over the thoughts in my own head. I didn't like the fact that he had turned up and I didn't know why. I couldn't believe it was all about Emiliya. Kapa had never run one game at a time. He'd always had something going in the background even when we were kids. If now was his time to try to talk Emiliya into the shadows, it was because it worked into something deeper.

I turned to Leda and Ceshame. "Get back to the station and check in. Start up the get-to files. Then you can check out, unless something new's come up." A riot, a murder, something like that.

They yes-captained me and stepped smartly out the gate. Bored secops, all of whom got this post because they were in trouble with their commanding officers, barely straightened as they passed. My crew's swaggers and stolen glances said clearly they were glad to be getting a half day off, which was why I'd given them one. I keep my people happy, which keeps their eyes fixed outward, rather than at my back.

"Well"—I turned to Hamahd—"let's not keep Commander Barclay waiting."

Hamahd bowed and stepped aside, as if I were actually someone he had to defer to. I started through the air lock, and he fell into place, the regulation four paces behind me, matching his stride to mine. I could just hear the clack of his hard-soled boots against the stone.

With Hamahd watching my every step I set off across the rooftops of Dazzle toward Upsky Station.

When Dazzle's purpose as an entertainment destination collapsed, its people reorganized themselves. Neighborhoods formed up according to tendencies and strata. The towers, domes, and parks just below the biggest light panels and black-sky windows were conquered and divided into private residences for those who had managed to hang on to some money and authority during the Crisis, the Split, and the Invasion.

Even up here, though, those chaotic times hadn't been good for the city and we never had enough people to really repair it, let alone clean it. Dirt tracked from the farms and gardens, or blown from pots and window boxes, built up in corners and odd pockets, allowing the local flora to spread. Cobalt-blue and blaze-orange lichen traced patterns on crumbling walls. Fleshy saffron feathers sprouted in dark corners, waving in the breeze from the irregular ventilation. Weeds, spread from the farms, made beards for the gargoyles and obscured the elaborate carvings, providing nest material for greasy feral parakeets as well as for the rats and mice, those eternal companions of human diaspora.

Predators had been imported to try to control the rodent problem. Now prides of wild cats wandered through the city. But the animals that had most successfully made Dazzle their home were the snakes—mostly small varieties, but every now and then you ran into a constrictor as thick as your wrist. Some of the old subway stations were nothing but huge nests of reptiles. Which were useful ways of getting rid of obnoxious new secops. One or two vermin-clearing assignments and they were glad to get back to Hospital, or even Market. So close to the black sky, they coiled up in the well-lit places, snoozing peacefully. They draped themselves on skylights and cornices, soaking up as much of the artificial light as they could.

In addition to the plants, handmade bridges and walkways had sent out tendrils across the roofs and balconies. As the trains and elevators became unreliable or hazardous, foot travel became more important. Some of these bridges were permanent, some actually artistic. Some were temporary and others more or less private property—enterprising families or gangs charged a toll for their use. This was the network I crossed with Hamahd following, all the time four steps behind me, no matter how fast or slow I went.

We passed the wealthy residents in their weighted, decorated clothes, as well as the more subdued but neatly turned out indentures who waited on them. They nodded in respect to my uniform. Some even raised their hands in greeting although they didn't stand aside. They didn't know me. I kept my rooms farther down, closer to the foundation streets. That made me unusual. Most of Dazzle's secops lived up here. That wasn't necessarily to be near the gentry, though. The last open tunnels to the farms were up here too. The farms were the most vital and most vulnerable point on Dazzle and have been ever since Oblivion died.

If you're an OB, that is, if your family's from Oblivion, you call the crossing to Dazzle the "Run" or the "Breakout." If you're a "Baby D," from Dazzle, it was the "Invasion." Whatever you called it, it was done on a massive scale. I was about seven, perhaps eight years old, when my parents, my older brothers, and I crammed ourselves in a ship, shoulder to shoulder with God-Alone knew how many other runners.

There was even less food in that hold than there had been back home, and no knowing if we'd be able to land, or if we'd be shot out of the black sky.

But there were thousands of us. We were sure some of us would make it. They couldn't get us all.

They didn't. They got a lot of us, but not all.

But what we arrived to was more disaster. When we starving refugees poured out of our ships, we ransacked the farm caverns. We staked out territory in them. Gangs rose up and fought over them. We, they, tried to bribe or enslave the growers.

This, as you can probably guess, was not a viable system. In the end it brought the Security and the Clerks, and Fortress itself, back to Dazzle. The initial Security Operation units landed with one mission and one only: make it safe to farm again. This was done with an efficiency that was cheered by all but the families of the dead.

Keeping the food growing and the water flowing is still the Security's major mission on this world. As long as this was done, Dazzle let the Blood Family take what they wanted and keep hold of it however they could.

Even the people.

Especially the people.

Upsky Station took up the top floor of the old Starfire Grand casino. As Hamahd and I crossed the arched metalwork bridge to the roof, I was met by two secops and their unusually dull-eyed Clerk. Out of the corner of my eye I saw Hamahd rake the man over with a stern glance. I spared a moment of sympathy for the other Clerk as I was palmed into the building on a check pad.

Upsky was unfortunately beginning to show its age. The walls needed paint, the carpets needed cleaning and repair.

So did most of the furniture. Much of the respectably shabby space was given over to the Clerks, who needed access to working screens so they could extract, compile, and record data on every aspect of the life and people of Dazzle. The murmur of voices, the clack of keys, the brush of fingertips and pages filled the hive. As usual, Hamahd left me here—with a respectful bow, of course, but without any explanation—and disappeared into the shifting swarm of his own people.

I tried to get myself to relax, but it was no good. He might not be following me, but he was in there, compiling his data, setting everything up in neat files just in case he needed them.

Just in case I made a mistake.

I kept walking along the old, faux-wood-paneled corridor until I came to the door with Favor Barclay's name and rank shining on its black screen.

I touched the knob. It recognized me and the door clicked open.

My thin, dark commander stood behind his desk, but he was not alone. In front of him sat the Grand Sentinel Torian Leidy Erasmus, Dazzle's Grand Sentinel.

"Come in, Captain Jireu," said Commander Barclay. "Thank you for coming so quickly."

"My duty, sir." I bowed to him, then turned and bowed much more deeply to his superior. "Grand Sentinel Erasmus."

The Sentinel was lean but fit, shorter than I was and much older. His face was lined and his eyes were dangerously alert and alive. He was not afraid to dress richly no matter where he went on Dazzle. Today he wore a shimmering ruby coat trimmed with onyx and gold and a black, full-circle cape made heavy with more gold and more gleaming scarlet thread.

Of course, all this wealth concealed body armor and God-Alone knew how many weapons.

Commander Barclay motioned me toward a smaller, harder chair than the one the Grand Sentinel occupied. I bowed again and took the seat indicated. A carafe of water and a glass waited on a table beside it. I poured myself a measure and drank the traditional welcome cup.

Both the commander and Sentinel Torian watched me patiently until I'd drained my cup, set it down, and smacked my lips politely.

Barclay nodded in approval for my manners and settled back in his chair, ready to get down to business. "The Sentinel is briefing me about the new arrivals we can expect from the Pax Solaris."

The saints again. The back of my neck prickled.

"New arrivals, sir?" I said. I wasn't supposed to know about this. So, until I got some signals as to how much trouble I was—or wasn't—in I was not going to let on that I did know about it.

"Yes. It's no secret," replied Commander Barclay. "The Pax is sending us an influx of new saints, and your patch is going to receive most of them."

"Yes, sir." I accepted this revelation as I would any other order, showing neither enthusiasm nor distaste. After all, I already had an abandoned hotel full of saints under my jurisdiction. In fact, it might have been Liang Chen who had sent for the newcomers.

I allowed myself a sideways glance at the so-far-silent Sentinel. Seño Torian was the overcommander of all the Security, including the Clerks. He studied me with an appearance of mild interest. I waited, focusing my efforts on keeping my face blank but attentive at the same time.

"Sentinel Erasmus tells me these may not be the ordinary run of Solaris saints," Commander Barclay said.

I raised my eyebrows. "No, sir?"

"No, Captain," said the Sentinel. He had a light voice, remarkably smooth for such an old man. None of us was sure of his exact age. He had most definitely had some Solaris-style life extension. Some even said he was the last living child of our Founders, Jasper and Felice Erasmus. But that couldn't be true. That would make him the very first of the first-degree Bloods, which would make him the *Saeo* of the Erasmus System, as opposed to the new pairing of Esteban and Mai. I could not for one second picture anyone taking precedence over Sentinel Torian without his permission. "In fact, we believe they will be sending us at least one spy."

I did not know how to answer this, so I said nothing. All the saints were supposed to be spies. I watched my herd of them faithfully. So far, all I had been able to find them guilty of was using the black market when they couldn't find what they needed elsewhere. I kept files in case I needed something to hang on one of them in the future.

"Nothing to say, Captain?" the Sentinel asked, raising his eyebrows. For a moment, I thought he might be mocking me, and the prickling beneath my collar intensified.

"I'm sorry, Grand Sentinel. I don't understand why Solaris would want to spy on us." Poor, crumbling, scrapping, enslaved *us*.

Sentinel Torian's voice went cold. "They see we are reunited and preparing to resume our place in the economic and political life of the diaspora worlds." Out here, we do not use the word "colony." "They are suspicious of our intentions and want to assure themselves that we don't mean to threaten their precious stability."

"And do we?" I asked. I don't know what made me do it. I was tired. I was frightened. I didn't want to be there.

Sentinel Erasmus laughed out loud. "Excellent question, Captain. I like how this mind works." He directed that comment toward Commander Barclay, who returned the smile briefly, looking relieved rather than pleased, I thought.

"What would you say," the Sentinel went on, a faint smile still in place on his narrow, smooth lips, "if I told you, yes, we do threaten that precious stability?"

I chose my next words with extreme caution. "I'd wonder why, Grand Sentinel."

"Because we mean to hem them in. We are in some very high-level and sensitive negotiations with other diaspora worlds. They are, like us, tired of this great hulk of Old Earth squatting in the middle of the Pax Solaris web, ready to take us apart if we are less-than-passive recipients of their commands and regulations." The Sentinel sat back in his chair with his clean and well-kept hands resting on its arms and regarded me triumphantly.

Commands and regulations? When had we ever done what the Pax Solaris told us to? Well, I was just a lowly Security captain. I couldn't be expected to be kept in the loop about diplomacy.

"We have reached agreement with enough systems that we will be able to create a cordon for the Solaris. Once it is in place, if they want to be able to run their ships, their goods, and their castoffs out to us, they must allow us equivalent access to the Solaris worlds."

Accepting our ships, our goods, and our castoffs.

Our criminals and spies.

It sounded perfectly reasonable, and well within the bounds of what the Blood Family was capable of. They didn't like the Pax worlds. The internal drive had come out of Solaris. The internal drive, more than anything else, was supposed to have caused Erasmus's collapse. The Blood Family could not forgive that.

But something nagged at the back of my mind, buried under all the other worries and wariness. An old report, an old investigation, something to do with the saints. I reached for it, but having the Sentinel's attention on me did not make thinking easy and it slipped away.

I turned to Commander Barclay. Now was the time to apply the first lesson I'd learned at the academy. Whatever your superiors tell you about policy, ignore it. It doesn't matter. Only one thing matters. "My orders, Commander?"

Barclay waited a moment to see if the Grand Sentinel would choose to speak. When he didn't, my commander said, "Your orders are to get to know this new group of saints. Keep an eye on them, but do not frighten them—and make sure they do not get themselves into any . . . trouble."

Of course. "And will I be informed what trouble is, Commander?"

"As necessary," said the Grand Sentinel.

And there it was. I was being made responsible for the new saints. If they did something successful—or unpalatable—it was on me.

"Is this clear, Captain?" There was an undertone in the commander's voice. Until the new saints were gone, his attention would be on me. He didn't like this either. He wanted to stay up here with the Clerks and the reports. He wanted to keep the markets open, and keep his home and family comfortable.

"Yes, Commander."

I waited in silence while the Sentinel studied me, and

Commander Barclay studied the Sentinel. Evidently satisfied that Sentinel Erasmus was satisfied, Barclay said, "Dismissed, Captain."

I stood and made my bow. Out in the corridor, my head began to ache again, the pain pulsing in time with my footsteps as I crossed back into the Clerks' territory.

Hamahd was waiting for me, of course. The Clerks had some comm network that the rest of us were not allowed to know about. I'd heard some secops brag they'd found its frequencies, but I didn't think it was possible. I suspected if that network existed, it was installed in one of those high-clearance wings on Hospital.

We walked out onto the rooftops. We took the arching bridge across to the Glorious roof, then a spiral stair down to the catwalk that we crossed to the Luxe. It swarmed with people lugging handcarts filled with jugs and cans, all coming back from the water market.

As we shouldered our way through the hubbub, Hamahd pushed closer to me.

"You should have told me about Kapa Lu," he said.

I started. I couldn't help it. Then I shrugged. "I didn't think there was any need. I knew you'd have the records."

"That, Captain, is not the point and you know it."

"I'm sorry. Will you need to write me up?" I ducked past a woman hunched under a yoke slung with about a dozen gallon jugs.

"Not this time."

"Thank you."

"Don't." We stepped over the ledge, taking a shortcut to the less-crowded roof on the old Fortuna, and walked on in silence for a moment. Then Hamahd said, "I like my post here, Captain Jireu. I like Dazzle and its amenities, faded as they are. You are a good subject and I do not wish to lose you as my assignment. Therefore, I am telling you to take this new matter seriously."

"I do."

"Yes. But not seriously enough, I think. Something is changing. Our new *Saeos* have a plan."

"There's always a plan, Hamahd."

"No," whispered Hamahd. "Not like this."

I waited for him to go on, but he did not. We crossed Old Cramer's Bridge, which juddered slightly under our footsteps. I licked my lips and tried to force myself to think. I never ate or slept well aboard the hyperwired ship. It felt too much like being in a cage. I wanted to go home. I wanted to get some dinner and go to bed early.

Except Hamahd—my Clerk—who never said anything he did not have to—had just told me I was in a bigger mess than I had believed, and he had started it off by talking about Kapa.

All right. All right. What do I know? Kapa is back and the saints are arriving. I've been ordered to keep an eye on the saints, and Hamahd is worried because I didn't tell him about Kapa. I can't talk to Kapa.

But I can talk with a saint.

We stepped off the spindly bridge onto what had once been a broad balcony and now was a kind of thoroughfare. I stepped to the side so a man with a load of reclaimed sheeting on his back could get past. I turned to Hamahd.

"Hamahd, please go ahead and make sure Liang meets me at the station, would you?"

His face was passive as he bowed, and I took it as a sign of approval. "Yes, Captain." He set off at a much faster pace than I had been using.

I stood there a moment, gripping the balcony rail until Hamahd was well out of sight. Hamahd's declaration that he liked his assignment was reassuring, but I was under no illusion. If it came to an audit, Hamahd would not save me any more than I would save him. And Hamahd had the power to call down that audit. For any reason, but especially if he thought I was not taking my duties seriously enough.

Fear spread like an old ache through my guts and I suppressed it. I thought about going home and decided I should risk the delay. It would take even Hamahd a little while to hunt up the saint. I had time to check in on Father.

In fact, given all that had already happened, I had better.

Most of the huge old buildings—the theaters and casinos and brothels—had been broken up, each becoming its own village with the interiors rearranged according to the evolving needs of the inhabitants. Every so often someone got a little too enthusiastic with their rearrangement, and whole floors came down. There was still a mound of rubble where the Ultima had been.

My own door faced the open street. The only way to it was to cross Bidden's sagging bridge, and climb down the rattling ladder to our balcony. Once a sliding crystal door had opened onto the tiled space, but I had replaced it with a new door of reforged and bolted metal. I rapped out our particular signal. Eventually, the bolts slid back and the door creaked heavily open.

"Welcome home, Captain." My father, Finn Jireu, bowed and held out his hands for my coat, just in case anyone was watching.

Fifteen years ago, my father and mother had sold themselves into bondage to buy a slot for me in the Security academy. The minute I got my rank and a steady posting, I started searching for them.

So far, I'd only found Father. Calling him my servant allowed him to live in my home, sleep in his own bed, have space and place and a little dignity. As a lieutenant, I was allowed a human servant. As a captain, I was allowed two. The arrangement twisted my guts, but if this game would keep him with me, I would play.

I touched his shoulder to assure him we were alone for the moment. He nodded and straightened up. "All right?" he asked in his thin and raspy voice. His coat was plain pale blue and his trousers straight buff brown. His boots were clean and new. Everything absolutely appropriate to his position as a waiting man, except for his sharp expression.

I shrugged. "I've got to get down and talk to Liang Chen," I said. "Something's up with the saints and God-Alone knows what." I pulled Emiliya's letter from my coat and handed it over to him. "Can you get this to Mother Varus?"

"Sure, sure. Sit down and eat, Captain Son." Our small dim flat smelled of hot duck and garlic and my stomach was already growling. "I know, you've no time to make a proper meal of it." He waved my words away before I could say them. "I'll take Mother Varus the leftovers as well."

I sat cross-legged on the carpet with my father, wolfing down steamed buns filled with duck and cabbage. For this brief time, I could pretend that there was nothing waiting outside the door. I poured him a cup of strong tea and heard the local gossip, although I only half listened. It was enough to hear his voice, steady if thin, and to know that for the moment, he was all right. No matter what came next, for right now, I had made at least one member of my family safe.

"Do you think they'll make us celebrate the birth, then?"

"Eh?" I looked up from the dumpling I'd been poking to pieces. Father cocked his head at me.

"The *Saeos*. This baby of theirs should be due in another month or two. Do you think we'll be required to make a turnout?"

Ah, yes. Sometime back, our rulers had announced they were going to have an heir. And weren't there three or four others in the first degree that were due at about the same time? Details trickled back.

"I'm sure of it. They've even hauled old Master Bloom out to design the party."

My father's mouth twitched. "The self-proclaimed Master of Dazzle running a baby's natalday party? Oh, I bet he's loving that."

I shook my head. "Don't underestimate him, Father. He has more disguises than any of us knows. I'd bet a gallon of pure water the best is his look of being a broken old man."

Father nodded, but I wasn't sure he believed me. There was no time or reason to argue the point. I got to my feet and Father rose as well and walked me to the door. I embraced his thin shoulders when I left, and he slapped me softly against the arm for showing sentiment. Feeling obscurely better, I made my way down to the foundation streets.

My Security house, No. 39, took up what once had been a string of boutiques for the tourists. I captained fifty Security, more than twice the usual number. This was because of the "OB troubles" down here, and because we had a water market.

Despite the Security and the Clerks, the way Fortress really controlled the Erasmus system was through the water.

Of all the moons in the system, only Fortress had its own supply. The rest of us had to import it.

Of course Fortress said they were committed to keeping a continuous and adequate supply of potable water, but somehow it never quite happened. The water markets only opened every other day, and it took every secop we had to keep them from turning into riots. The Security had to escort the carriers to fill the tanks. The Security had to keep order in the square where the excess was bought and sold at approved times. There was always talk of reservoirs and of getting the central plumbing working again. I did not expect to live long enough to witness these miracles. Why would Fortress voluntarily give up so much control?

My official job was to keep the streets peaceful. What that meant was I had to make sure that Dazzle's children did not kill too many of Oblivion's, and vice versa. I spent a great deal of time talking. I spent almost as much time tracking the shifts of turf, following the rise and falls of gangs, guilds, and families. My runs in the black sky were fairly regular too. I was one of the few licensed pilots on Dazzle—a status that allowed me to see Emiliya and other old friends. A status I kept in part because of Hamahd's good reports.

One more thing to keep in mind during . . . whatever was to come.

I entered the Security house through the central front door, stopping to palm the active pad on Hamahd's desk. Hamahd gave me a cursory glance and added his print for confirmation. We nodded to each other and I walked to the former storeroom that was my office.

It was a comfortably furnished storeroom now, with a desk and a screen, chairs, a cabinet, and at the moment, the cross, pacing Solaris saint I had sent Hamahd to bring me.

"Thank you for coming, Seño Chen," I said. "I'm sorry if I've kept you waiting."

"I hope there's no problem, Captain Jireu?" One of the things I like about the saints is they are reflexively polite. Liang Chen was angry, but because I had been courteous, he was incapable of being anything else in return.

"Nothing new. Will you please sit down?" I took my seat behind my scarred and listing desk and gestured him to the best and newest chair.

"Thank you." Liang sat, crossing his legs and his arms. He was not tall, but he was solid in a way very few of us from Erasmus are. "How can I help you?"

I had considered and discarded multiple approaches on my way down. My relationship with Liang was complicated, to say the least. We neither liked each other nor hated each other. We both pitied each other for very different reasons, and we needed each other.

Finally, I decided I would imitate the Grand Sentinel and be direct.

"I have been told that a new group of workers is arriving from the Pax Solaris."

Liang shrugged his shoulders, plainly irritated I was talking about such a small thing. "It's the usual rotation. We aren't allowed enough hands to do what we really need to, so the people we do have burn out pretty quickly."

I watched Liang for a moment. In addition to polite, he was inherently honest, something else I liked about the saints. They said what they meant and meant what they said, and if they didn't, you could tell right away.

"So there's nothing about them I should know?" I could make Liang's life difficult and chose not to, and he knew that. He did help the people down here, kept thirst and the worst starvation at bay. I was grateful for that, but it was no different from the gratitude I felt for Hamahd—it only went so far, and no further.

Liang shrugged again. "I don't know for sure. Might be they've finally decided to investigate Bianca Fayette's death."

I blinked. "Bianca Fayette?"

He frowned. Real anger deepened the lines on his brow and stiffened his shoulders. "Yes. A member of the Guardians who was . . . found dead a year ago."

That was it, what I had been trying to remember.

A dead saint. It happened now and again. The foundation streets were not necessarily safe, even for those who understood them. I had seen the report. I had seen the place it happened and supervised the transfer of the body to the saints. When they did not raise a stink with the guard or Commander Barclay, I had forgotten about it.

"I take it you were not satisfied with our investigation for . . . I'm sorry, what was her name?"

"Fayette," Liang said, slowly and clearly. "Bianca Fayette."

"You were not satisfied with our investigation for Seña Fayette?" Not that there had been any. The body had been more liquid than solid by the time we'd been notified of its existence. Whoever or whatever had killed her was long gone.

Then it occurred to me that no one had come to investigate any of the other deaths we'd had among the saints in the past five years. But then again, none of them had been Guardians.

"Your people said it was simple robbery." Liang lifted his shaggy eyebrows. "Is there any reason to believe otherwise?"

"You must think there is or you wouldn't have made the request for an additional investigation. At least, I assume you did?" I didn't assume anything. I was fishing, but Liang didn't seem to notice.

"Just for form's sake." Liang looked away. As I said, you could tell immediately when the saints tried to lie. "We are in a dangerous neighborhood. Coordinator Fayette wasn't careful enough."

Which was what I had been thinking, but hearing it from this mild, polite little man was both incongruous and uncomfortable. "That's a little cold."

"For a Solaris saint, you mean?"

"Yes."

Liang blew out a sigh and rubbed his hands together. "I suppose it is. But I've got no time for those who can't remember the difference between immortal and invulnerable." He put his hands on the chair arms, getting ready to push himself back up onto his feet.

"I beg your pardon?"

"Sorry." He grimaced, probably because he realized he'd just delayed his own retreat. "Bianca Fayette was a licensed immortal. Some of them forget that just because they've been chemically fiddled with, they are not immune to being bashed over the back of the head. Which is what you said happened to her?"

"I'd have to look it up, but yes." I watched him. I'd never heard a saint speak this way about anybody. I'd never heard them speak openly about their immortals either. I wonder what that did to them, the knowledge that death was a choice. What must it be like not only to own your life, but eternity along with it?

Liang finished standing up. "Bianca Fayette tried to turn a profit from her time here. That's not what we're here for."

It took me a moment to digest this. I suppose, if I had

bothered to think about it, I would have thought saints were human and therefore vulnerable to corruption. I had never considered the possibility I would hear one of them talk about it. I didn't want their secrets. But now it looked like I would have no choice but to take them.

"Why didn't you ship her home?" I asked.

The corner of Liang's mouth twitched. "As if any of us would have real jurisdiction over a Guardian."

"I see." For once, something Liang said about the Solarans that made perfect sense.

"Maybe." But Liang's eyes did not hold the benefit of even that much doubt.

"Sorry to have dragged you down here for this."

He sighed one more time, deflating into himself. "That's all right. I was coming down anyway. A friend of mine sent a message from Werethere. They've gotten a shipload of emergency construction workers from Oblivion. He's asking to see if there's any word of your mother."

"Thank you." I had to work to keep my gaze steady. There was no way Hamahd was not listening to this conversation.

There is also no way he doesn't know you've had Liang helping look for Mother, I reminded myself. *It's just that until now he hasn't decided to care.*

Liang shrugged, irritation and anger adding force to the gesture. "It's hard. They're playing games with the names. Have you managed to get her ID number?"

"No." I managed to remain calm. "It is not the sort of thing the Clerks are inclined to share."

Liang snickered. "Yeah, I've noticed. I'll keep the channels open."

"Thank you."

We stayed there in silence, not friends, but not enemies,

using each other, but wishing we didn't have to, each trying to understand the other as best he could.

"I'm on your side, Amerand," he said.

I said nothing. I believed him. The problem was he had no idea what he was talking about.

"I need to get back," said Liang at last. "They're shutting off the water in fifteen, and I want to make sure the crowd doesn't get restless. Unless there's anything else?"

"No. Thank you." I stood to acknowledge his departure. "Do you need extra Security?"

"I'll let you know."

"If any OBs become a problem, send them to me."

"I will. Thank you."

Liang left me with only one sideways glance, which I couldn't read. I rubbed the back of my neck and stared at the closed door.

Something was changing. It involved Kapa. It involved the saints. It involved Fortress and the Clerks. It involved me and Emiliya and Kapa and by extension all of our families.

In the heights, I hadn't thought I was in trouble.

I had been very, very wrong.

SEVEN

TERESE

No matter how desperately you want to get your mission started, get your boots on the ground somewhere else, it never goes fast enough. When you need a total physical makeover, it takes even longer.

To make matters worse, medical rebirth is boring. And painful.

I had to go through seventy-two solid hours of anesthetic dreams before I was allowed to awake fully to my new physical self. The human body does not like to have its clock reset. It protests and struggles and begs the brain for help. They have to keep you either completely out or fuzzily numb for days while the nanos and the doctors do their work, but even then you are aware in some subbasement of your mind that what is happening is *wrong*.

I had been told I was being put back to the physical equivalent of a woman late in her third decade, but when I first tried to get out of my bed, I felt like I had been accelerated toward death's door. I swear, my veins burned. Childbirth? Nothing. I'd've done it three more times rather than face that new pain.

The therapy to get myself and my body up to speed was much the same as the medical rework: prolonged, painful, and boring. Multiple therapists and trainers worked with me and on me, blithely unaware how close they were to grievous bodily harm. But then, I expect they were used to that.

David did not come to see me. He didn't call either. I shoved the fact of his silence into the background and struggled to get on with the job of getting my body and mind into full working order again.

I didn't call him either.

Before I went under the needle, Allie and Dale came down, having obviously resolved to try a concentrated-intervention strategy. They argued with me for hours. They reminded me what I was doing to them, what I was doing to their father, what I was doing to myself. They insisted I was not fit to meet the challenges of impending war. Was I aware I might just make things worse?

I pointed out I had a duty to not just the past, but the future. I was doing this to keep them safe, and their families yet to be. I pointed out I hadn't volunteered for this, not entirely. I was being called back to active duty.

They left—sober, disturbed, and more convinced than I would have believed possible, which gave me the strangest twisted feeling in my heart.

Jo came alone, of course. She waited until after the major treatments, and until I was on my feet again. She walked into the hospital room and looked me up and down intently, memorizing every detail of every change. Then she turned on her heel and left without saying a word.

I huddled under the covers and sobbed with the pillow stuffed in my mouth for ten full minutes before the nurses came and pulled me out.

Slowly, I did adjust to my rejuvenated body. The pain faded and I began to enjoy the strength and energy. I wasn't that much lighter, but the weight I carried was muscle mass, so I was stronger and less . . . worn. I ran through the terrace parks, braving the driving Lake Michigan winds and sometimes risking my new ankles on the ice. I walked through the chaos of the lower city, plowing through drifts for the sheer hell of it, and once getting into a snowball fight with a mob of schoolkids who had slipped the leash for a moment.

Everywhere I went, memory stirred. Not huge things. Most of the actual places I had frequented when I was assigned here—the bars, restaurants, and clubs—were long gone. It was more the feeling. The walkways felt familiar under my shoes. Smells created waves of pleasant nostalgia. Even the air that carried the rush and rigor of the city's presence felt comfortably familiar.

The doctors said it was a side effect of the medical rebirth. My body had been reset to a previous time, and it was the physical sensation of being that age strengthening the memories of the place around me.

I hoped that was true. Because I didn't like what the alternative meant. It meant David was right, and something inside me was burrowing through my time with him to the old life underneath. And it felt good.

Indoors, I played in old Xperiensors I'd enjoyed in my second and third decades, and tried some new ones Siri recommended. I took the stairs instead of the elevators and reveled in my speed.

Vijay and Siri came around regularly and we would go out and get dinner, or sit around the room and talk about old times and catch up on the unit gossip.

We did not talk about our personal lives. We never had. For this, I was grateful. I caught all the playful slaps and arm punches that passed between them and hadn't been there before; all the looks filled with things they were never going to say in front of me. I pretended I didn't notice. They let me pretend and we were all satisfied, for the moment anyway.

It wasn't like we didn't have plenty to keep ourselves busy. There were hours upon hours of reports in various formats to be reviewed, walked through, and talked over, from plain text to full-sensory, composite XPs. We had to review Siri's dossiers on key power figures on Dazzle where we'd be based, like Commander Favor Barclay ("He'd like to be a good guy, but he's too frightened"), as well as potential information sources like Natio Bloom ("the 'Master of Dazzle'; spends a lot of time trying to convince everybody, himself included, that title still means something. Kind of sad."). Then there were personnel decisions, equipment decisions, strategic and logistical decisions. I needed to brush up on at least one of the Erasmus dialects. Siri, of course, already spoke the slang fluently—and more than a little smugly.

In addition, I had to spend time coordinating our operation with the Common Cause Assistance Foundation, which was running the current aid mission to Erasmus. I had a few old pangs when I sat down with the board. During the Redeemer crisis, I'd also gone in with an aid mission. It is, in fact, the most common way to insert Guardians into a non-Pax environment. This is not to say the aid is disingenuous, or that the people who give it are not dedicated humanitarians. They are, deeply so. They are our open hand.

This time, oddly, I wasn't going to be given a cover in the aid mission or even a formal designation with them. I was going under my own rank as Field Commander with an open and visible mission: to find out what had really happened to Bianca. But, as much as possible, we try to work with any humanitarian agency in place when we go. They have a solid knowledge of the local community and the local power structure. That was important because Siri and Vijay's personal experiences were almost two years out of date.

And, of course, the fact that I was not going in undercover with CCA did not mean that no one was going in with them. I just had not been officially informed about it.

I remained uninformed until six weeks before our scheduled departure, when Vijay abruptly stopped showing up to meetings and ate his meals out. It was part of the deal. He and his were going to be our connection to the black market, the smugglers and the pirates. I couldn't know where he was or what he was going to look like. He'd get his reports to Siri, and she'd get them to me.

I gave her a week to mope. She, of course, denied that she was moping. But his leaving hurt her. I tried not to imagine their farewell: how they had held each other, laughing and joking together. Siri would have threatened him with assorted interesting and impossible punishments if he didn't take care of himself. He would have mocked her ruthlessly until she had no option but to give him one of those playful slaps I'd seen, and he would have grabbed her hand, and then . . . and then . . .

It wasn't that I minded that they were lovers. It was the contrast between what I imagined for them and the way I had taken leave of David that was too much to bear.

I turned my face to the world again, and I kept on going.

We were three weeks away from launch when Siri arrived on the threshold of my hotel room and asked to be let in. It was late, but I was up, with my glasses plugged into my set so I could go over the unsteady XPs from one of Bianca's trips to Fortress.

I unplugged as Siri dropped onto the sofa. She rubbed her long hands together in a way that was more a sign of restlessness than of trying to get rid of Chicago's February chill. I tried not to notice as I folded my glasses away into their case, but the warnings were already sounding in the back of my mind.

"So, what's up?" I asked as casually as I could.

"I had a meeting with Misao, about Jerimiah."

"And?" Siri had been working with Jerimiah over the past weeks, distilling the information that he—it—still held, matching it against her own experiences in Erasmus. I read the reports closely, but I had stayed as far away from the meetings as I could. I couldn't stand to be in the same space as Jerimiah, let alone when Siri brought out Shawn, her own Companion, to help with analysis and what passed as inter-rogation between the two artificial constructs. At those times, the loss inside me opened so wide I felt like I'd start bleeding from my heart.

"I think it would be valuable to have him on the mission with us."

Him. Jerimiah.

With an effort, I set aside my emotions and tried to think in purely practical terms—about logistics, about advantages and disadvantages. "That means a lot of extra equipment to keep him coherent and to be able to tap in and communicate securely, especially going into a place with such a fragmented datascape. Will Misao authorize that?"

"We wouldn't need the extra tech if you carried him."

I frowned. "What?"

"If you had Jerimiah installed."

I stared at her. I heard what she was saying, but for a long moment, there was a wall between her words and any form of comprehension. Slowly, understanding leaked through. She wanted me to carry Jerimiah with me, inside me, as I had once carried Dylan.

She was asking me to take on a Companion. *Bianca's Companion.*

"I cannot *believe* you did that." My voice shook. Cold surged through me. "Even if it wasn't completely morbid, even if it wasn't indecent and disrespectful, and . . . What in God's name were you thinking?"

Very softly, Siri said, "That Bianca might still be alive."

I stared at her until my head ached. She just sat there, calm and collected. Like she believed what she said. Like it was possible.

"Have you lost your mind, Field Coordinator?" I asked quietly, matter-of-factly. It was the only explanation I could come up with.

"No, I haven't." Siri had clearly been ready for that assessment. Her eyes gleamed with the light of discovery. "Think about it—about Jerimiah, about his condition, about how he was found." Siri leaned forward, ticking the points off on her fingers. "He was found damaged, unable to even say how his principal died, in a body that was barely still a body. Even now he is disassociated from himself."

"I've seen all that." I'd made myself look at it. I'd needed to know where and how Bianca was found if I was to begin an investigation into her death. Now the sight of her decayed body weighed heavily in the hole in my head, and it would probably never go away.

"If someone took her into captivity, if they removed the Companion network and implant . . ."

"You can't just remove a whole Companion network." Pain. Knives and dirty, bloody fingers, and pain and pain until I passed out and woke to more pain and the hole in my head . . .

"They have a hospital the size of a small planet out there. They might have been able to do the surgery." *Instead of butchery,* said the silence of her pause. *Instead of what was done to you.* "They had a look, managed the data alterations in the inorganic components, and put him back. He'd already been through enough trauma. Any mismatch between his organic and inorganic nodes could easily be put down to that.

"Plus," she went on, gathering steam, "the people who provided the identification of the body aren't exactly on our side."

"Her body was shipped back here." By now I had rallied enough to put some force and incredulity back into my voice. "Are you saying our people can't run DNA matches?"

"Things can be faked. Things can be grown."

"They faked a human body? A well-known and thoroughly IDed human body?"

The gleam in Siri's eye brightened. She was sure she had me. "A body in an advanced state of decay, shipped back in puddles and pieces. Hospital the size of a planet, remember? You've never heard of stem cells? You know, the little bits of you that can be used to grow other bits of you?"

I sat there biting my lips against the ideas that swirled through my mind. Me carry Bianca's companion? What about Dylan? Dylan screamed when they cut him out of me. I screamed. He died. I died. The hole was too deep, too permanent. There was no filling it. I would not have another Companion trying to straddle that abyss inside me.

The thought twisted my guts, and yet . . . there was something in it. I didn't want a Companion. I didn't want to face that dependency or that loss, again. But what if I carried Bianca's Companion? The one who had been there with her, the one who knew all the secrets she had kept to herself?

The idea repulsed me as it beckoned me. To have even that much of Bianca back. Could I stand to have a part of Bianca with me?

If there was even the smallest possibility that Bianca might be alive, could I refuse?

No. Get past this. Remember what is real. I took a deep breath. "If you're so sure about this, Siri, why didn't you tell Misao?"

"I did." But for the first time since she came in, Siri wasn't looking at me. "He didn't believe me."

Relief like a tidal wave washed over me. Not because of what she said, but because as she shifted her weight and rubbed her hand back and forth on the sofa cushion next to her, I understood that she had not only been turned down, but turned down flat, and this was a desperate attempt to revive a dead cause.

"That's it, then," I said.

"No," snapped Siri. "It isn't. If you'd just *look* . . ."

"No."

"Listen, Terese . . ."

I shook my head, hard. "It is not possible," I told her. "They would have had to fake the memory node that had her last words stored in it. They would have had to have known my name and our relationship. There's too much."

"Hospital the size of a planet," repeated Siri. "With a hell of a reputation for doing the impossible out in the colonies. I know, because I looked. We don't know what they can do out there."

"If you think Bianca's still alive, why would you want me to carry Jerimiah? Why wouldn't you want him safe back here waiting for her?"

"Because then we'd have his memories, *Bianca's* memories, to work from. You worked with her longer than anyone. You'd be able to interpret the fragments better . . ."

I couldn't stand it. The pain was too much. "Why in God's nine billion names are you doing this, Siri?"

Siri licked her lips. "Because she sent me away and I left. I didn't ask, I didn't think about it. I just sulked and I went, and she was caught and maybe cut up and maybe worse, and I wasn't there to stop it."

I nodded. "I know just how you feel."

"Then will you at least consider it?"

For a moment hope, bright and cruel as a knife, presented itself to me. It took every ounce of strength I had to turn away. "No, Siri. I cannot believe it. I can't."

"Why not?"

I swallowed. This was no time to lie. "Because if I do, I will go in there ready to tear the place apart with my bare hands. I won't give a shit about any other part of this mission."

I straightened my spine and my voice sharpened, taking on the tone I use for giving orders without my conscious will. "You don't bring this up again. Not to me, not to Vijay, not to anybody. And if you aren't going to be able to keep your mind on the real mission, you say so right now, do you understand me?"

Anger sparked deep in Siri's gaze, but she simply said, "You have no idea how much she did for you."

"I do."

"No, you don't," she said in a hot, harsh whisper. "If you knew, if you *really* knew, you'd do anything to find her."

I could not hear any more of this. "Understand me clearly, Siri." I spoke each word with as much force as I had in me, so I would obliterate the temptation she'd held out to me. "I catch you giving less than one hundred and ten percent to our stated mission—I catch you doing one bit more than you've been authorized to do—and your time as a Guardian will be over. This is a hot spot and we *cannot* be screwing around."

I had her gaze and I held it, watching every shift of her eyes, watching her shoulders slump one millimeter at a time.

Siri squared her shoulders, coming to attention even though she remained seated. "Yes, ma'am," she said, and I nodded, just like Misao.

We talked a little more, about this and that, minutiae about the mission arrangements blended and blurred with trivia about the new XP games she'd gotten me to try and the new restaurant we'd ordered from last night. She left without referring to her theory again.

But even as the shield opaqued, I knew she wouldn't give the idea up for as long as the mission lasted. I sat there with my hands on my knees, trying to blink the conversation back into forgetfulness.

David, you were right. We live too long. We serve too many masters, have too many families. We think we can walk away. We want to walk away, but we can't.

I could not believe Bianca was still alive.

I could not believe it for all the reasons I had given Siri, and one more. Because it meant I had done less for her than she had done for me, and I didn't know if I could live with that.

I had to forget Siri's words. If I remembered them, I would forget everything else, maybe even my oath—maybe even the First Precept—and then God help me, and God help Erasmus, and maybe even God help the Pax Solaris.

EIGHT

EMILIYA

Emiliya Varus sat at her heavy, sharp-cornered desk. A single light square from the fully paneled ceiling shone down on it. The room around her was small, providing just enough space for a narrow bed, the desk, the chair, a tub, and a toilet behind a folding screen. A few shelves and cupboards were attached to the walls, but they were mostly empty. Emiliya owned a couple of extra sets of professional whites, a few knickknacks given as gifts by friends from the Medical, and nothing else.

The room was stifling, but Emiliya did not turn on the vents. Running the vents cost. Instead, she'd opened the door behind her. Voices drifted in from the hallway and from the rooms next door. She ignored them. Instead, she kept her mind and her eyes on the fold-up screen in front of her, studying her day's reports, making sure she had filled in all the lines and boxes correctly so that she was not fined for mistakes.

On Hospital, the Clerks didn't follow lowly scan-and-stitch physicians personally. They followed their records. Those records controlled appointments, postings, future opportunities, and, most important, debts. It was vital that she not give them additional opportunities to up her load.

You're going to get us all out of here one day, Emiliya, her mother said. *That's your job.*

Except she hadn't done all that well at the academy. She'd tried and she'd tried again, until she made herself sick and broke down, and adding to her debt because she became a patient as well as a student. In the end, she could only scrape out a general degree, which was nothing. The kind of work she was given barely covered the cost of supplies.

"Hey, Emiliya!"

Emiliya jerked her head up and around to see a young man leaning in from the brightly lit corridor.

"Hey, Piata," she answered with much less enthusiasm.

"Records?"

Emiliya grunted an affirmative and faced the screen again, hoping that Piata would take the hint and leave her alone.

He didn't. He strolled inside and squatted down next to the desk, folding his gangly arms to rest on the edge. He had a sharp face and tan skin. Dark freckles dusted his cheeks and the backs of his delicate hands. The prominent bones of his wrists stuck out from under the weighted cuffs of his professional whites. A gold-crystal-studded cap covered his ginger hair.

"Got the word that you're heading up the team on the new saints."

Emiliya sighed and leaned all the way back.

"Looks that way." She folded her arms and cocked her head toward him. "You want the job?"

"You're kidding me, right?" Piata's eyes opened wide with surprise. His irises were a strange tarnished-gold color. Emiliya expected they were a modification, possibly a home brew, that didn't go quite right. "You've hit the jackpot."

"No jackpots in Erasmus anymore, Piata. You know that."

His cocky grin didn't falter. "There is if you get your debt cleared."

"What?"

"You get debt-free, you stand a chance. You can even leave."

Emiliya rubbed her eyes. *I don't have time for this.* She hadn't had a whole lot to eat today and even though she was used to it, it was making her short-tempered. "What are you talking about?"

"Brahm Rajandur."

"And what's a Brahm Rajandur?"

"Brahm Rajandur is the guy who brought the last saint into Hospital."

Now I know you're just kidding me. "We've never had a saint here."

"Oh yeah?"

Emiliya held on to her temper with difficulty. "Look, either make sense or go away."

"Brahm Rajandur." Piata straightened himself. "Look him up." He tapped the edge of her screen. "He got publicly cleared of all his debts, and he's in a positive salary now."

Emiliya faced her screen and her report. "Go away, Piata."

"Okay. Okay." He held up both hands and backed away. "I'm going."

Emiliya didn't watch him leave. She scrolled down through her work. The mountain of red tape and registry work was going to make her late for the discount hour in the cafeteria. She sighed and called up her accounts, looked at the negative balance, and sighed again, smoothing her hair back with both hands.

Maybe just skip dinner. She thought about Amerand and how he'd looked at her last time, a little concerned but mostly disappointed. He never thought about what made her so thin. *Just assumes it's because I don't train enough.* He never thought that she might be skipping meals to try to save money.

I work on Hospital, after all. Why would I be starving?

And as if her hash of feelings about Amerand weren't enough, Kapa showed up.

She'd been having tea with Amerand when she got Kapa's ping. It had taken all her will-power not to run out of the room then and there. It had taken her hours to work up the nerve to go down and see him. What a joke that Amerand caught them together.

Of course, Kapa might have arranged that. He did things like that.

Kapa.

He had broadened out, a lot. His hands were thick. The muscles on his neck stood out and he'd already started to get wrinkles around his eyes. He'd lost a tooth and had a stupid, flashy amethyst replacement. He looked terrible.

He looked magnificent.

"Kapa." She had said his name softly, almost hoping he wouldn't hear her over the constant noise of the crowded port. But his head swiveled around, and his eyes lit up.

"Emiliya!" He strode over—long, easy, light-footed strides despite his weighted boots. "I was starting to wonder if you got my message."

The last time she'd seen him, he'd been a skinny boy. That time, she'd kissed him hard and buried her fingers in his hair. This time, she couldn't move. "What are you doing here?"

His grin broadened. "I promised, didn't I?"

Oh, he'd promised. *I'm getting us out of here, Emiliya,* he'd said. *All the way out.*

"That was ten years ago!" *And you've been gone for seven of them. You left and you didn't take me with you.*

But he'd just shrugged, like it was no big deal. "It took longer than I hoped. But I'm here now." Kapa stepped close, and took her hands. His touch was heavy, slow, nothing like she remembered. "I've got a license and I'm a pilot, and I've got a berth for a doctor." He lifted her hands as if he meant to kiss them.

"I can't go with you!" She remembered how she pulled away, how it was a relief and terribly painful at the same time.

He stared at her then. "Why not?"

"I'm on contract with Hospital until my debt is cleared. I can't move a pinky unless they tell me to!" *You're too late!*

"God-Alone, Emiliya."

"And I've still got family," she barreled on. "My mother, my brothers and sister back on Dazzle. If I go AWOL, what happens to them?"

He threw out his hands like he always had when they argued. "Did I say AWOL? Do you really think I'd come back here if I couldn't get you out clean?"

"This is not clean. Clean is getting a request through channels. This is . . . shadows."

"Sorry I didn't fill out all the proper forms, Emiliya." He sneered at her, the curl of his lip revealing a hint of that stupid purple tooth. "But I'm here and I'm asking anyway. You say yes and the rest is just that: forms."

"Except you'd have to buy me, Kapa."

He shrugged again. "So what?"

"You'd have to buy me and pay rent on me. And if you didn't, it'd all pile onto my mother."

Kapa snorted and kicked the wall. She recognized that gesture and she didn't want to. She didn't want to see the boy she'd loved in this careless man. "Now you're sounding like Amerand."

"Maybe it's time I did."

"You with him now?"

She shook her head. "No. Now I'm just alone."

Except she wasn't alone. Amerand stepped up, and, standing between light and shadow, she chose light.

But why the hell did that light have to be so cold?

Since then, she'd gone over the scene a hundred times. She should have taken Kapa's hand. She should have turned him in for spite and for the bounty. She could even have told Amerand what Kapa had said before he got there. But he hadn't asked, and she'd gotten so used to hiding things from him she couldn't make herself speak.

She shut the screen off because leaving it on made the numbers on her debt account click up even higher.

Once, Kapa had been the one who made her safe, but he'd been gone too long. Now seeing him for the pirate he'd become terrified her. There had to be another way out.

But in the pit of her heart, she knew there was no legal way. There never would be. She'd have to run for it, and her best chance for making that run hadn't been back for a month.

"I'm so sorry," whispered Emiliya to the memory of her mother's hopes. Mother, Kim, Parisch, Geri. Maybe there were more by now. Mother somehow always managed to be unlucky, or careless. Or maybe she thought her general-degreed daughter could free two or three more while she was at it.

I thought it could work, too.

But the anger was born of guilt and frustration and it did nothing to warm her. What her mother did was one thing, but the kids . . . her brothers and her sisters . . . It wasn't their fault. They didn't deserve indenture. They didn't deserve to lose that last sliver of hope.

What the hell is Piata thinking coming in and spreading hallway rumors? She lifted her head and glowered at the door. Everybody whispered them, in the corners and behind desks, trying to dodge the drones and the ears. Did you hear, this guy, he found a new way to work RNA transfers, and they cleared his debt? Do you know, there was this one woman, she got this new live mitochondrial-imaging system going, and they cleared her debt?

Except none of them ever had names attached. They were just "some tech," "this one doctor," "this guy" . . .

Piata's guy had a name. Brahm Rajandur.

She hesitated—it would cost. "What the hell." She flipped open the screen again, lighting it up and starting the meter. She entered the name and sat back.

NOTICE OF POSITIVE STATUS

In recognition of his outstanding service in the advancement of Moontwo's medical team, Brahm Rajandur is effectively and officially cleared of all public debts owing the Governing Board and Public Finance Committee of Moontwo as of 11:21:30:14:09,

Emiliya was on her feet so quickly she barely remembered to slap the screen down to shut it off. She was out the door and sprinting down the narrow dormitory hallway to hammer on Piata's door.

Piata slid the door open. He was grinning.

"Gotcha."

She was panting and had to swallow before she could speak. "What is this? Is this a fake?"

Piata shook his head. "It's for real."

"How? What? Did he discover a better cure for ugly? What?"

Piata's tarnished-gold eyes flicked right, then left. "Come on in." He stepped back, giving her room. "We don't need to share this with the whole world."

The light panels were all on and Emiliya blinked in the simulated sunshine as Piata slid the door shut. Piata's room was a match for hers in size and furnishings, but he'd splashed out for some active screens. The walls showed scenes of Dazzle in its heyday, just as if he had a window onto a street.

"Have a seat." He nodded toward the bed. She sat stiffly on the edge. Piata leaned back against the desk and folded his arms, grinning at her. "And it's okay to talk. As far as the ears know, I'm spending the evening with a good vid." He nodded toward the shining street scene on his wall.

You wired the room? It was a hell of a risk. If they caught you, when they caught you, you could be kicked right off Hospital, credentials revoked, which left you with no legal way to make a living.

Get out of here. You shouldn't even be talking to him. But she could still see that public notice in her mind.

"You talk," she said, trying to sound much cooler than she felt. "You're the one who's so in the know."

Piata nodded. "I've been trying to keep an eye out for . . .

extras. Stuff I can do, or get, that might just help my balance with the Clerks and the Administrators."

Translation: You've been hacking the databases looking for something you might be able to get hold of that somebody up the chain might want to buy. Emiliya shifted her weight. She knew Piata was a bit on the fringe, and that he liked to play up being the pirate, but she'd thought that was all skin.

Seems I've misjudged you. For a moment, her mind's eye transposed Piata's pretend-pirate face over Kapa's real-pirate one. The similarities made her shiver.

"And in the course of so doing," Piata went on, "I've gotten hold of the criteria the cell-masters are looking for in the saints."

"Criteria?"

"Yes. You don't think all this scanning you're going to be doing is for smuggled goods, do you?"

"I thought it was just for data." Everything was about data. Every person, every living thing Hospital got its collective hands on, was scrutinized to see if it could yield some new scrap of information that might become valuable. A bunch of healthy specimens from the rich and well-cared-for Solaris worlds would be too good to waste. She'd heard rumors that the marketing wing was setting a "Solaris Standard" for health treatments.

To make a standard, you needed a baseline.

But Piata shook his head. "They're looking for some very specific stuff. And when they find it, they'll want the body it's in for analysis and replication." He met her gaze. "And we figure they will be more than willing to compensate whoever brings that body in."

Emiliya pulled back. "You are not talking about kidnapping a saint."

"What if I told you it wasn't the first time?"

"Are you out of your mind?" she exclaimed. "Even the Blood Family wouldn't risk cutting up a saint. The Solarans take worlds *apart* for that kind of crap."

Piata leaned forward. "Look at me, Emiliya. Do you think I'm joking you now?"

She looked. She looked for a long time. "What *exactly* do you want from me?"

"I just want to know if you find a match to a set of criteria and which of them it is. That's all."

"Then what?"

"Then you're part of the team, and we all get our debts cleared and go positive."

Go positive. Cash instead of debt. Cash is freedom.

Getting caught was the end of it. Even having this conversation, even thinking the thoughts that filled her mind was dangerous.

"Piata, I've got family back there. The idea was I'd be able to buy them out."

"So, you give the positive balance to them." He spread his hands. "What do I care? There'll be plenty to go around."

Her own hands gripped her forearms, nails digging into cloth. It took every ounce of will she had to suppress the eagerness rising in her. She could go positive. She could save them after all. And she wouldn't have to crawl to Kapa or to Amerand, didn't have to go into yet another kind of debt . . .

"I can't risk it," she said out loud to Piata.

"Go back to your room and take a look at the announcement about Rajandur. Take a good, long look." Piata leaned forward, and his voice dropped into a seductive murmur. "They want a saint. They can't just take one themselves. The saints will balk a little, you know? Maybe even pack themselves up and head back home. Out of reach. If we do it, if we make it look like a kidnapping for ransom, or a robbery gone wrong, then *their* hands are clean and we've got the most precious commodity in the system. We will be rich, we will be free, and we will most definitely be *gone*."

"Why me?"

"Because you're heading up the scan team and in a lovely confluence of events, your boyfriend's their babysitter."

"He's not my boyfriend."

But if I get out . . .

If she was free and out among the black-sky worlds, she could bring him out with her. They'd be free together. Free to be together. And she wouldn't have to be grateful to him, or dependent on him. They'd look out for each other because they wanted to, not because they had to. It'd be what she wanted to have with Kapa, before he vanished and left her stranded.

Free. Black-sky free.

Piata shrugged. "He's your friend, and their babysitter. You're going to be able to get closer than any of us." His sly grin turned positively feral.

Emiliya sat there, hearing the sound of her own harsh breathing, feeling the hammering of her heart. She heard what Piata was offering. She saw the picture he was drawing, and it was beautiful, especially when she added her own details.

But Emiliya was a daughter of Oblivion and there were things that would not leave her. Running the tunnels she learned that the best thing to have was something somebody else wanted. It gave you power, and a way to make them pay.

But the other thing she'd learned was that the worst

thing to have was something somebody else wanted. They'd kill you for it.

Emiliya looked up at Piata and saw him in a whole new light.

"I'm in," she said.

NINE

TERESE

As such things go, the trip out to the Erasmus System wasn't too bad. Like long medical procedures, space travel is essentially dull. The destinations can be exciting, even awe-inspiring, but the actual transit involves sitting in some variant of a tin can while falling through vacuum, for a long time.

In our case, the tin cans were roomy and designed to be comfortable for bored or nervous passengers. The acceleration was gentle, to give us time to adapt to the lighter gravity we were heading for. With all the personnel we were carrying, there were plenty of people to talk to and get to know, which meant you didn't have to make yourself jittery playing XPs or spending too much time with the same couple of people.

Plenty to keep me distracted from the fact that I had waited until after we left to finally send a message to David. It was short. *I'll be back,* I said. *I promise.* It was all I could do.

Once, the faster-than-light part of this process had been handled by massive gates. A ship could jump out to anywhere at all, but it could only get back to its point of origin if there was a gate to jump back through. This meant the worlds nearest the gates saw a lot of traffic—and a lot of money.

Jasper and Felice Erasmus had built their little empire around the gate system. That empire was brought down by the basic fact that human beings can never leave well enough alone. Understanding improved. New power sources were developed and the size of power cells shrank. The internal drive became reality and the need for the gate network—and gate port worlds—vanished.

Despite the comfort of my surroundings and the available distractions, I had far too much time to ruminate on my last, and very unofficial, meeting with Misao.

I had been on my way back from a run, short of breath and slightly sweaty. Spring was making its first slushy inroads into Chicago airspace and I'd been out to see the ice breaking up on the lake. At first, I hadn't recognized the man who turned toward me from where he had been standing at the entrance to the Palmer House garden. For a second, I even had the wild hope it might be David, but when I saw who it really was, I pulled up short and stood there, wordless.

"Walk with me," Misao said.

I obeyed, too startled to do anything else. I fell into step beside him as he turned west up the Owens Street walkway.

He didn't seem to have any destination in mind. We just strolled through the chilly wind toward the glorious pink-and-gold sunset. A few kids ran past on one side. I hunched my shoulders, the sweat cooling my skin down to the point of goose pimples, and wished he'd suggest we go back to the Palmer House, or just tell me what the hell was going on. Misao was only wearing a thin, open coat and hadn't seemed to feel the cold. He just walked with a measured pace, his eyes straight ahead.

We reached the escalator for the El station. I stopped, rather awkwardly. "I think this is your exit," I said, gesturing toward the rising stairs.

Misao faced me and I saw a strange sharpness in his green eyes.

"This situation is bad, Terese," he said softly. "Not just because of the hot spot. The whole thing stinks. If I could, I'd pull all of you out. I just wanted you to know that."

I had no answer. I didn't recognize the angry, diminished man in front of me.

"We've missed something and we're still missing it," he went on. "You're being sent in blind, and I can't do a thing about it."

He didn't want anyone at HQ to hear us, I had realized belatedly. He didn't want anyone to hear *him*.

I tried to shrug it off. "We've gone into the dark before," I said softly. We had—I had—and we'd come out in one piece. Mostly.

How had I come to be the one reassuring Misao?

"Not like this." Fury roughened his voice. He hadn't been angry at me. He was angry at the world, at the higher-ups and the lower-downs who couldn't tell him what he needed to know. "Our best people have said we've got all the intel there is, but I can't make myself believe that. The situation is focused around Bianca, I'm sure of it."

As soon as he'd said Bianca's name, I heard Siri again. *You have no idea what she did for you.*

But Misao would know.

"Was it your idea, Misao? Did you ask Siri to tell me her little theory about Bianca? As if I might not be motivated enough?"

All the anger I'd seen in him a moment before dissolved slowly into disappointment. He looked away quickly. When he spoke again, I barely heard him.

"Of all my people, I thought you were one who was not convinced that I am a manipulative mastermind. I brought you back because I need you. Because despite everything, you remain one of the best coordinators we have." The wind gusted hard, and Misao sucked in a great breath. "Two years ago Bianca tried to tell me that Erasmus was ready to explode. But she didn't have the proof, and even if I wanted to believe her, there was nothing I could do."

He drew one tan-gloved hand out of his pocket and laid it on my arm. I couldn't remember a time he'd touched me. Misao was my distant, steady boss. He did not come down to us, he did not come out with us. He was apart, distinct.

"Be careful. Be thorough," he said to me that cold afternoon. "Be sure, Terese. Before you make any move."

I swallowed and nodded, and I had gotten out of there as fast as I could, so I wouldn't have to witness for one heartbeat longer the inconceivable sight of Marshal-Steward Misao pleading.

Finally, there came the hard lurch between the end of the jump and the beginning of slower-than-light acceleration. Siri and I sat side by side in the cabin we'd shared, in two swaddling loungers with the webbing drawn tight over our legs and torsos. I had claimed the couch closest to the window. With the active screen pulled open across my lap and the window in front of me, I took my first look at our hot spot.

Whatever else may be said about it, the Erasmus System *is* beautiful. Its sun is a vigorous, young yellow. Its ten planets are all gas giants: the Divine's own jewels floating in the blackness. Our ultimate destination was truly impressive. R3ES3—which the pilots and the returning aid workers called "Reesethree"—had probably been destined to be a star, but it hadn't quite cleared the final hurdle to start its gases fusing. It remained a huge gas giant turning lazily on its axis displaying chaotic bands of sulfur yellow, rusted orange, and startling scarlet. Many-armed hurricanes—great swirls of black, white, and tan—crawled across the lanes of color.

Even from this far out, we could make out some of Reesethree's moons. Five of them were almost Mars-sized and seismically stable. But more important, one of them was Europan—it had a world's worth of water concealed under a shifting layer of ice. This was enough to make the moons suitable for human habitation, at least by sufficiently determined human beings.

I didn't spend too much time on the scenery, as spectacular as it was. What I really wanted to see were the jump gates. We were heading straight toward them, so I was able to tap the fleet's scopes and get a good long look.

There is no mistaking jump gates for anything but artificial constructs. Mother Nature does not make cubes, and even if She did, She would not cut perfect circles out of each side, then make the things float.

The Erasmus gates were old. They tumbled through the darkness—giant dice in a game the gods had finally decided to let us in on. Their extinguished lights made dark spots and lines on their scored and pitted hides. One sat with a side perpendicular to the plane our ship traveled on, another pirouetted on its corner, showing me each of its blind eyes in turn as we flew past.

I stared at them, searching for some sign of activity, any sign of life. Because if we had gotten it right, the Erasmans were going to launch their war through those gates.

The three of us—Vijay, Siri, and I—had been in one of the endless briefings in Misao's office. At that point, I was still in enough pain from my rebirth to be . . . overly direct.

"How could a little piece of chaos in the third ring be able to launch a war that could reach the Solar System?"

Vijay had folded his arms and crossed his legs, businesslike, distanced, and a little disgusted. At me or the situation? "Alone, they probably can't," he said. "But while they've been trying to keep some kind of hold on power in their own system, they've also been expanding their influence into some other little pieces of chaos."

"Little pieces of chaos which, coincidentally, also still have jump gates on the edges of their systems," added Siri. "And which could be brought back online fairly easily and used to launch . . . anything at all."

I had stared at them. They were talking science fiction. The idea that someone could launch a fleet of microdrones, or infectious spores, or something else exciting, using old jump gates was a horror XP staple. Such an attack might not take down an inhabited system, but it would tear it up badly, and it would be extremely difficult to tell where the attack had come from, let alone to stop it once it got started.

"They'd destabilize the entire FTL-transit network," I said. "Nobody would allow outside ships into their system. Trade between the diaspora worlds would grind to a halt . . ."

"Which may be part of the idea. Destabilize the whole system, then be smack-dab in the center when it comes to building it back up again." Misao worked his desk's commands, cross-loading more scenario workups.

There was a kicker that the horror shows seldom bothered to consider. The internal drive works on the same principle as the gates. Anything you can do with a gate, you can do with an ID ship, only it would require fewer people and leave fewer witnesses.

"Why not take apart their gates?"

Siri's smile had been bitter. She brushed a speck of dust off her neat cobalt-blue slacks. "Because if this is a viable plan, they could simply smuggle the plans out to one of their partner systems."

"Then there is the diplomatic question," said Misao. The frustration in his voice had strained to get out. "If we start taking apart all the old gates we can reach, we are going to undo far more than some antiquated hardware."

Of course. I rubbed my forehead. Interfering with something an independent system considers its property inevitably makes you more enemies than friends. And worse, it can also cascade in an uncontrollable manner. And just going around saying, "Hey, someone might be trying to weaponize the gates, let's take them apart, okay?" was probably a diplomatic nonstarter.

A cold, even voice pulled me back to the present.

"Erasmus traffic control to ship provisionally identified as *Miranda I*. Your approach has been recorded by our scopes. You will respond with the identification codes for your ship, the fleet vessels, and the piloting personnel within sixty seconds or we will begin countermeasures."

I dropped my gaze from the window to the screen lying across my lap. I brought up the view of the habitat where this message of welcome had originated, and followed as one of the pilots zoomed our scope in on the gently spinning series of tin cans and golden sails to show its missile ports open, ready, and pivoting toward us.

"Countermeasures," said Siri. "I do love the old-fashioned rhythms of diaspora dialects."

"Not to mention their old-fashioned notions about hospitality," I replied.

Of course I had every confidence in our pilots, but I still had to work to keep from clutching my couch arms as the long strings of identification codes were reeled off for the five fleet ships. After all, what better justification for a war than to accuse a bunch of Solaris ships of smuggling or some other sovereignty violation, then blowing them out of the black sky? It was cost effective, and could have a positive propaganda effect with allied systems.

"There are days I hate having an imagination." I loosened my hands for the twentieth time.

"You too, huh?" muttered Siri.

We grinned at each other, and with a jolt, I realized I was excited. I had thought I'd never get to do this again. For years I had looked toward a future without any missions, without any chance to use my skills, to protect my home and all the people of two dozen worlds who carried peace as their birthright. And no matter what else I'd worked at, I had felt bereft.

In my mind's eye, I saw David standing hunched and alone in the rooftop garden. I saw the strangled anger in Jo's eyes, and guilt threatened. It raged and it stamped, but I beat it back.

Let me enjoy this, I told it. *Just this once, if never again, let me feel that it is good to be on the job.*

"*Miranda I,* you are confirmed," said the voice of Erasmus Flight Control. "You may begin your docking orbit with Erasmus Habitat 2, staying within designated coordinates and parameters."

I started unhooking my webbing and looked across at Siri. "Time to dress for dinner."

Long-term exposure to microgravity is not good for human physiology, even if you are willing to shoot yourself full of physioactives to keep your heart and bones in condition. All the "little worlds" find ways to deal with the problem. The most common method is to adapt the clothing. Shirts, trousers, and shoes can easily be made heavier, and you can make use of local stones and metals to do it. Erasmus had elevated this necessary adaptation not only to an art form, but to a status marker, which we needed to match if we were to be taken seriously.

While the pilots guided us into docking orbit with Erasmus Habitat 2, we donned our field-dress uniforms. These are not the sleek uniforms we wear when we're on public parade. Field dress recognizes the possibility of sudden violence and involves black body armor that is specially reinforced and weighted for the environment. The shining boots are thick-soled, hard-toed, and square-heeled. The armor is softened by a neatly tailored blue dress tunic with a flaring hem that is weighted on the inside and stiffened with gold-and-white braid on the outside. There is also, of course, the venerable tradition of the "fruit salad," on the chest, showing honors earned and tests passed. We even had our peaked blue-and-white hats on our heads, since docking bays are designated "outdoors" for protocol purposes.

Then there was the gun. Not a lethal armament, but an armament nonetheless, slung across my back with a wide white strap. We all carried one. Just in case.

Most of the diaspora populations have heard that Guardians cannot kill. We don't keep that a secret. But outsiders have a tough time reconciling "cannot kill" with a group of overtly armed people. It makes them wonder if that whole not-killing thing might just be a rumor, or if we are a branch with some kind of special license. This means the smart ones hold off from any violence, at least for a while, and only the stupid ones rush in.

I can tell you from experience, it's a lot easier to deal with the stupid ones.

The half dozen of us "official" Guardians assembled in the main dining hall. I surveyed my tiny contingent. We should have had three or four times as many operatives for this mission, but the personnel simply was not there. They were out in Freedom and Ganges Heart and Dragon's End and a dozen other diaspora worlds. I had to threaten to resign my commission again to Misao and four others above him to make sure we even had our own doctor. Gwin wore gleaming white gloves on her hands and stood head and shoulders above the rest of us. I wondered if she'd chosen that build.

The docking clamps clanked as they sealed and whirred as they pulled us in. The ship ran through its cycle of signals and announcements. I used the time to line up my five subordinates for inspection. I tweaked Siri's hem and brushed some dust off her shoulder. She muttered something under her breath I could have written her up for.

Once they all passed muster, we fell in: our short double lines straight, our shoulders square, our heads up, standing at the ready, waiting for the doors to open.

We let the civilians exit ahead of us. This is standard operating procedure. After all, what's the point of getting all dressed up if you're not going to make an entrance?

Even though we were only six, we made an impressive noise as we marched down the ramp into the cavernous white docking bay. Our civilians, the thirty that were already down on the deck bay, stood up a little straighter, proud of the show. Several people lounging by the gates also straightened at the sight of us.

As I led my people past the civilians, I glimpsed Vijay far in the back of the crowd of aid workers. If it hadn't been for his height, I wouldn't have known him. His skin had been dyed a mellow brown and his shaved scalp gleamed in the flickering lights. The real change, though, was his face. They'd scarred him. Angry white slashes crisscrossed his cheeks under his eyes. His nose was a squashed lump. Erratic, snarled lines decorated his forehead and throat, as if someone had given a toddler a knife instead of a crayon and let him draw on Vijay's skin.

The resulting impression was of an optimized kid who'd gone way far down into the anger and the self-mutilation that came with it. He caught me looking at him and for a moment his eyes, undamaged and dark, narrowed. We both glanced away and I focused on the little committee that stepped up to welcome us.

There were four of them—two Solarans and two Erasmans. The Erasmans stared. The Solarans grinned.

I recognized Liang Chen from the videos and messages we'd passed back and forth. His dark hair was combed back into a long ponytail and his trousers, shirt, and boots had clearly seen hard use.

"Welcome to Erasmus, Field Commander Drajeske." He held out both callused hands to me and I took them, but he didn't hold on for a second longer than was necessary. "Let me introduce you to Commander Favor Barclay of the Erasmus Security."

Local protocol called for me to bow at this point. "Commander Barclay."

Unlike Liang, the Erasmans had dressed to impress. Their black-and-scarlet uniforms with gleaming gold braid stood out against the white walls that were being polished by stumpy cleaning drones. Most dramatic, though, was the full-length black cape that hung over one shoulder, only partly concealing the compact gun holstered at his hip, a gun that was probably a lot more lethal than the weapon I had slung over my back.

Barclay responded with a polite bow of his own. "Field Commander Drajeske. This is Captain Amerand Jireu." Barclay gestured to the man behind him, who stepped forward smartly. "He will be your main escort and contact while you are with us."

I bowed and he bowed. Captain Amerand Jireu was tall and lean, with that particular kind of wiriness that belongs to a strong man who has seldom known the full gravity humans evolved under.

"I hope I won't be taking up too much of your time, Captain."

"Not at all, Commander. It's part of my job."

"And you know Orry Batumbe." Liang was gesturing toward the second Solaran and I turned my gaze back where it belonged.

We clasped hands. "Good to see you, Orry."

"Good to see you too, Field Commander." He was wrinkling and graying and was maybe fifteen pounds thinner than when I'd known him during a stint on New Atlantis, but his eyes were bright and clear, if a little harder than they had been.

"This is my second, Field Coordinator Siri Baijahn," I said to the little welcoming committee. Siri bowed smoothly, her expression politely neutral, but her gaze flickered over the men in front of her, storing the details for later. Details, for instance, of the six people standing behind the welcome committee, all of them Erasmans, wearing high-collared black coats with hems so long they brushed the backs of their black boots.

All of them carried data pads. None of them was introduced.

These, then, were some of the Erasman Clerks, who were almost as famous as their heavily armed Flight Control, and at least as dangerous.

Liang turned to the Erasman commander. "Well, in the interests of not taking up too much time, I'll stay here and supervise the unloading."

"Very good," said Barclay briskly. "We've three Clerks to assist you." *So what are the other three going to be doing?* I wondered. "We have, of course, received your cargo and crew manifests, but we'll need to double-check them." Barclay gave a shrug that said, *Bureaucrats, what can you do?*

He turned to me. "Captain Jireu will be piloting you to Moonthree after you've been through your screening."

"Screening?" This was a twist.

"A routine security screen," said Barclay blandly. "Surely you were informed?"

No, we had not been informed, and I was sure he knew that. However, if I said anything, I was equally sure his eyebrows would lift and he'd say "I'm shocked." We'd wrangle, and I'd end up doing as they said anyway, because otherwise we wouldn't go anywhere.

"We received a large number of security protocols . . ." I said lamely. When all else fails, be willing to look like a fool. Maybe they will underestimate you later about something really important. "This one may have gotten skipped. My apologies." I put on a sheepish air and said to Captain Jireu, "If you'll just show us where to go . . . ?"

Captain Jireu bowed again but kept his face lifted. I noticed his skin was the color of golden sand, which made his deep-set eyes look especially dark. His thick, tightly curled hair was cinnamon brown and cut close to his scalp.

Handsome.

I told myself this person was too young for me to be having that thought, but that didn't make me feel any better. Then I thought about the light-years' worth of silence stretching between me and David and felt even worse.

Orry was watching me closely and I wondered what he was seeing. Probably too much. Orry was a romantic and a sensualist, given to believing everybody chased parts and parcels as much as he did.

Fortunately, this was neither the place nor the time for Orry to indulge himself, and he peeled off with Liang and the rest of our team to head back for the docked ships.

"Follow me, please," said Jireu. I motioned to Siri, who was the only other member of the team authorized to go to Moonthree. We were not allowed to bring our own ships any farther than the habitats, at least until they'd been thoroughly inspected and the licenses were issued for our personnel and their transport. I had a bet on with Siri that those licenses would not appear in less than two weeks.

There was a very practical reason Jasper and Felice Erasmus had set up their empire among moons and stations. It made controlling the movement of people, cargo, and information that much easier.

Behind us, the busy sounds of organization and unloading echoed off the white walls. Liang was already getting into it with Barclay and the Clerks, and Orry was trying to smooth things over. Oh, this was going to be a long day.

Out of the corner of my eye, I saw Siri glance at one of the cleaning drones and glance again. She caught my gaze and blinked rapidly, resetting her cameras. She nudged the drone with the toe of her boot. It beeped a warning and drifted away, but not too far.

Ah. More minders. But for us or the Erasmans? I eyed Captain Jireu, but he faced rigidly ahead.

Captain Jireu led us through a battered air lock into a second, smaller, curved white room, just as gleaming and sterile as the first one. All that blank whiteness began to prick the back of my mind. What came through here that needed quarantine?

What do they expect to come through here that might need quarantine?

An active desk and a scanning arch had been set up in the middle of the subchamber. The desk, a block of polished metal and blanked-out screens, was occupied by a thin, pale woman in traditional medical whites. She looked like she could have been made for this unsettling white space.

"Dr. Emiliya Varus will be doing the scans for you and your people," said Captain Jireu.

I bowed to Dr. Varus. She had hard lines to her face. Her bones showed sharp and close under her skin and her keen eyes sat too deep in her skull. Whatever this woman had been through in her life, it had left nothing soft or easy in her.

"For the record, we are Field Commander Terese Drajeske and Captain Siri Baijahn," I said briskly. "You should be in receipt of our biological records and signatures. A complete list of all inorganic modifications was provided with the approval order for our arrival." I spoke clearly, for the benefit of all present and remote listeners.

"While I'm sure that's true," said Dr. Varus, "we need to verify that information for security purposes."

"The last thing I want is for anyone to feel insecure." I flashed my best diplomatic smile.

Dr. Varus frowned more deeply toward Amerand Jireu.

"I'm sorry," I said at once. "That was uncalled for, and of course we understand about the scan. We're frequently suspected of being walking transmitters or weaponized."

Jireu looked pointedly at the gun butt visible over my shoulder. "And are you?"

It was a refreshingly direct question, and I gave him a small smile. "Not this week."

His mouth twitched. "So, what are you this week?"

"This week, I'm just trying to help." Siri stuck her tongue in her cheek and looked away, her camera-eyes tracking the cleaning drone on the floor, and the one on the walls.

"This week," Captain Jireu repeated, but I just turned toward Dr. Varus.

"What's the procedure?"

"Under this archway, please." Varus's gaze slid to Captain Jireu again. I wondered if the two knew each other, or if she somehow trusted him less than she trusted us. There was *something* about this she didn't trust. She moved sharply, discreetly, like she wasn't sure of distances or angles.

I unstrapped my weapon and handed it to Siri. Jireu frowned again but made no move to ask for custody of my weapon. It had been preregistered and cleared with Erasmus Security. Bianca's death had accomplished one thing for us: The Erasman authorities were ready to allow us a certain amount of self-defense.

The "archway" Dr. Varus directed me toward was smooth and—unsurprisingly—white, but its display screens and input panels glowed in a whole rainbow of colors. I walked into the cabinet like a magician's assistant and the door clicked shut behind. I closed my eyes and focused on the infinite space inside myself. I made myself breathe deeply while around me the machine hummed and shined its lights and vibrated under my feet.

The door will open again. It's almost done. The door will open.

"We've got no direct information on Hospital," Siri had told me back during the initial briefings.

"They've restricted the hospital?"

"For security reasons, *they say*." Siri had leaned hard on the last two words. "To prevent the 'agitation' that passed between Dazzle, Market, and Oblivion from claiming the one place that still brings money into the system."

"How? What have they got that anybody finds it's worth the expense of having their people shipped in there?"

Siri had rolled her eyes at me. "It's more a case of what they don't have."

"Ah."

Most countries, most worlds—the worlds of the Pax Solaris included—impose strict regulations on medical procedures. There are things their doctors can be arrested for doing, or are not trained to do. This led to a black market in providing doctors trained above or beyond local regulation. Moontwo, Hospital, evidently was one place you went to undergo procedures your home system might have interdicted.

This memory did nothing to calm me down as I stood there in the white scanner cabinet. I was clenching my fists and gritting my teeth by the time the door did open.

The first thing I noticed when I stepped out into the open bay again was that Dr. Varus did not look pleased. She stared at the numbers that flashed on the screen along with the colorful outline sketch of my body and murmured questions for the bulky set clipped over her ear. I waited.

"You've got some serious scar tissue behind your right ear."

They couldn't get everything out. No one wants to mess around near the brain more than necessary. "Yes."

"Where'd that come from?"

None of your business. "I was on assignment in a city that had a lot less forbearance than you do. I was imprisoned and tortured."

I was expecting some sign of pity, or perhaps respect. I got neither. Dr. Varus's face creased with distaste as she scanned the numbers and telltales on my profile. "You have had extensive work done recently."

"All of which is detailed in the authorizations you were sent," I answered, my patience evaporating. "As was my scar tissue."

She turned back to her desk, unfolded another screen, and typed in some more entries, using the ancient keypad. "That is correct," she said finally. "Next, please."

Siri sighed, handed the weapons over to me, and took her turn in the white cabinet. I felt my palms begin to sweat in my gloves, but I couldn't understand why.

"What for?" asked Captain Jireu abruptly.

"I beg your pardon?" I tore my gaze away from the white cabinet.

"What were you imprisoned for?"

"They never told me."

Dr. Varus clicked her keys and murmured into her set.

Variously colored outlines of Siri came up on one screen, and she matched them with those on the second, and again on a third. I moved Siri's weapon to the crook of my arm so I could activate the watch on the back of my glove. Seconds clicked by. Two minutes, three, and four. I hadn't been in there that long.

At last, the scanner door hissed open and Siri strode out to reclaim her weapon. I handed it over, with a meaningful glance toward Dr. Varus, who still had all three scans up and was turning her head to face one, then another.

I touched my gloves to activate the message keys.

Siri, what're you carrying? I tapped.

She cupped her palm to read her screen, then tapped back. Nothing.

No BS. This could make HUGE trouble. *Goddamn it, Siri, if you've smuggled something unauthorized in with you, I will strip you of every rank you've ever carried and boot you back home with my own boots!*

Nothing!

I strangled a sigh and tapped again. I kept my eyes on Dr. Varus. All her scans had gone to black. She stared at nothing. Beside her, Captain Jireu shifted his weight uneasily. His gaze flickered up and met mine.

I'll back you, Siri, I promise. But I can't help if they can ambush us.

Jireu watched my fingers move.

Siri's message came back. On my oath, I've got nothing I haven't declared.

To them or to Misao?

The fury on Siri's face could have peeled paint, but I didn't back down. I could not forget how she had talked so urgently about Bianca's maybe being alive on Hospital, a place we knew next to nothing about. I had turned the idea away because it would make it impossible for me to do my job. But I knew she hadn't let the idea drop. Siri did not let things drop.

But even as I moved my fingers to start another message, Dr. Varus had caught Captain Jireu by the arm and pulled him out of our earshot, speaking urgently. Jireu frowned, then the frown softened. He touched her hand in a way that spoke of friendship, or, possibly, love. I glanced sharply at Siri. She nodded, a bare hint of movement, and touched her set. I touched mine, and I heard:

"Amerand, can you hang until I'm done with the scans? I'm going to need a flight to Fortress."

"Are you cleared for that, Emiliya?"

"I will be." Her tone was flat and tense.

Jireu hesitated. "What's going on?"

"Nothing, but I'm going to have to report in person rather than over the line, and I was hoping to get a decent pilot."

That sounded lame, even to me. She'd found something unexpected. If Siri was hiding something from me... Maybe she'd managed to bring Jerimiah in the middle of this paranoia.

I had no chance to get her another message, because Captain Jireu was walking back toward us.

"There's been a change in the scheduling requirements," he said. "No one is being permitted to fly out until everyone has been cleared. I'll have to ask you to wait aboard the ship." His gesture toward the docking-bay door was as smooth as his lie.

I watched him long enough to see his smooth expression falter, just a little. Did he think we didn't notice? Yes, he did. He didn't take us seriously yet. I felt the claws of my pride extend.

I thought about stalling, about making demands. I ran through half a dozen scenarios in those few seconds, but in the end there was nothing I could do but accept the delay.

"Of course." I pasted a false, pleasant smile on my face. Captain Jireu walked past us, his shoulders stiff, and we fell in behind, heading back toward the bustle and chaos of the main bay.

What do you suppose all that was? Siri's message glowed faintly on my palm.

I closed my fist around her words. *That, Captain Baijahn, was just the beginning.*

TEN

AMERAND

I led Field Commander Drajeske and her Field Coordinator to the passenger compartment of the shuttle. They looked around casually, their faces masks of unimpressed politeness. Emiliya hurried in just a moment behind. She did not say one word to me, or to the saints. She just shot me a glance that was both apologetic and frightened as she slipped past us and settled into her couch, making far too much work of getting her frayed webbing straight and settled.

Field Commander Drajeske cocked her head at me, clearly looking for an explanation, but I had none to give.

"Excuse me." I bowed, and turned away to climb the ladder to the cockpit.

Of all my Security duties, I hated piloting the most. I knew others who thought it was liberating. They created elaborate fantasies of how one day, they'd beat the cameras, scam an internal drive, and just . . . leave, make their way to another system to become black-sky gypsies and never look back.

I knew of only one pilot who actually tried it. It turned out the Blood Family was perfectly willing to sacrifice ship, crew, and cargo to make a point. I had every faith they'd be willing to do it again.

The shuttle I had license to pilot was a standard design: three large, mostly spherical pods hooked together in a straight line. The main crew area was in the center with passengers and cargo on one side and engines on the other. The cockpit made a large blister on top of the central pod.

It was an ungainly design, good only for the barest of atmospheres or pure vacuum, but it had two advantages: It was cheap and it was modular. If necessary, the engine compartment could be detached at the heavily guarded shipyard that had been made of Habitat 1 and replaced with a compartment containing an internal drive. This meant Habitat 1 didn't have to keep whole ID ships around. After all, the last thing the Blood Family wanted was anybody tempted to steal one.

I had piloted and crewed ID ships for a while before I got my posting on Dazzle. The flights were not pleasant. But then, I understand transporting slaves never is.

And of course, whether FTL or STL, all the ships were equipped with so many eyes that I was surprised they didn't glitter.

Leda and Ceshame were already in their chairs by the time I climbed into the cramped cockpit. We had to move carefully to avoid elbowing each other, but it was a dance we were used to. I took my chair and strapped myself in.

"Any thoughts, Captain?" said Ceshame.

"All of them my own." I moved my hands over keys and screens, running through the prelaunch checks.

Leda was eyeing me. "Any about these new saints?"

"Big guns," remarked Ceshame before I could answer.

"I'll say." Leda shook her head. "So much for 'Ooo, we are happy, peaceful, and wise. We don't kill anybody.'" She folded her hands prayerfully, then added a rude gesture in the direction of the passenger compartment.

"Ah, they're for show." Ceshame waved the whole idea away. "Scare the ignorant locals."

"Or they shoot tranqs or something."

I swiveled my chair and raised an eyebrow at Leda. Leda was as trustworthy as anyone I knew in the Security, but she had a reckless streak. "Planning on finding out?"

Leda snorted. "I'll leave that to you, Captain."

"Lock it down and prepare for launch," I said.

"Yes, Cap'n."

Behind me Ceshame chuckled.

After that, it was all business. There was no place for humor while Flight Control was paying attention. We recited our ID codes, made sure that the backup codes for the ship and the engine were received and confirmed. Our launch and descent path were received, loaded, and locked into the computers. I opened the scope I had access to in the passenger cabin. The saints and Emiliya had themselves strapped in. I couldn't see the weapons, so I scanned for them. The saints, experienced travelers, had stowed them securely in the floor lockers.

Why wasn't I told they'd be armed?

I found myself wondering if I should have confiscated the guns. I had never dealt with armed Solarans, or armed travelers of any kind. There was no procedure. *Did I just endanger my mission?*

As I remembered Terese Drajeske facing me, to my shame, my ears began burning. When I first looked at her, all that I saw was the uniform, and the shining black body armor beneath the blue tunic. I hadn't thought Solaris saints might have uniforms, let alone people to wear them. But when I was able to see past that, to the woman who wore it . . . she was beautiful.

Then I pictured Field Commander Drajeske's serious gaze and sardonic smile and reality quickly righted itself. Whatever these new saints had in their mission logs, diverting this pathetic shuttle was not on the list.

The docking clamps finally let us go, and we fell away from the habitat. The computer handled acceleration and direction. We accelerated to create a match for Moonthree gravity and the nauseating drift of zero g faded. As the authorized pilot, I had to do the checkback with Flight Control, reciting all the codes again, confirming all the readouts while my people settled down into patient boredom.

After I closed off with Flight, I officially passed cockpit watch (calling it piloting was an exaggeration—I was there to make sure no one hacked the ship's systems to divert it by remote) over to Ceshame. He shot me a dirty look as he palmed the authorization plate. This meant he was trapped up here until I decided to relieve him, but he didn't complain. Rank has its privileges.

I unstrapped myself and climbed down into the main crew compartment. It was little more than a narrow aisle with coffinlike bunk compartments bolted to the walls on one side. The rest of the room was taken up by a hyperefficient—and consequently nearly impossible to use—cooking and eating area.

To my surprise, Emiliya was already there. She stood at the galley counter, tracing the circle on the sealed burner with her long fingers.

"Emiliya?"

She glanced up, unsurprised to see it was me. "Sorry. I just didn't feel . . . it was awkward sitting in there with the saints. Something's going on between them. It's pretty tense."

"You insisted on coming," I reminded her.

"Yeah. Mistake probably."

I waited a long moment for her to turn around, but she didn't. She just stayed as she was, one hand pressed against the counter's rounded edge, one hand tracing the cold and covered burner.

"Emiliya," I said at last, hoping she would hear the plea to turn around in my voice. "What is going on?"

She shook her head. "Nothing. Sorry. Tired."

"Why did you want to come back with me?"

"So I could ask you a question."

"Here?" The word blurted out of me, but I couldn't help it. She knew how wired the ship was. Even if Flight wasn't paying attention at this moment, the Clerks would be reviewing every micropixel of data when we got back.

She hung her head and planted both hands against the counter, leaning her weight on them. "Can we trust any of them?"

"Who?" I asked, confused. "The saints?" *Why would you be wondering about the saints?*

"The Family," she whispered. For the first time I saw how tightly her skin stretched over the bones of her face. "The people on Fortress. Can we trust any of them?"

I cannot believe this. Emiliya, why are you doing this to me? Why are you doing it to yourself? Maybe she thought I had managed to rig my ship in some way to cut off the ears and eyes. She was wrong. Oh, I had the skills, but I didn't dare. I had too much left to lose.

But she was serious, and she was frightened. I looked away, to the screen, and the window, and the screen again.

We were on course, our path was clear. There was nothing out there that was not licensed. Moons, ships, planets, stars—all moved in their proper orbits. The only thing off course was our conversation.

"Does this have something to do with Kapa?" If he was legal, no harm in asking. If he wasn't, no harm in trying to find out what he was really up to. Investigating the shadows was part of my job.

"No," she answered flatly. "This is just me. I just need to know."

I didn't want to answer, but I couldn't refuse. All I could do was take my time putting the words together.

"If I were going to speak to any member of the Blood Family about something that was important to me, it would be Grand Sentinel Torian." Torian at least left Fortress sometimes. He at least knew something about what our lives were really like.

"Thank you." Her smile was reflexive and weak. "Is it okay if I borrow one of the bunks? I haven't been sleeping well lately."

It wasn't strictly regulation, but it wasn't forbidden either. "Sure. Take this one." I tapped the sliding door on the middle bunk. "Leda and Ceshame are pigs."

Her smile was quick and mirthless. She didn't look at me as she swung herself into my bed, but she did whisper something, just before she shut herself in.

I believe, but I do not know for certain, that last thing was "I'm sorry."

I stood beside the closed door for a long moment, trying to understand what had just passed between us. I needed to move, to walk, to do something, but my options were extremely limited in this falling tin can.

The idea of going back up into the cockpit with my two subordinates most definitely did not appeal. Instead, I climbed over the thresholds into the chamber Emiliya had ceded over to the new saints. I was, after all, supposed to be minding them.

I was not surprised to find that Field Commander Drajeske and her captain had already abandoned the couches in favor of the fold-down seats by the "window." It was a live but inactive screen that displayed whatever the navigation 'scopes saw. In this case, it showed the appearance of Moonthree from around the massive curve of the gas giant. The Field Coordinator—Siri Baijahn, I remembered her name was—had her legs stretched out in front of her and a set of flat dark goggles covering her eyes. Her lips and fingers both twitched in time with whatever she saw on that private screen. I had a moment of imagining the Clerks grinding their teeth in frustration at the sight of a screen they couldn't spy on.

Field Commander Drajeske had discovered the small store of beverages in the cold locker and sat with her back to Coordinator Baijahn, sipping from a drink box and watching the stately emergence of Moonthree, like a white egg from the larger world, lost in nothing more complex than her own thoughts.

Something's going on between them. It's pretty tense, Emiliya had said.

Commander Drajeske turned when she heard my footstep on the deck and raised her drink to me in salute. She reached out to touch her second on the arm, but I gestured she should leave the other woman be. She shrugged easily and got up to join me instead.

"All well, Captain Jireu?" she asked. Her hands were

smooth, with rounded fingertips and short nails. A heartbeat later I realized I was staring at them.

What the hell is my problem?

"Yes, thank you," I answered, remembering to meet her eyes. She was looking keenly at me, assessing me, judging me. That thought stiffened my spine. She had no business, no right to judge me. "But I need to see where you've stored your armaments." I already knew, but I wanted to make sure she knew I was keeping an eye on her; that *I* was in charge in this place.

She blinked. "Of course." She slotted the drink box into the table compartment. In her chair, Coordinator Baijahn twitched and smiled.

The Field Commander shook her head. "I'm going to get her help for her game addiction, I swear." She pulled open the floor locker and showed me both weapons strapped and secured. I rattled them once for form's sake.

"We don't normally go into a new situation armed," she said as I closed the locker. "But Liang Chen reports there's still some violence where we will be stationed."

"Some?" The diplomatic language sounded very like Liang. "Yes. There's some." I faced her, mindful of the surveillance around us but intensely curious. No one could fault me for getting a little extra information out of her while I had the chance. "I thought you were not permitted to defend yourselves in your service."

"We're not permitted to kill," she corrected me. "We're trained to avoid inflicting unnecessary harm in case of physical conflict. That is not the same as not defending ourselves."

I folded my hands behind my back. "So, what kind of gun is that?" I nodded down toward the weapons in the locker.

She raised her eyebrows at my blunt curiosity. "Part of its function is to make you wonder."

"And is that part of your function as well?"

That drew a smile from her. "On occasion."

"Who were you expecting to have to confuse?"

She shrugged. "I seldom know until I'm on the ground."

"You've done this before?"

She cocked her head at me, her eyes wide with mock horror and surprise. "Are you asking if you're my first?"

Is she flirting with me? The thought flickered through my mind, almost too fast to catch.

The corner of my mouth flicked upward. "It appears so, yes."

She nodded, her lips pursed as if acknowledging a point. "Sorry to say, Captain Jireu, you are not. I have done this sort of thing before."

"And exactly what is 'this sort of thing'?"

I expected another joking or evasive reply, but it didn't come. "I'm here to find out why one of our best officers is dead, and to help with an aid mission your people requested. I'll do that in whatever way works."

I turned my face away. On the screen, Fortress had fully emerged from behind the gas giant and waited like a pearl on black velvet as we slowly fell down toward it.

"My people requested nothing from you," I whispered.

"Someone did," she answered. "We don't go where we're not invited."

I had to shake my head. "That is either naive or dishonest."

"Which would you prefer?"

To my own complete surprise, I laughed. "I'd prefer naive, but somehow I don't think that's what I'm going to get."

"You've only known me for ten minutes, Captain Jireu. You don't know what you're going to get." This time, her smile was sharp enough to cut.

"No, I don't think I do." *What are you really here for, Commander Drajeske? Are you and your gun and your coordinator here to take Erasmus apart?*

The thought sent a jolt through me. Did the Family suspect? They must. If the thought had crossed my mind, it had certainly crossed theirs.

And they had given her over to my keeping, probably quite secure in the knowledge that if they decided she needed to die, I would do the job. I didn't like saints, and I had never refused an order, no matter how distasteful, because my father lived in my back room, and I didn't know where my mother was except that she was still in their hands.

Did Terese Drajeske suspect me of being a potential assassin? She couldn't possibly. She was a free person. No person who had a choice would walk into such a threat.

Would they?

I shot to my feet too fast and nearly overbalanced. Terese reached out to steady me, and I snatched my arm away. She folded her hand and lowered it. I was staring at her again, half in horror, half in confusion.

"It's all right, Captain," she said softly. "I understand."

"Excuse me." I bowed and strode out of the cabin, cranking the door shut behind me hard enough to slam. I pressed my fist hard against the wall and my forehead against my fist.

You don't understand. You can't understand because I don't understand. Something's happening, and I don't know what it is.

I straightened up. The cameras, the Clerks, the Blood

Family had already seen far too much. I couldn't undo it, but I could limit further damage. With the discipline of a lifetime, I made my face blank and still.

As I moved toward the cockpit ladder, I touched my hand to Emiliya's sealed bunk, my sealed bunk.

I'm sorry, too.

ELEVEN

TERESE

Power looks startlingly similar wherever you go. Power does not want you to forget for a minute that you are small and alone. The palaces of Moonthree are meant to impress, amuse, and inspire continued excess. The Great Hall, the official reception point for government representatives and other dignitaries, is built to inspire awe.

If I had thought the precautions taken by the Flight Control for entry into the Erasmus system were a trifle . . . overdone, they were nothing compared to the precautions around Fortress. I tried to calculate how much fuel Captain Jireu burned to negotiate the maze of satellites and patrol ships and gave up. We, of course, were not privy to cockpit chatter in our threadbare passenger cabin. I had a feeling Siri could get to it if she wanted, but there was no point.

"He might not even be flying," she pointed out. "They might be doing it by remote."

I raised my eyebrows to her. "Are we that scary?"

Siri chuckled and I looked away before she could see me wince. I hated not being able to speak to her directly, but we were being watched. Whatever she was up to, if she was up to anything at all, I had to let it go for now.

Even the spaceport on Fortress was a tribute to the resources lavished on that world. The ice skin on which the hangars and landing fields floated had to be kept smooth and steady. Huge sealed Zambonis were constantly at work, maintaining the shining ice sheet. The port was filled with workers. There were no cleaning drones here—everything was done by hand or with mechanical assistance. I counted half a dozen different kinds of work uniforms, and that did not include the uniforms of the soldiers who stood watch beside every door, their guns at rest in their hands.

I wondered briefly if this display had been arranged for our benefit. Not even Bianca had managed to record anything inside Fortress. From the way Siri was blinking and rubbing at her temples, I had the distinct feeling she was suffering equipment trouble.

The second elevator shaft was glassy, and let us see the mottled white-and-silver ice as we were plunged through it into the deep turquoise of the living water. The Hall itself was high enough up that the sunlight penetrated the ice, but far enough down that its ocean waters protected us from the gas giant's overenthusiastic particle discharge. When we emerged into the corridor, a Clerk bowed to us and took our palm prints, including Captain Jireu's. Once we had all been verified, he bowed again and took point in front of us, leading us deep into the palace, past the soldiers, past the servants, who did not lift their eyes to watch us. Captain Jireu walked beside us, but Dr. Varus did not. One of the Clerks had led her away. I noticed how Captain Jireu tracked her until she was led out of sight around one of the steeply curving corridors.

Uniformed servants stood by each door to open it before us and close it behind us. They lined the walls, making a stiff and silent audience for our passage, turning the act of walking down a hallway into a parade.

Captives, every single one of them, held hostage to the good behavior of their families on the other moons. That fact weighed heavier on my mind with each step. I wondered if

Dr. Varus had family here, and if that was where she disappeared to. I hoped that was it. She had bioscanned me and Siri, had been all but invisible on the flight across, and now had been taken away. It was not a sequence of events that made me feel comfortable.

It took a team of six men to pull open the huge gilded doors to the Great Hall. Three-quarters of the circular chamber had a wall of clear arched glass edged with something that shone like frosted silver. As a concession to the human need for edges and boundaries, the floor was solid: a gleaming surface much like marble but in swirling blues and greens. It had been inlaid with a pattern of sweeping tree branches and names so elaborately scripted they'd become decorations rather than text. A rail that might actually be wood ringed the room, cut and bent into fantastic abstract waves and curls and polished to a high shine. Transparent pillars filled with bubbling water extended from floor to ceiling, where proud and benevolent faces I took to be gods were painted to look down on us.

The materials engineers must have had a field day. I was sure the view into this place was nowhere as clear as the view out of it, but I couldn't catch how the trick might be accomplished.

It was the only place we had been so far that was empty of servants. As the doors clanged shut behind us, Siri and I were left alone with Captain Jireu. It was a nice trick, very effectively disconcerting, especially when you were being reminded everywhere you looked that you are alone in a bubble of air beneath the ocean.

But what struck me most in that first glimpse was the life.

Outside in a world of indigos and greys, there swayed a forest of broad-leafed, ruby-red kelp, its edges glowing gold. A tangle of blaze orange drifted past, bumped against the glass, shuddered and re-formed into a sail that shot away into the forest. Silver fish turned their glowing faces hopefully up toward the white ice. A rain of white stars drifted down and the fish burst into motion, snapping them up. A jet-black eel at least three meters long undulated slowly toward the seaweed, ignoring the rippling, color-shifting mounds that floated along underneath it.

I splayed my hand against the cool window and stared. I couldn't help it. I had seen alien life before, but not much of it. Siri stood beside me, not blinking, just taking in all the silent wonder. Amerand stared too, but his was a hungry stare. He didn't see the fantastic life that swam and hunted, bloomed and played out there. He saw the water, which was life and wealth and freedom, and power. Power above all. All that water, the only natural water source in the Erasmus System, was the way the Blood Family kept control.

I found myself wondering what he would make of the home I'd had in the middle of Lake Superior, or the one in the living darkness of the Mariana Trench. I didn't know what to make of him. He was so used to being watched that he wore a permanent armor over his thoughts, and yet he was still a very young man, not even through his third decade, and as thick as that armor was, I could still catch a glimpse of the struggling human heart underneath.

When he noticed me staring at the ocean—and at him— the hunger vanished behind a kind of bleak amusement for the tourist. His expression sobered me and reminded me where I was. I pulled back my hand and collected my wits.

"Amazing, isn't it?" said a man's voice behind us, and I turned to greet the ambassador of the Pax Solaris to the Erasmus System.

I hadn't seen His Excellency, Ambassador Philippe Diego y Bern, for four decades. He was still a solidly built man, although his chest and slight belly now formed a single gentle curve out in front of him that was going to soon turn into a paunch if he wasn't careful.

"Field Commander Drajeske." He held out both hands as he crossed to me, the soles of his heeled boots ringing on the marble-patterned floor. Gold buttons made a sparkling line down the front of his knee-length coat and his straight grey trousers were trimmed in silver braid. The scarlet, blue, and gold of his sash made a swath of color diagonally across his chest. "It is good to see you again."

"Good to see you too, Ambassador." I clasped his hands. Ambassador Bern had been Assistant Secretary Bern when we'd worked together during the Redeemer crisis. He was cool, strong, and utterly determined. His facility for diplomacy was all that kept those he worked with *and* against from applying the term "ruthless" to him. At that moment I saw sorrow and regret written across his face. I squeezed his hands, trying to tell him that, whatever had happened, I knew he had done his best. We would talk later, but I already had the feeling whatever he would tell me was not good news.

"Field Coordinator Baijahn." Bern turned to Siri and took her hands as well. "I am glad to see you again."

"Thank you, Ambassador," replied Siri stiffly. I bridled at the enforced silence. I knew what Ambassador Bern had done for me. For Bianca, he would have moved whole worlds.

The ambassador turned from us to Captain Jireu. "Thank you for your escort, Captain Jireu," he said.

Captain Jireu bowed. "You are both most welcome. Field Commander, I will leave you and the ambassador to make your formal presentation. You can ping me when it's time for us to travel to Moonfour." With a final glance at me, he turned crisply on his heel and marched away, becoming a shadow behind the aquamarine glass walls as he turned the corner.

"Our hosts are waiting." Ambassador Bern gestured toward the far side of the chamber at a second pair of huge, gilded doors. The panels were embossed with more branching trees. Crowds of men and women stood among the foliage. Before I had a chance to look closely at them, the doors were pushed open by another team of servingmen, letting us know we were expected, and that somebody else controlled our movements.

I saw Siri flex her right hand once, a small motion like the raking of claws.

The rooms in front of us were built on a more human scale. The ceiling had a skylight dome to show the textured-ice sky and the occasional ocean denizen that glided over, casting a shadow like a cloud across the patterned floor. But the walls were opaque, decorated with framed screens, most of which displayed static art. Some of this was in the form of hieroglyphs or ancient Chinese watercolors, but much more was portraiture, with the forest theme repeated and reworked into every surface.

Reminders of empires and dynasty and the long history of power held by an individual family. Not subtle.

Two people sat on the curving sofa at the very center of the room. They were a matched pair: Esteban Donnelly Erasmus and Mai Godsil Erasmus. Their dress was elaborate, as was the style here, but the most striking feature of it was the collars of rank each wore. These were broad Byzantine creations that covered breasts and shoulders. *Saeo* Mai's had been made in all shades of blue and green trimmed by white above and black below, all sweeping and shining like the currents in the water outside. *Saeo* Esteban's was a match, only it was all done in shades of red, orange, and gold made to mimic the skin of the gas giant we orbited.

Because of Jasper and Felice Erasmus, it was decided by their heirs that the rulers, the "*Saeos*," of the system's governing board would always be husband and wife. The solidification of families through political and corporate marriage was an ancient idea that had never quite died. It certainly made for a very potent symbol, but only as long as the people in the primary relationship agreed to hold steady.

Esteban and Mai must have been fairly steady, because underneath her beautiful robes, *Saeo* Mai's belly showed her to be profoundly pregnant.

I folded my hands and bowed, dipping my gaze from *Saeo* Mai's bright smile, and *Saeo* Esteban's suspicious demeanor. Siri stood behind me, the good subordinate, silent, respectful, and watchful.

"Welcome to Erasmus, Field Commander Drajeske." *Saeo* Esteban Donnelly Erasmus's voice was deep, authoritative, practiced.

"*Saeo* Esteban, *Saeo* Mai," I said. "Thank you for receiving us into your system."

"Please believe that we are truly sorry for the circumstances necessitating your presence." *Saeo* Mai also had a deep voice, but with an edge. This was a woman who knew exactly who she was. She was less certain who I was, and that bothered her. Which was only fair, because something about this entire scene was bothering me.

"We are ready to assist you in whatever way possible," *Saeo* Mai went on.

"We have accommodation for you here on Moonthree," added *Saeo* Esteban. "And we will be able to place a shuttle at your disposal as soon as you need it."

Ambassador Bern bowed again. "You will understand, I hope, that the Field Commander is still determining the scope of her investigations, and may need to spend at least her first few days on Moonfour, talking to the aid mission to which Bianca Fayette was attached. We need a more complete picture of her circumstances. I'm certain, after that, we'll find this was a tragic accident and nothing more."

And it buys me a little time before I have to walk into whatever cage you two have prepared for me, I thought.

You two.

Now I knew what was nagging at me.

Where are your people? Where is your government? What are you two doing alone in this cavern? We knew that most of the family was kept from contact with ... anyone. It was like the ancient Persian courts, where the more precious a person was, the more isolated they were kept in order to preserve purity of blood and ideology. But this was a place where work was done directly by humans, by living hands and eyes, not by computer surrogates like back home. The slaves they'd surrounded themselves with were not doing the governing. And somehow I didn't believe the real work was being done by the Clerks.

Seats of government are busy places. This one was practically a museum. We were seeing servants. We were seeing figureheads. We were not anywhere near the real power.

"I sincerely hope you are correct," said *Saeo* Esteban, and I know I did not imagine the brittleness in his tone. He did not like Ambassador Bern's diplomatic response. Probably he was the sort that preferred to be the only liar in the room.

"It is extremely regrettable that anyone here to help the people of Erasmus should meet with such a pointless end."

"Field Coordinator Fayette was also presented to you?" I asked, with the air of checking things off my list.

"She was not," replied *Saeo* Mai.

"We generally meet only with the heads of the Solaris missions," said *Saeo* Esteban. "Is there a reason we should have been given her credentials?"

"Yes." I frowned at Ambassador Bern. "As a representative of the United World Government for Earth, she should have been formally presented, or at least her credentials should have."

Bern picked up on my tactic and actually managed a squirm, which was made highly noticeable by the lines of his formal coat. "I was unable to formally present her credentials, because they were not presented to me."

"I beg your pardon, *Saeo* Mai, *Saeo* Esteban." I made sure I sounded angry, like I was surprised I'd been left out of this particular loop. "Clearly, I need to spend more time assessing the situation. I hope to be able to meet with your representatives in a few days to give you a full update."

"Of course, Field Commander," replied *Saeo* Mai smoothly. I saw the subtle signs of smugness in her courteous manner. Now it appeared as if I had no idea what was going on. Hopefully, they'd believe I possessed an honesty born of naïveté and that I would spend more time investigating my people than theirs.

You see? I could practically hear *Saeo* Mai thinking as she laid one hand on her husband's and the other on her pregnant belly. *You see? Nothing to fear.*

The problem was that Esteban was still watching me, and he was nowhere near as sure.

Surprise, surprise.

We made our bows and murmured our pleasantries and were ushered out. The doors were closed behind us.

"Ambassador, we clearly need to talk about this," I said aloud. Aloud and with a serious overtone of annoyance. "Maybe your office?"

"Of course. This way."

Bern pushed open the door and once more we found ourselves in the middle of an escort of Clerks and servants. We marched forward with Siri three paces behind, not saying a word.

The Solaris embassy was in the bureaucratic wing: a huge suite of interlocking chambers dropped right into the middle of the main hive of Clerks. To get to their own space, every embassy staffer had to walk past the sprawling open office filled with the Clerks in their black uniform coats, working in a silence that was positively eerie. The Clerks spoke no more than the servants did. The difference was, the Clerks watched you as you walked by, with bright and very interested gazes.

By the time we reached the plush—and much more private—offices on the other side of the Solaran embassy doors, the sound of human voices was a sweet music. The door shut and sealed behind us. I turned a little to Siri, but she spoke up before I could.

"Ambassador, I'd like to spend a little time with your staff," Siri said. "To get up to speed on the security and some of the interaction questions."

"Of course, of course." I could have sworn Bern actually looked relieved at that. He beckoned over our heads and a brisk young man with straight black hair and half-moon eyes stepped up to us. "This is Marin Shun. Marin, this is Field Coordinator Baijahn of the Solaris Guardians. See she has access to what she needs."

Seeing Siri effectively paired off, I followed the ambassador to his private office.

Ambassador Bern's private office was rigidly traditional. Faux-wood paneling and shelves filled with books made the room look like an antique office from Earth's European empires. The chairs were solid, deep, comfortable, and probably locally made—such weighty furnishings would have cost a fortune to import.

Ambassador Bern motioned me to a chair as he moved behind his desk and selected a book from the shelf. It fell open at once in his hands and I seriously doubted it was anything so archaic as the paper volume it appeared to be.

"We've been running a most interesting race with the Erasmus Clerks." He moved his finger down the page as if checking some reference. Which he probably was, most likely an up-to-the-heartbeat reference on security conditions. "Sometimes they are ahead, but at the moment"—he snapped the book shut and replaced it—"we have the upper hand. This room is as secure as I can make it."

He came back around the desk. I had a whole list of questions, mostly about how we would get into the real halls of power once we were forced to move operations to Fortress, but I never got to ask them.

Slowly, with joints that creaked with unaccustomed effort, Ambassador Bern lowered himself onto his knees.

"I am here to tell you," he said hoarsely, "I am the one responsible for the death of Bianca Fayette."

I stared at him. He was *not* doing this.

It happens, sometimes, that a Guardian kills someone. No

matter how hard we try, we make mistakes, or we misjudge. Sometimes, we lose control. When it happens, we must find the family of the victim, and we must kneel, and say just what Philippe Bern had said. Then we must wait, and we must take whatever comes, whether words, blows, forgiveness. If a family member wants to beat one of us to death, it will not be stopped because it's the only way to end the chain of killing before it begins. Any death, *any* death can be the fuse that explodes the war. All deaths must be claimed, and we must take the punishment for them so the innocent will not have to.

But none of us has to accept responsibility that is not ours.

"How?" I croaked. I had to stop and try again. "How could that be possible?"

He lifted his face, and I saw the genuine anguish there. "Because I knew what she was doing, and I did not stop her."

"Please, stand up. Tell me what happened."

He stood as slowly as he had knelt. I saw his hands shake.

"What happened?" He wiped his palms on the sides of his long coat. "What happened was I was tired and she was revolted." He looked at me, his gaze direct for the first time since I had entered this room. "You have absolutely no idea how bad it is here."

"I'm starting to get the picture."

"If you can say it so calmly, then you haven't," Bern said, half-pitying, half-disgusted.

"It's vile," I agreed, trying to keep the tremor out of my own voice. "Slavery is always vile. But how does it make you responsible for Bianca's death?"

"She came to me . . . she came to me and told me she was going to take the Erasmus System apart."

There are moments when reality shifts so abruptly that you cannot understand it, let alone accept it.

"That's impossible," I said, certain it was true. "She had no orders. If this was a takedown mission, they would have told us before we ever came in." Takedown is the last phase. Takedown is the thing we do only when there are no other options. It's incredibly hazardous, because if it isn't done just right, it can raise new threats that are ten times more dangerous than the old.

Ambassador Bern's face had gone slack, weighed down with pure regret. "It wasn't a mission, at least, it wasn't an official mission. It was *her* mission."

Words and strength ran away from me like water down a drain. This was not possible. This was not happening.

We all join up because we want to help, we want to save lives, save humanity, to share the peace and prosperity we've known all our lives. Then we find out that's not our job. Our job is not to spread peace but to watch it. We must apply its principles in such a way that it creates a shield around our worlds. We do not, we *cannot* go out and save the worlds that will not agree with us.

Especially if we might get caught doing it.

Bianca had lived this reality for five centuries. She had taught it to me. She had given me the strength to hold on even during the Redeemer crisis, until the orders and the backup came.

"Bianca had tried to tell the Guardians that Erasmus was a highly active hot spot, that a takedown needed to be initiated, but they wouldn't listen. They said she didn't have enough proof."

I knew this much. Misao had told me in that last meeting. Had he suspected . . . no. He couldn't possibly have. Not even Misao could have suspected this.

"She came to me for help," Bern was saying. "I thought

she was just going to ask me to help with the spying, get the data for her, help build a case . . ." He turned away, looking at the books on his shelves. He shrank into himself, hunching around his own center.

"But she said she was cutting herself loose. She said she'd volunteered for the Tour so she could decide if she wanted to continue with the Guardians after her next Turnover." Every hundred years, licensed immortals must turn their lives over. They must divest their assets, and either quit their jobs or start over from the bottom. It's how we keep wealth and power from becoming concentrated in a few hands. Immortals among the Guardians go on the Grand Tour of the diaspora worlds before their Turnovers, to educate their replacements and see if they still love their work enough to continue, even from the bottom of the ladder.

A hundred years ago, Bianca had taken her Grand Tour with me. This time she'd done it with Siri and Vijay.

Siri and Vijay.

Siri.

Does Siri know about this? Is this what she's been hiding? Why she wanted Jerimiah to be brought with us?

"She said she couldn't leave this place standing. She said if Command wasn't going to do anything about it, she'd take it apart on her own."

"Why?" I demanded. "This place is falling apart anyway. Even if they're a threat right now, they're not going to stay that way for much longer. They're spending themselves into free fall. They've already taken some massive internal hits, and they're probably going to take another soon. If the reports are right, Dazzle is not happy with the kind of shots Fortress is calling, and now that Oblivion's gone, they are getting restless. All we've got to do is contain them for a few decades and they'll go down like a house of cards." I spread my hands toward him. "I could see that from back home. Why couldn't Bianca see it here?"

Bern shook his head. "I don't know."

"Why didn't you turn her in?"

Bern turned his face away. He looked old. He looked overdue. I felt a wave of sympathy for him, but it wasn't strong enough to damp down the confusion or the anger.

"I'd like to say she seduced me," he said to the desktop. "I'd like to say she used me, but it wouldn't be true."

I forced my brain to move. I made my mind's eye open and made it see what was in front of me. This had happened. It had been done. By Bianca Fayette. I had to accept that. I looked again at Bern, a fit man, a smart man in his fortieth decade, and I thought about Bianca.

"Were you lovers?" I asked. Bianca liked men, and she enjoyed love, both the act and the emotion. She liked the joy and the passion of it, but I had never known her to abandon herself to that love. Even in the throes of a new affair, part of her remained detached.

He nodded. "Yes, we were lovers."

"But that's not why she thought she could tell you what she was planning."

"I told you, you do not understand this place. They have gotten the commodification of human beings down to the sharpest science. The entire system runs on it. They . . ."

My patience snapped. "That's not the point!" I jerked to my feet, nearly overbalanced by emotion. "Listen to you! What did she, did *you*, think you were doing? The Guardians are stretched and starved, and you thought taking apart this fucked-up central authority on your own was going to *help* somebody? When do anarchy and deprivation make things *better*?"

"It seemed better than leaving it be." Calm had returned to Bern, the kind of dreadful calm that comes when there's nowhere to go and nothing to lose.

I wiped my mouth. The buttons on my tunic sleeve dragged hard across my lips. "I'm going to have to turn you in, you know that. I can't let this go."

He shook his head, just a little. "I had hoped . . . you and Bianca were so close, but . . . well, you've been gone for so long . . ."

I cut him off at once. "Don't you dare try to make this about my loyalty, Bern. I am a Guardian, and you . . . ," *and Bianca*, "broke the first rule, the *oldest* rule." I have seldom been so fully in my own self as I was speaking those words. I was solid and present, body and soul, and everything rushed and turned around me; it roared inside me. "You pull together your resignation. Make whatever excuse you want to your staff, but you do it."

For a moment, Bern actually looked angry. "I am all the backup you have in this system. You'll be on your own if I have to step down." Oh, he was good. Diplomat to the core. Give them a carrot, show them the stick. Oh, yes.

"You think I don't know that?" I shot back. *If you'd kept your mouth shut, I wouldn't have to do this, be this, think this . . .*

If you'd kept your mouth shut, I wouldn't have to be doubting Bianca's sanity.

But I knew there was something else. He'd done it because he believed I'd go along with what they had planned between them.

I felt Bianca's ghost behind me, willing me to action. My guts clenched and for a moment I thought I was going to be sick. Was this why Bianca wanted me back? Because she thought I'd go forward with her unauthorized takedown?

Was *this* why Jerimiah couldn't remember what had been done here? Had Bianca sabotaged her own Companion?

I couldn't breathe. I couldn't see. Her ghost was reaching out of the black hole in my head. I desperately wanted to take her hand, but instead I clenched my fist.

"You are done here," I told Bern. "As of now."

I didn't have the authority to do this, but it would have been pointless to argue it. As soon as I told Misao, the Diplomatic Corps would be notified, and he would be out anyway.

He bowed. I remained straight backed.

"Go," I said hoarsely. "And send Field Coordinator Baijahn in here immediately."

"Yes, Field Commander."

He turned on his heel and exited his office.

Behind me, the door thudded closed. I doubled over, pressing my hand against my mouth as I choked down my bile.

Gradually, I was able to straighten up. The solidity I'd felt moments before deserted me. Despite my weighted uniform and my heavy boots, I felt like I was going to float away. I sat down again and stared straight in front of me. I couldn't shift my gaze, couldn't move my hands. I could barely blink.

I had thought I had done with mourning for my friend. I thought I knew the worst. I hadn't come anywhere close.

Why didn't you tell me?

But Bianca didn't answer. She wasn't a Companion, after all, no matter how badly I'd wanted her to be. She was a memory, an echo of a person, and, as it turned out, a distorted one.

I'd come back to save my world and avenge my friend. I thought she'd fallen in the line of duty.

Now . . . now, what was I supposed to think?

At the very corner of my vision, I saw the door open. Siri stepped into the office and closed the door gently behind her.

"What's going on?"

I made myself stand. I folded my hands behind my back so she wouldn't see how they clenched. With all the strength I had left, I lifted my head and met her gaze.

"Siri. I am going to say something to you now, and, if you even think about lying to me, I will be sending you right back to Earth."

She turned her head, first one way, then the other, looking at me out of the corners of her vision, trying hard to come to her own conclusions. "Permission to speak freely?"

I nodded once. "Yes."

"With respect, Field Commander, I'm getting a little sick of your accusations that I'm a lying screwup."

"Bianca was working a takedown of this system."

"Impossible!" Siri shot back immediately. "We had no orders!"

"She wasn't waiting for orders."

I watched the blood drain from Siri's face. I watched her lips move silently, and I watched the naked fear strip all other expression from her face. "No," she whispered. "Not even . . . she wouldn't do it. She wouldn't."

"That's what I said." My knees buckled and I dropped back into the chair. Siri's shock was too raw to be faked. She hadn't known.

Siri wasn't in on it. Siri hadn't betrayed us.

Thank you, I murmured in the back of my mind, to Siri and God and all the ghosts following me.

Siri paced around my chair until she stood facing me again. "You're serious."

"Yes."

"Did Bern tell you this?"

"Yes."

"Where is he?"

"Resigning."

I have to say this for Siri, she was able to take all of this in stride much better than I had. Maybe it was because she'd been active and I hadn't. Maybe there were things in the back of her mind that suddenly made sense. I don't know. What I do know is that she'd been hit hard by this new truth, as I had, but she was already up and on her feet.

"Bern could have been a huge help to us, you know," she pointed out. "He knows what goes on here, and he would have had to do what we wanted."

"And he is either telling the truth about Bianca, or he's lying." I rubbed my gloved palms on the chair arms, thinking of the way Bern had rubbed his palms on his coat. What was he trying to clean off? "If he's telling the truth, he's broken so much of the Common Cause Covenant that he's going to be lucky to get off with only one natural lifetime's worth of imprisonment. If we'd worked with him, it would have been us next."

Siri nodded thoughtfully in agreement. "And if he's lying?"

"Then he's either insane or corrupted."

"Shouldn't we find out who corrupted him?"

I met her gaze, feeling my own steel hardening inside once more. "We will if and when they make a move on his replacement."

She nodded again. "So, what do we do now?"

"You find Miran and get as accurate a picture as is available about how the power is structured here, physically and in terms of data flow. I'll get an encrypted report back to Misao. Then we go on with our mission."

"Will do." Siri turned toward the door.

I stood again. I wanted to be on her level when I said this. "Is there anything, and I mean *anything*, else you should be telling me right now?"

Siri stopped, her hand on the doorknob. I saw her shoulders shake, but she met my gaze without hesitation.

"I swear, Terese. On God's word and Bianca's soul, I swear, I have told you everything I know."

"Thank you." I reached out, and she laid both her hands in mine. We stood like that, hands clasped, the old gesture of trust, of respect, and of friendship. "And I'm sorry," I said.

Siri smiled, a lopsided cynical expression. "It's okay. It's why they pay you the big bucks."

She let go and left me there, shutting the door carefully, and I moved to Bern's desk, trying to find words in my mind to officially betray the trust Bianca had placed in me.

TWELVE

EMILIYA

Emiliya Varus stood in the center of a small room in Fortress's central administrative palace. Its low, transparent ceiling allowed a view of the ice and the ocean. It was impossible not to feel their chill seeping down her spine. The room's chairs were grouped for comfortable conversation, but she had not been invited to sit.

The Grand Sentinel Torian Erasmus also stood.

Emiliya watched with a mixture of fear and hunger as he read the bioscan data spilling across the active pane he'd opened on the curving wall. Without looking up, he made a small gesture with his hand, and the servants lining the walls all bowed and filed out. Emiliya's throat tightened. The last to leave were the footmen, who closed the doors behind themselves.

Torian closed the pane and turned around.

"I want to thank you for coming forward, Dr. Varus." The Grand Sentinel gestured once more, this time indicating the nearest chair. It took Emiliya a moment to realize this was the delayed invitation to sit down. She did so, too quickly and too stiffly. "Your information is invaluable to us."

"Thank you, Sentinel."

Torian regarded her a moment longer, then moved to the sideboard. He selected a corked jug and poured out a measure of milky liquid into a rose-crystal cup. He handed this to Emiliya, who accepted it and held it in both hands.

Torian looked pointedly at the cup, then at her face.

Emiliya blushed, and drank. The beverage was some kind of eggnog. It was sweet and rich and the part of her that was starving wanted to gulp it down. She forced herself to sip, aware every instant that the Sentinel watched her.

"Somehow, Doctor, I think you did not do this out of loyalty to Erasmus."

"No." Emiliya had come to him intending to be smooth, to be strong. For once in her life, she had the upper hand. But she had no experience with power and didn't know how to hold on to it, and she knew she had already failed.

"No," Torian repeated with a sigh. "I am disappointed, but not surprised. However, as we have made our wealth from using you, I don't see why I should scold you for using us."

She made no answer. In the face of such shocking honesty, there was none to make.

"I expect you want debt clearance?"

"No, Sentinel," she answered softly.

Torian lifted his eyebrows. Now he was surprised, and perhaps a little impressed. "What do you want, then?"

Emiliya laced her fingers tightly together around the cup. "I still have family on Dazzle."

"Ah." Torian nodded, comprehending. "And how many family?"

"Four." She tried to picture her mother on her knees by the light of one flickering bulb. *Don't do this, Emiliya. It's too dangerous. We'll find another way.*

But Mother would never say that.

"Four." Torian touched the wall, opening another pane. Bright squares of video and charts crowded the blackness. "So many?"

"You said 'invaluable,'" she reminded him, and her empty stomach clenched at her daring.

But the Grand Sentinel just chuckled. "So I did." He gazed thoughtfully at her. "Do you know, I argued against publicly clearing Brahm Rajandur. It set too high a standard. But then, I've been against a system built on debt slavery from the beginning," he added softly, as if he had forgotten he was still speaking aloud. "It was never the way to true, long-term stability."

"So why don't you end it?" whispered Emiliya.

He cocked his head toward her. "What would you say, Emiliya Varus, if I told you that was my plan?"

I don't believe you. Her hands clenched so tightly around the cup she feared for a moment she would shatter the stone. "I don't know how you could."

"Yes. There are many . . . issues. Not the least of which is that my family must be taken care of. That is primary, and for them to be truly cared for, we must have that long-term stability." Torian touched the pane to close it. "Very well, debt clearance for your relatives. I will need their names and IDs."

Emiliya stood to make a deep bow. "Thank you, Sentinel." *That's all that matters. Nothing else.*

"You have not heard the terms yet."

Startled, she looked up without straightening. "Terms?"

"Four free lives requires more than telling tales on your fellow Hospitallars."

Emiliya bit her lips. *I should have known.*

"What do you want?"

"The saint will be kidnapped and rescued, much as your friend Piata planned. But afterward, she'll need a doctor."

"Me?"

He nodded. "And you will give her a painkiller."

"I see." And she did see. Hospital, meaning the Blood Family, had some specific use for this saint. Whatever was riding on this, it had been thought out long before. Piata's plan never had a hope of working. "What if she doesn't want it?"

Torian shrugged. "That's your job, and that's the price. Four lives for one dosed saint."

"They won't trust me." Suspicion rolled off those soldiers in waves. Suspicion and condescension.

"They will."

"Why?"

"Because Captain Jireu trusts you, and they already trust Captain Jireu."

Emiliya sucked in a deep breath. "What . . ."

"No," Torian cut her off. "You either do this thing and free your family, or you go home and keep this encounter to yourself, because if you let slip one word, I will make it known who was responsible for spoiling the chance of debt clearance for a set of Hospitallars. Choose."

There was no real choice, and they both knew it.

"I assume I will be given the dose in time." Emiliya was surprised at how easily she dropped into a tone of brisk professionalism.

"You will be given it immediately."

"Then I suppose I should go to the dorms and wait for my instructions."

"Very good, Doctor." Torian nodded again, a professorial gesture to a struggling student who has finally understood the question. "We will talk again soon." He touched the wall, and the doors swung open, letting in the squadron of servants and footmen.

"Thank you, Grand Sentinel." Emiliya bowed, stiff and correct, and let the servants and a pair of Clerks lead her away.

THIRTEEN

AMERAND

As soon as I had transferred my saints to the tender care of the Chairs and their people, I went looking for Emiliya.

There were multiple Security houses around Fortress. The Family liked to have us salted through their domain, just in case we were needed. They had never completely relaxed since the Breakout. Despite what ultimately happened to Oblivion, they never stopped thinking that another fleet might rise up and come at them. So the missiles were all armed, the doors all had triple security, and every palace had its watch houses—relatively spartan places with screens instead of windows, barracks for the noncommissioned and private rooms for the officers. Clerks had desks beside the secops' monitoring stations, watching the watchers and making sure the defenders stayed in the prescribed bounds.

At Security Station No. 23, I checked in with the Clerk on duty at the door, then walked into the front monitoring room. The battered old lieutenant at the desk glanced away from the shifting images on the screen walls and gave me a brief wave.

"How's it holding on, Iver?" I slid into the seat next to him and entered all four of my security codes on the keypad.

"Pretty tight." Iver was white-haired, scarred, and crooked, with a permanently hunched back and wry neck. He'd been on frontline duty during the riots, only pulled off when Hospital said his bones couldn't take being broken anymore.

I don't know why he'd never risen above lieutenant. I suppose, sometimes, if you're smart, you find your level and stay there.

Iver watched the screens for a while. Long lists of routing privileges and protocols scrolled in from Flight. Other screens watched over the rooms in our quadrant of the palace. Servants passed back and forth between members of the Blood Family. We ignored the Blood, unless we were specifically assigned to them. Even on Fortress—especially on Fortress—our business was not with the Blood but with the indentured, the OBs and lawbreakers. The Erasmus Blood took care of its own.

Iver's gaze slid over to my hands as they worked the keys, and from there to the corner of the screen I commandeered.

"What's doin'?" he asked.

"Just looking for my cargo." I frowned at the arrival lists and tracking prints. Emiliya seemed to have gone off the map.

"You hauling something besides saints?"

"Hospitallar."

Iver grunted and hit a few keys to clear a new space on the wall. "Got a name?"

I didn't like sharing my business, but Iver had always been all right, at least with me. "Emiliya Varus."

Iver hit the keys. A new tracking map came up with a new set of IDs and codes, none of which had shown up on my screen. Behind us, I heard keys clicking from the Clerk's station.

"Mmmm . . . precious cargo." Iver swiveled his chair to face me. "She's in Room 36. That's the Family section."

It took everything I had to keep my face still. "Who's she with?"

Iver cocked his head toward me, eyes narrow and dangerously curious. "Couldn't say. That's on privacy."

Which meant she was in there not just with any Family Member, but with one who was fairly high-level, second-degree Blood or better. It could, in fact, be Grand Sentinel Torian.

"Was she called in?" I was spying. I was spying on Emiliya. I should have felt guilt, but I didn't. What I felt was fear, cold and hard in the pit of my stomach.

Iver sucked on his cheek, making a loud smacking sound before he turned toward the board again.

Before he could lay his fingers on the keys, the door opened behind us and another pair of Clerks entered. I jerked around to stare at Iver, but he just watched the screens, stone-faced and silent.

The new pair of Clerks passed us by like shadows and stood beside their colleague's desk. He looked up at them, and for the first time in my life, I saw a Clerk look nervous. One of the two newcomers—a dusky-skinned woman with her curling hair cropped short—put her hand on his shoulder, whether in comfort or to hold him in place I couldn't tell. I couldn't read their faces at all. The Clerk bowed his head, clacked a few keys, then stood and squared his shoulders. The woman nodded and walked him out the door. The remaining Clerk, a soft, plump, pale man with a shock of yellow hair, slipped into the desk, poised his hands over the keys, and looked at the screens with shining eyes. He began to type.

I glanced at Iver. *What was that?*

Iver moved his head back and forth, a minute gesture I would have missed if I hadn't been right next to him. Then his eyes flickered toward the Clerk, who hadn't even looked up from his keyboard.

"Got no record on whether your Hospitallar got called in," Iver said. Then he leaned back in his chair, hands folded across his belly and looking at me, almost daring me to ask another question.

I mustered thought and nerve. Whatever that changing of the Clerks meant, I couldn't worry about it just now. I'd drive myself insane. Worse, I'd drive myself to take risks trying to find out. I was looking for Emiliya, who had actively sought out one of the highest up of the Blood Family, and hadn't told me why.

"Problem?" asked Iver.

What could I possibly say to that, especially with this new yellow-headed Clerk in the room? "No. Just trying to get a bead on how long she's going to be. I'd hate to strand her, but if the saints need to leave . . ." I shrugged, and Iver shrugged in answer. We all had our orders, and those set our priorities.

Iver and I talked a while longer. I don't remember about what. I wandered over to the canteen and had a meal. I exchanged some gossip and took some messages for some of the other OBs in the ranks. I heard a lot of grumbles about a new smuggling rig, and plenty of wishing that the attendant ship would come in and get its load so it could be sweetly and simply blown out of the black sky and the Clerks would get off everybody's backs.

Whenever a new smuggling rig was spotted, the Clerks went into overdrive trying to ferret out the corrupt officers who had looked the other way while the pump ship had landed. They always found someone.

What never failed to amaze me was how they would let several loads of water be carried off while they concentrated on rooting out the corruption. It practically guaranteed that the smugglers and pirates would keep trying.

None of us ever speculated out loud how well plumped the Clerks' pockets were, or how frequently they got laid. It wasn't worth it.

Neither Emiliya nor further orders came by the time the lights were dimmed for night shift. I bunked down in the guardhouse barracks instead of taking one of the officers' rooms. I did not like to sleep alone. I never have. In the barracks, I could lie on my back in the darkness, hearing the sounds of sleep all around me. This to me, no matter where I lived, was the feeling of home.

Eventually, I slept.

"Captain Jireu?"

Light shattered sleep. I cracked my eyes and squinted up at a Clerk who looked barely old enough to shave.

"You are to get your ship ready to leave," he said.

I swore at the universe as I hauled myself out of bed. The rest of the secops in the room swore at me as I sent the Clerk running off to find Leda and Ceshame.

I pulled on my clothes and boots and headed back to the port yard, punching in my codes over and over as I passed through the various security gates. Over and over, I waited for clearance, and fumed and wondered what my saints were thinking of.

Terese Drajeske stood in the elaborately tiled waiting area looking grim and disheveled. Whatever she'd been doing, it wasn't exchanging pleasant gossip with colleagues. Beside her, Coordinator Baijahn had her hands folded behind her back. Her eyes darted all around the room, as if looking for some way out.

"My apologies, Captain Jireu," the Field Commander

said, with that reflexive Solaran politeness. "I would have waited until morning, but . . ." She shrugged irritably.

"We can sleep aboard ship," I replied by way of letting her know it was all right, even if it wasn't. "We should be stocked and ready?" I turned to Ceshame, who glowered at me from the gangway threshold. I should not be asking those kinds of questions in front of cargo.

"Yes, Captain," he said with hollow briskness.

"Then if you'll board and get strapped down"—I bowed to the saints—"I'll get the permissions and coordinates from Flight."

Terese nodded grimly to her second and they climbed into the passenger pod. I tried not to wonder what had dragged them so far down. I had more than enough home-grown worries.

I climbed into the cockpit, but instead of punching in for Flight, I tapped the Security network. This time I found Emiliya easily. She was in one of the medical hostels. The Families liked to sort us—separate and isolated—according to world and job.

Against my better judgment, I checked the times on the tracking map. According to this, Emiliya had been in the hostel since ten minutes after we arrived.

I closed the tracking map.

I pinged the room. There was no answer. I pinged it again. The screen stayed black and dark, but Emiliya's weary voice answered. "What is it, Amerand?"

"We're about to launch for Dazzle, Emiliya. I wanted to make sure you're all right before we fall away."

She sighed. "Yeah. I'll be there in five minutes."

"Don't you have to go back to Hospital?"

"Not yet. They want new scans of all the Dazzle saints.

Apparently . . . apparently we didn't do it right the first time. I'm due over there, and I'd rather go with you."

"Okay, then," I said softly. "But make it five for sure. I think our saints are not feeling patient right now."

"Five." Emiliya shut the connection down, leaving me staring at the console.

If she needed to rework the scans, she shouldn't be going to Dazzle, she should be going to the habitat, where her rig was. What she had said made no sense. It was a lie, and a clumsy one.

The chill returned to my blood. I could not brush it aside. Whether she wanted to or not, Emiliya was on assignment for the Blood Family. I had no idea what her orders were or how she intended to carry them out.

More than likely they had nothing to do with me. What was I? I was an extra pair of eyes, a kind of backup for the Clerks and all the other systems watching the saints. Why should I worry about what Emiliya's orders were with regard to them?

I'd have to find a way to talk with Emiliya. When we got to Dazzle, I'd get her into a blind spot and make her tell me what she could. And then . . .

And then what? When I knew what she was doing, what would I do? I couldn't possibly be thinking of *warning* the saints.

Could I? Could I really?

Leda and Ceshame were coming up the ladder, growling and swearing. I had to move my hands across the console, give the ship's ID and priorities up to Flight, and try to get our permissions back. They were slow in coming. It was the midnight shift, because the habitats set their clocks by Fortress, and no one was happy to be here.

The cameras showed Emiliya stepping on board and palming the plate to register that she was aboard a ship authorized to carry her. She looked into the lens for a split second before clambering into the passenger cabin. I couldn't help myself. I switched the camera over to follow her.

Terese Drajeske and Siri Baijahn were already in their couches. Terese nodded to Emiliya, who nodded back and took her place in the third couch. While I watched, Captain Baijahn's gloved fingers moved restlessly across the back of her other hand. Something was being activated down there and nothing on the screen could tell me what it was.

I sent the launch signals down to our passengers and out to the port. The thrusters lifted us smoothly and the automatic systems cut in to start us on the long, sweeping fall toward Dazzle.

"Whoever takes first shift gets a full day off when we get home," I said to Leda and Ceshame.

They eyed each other and held up their fists. The finger-pointing game of odds and evens went the traditional three rounds. Leda won, and Ceshame and I climbed down into the crew compartment.

I stared at the hatch to the passenger compartment.

"You wanna go in and get her out, I'm not saying anything," he remarked.

It took me a moment to realize he thought I was itching after Emiliya.

"We're on duty," I growled, and pulled myself up into the middle bunk. I shut the door on the world.

I closed my eyes and willed myself to sleep. I felt like I was standing on the edge of an empty shaft. Tomorrow I would fall, I was certain of it.

Maybe I could put tomorrow off for a little while longer.

But I could not get away from the fact that the last person to sleep in here was Emiliya. I hated myself for not trusting her, and I hated myself for caring at all about the saints, because that was what was making me distrust the girl I'd held in my arms when we'd heard that the last light had gone out on Oblivion.

I had to remember that. I couldn't forget that she was one of Oblivion's children and that we had to hold it together for ourselves. We had no one else, not really. In the end, we would always turn to each other, whatever else it looked like we were doing.

A furious buzzing shot through my head. My eyes snapped open.

"What is it?" I demanded, my hand groping for the bunk capsule's light panel.

"Captain," came back Leda's voice. "We've got an unauthorized ship in view."

I swore and slammed the door open. I didn't bother getting my boots back on, I just climbed barefoot up into the cockpit.

As soon as I got there, Leda gave over the central seat, dropping into the copilot's spot. I sat down without looking. Ceshame swung up the ladder behind me and dropped into the number three station.

The window was almost filled by the gas giant turning below us. The riotous stripes and swirls slid silently around its perfect curves. A ship—a bundle of blobs and lights made indistinct by distance—flashed past, finishing its burn to drop into a transfer orbit. I looked up and down, and up and down again, comparing the data I saw on the screen against the reality I saw out the window.

"Shit," I said flatly. "Get me . . ."

Leda was ahead of me, her fingers rapidly tapping keys. A string of letters and numbers spilled across the bottom of the screen.

"Says it's with the water authority," Leda told me. "But we've got no routing for it."

"If it's a smuggler, they're fuckless idiots to be running where we can see them," Ceshame muttered.

"We didn't exactly give Flight a lot of warning," Leda reminded him. "Maybe they'd already started out."

I knuckled my eyes. Flight and the Clerks had been waiting for a month for a ship to come and snatch the cargo from that rig on Fortress. Why'd it have to be passing through under my nose?

"Let's hope they'll see reason." Most smugglers didn't want to die. Most of them gave up when they were spotted, preferring an indenture they had a chance to escape to being blown to bits in the black sky.

I turned the intercom over to an active frequency. "This is the *Iphigenia III* to ship ID string 614780J. Identify yourself. We don't have a registered flight path for you."

There was silence, then static, then, "Hey, Brother Amerand."

Kapa. I froze, my heart beating hard at the base of my throat.

"Kapa! I see you, you stoneless pirate." *With a tanker ship, smuggling water.*

When his voice came back, it was the kind of smooth that makes your skin crawl. "You see nothing, Captain. Nothing at all."

A faint voice in the background was less sure. "You said no hassle. You said . . ."

"Shut it!" hissed Kapa.

I gritted my teeth. "I'm not playing games, Kapa. You've got a load of water you're not authorized to carry. Reverse burn and park your ass. We're coming to get you."

"If I was you, *Captain*, I'd check with Fortress, see what they say."

I stared at Ceshame, and he stared back at me. He moved his hand toward the keypad, his eyebrows raised in question.

Was it possible that Kapa had permission from Fortress? If he did, it was because he'd worked a deal with somebody at Flight; otherwise, there'd be an open plan. What the hell kind of smuggler didn't think to manufacture a flight plan?

"Reverse burn, Kapa. We're carrying and we've got you spotted. Don't make me shoot you."

Shoot you. Hull the ship, maybe too badly for a rescue. Maybe not. I'd try not to, but I didn't actually have a lot of choice. I wasn't carrying small arms.

Don't make me kill you. My gorge rose and I had to force it back down. It hadn't come to that. Nothing had happened yet.

"I'm telling you to call Fortress, you dumb screw!" shouted Kapa. "You think I'd be out here where everybody can see if I didn't have the word?"

"I'm looking at the run specs, Kapa, and you are not there. For the last time, reverse and park it. We're loaded and aiming right at you." Leda had the ship in her sights, and the screens in front of me showed how she was tracking him, and how she had already alerted Flight that we had a shooting situation, getting the authority before she had to pull the trigger.

Silence. A cold sweat prickling my scalp. *Park it, park it, park it,* I silently willed the idiot on the other side of the void. *Not worth it. Not worth your life. You can get out of this as long as you're still alive.*

"Fuckless!" shouted Kapa, and a fresh burst of static flooded the speakers a minute later. Through the window, I watched the other ship turn swiftly on its axis. I saw the burn flash from its rear jets, but it was too long, too bright, and too hard to be just finding a parking orbit. The ship shot out of our view.

I didn't even have to order Leda to swing our head around with a short, sharp burst. We were all shoved back hard into our seats for about four seconds before Kapa's ship was centered in the view again, blazing bright over Dazzle's curve of mottled bronze.

Something was wrong with the burn. It wasn't a smooth flame anymore. It was shattered somehow, sharp and sparkling.

"What are they doing?" Ceshame squinted at the screen.

I felt the blood leave my face. "They're burning the water. They're using the *water* for extra fuel to speed up their run!"

If I'd gone white, Ceshame flushed red. *Wasting lives,* I saw him thinking. *Lives burning out in the vacuum.*

"I've got them targeted," announced Leda.

I should shoot him down. He'd not only stolen the water, he'd wasted it. He'd completely and utterly wasted it.

And if I did, I might just be setting Emiliya free from whatever hold he still had on her.

"Kapa, you can't outrun us. You've burned the damn cargo. Stop this right now."

The silence on the other side stretched out endlessly. *Don't be an idiot, Kapa. You were always the smart one. You were the one who could work the angles. You were the one who had the nerve to get out. Have the nerve to stay alive.*

You should never have come back.

At last the silence on the other end broke. "Okay. Okay."

I could hear swearing and yelling in the background. Kapa ignored it. "What do you need us to do?"

I eyed my screens, my lists, and my permissions, and all the back-and-forth between Leda and Flight. "Cut your acceleration, let us catch up and dock. And Kapa . . ."

"Yeah?"

I leaned close. I wanted to be sure he heard me. "Flight's got you pinned now. If you try anything, they'll shoot us all down."

"Yeah," he muttered. "I bet they would."

"Just so we understand each other."

"Oh, I understand you."

"He's slowing down," said Ceshame. Our thrusters rumbled and the ship slipped sideways, lowered, and banked. I checked the rate of our fuel burn. We were going to have to coast most of the way home at this rate.

"Got 'em!" Leda cried happily. "Bonus time all around!"

Then she saw my face and swallowed thoughts of extra pay. She turned back around with a shrug.

Out the window, Kapa's ship looked like it was sitting still. Ceshame and Leda had their eyes pinned on it, and every scanner was up and open, looking for weapons or traps.

"Can't get an internal scan," muttered Ceshame.

"No weapons ports," said Leda. "They got some serious crypto coming and going though. I can't make out anything but static."

"Keep listening, in case they're bringing in friends." I got out of my chair. "Or in case he wasn't bluffing about Fortress. Ceshame, you're with me. Leda, dead man's switch on the clamps. If that ship so much as twitches, drop us back."

"Yes, Cap'n."

"Yes, Cap'n."

I climbed down with Ceshame behind me. As we stepped over the threshold to the connecting passage, the door to the passenger cabin swung open. Terese Drajeske, wearing nothing but black leggings and a skintight black top, said, "What've we got?"

I hesitated. She was a trained soldier, but she was not allowed to kill, and I didn't think that would slow Kapa down for a second if he decided to put up a fight.

"We have to take a smuggler into custody," I said. Over her shoulder, I could see Siri Baijahn, dressed like Terese was, and Emiliya, looking pale, thin, and haggard next to the other two, still in her medical whites with her shoes on her feet.

"I'm going to ask you to remain in the passenger cabin," I told them all.

I half expected Commander Drajeske to protest. But her eyes flicked from me, to Ceshame, to the closed air lock.

"It's your ship," she said.

I met Emiliya's eyes. Beads of perspiration stood out on her forehead. Something very close to panic tightened her face.

Commander Drajeske closed the door.

I pulled my pellet gun from its holster and worked the action. "Have we got a picture yet?"

Ceshame hit the switch on the pad by the door with his left hand while he drew his sidearm with his right. "Not yet. He probably disabled the camera systems as soon as he got his hands on the ship."

"Probably. Stay sharp."

Ceshame took up his position to cover me. I tapped out the ID and authorization codes. With a grind and a hiss, the air lock opened to reveal Kapa standing in the frame of the threshold. I pointed my sidearm straight at him and he spread his clean hands to show them empty. Kapa smiled, flashing his shining, lavender tooth. At the same moment, I heard a shrill whine coming from somewhere in the belly of his ship.

I grabbed Kapa's arm, swinging him through the hatch into my ship and hurling him across to Ceshame.

The world lurched and shook and the bottom dropped out.

My head hit the ceiling, and I saw stars.

FOURTEEN

AMERAND

I cursed and tried to roll myself onto my knees, but the gravity was gone and I slammed off the wall instead.

Kapa was ready for it and we weren't. He had his knife out and he drove it straight into Ceshame's guts.

Ceshame screamed. Red bubbles of blood exploded into the air. Kapa took a faceful and choked. I grabbed the edge of the threshold and forced myself to see straight. Leda swam headfirst down the ladder in time to see Ceshame curl in on himself, clutching his stomach.

Kapa kicked off the wall toward Leda, knife first. Leda, the fool, yanked out her pellet gun and took a shot, which, of course, went wild. The kick drove her back into the wall, knocking what was left of her breath out of her.

I launched myself, slamming my shoulder into Kapa, shoving us both against the wall. I got my hand around his wrist and twisted hard. Bone snapped and he screamed and the knife was loose and floated away. I reached for it with my free hand.

Which was when the rest of Kapa's crew flew through the air lock. The deadman's switch had failed, or they'd been ready for it, and they still had hold of us.

A noose looped around my neck before I could get my hand up. My momentum slammed the line against my throat and pain blinded me. I gasped and gagged, and got a mouthful of Ceshame's blood.

"For fuck's sake, get the acceleration on!" shouted Kapa.

I tried to flip myself over, but the noose choked me. I couldn't reach my captor. A rumble vibrated through the hull, and we all dropped to the floor. My captor missed his footing and fell. I fell with him, landing on top of him. I dug my fingers under the noose as I rolled. It came loose and I jerked it away, forcing myself to my feet, coming up to face Kapa, who pointed my sidearm at me.

"I'd rather not do it, Brother," he said.

Ceshame was on the deck, spattered with his own blood and not moving. Leda had collapsed on the deck beside him. Pain hazed her eyes and she tried to get up, but only fell back panting. Kapa had two men and a woman behind him, and out of the corner of my eye I could see two more of his crew just waiting for the room to fit themselves in.

I held very, very still. I caught Leda's pain-wracked gaze, and prayed she'd understand she should be still too. She panted hard, and spat and curled more tightly in on herself. Gradually, her breath slowed. Then it stopped.

Her sightless eyes rolled open.

I could do nothing at all.

Kapa just turned to his crew. "Go get the saints," he ordered. "If they've locked themselves in, tell them I'll shoot their minder if they don't come out." He winked at me. "Don't worry. They won't let it come to that. Against their codes."

Disbelief surged through me. "You are not talking about kidnapping a pair of saints, Kapa."

He shrugged. "You pick your hole, I'll pick mine."

"Either way, we both go down."

That only made him grin wider. "Unless you change your mind. Door's open for about sixty seconds longer, Brother. Put in and we can go get Emiliya out too. Be just like the old days."

He didn't know she was with us. I licked my lips. Would it make a difference if he knew we had Emiliya? Probably not. He'd find out soon enough anyway.

I felt sick. I had screwed up, utterly and completely, and now Kapa was trying to recruit me over Leda's corpse.

"Shut it," I croaked. My throat burned like fire from the noose. "Even if they didn't have my parents, you'd be asking me to turn on my own people."

Kapa shrugged. "Well, at least you get to go out on a clear conscience."

One of the women had gone to the door. Had Emiliya and the saints locked it in time? I had no way of knowing. I had no way of moving without getting shot. Kapa was not going to miss me at that range, and he wouldn't give a damn if he pinholed the ship doing it. After all, he had another ship. An internal drive ship. That whine I'd heard was the jump engine ramping up.

Where did Kapa get an ID ship?

Kapa's crew member was banging on the passenger compartment door. "Come on out!" she yelled into the intercom grille. "And you won't have anything to be sorry for!"

I thought about Terese Drajeske and Siri Baijahn, and the weapons they had stashed in the lockers. I thought about the fact that they were forbidden to kill, and that Emiliya was in there and I had absolutely no idea what any of them could, or would, do.

"Okay, okay," came Terese's voice over the intercom. "I've unlocked the door."

"Good girl," sneered the pirate, and she cranked the latch.

"No!" yelled Kapa.

Too late. The door pulled back and Terese, fully dressed, slammed the muzzle of her gun directly in the pirate's solar plexus. The blow doubled the woman over and dropped her to the deck. Terese hit the deck full length, giving me a perfect view of Siri kneeling in a firing position and taking a bead on Kapa. Kapa swung my pellet gun around and I raised my fists, but there was a sharp crack, and the gun vanished out of his hand, and Kapa was knocked back against the wall.

From her position on the floor, Terese rolled, swinging her gun out to sweep the woman pirate's feet out from under her. I spotted the gun Kapa had dropped and darted for it. I heard the firing crack behind me. Kapa was swearing and shouting. Another crack, and I turned, gun up. Kapa was struggling to pull himself from the wall. He couldn't seem to move his good hand. A massive blob of shiny mucus covered his fist and wrist.

Glue. She'd glued him to the wall. His broken hand dangled uselessly. The pain had to be intense. Hate distorted his features.

The last pirate still standing struggled to pull his feet free from the deck. Glue covered his boots.

A rush of wind told me the air lock had closed. I whirled around in time to see the warning light blink over to yellow. I dodged over to the panel. That wasn't our door. Whoever was still on board Kapa's ship had cut us off from their side.

I spun again to face Kapa. Death had slackened all of Ceshame's features, and his corpse slumped across Leda's. I swore, bitterly and silently.

Terese was breathing hard and she and Siri had their guns up, covering all three of the pirates: the one glued to the deck, the one groaning in pain between Ceshame's and Leda's corpses, and Kapa, glued to the wall.

Emiliya was nowhere to be seen. And the door to the internal drive ship was shut and locked.

"You got us," said Kapa, his grin firmly in place. "And we look like pretty good chumps, too. Now listen to me. You're in the middle of fuckless nowhere right now. If my ship leaves, you've only got a slower-than-light engine and a slower-than-light transmitter and we'll be left with the choice of suffocation and starvation, *if* my guy doesn't decide to be nice and put us all out of our misery."

"He'd be killing you too," Terese pointed out.

"What makes you think he'd give a damn? You think I hired a bunch of Guardians?" He sneered the last word. "Make your decision now, Lady Saint. Play tough and you're killing us all."

"Is he bluffing?" Terese asked me.

Kapa met my gaze without blinking. I expected his expression to be cold, but it wasn't. His face was warm and open, absolutely sincere, like a friend's.

"Kapa," I said. "What do you think you're doing?"

He shrugged and winced as his broken hand flopped. "And I'm going to tell you now? Answer the seña's question."

My jaw worked back and forth a few times before answering.

"No, he's not bluffing," I said. "He's gambled everything on this. If it doesn't work, he's dead anyway and he knows it."

Where's Emiliya?

"Make up your mind fast, Lady Saint," said Kapa. "I did not leave a patient man over there."

Terese looked at me. I looked at her. Siri was still kneeling in her firing position, waiting. A bead of sweat ran down her brow.

Where's Emiliya?

"Stand down," said Terese hoarsely. She laid her gun on the floor, but I thought I saw her finger make an extra tweak on the trigger. She met my eyes, but I saw no fear, only grim determination. As far as she was concerned, this fight was a long way from over.

Anger rushed through me, together with a hot, ferocious adrenaline wave, and I had to suppress the most bizarre urge to smile.

"Up to you now, Brother Amerand," said Kapa. "You gonna shoot, or give Isha there your gun?" He nodded toward the woman pirate between my dead crew. She'd risen to her knees, gritting her teeth against the pain. The look she sent toward Terese was pure hate.

I could stop this now, but I would end as a corpsicle, and I wanted to live. I wanted revenge for the death of my crew.

I laid my gun on the deck and kicked it over to Isha. Moving slow and lopsided, she scooped it up, checking the trigger and the load.

"Now get me out of this." Kapa jerked his chin toward his glue-covered hand.

Terese shrugged. "I don't have the release."

"I don't believe you," answered Kapa, and Isha pointed my gun at Terese's face. Isha's arm shook. Her finger on the trigger shook.

Terese met the woman's eyes, letting Isha see she was not afraid. She shrugged again and nodded to her second. The Field Coordinator had also laid down her weapon. Moving slowly, Siri Baijhan crossed the deck to Kapa.

"It's in my pocket," she said. Keeping one hand up and out, she pulled a capsule about the size of her thumbnail out of her belt pocket and smashed it against Kapa's trapped hand. A sharp ammoniac scent burst from it followed by a soft hiss, and the epoxy turned to a clear jelly and sloughed off down the wall.

"Now him."

Siri performed the operation on the other pirate's boots. His foot lashed out and caught her right on the temple, snapping her head back and sending her sprawling onto her back.

"Siri!" Terese was beside her in an instant. Coordinator Baijahn blinked unsteadily at the ceiling.

"None of that," said Kapa mildly to his man. "No unnecessary waste." He tapped on the intercom. "Open it up. We're in control here."

The warning light blinked over to green and the air lock whooshed open again. Kapa's remaining crew member—a squat, scarred man with a bird icon tattooed on his temple—came out, pellet gun pointed at us. I looked toward Terese, but she was helping Siri sit up. Siri blinked unsteadily at her surroundings. Blood trickled down her cheek.

"What the hell?" she said. "What the hell?"

Kapa paid no attention. He was busy taking charge. "All right, Gull, search the passenger pod. Make sure they haven't stowed any other little surprises in there." Gull was the new arrival. He worked the action on his own weapon by way of response.

"Then we stow these three in there," Kapa went on, nodding toward the passenger cabin. He cradled his broken hand in the good one. Pain turned his face grey, and his forehead was slick with sweat. "After pickup comes, we can strip the rest of the shuttle." His gaze wandered over his prisoners and lingered on Siri Baijahn where she sat beside her commander. "And maybe now you've learned a little lesson?" He smiled at Terese where she crouched next to Siri, who still blinked dazedly around at all of us.

Terese's smile was sharp and dangerous. "And here's one

for you. Touch one of my people again, and I will cut your balls off."

Kapa flashed his amethyst tooth at her. "No good. I know you can't kill me."

Terese's smile did not waver. "So you'll be alive, and without your balls. Think about it."

Kapa narrowed his eyes, turning his face genuinely ugly. He leaned in close to Terese, trying to make her shrink back. "You're so lucky I need you."

"Thanks for letting me know," she answered evenly. "Gives me a whole world of latitude, that little factoid does."

"I need you alive, but you don't have to be in one piece," Kapa said quietly, seriously. "Think about that little *factoid* while deciding how much *latitude* you really have."

Siri finally seemed able to focus again on what was happening. She and Terese both watched Kapa as he straightened, their expressions hard and cold. I wondered how many things you could do to a man before he died, and how many of them the saints knew.

Gull was in the passenger compartment now, gun ready, eyes sharp, the pirates backing him up. The obvious place to hide was in the bunks. But Emiliya was a tunnel runner. She knew how to hide. She wouldn't be waiting in the most obvious spot.

The pirate opened the first bunk.

Nothing.

He opened the second, the third . . . nothing.

He moved to the lockers, and opened the first, the second, the third.

Still nothing.

I was beginning to wonder if I had dreamed Emiliya's

presence. I stared straight ahead. I could not betray the possible hiding places with my glance.

Then I noticed Terese Drajeske's mouth moving. None of Kapa's crew was looking at her. They were all watching Gull. Terese Drajeske was watching the passenger compartment, and slowly, softly, counting down.

Four . . .

Gull bent down and hauled up the floor plates with one hand.

Three . . .

Two . . .

He slammed them shut and straightened up.

One . . .

A white blur dropped from the ceiling. Gull gave a strangled shout and toppled over. Emiliya rolled to her knees, his gun in her hand. Gull was flat on the deck with a needle in his throat.

Terese dove across the deck, grabbed the pirate nearest her by the ankle, and twisted hard. I heard the snap and he screamed, and Kapa swung his gun around at me, but I launched myself forward and tackled him. The firing crack sounded and metal snapped. I rolled him over, twisting his broken wrist and making him scream high and sharp. Around me they were shouting and another shot whizzed overhead. Siri hauled herself to her feet and lurched forward. Terese swore and Emiliya shouted a warning, and I shoved Kapa against the wall. When he slammed his good fist into my gut, I saw stars and barely managed to hang on. I smashed the heel of my hand against his nose. I felt the bone break and he screamed and gurgled, but I had the gun, and somehow found my feet.

And Emiliya was on her knees, staring at Kapa.

And Kapa was staring at Emiliya.

"What are you doing here?" he demanded, his voice harsh with pain. Blood dripped from his mouth. "I swear, Emiliya, they didn't tell me you'd be here!"

"Move!" bellowed Terese Drajeske, snatching up the epoxy guns where they'd been dropped on the deck. "Into the other ship! Go, go, go!"

I was still half in a daze, but I obeyed, stumbling across the threshold with Siri Baijahn. A strained heartbeat later, Emiliya shoved her way in. Terese leapt in after us, and I leaned hard on the active pad by the door, and to my relief, the air lock ground shut.

"We've got the door," Terese said. "Better find out if you can fly this thing."

Kapa's tanker had been made out of standard shuttle modules, and the ladder to the cockpit was right where it was supposed to be. We had two chances, and which one would work all depended on how overconfident Kapa was.

I swung myself up into the cockpit, adrenaline singing through my blood and my mind racing. I'd known already it would be empty. You couldn't cram more than six people into a ship this size. Kapa had brought over his whole crew in the boarding action. That boded well for our chances. If he'd been careless enough to empty his ship . . .

I dropped into the pilot's chair and laid my hands on the keys, hitting the commands for the clamps and the air locks.

And nothing happened.

I tried again, and still nothing happened.

So Kapa wasn't that overconfident. He'd locked down the system.

And probably had a backdoor command so that he could open the air lock from the other side, just in case anybody tried to shut him out of his own ship. Which was why he had been willing to empty it out in order to board us.

"Engine compartment!" I leapt out of my chair and dove for the ladder. "Engine! Now!"

None of them hesitated. Emiliya led the way, bouncing off the floor and caroming off the walls in the way tunnel runners knew best, not quite running, not quite flying. I watched Siri Baijahn's jaw drop as she and her commander followed, more slowly and much more clumsily. Siri was starting to sag, and her face had taken on a nasty grey color. *Concussion,* I thought. *Maybe a bad one.*

I shoved Siri ahead of me into Terese Drajeske's arms. I dove headfirst toward the door behind them, rolled over the threshold, bouncing to my feet in a way I'd forgotten I knew. I spun around in time to see the main air lock creak open.

Kapa, covered in his own blood, staggered inside.

We hadn't gotten all the weapons. He aimed his gun at me. I darted behind the bulkhead and slammed both hands against the active panel.

Luck was with me this time. The air lock groaned and hissed, but it closed, putting a heavy metal door between us and Kapa.

Cutting us off from the cockpit, where Kapa could open the door with a single command.

Terese was beside me. "I got this," she said. "You activate the lifeboat."

I stepped back, and she aimed her epoxy gun at the door seams and shot, and shot again, gluing the door shut. Then, for good measure, she brought her gun butt down on the access panel, lifting herself off the deck with the force of the blow. But it did the job with a shower of sparks and a flash of red lights.

I left her to it and turned to the internal drive. It was an absurdly small thing, an irregular metal housing, all knobs and tubes and bulges. Metal pipes branched out and embedded themselves into the ceiling and the decking.

Every ID ship had a lifeboat function, and an access pad to allow you to activate and fine-tune it. If something went wrong with the ship—say, if she got hulled somehow—the engine compartment acted as the lifeboat. The engine would jump that module back to its previous location.

I punched in the standard emergency codes on the pad as fast as I could, and as the readout came back, I swore.

"Problem?" asked Terese calmly.

"They've gutted the programming. I'm not sure they've left the lifeboat functions."

There were crash alcoves in the walls and Emiliya was already swaddled in. Siri Baijahn had her feet in the ankle straps, but hadn't pulled down the mask or the webbing yet. She had her epoxy gun pointed at the door, but her face had gone green, and the muzzle dipped and wavered.

The door creaked, hydraulics straining against the epoxy seal. I made my fingers move across the keys, frantically working to match up the fragmented code.

The door creaked again.

"Well. This is going to be interesting." Terese stationed herself right in front of the door, raising her gun. She could not kill, even to save her own life, but was going to put herself between us and whatever came through that door.

I looked back down at the internal drive's screen. I could not think about what she was doing, nor about the creaking door or Emiliya in her cradle. I had to find the fragments and crumbs of functionality Kapa had left behind. I had to knit them back together with language half-remembered from the few short years I was an ID pilot.

And I had to do it now.

The door buckled. A crack appeared in the epoxy. Terese stood there, gun up and ready.

I beat in a final connector, forcing two commands together. "Done!"

Terese spun and kicked off the deck, leaping into the center of the chamber. I bolted after her, hitting the seal on the inner door. Terese slammed into her cradle, and only then did her hands begin to shake so badly she couldn't work the buckles. I dodged over, slapped the clasps together, and dropped the pressure cap. Our eyes met for an instant before I swung into my cradle, slammed my buckles shut. I grabbed my mask, hauled down the cap, and pressed the red button.

The world lurched and dropped and rose again, and gravity was gone and I was falling . . . falling.

Falling.

I wasn't falling.

I was floating.

I tumbled, over and over. There, turning over me, visible through the one window, was the orange-and-red curve of the Reesethree gas giant. Then it was gone, replaced by blackness. Then it was back again.

We were out of the trap, and into the pit.

Because we were a completely unauthorized object tumbling through the Erasmus System.

"Please, let that intercom work," I murmured.

A split second later, the warning voice came. "This is Erasmus Flight Control to unidentified ship. You will identify yourself and all members of your crew and state your purpose, or you will be tagged as unauthorized."

"Captain Amerand Jireu of the Erasmus Security." I reeled off my ID code, praying I was giving them this month's. If it was last month's, they might just . . . no, we hadn't escaped from those idiots to be shot down by Flight.

Those idiots. Kapa. Set up and waiting to kidnap the new saints, now out in the middle of nowhere in a standard old hyperwired shuttle, and with Ceshame and Leda lying dead on the deck.

"Jireu? What happened?" said the voice on the other end. My blood roared so loud in my ears, I could barely recognize it.

"Caulder?" I said, praying I had it right. Caulder was okay. Another one who kept his head down, just like me. "Is that you?"

But it wasn't Caulder who answered. It was a stranger's voice, hard and clipped, almost mechanical. "You have been identified, Captain Jireu. I require identification for your crew and ship."

"I don't have ID for my ship! We're a peeled core! We need emergency assistance!"

"I require identification," replied the voice without any inflection whatsoever.

"Doctor Emiliya Varus of Moontwo," Emiliya called out and reeled off her ID.

There was a pause, then the voice reported. "I have confirmation. Is that all your crew?"

"We also have Field Commander Terese Drajeske of the Solaris Guardians, and Field Coordinator Siri Baijahn, who is injured. We need a rescue ship now!"

"I need their ID numbers, Captain."

I shot Terese a pleading look. We turned over again, and my stomach lurched and she slowly shook her head.

"Get the cameras on, Caulder!" I called, hoping he was still in earshot. "You can do a visual ID."

Another sickening pause. "You've got no cameras I can hook into, Jireu. You've got thirty before I have to log an unauthorized. You've got to give me something." He was pleading. That clipped voice must have been his Clerk. I could picture Caulder standing back of the controls at Flight, unable to shove the black-coated, hard-eyed stranger aside.

"Contact Grand Sentinel Torian Erasmus," said Emiliya abruptly, and she reeled off a code. "He will pass emergency authorization."

I stared at her. She did not look at me. She looked at Captain Baijahn hanging in her straps. Our spinning and weightlessness were not doing her injured head any good. She looked like she was a few seconds from vomiting.

"On it." Underneath I thought I heard Caulder whisper, "Come on, come on, don't make me do this, don't make me do this . . ."

Seconds crawled. How many had it been? I lost track. I didn't dare make a move to stabilize us while we were unauthorized. We turned and turned again, and my head was reeling, and in a moment I was going to heave up whatever I had in me.

I knew Caulder, but I didn't know who was with him or who was watching him. We continued our slow tumble. Captain Baijahn lurched and gagged.

"Authorization complete," said the clipped Clerk's voice.

It was Caulder who said, "We got you, Captain. You are authorized to stabilize your fall and wait to receive assistance."

Terese let out a long, wordless whoop of relief.

"Thank you, Flight." My fingers moved across the keypad beside the alcove. The code was still shredded, and the equipment still bad, but there was a little emergency ballast we could expel. It was enough to slow our tumble to a much more gentle rate, allowing nausea to fade.

Emiliya hit the green switch on her cradle to open the pressure cap. She undid her straps, pushing herself over to Captain Baijahn. Terese also opened up, unbuckled and pushed off, catching up with Emiliya. Our eyes met, but Emiliya said nothing and I said nothing.

Emiliya strapped herself into the alcove next to Siri Baijahn and opened her high-necked white jacket. The inside was lined with little pockets; the emergency medical kit all doctors carried when they were off Hospital. With competent fingers she touched the spreading bruise and the split skin on the Guardian's temples. "That's got to hurt."

Siri swallowed and coughed. "Yeah."

"I can tell you now, you're concussed. I can't do anything about that here, but I'll give you something for the pain, then I can close up that cut."

Siri looked at Terese. Terese hesitated, and looked at me. I nodded to her, and she nodded to Emiliya. Emiliya reached into one pocket and brought out a sprayer, which she pressed against Baijahn's neck. The Solaris captain grunted against the pressure, then let out a long sigh as the stabilizer hit her system.

"Thanks. I thought I was going to . . ."

"No need to go into details, Siri," muttered Terese.

Emiliya didn't answer. She just reached for a swab and got to work cleaning the wound. Little flakes of blood drifted about the chamber.

"Anything I can do to help?" Terese asked.

"No. Thanks. It's done." Emiliya lifted the swab away. It was probably coated with a glue or clotter, because instead of an open cut, there was a bright green smear on Siri Bai-jahn's temple.

"How are you feeling?" Terese asked Siri.

"Like crap," Siri answered. "But I'll bet that pirate feels worse."

"Oh yeah." Terese grinned and twisted toward Emiliya. "Thanks for the help."

"Glad I could," murmured Emiliya, closing up her jacket.

Now that we were safe, curiosity reared its head. "What was that thing . . ." I sputtered at Emiliya. "You fell off the ceiling."

But it was Terese who answered. "Cadet trick. If you do it just right, you can epoxy someone to the ceiling with a couple of release capsules under their waistband. The shot cracks the capsule, but it takes maybe two minutes for the release to leak through and drop you. No one ever remembers to look up."

I was staring. I couldn't help it. Terese grinned at me and held out her hand. "Hello. I'm Terese Drajeske of the Pax Solaris Guardians. I don't think we've met properly."

"Captain Amerand Jireu of the Erasmus Security." I took her hand and shook it up and down. It was an antique gesture I'd only ever seen in the XPs. "No, I don't think we have."

As I hung there, holding her hand, the thought shot through me: *There is no camera here.* There was no drone, no Clerk. The connection with Flight was faulty at best. Whatever I said next, no one beyond this fragile chamber could hear it. Whatever I did next, no one could see it.

"I cannot say this again. There may not be anywhere else unwatched. If you need help, I will help you."

Terese was silent for a heartbeat, then another. Her eyes flickered toward her second, who just cocked her head.

I looked at Emiliya and saw her devastation. The bottom dropped out from my heart, but I could not take what I had said back. I would not.

Terese raised her eyebrows. "What if I'm here to shore up and support the Blood Family?" she asked.

"Are you?" I asked.

Her smile was small and fleeting. "No."

"Help us," I whispered. "We are alone."

Terese nodded. Her gaze was calculating but not closed. "No matter what happens, I won't leave you here."

I was breathing hard. My heart pounded more quickly than it ever had.

Emiliya turned her head away, but not so far that I missed the tears shining in her eyes.

"Jireu?" Caulder's voice and a burst of static came through the intercom. "We've got the rescue ship launched. We'll be there in about six hours. How's your air?"

With that, thoughts of the future and how I had just changed my world had to be shunted aside so the business of survival could be tended to. But I knew this: In that moment, I ended my life as a slave.

I wish to all the gods in all their many Heavens that that was all I had ended.

FIFTEEN

TORIAN

Grand Sentinel Torian Erasmus strode into the luxurious, busy birthing room. Mai Erasmus, exhausted and disheveled, sat propped up on pillows in the center, holding her infant daughter. Triumph filled her smile as she looked down at the baby. The infant had her own eyes screwed shut as tightly as any newborn kitten's and seemed to be trying to see how far she could push out her lower lip. Estev stood to the side with a cluster of half a dozen doctors, listening intently as they pointed to a series of numbers on an active pane.

Mai barely glanced up as Torian approached her bedside. She was lost in the wonder of her new child.

"How are you, Mai?" Torian laid a hand on her shoulder. The infant wriggled in her arms and kicked rosy feet.

"Exhausted. Hoarse," Mai admitted with a grimace. "Next time, I want the full range of drugs."

Torian chuckled briefly. "I promise. And your daughter?"

"As fit and beautiful as could be wished," announced Estev, moving to join them. He kissed his wife, deeply and openly for a long moment, and they both beamed down at the infant, nothing in their faces but parents' proper pride at the new life they had brought into being.

"And they say they can do the monitoring through something other than blood samples." Estev jerked his chin ruefully at the doctors, who had removed themselves to the background. "I think she'd object. She's got her mother's sense of propriety."

Torian chuckled briefly. "I have no doubt." He leaned closer, unable to help himself. As old as he was, as aware as he was of the totality of what this child represented, an infant exerted an attractive force on its family. "But, from what I have seen, the prognosis all seems good."

Mai let out a long, slow breath. "Then we have succeeded?"

Torian smiled, allowing himself to drink in the deeply satisfying scene. *The future is here. It is finally here.* "There's going to be reason for caution for a long time yet, but I think you may safely go ahead with your plans for celebration."

"Bloom will be pleased," Estev remarked.

"Possibly." Torian stood up and back. "I will need to divert him for a little bit, though."

"Oh?" Estev raised his eyebrows.

"Yes. I want to start putting a little pressure on Drajeske's second-in-command."

"Why her?" asked Mai.

"Because if you want to weaken the top, you work from the foundation," Torian answered. Mai's eyes narrowed. She had very fine instincts when it came to hearing the unsaid, very much like Felice had had in her time. Torian counted himself lucky that she was still dealing with the aftereffects of childbirth. Otherwise, she would have pursued the question much further.

"What form will this pressure take?" Estev inquired. Estev did not like subtlety. It took everything Torian had to persuade him that they could not do to Dazzle as had been done to Oblivion. They were still dependent on other independent beings for labor and biological resources. The spread of the Pax Solaris had made new stock difficult to come by.

Torian waved his hand, indicating that this was a minor thing, nothing for the *Saeos* to bother themselves with. "A little seduction, a little misdirection. Nothing Bloom can't handle."

Estev smirked. "And will relish, I'm sure. Next best thing to a party. But I am wondering . . ." He drew the last word out long and slow. "If everything is going so well, why are you perspiring?"

It was true. Sweat rolled down Torian's temples and stood out in great beads on his forehead.

He wiped his brow with the back of his hand, looking unusually sheepish. "Damn. Some of the new modifications haven't settled in yet. Problems with the heat exchange."

"Nothing you can't handle, I'm sure."

"As you say," Torian replied easily. "By the way, did I give you my congratulations?"

Mai smiled up at him. "No, I don't believe you did."

"Congratulations, then." Torian rested his hand on her shoulder and gazed down at the tiny bundle of humanity in her arms. "It is an amazing thing to see your children live forever."

Estev was the one who answered. "It is indeed. We couldn't have gotten this far without you, Torian."

Torian felt his throat tighten. Memory threatened: Hadn't Felice said the same thing to him once? Jasper, perhaps, when they'd concluded the first deal, when the first cargo of prisoners arrived through the new gate. "It is my duty," he murmured. "And my debt to your parents."

The baby squeaked, a sound somewhere between a grunt and a chirp. "One of these days you're going to tell me all about that debt," Mai said. Awkwardly and one-handed, she loosened the top of her nightdress so the baby could nurse.

"One of these days probably, but not today." Torian tried

to keep his tone casual, as if he might actually do it. "Now, you need your rest and I need to contact Bloom."

Torian said his farewells and strode out of the room. His heart swelled and constricted with emotion, and he tried to suppress it. This was not the time for sentiment. He must be more clearheaded, not less. They had already rushed things more than he would have liked. Before this, he had been able to test and retest every phase of his long-term plan, but events were in motion that could not be halted. Some things simply had to be fixed on the move.

This did not, however, mean that Mai and Estev needed to be bothered with every detail. Especially not with the birth of their daughter and the other infants born to the First Bloods this week to keep them busy.

He pressed his palm to the back of his neck and the spot behind his right ear. The skin there was as hot as if sunburned, and the discomfort was becoming serious.

Natio Bloom was already in the audience chamber, chatting with the servants and, ever the performer, telling jokes to see if he could make them laugh even though he knew it could get them into trouble.

Bloom always did have a mean streak.

However, he also had a faultless sense of occasion, and he bowed to Torian with perfect grace. Bloom wore his customary black and white, but also carried a black cane tied with white ribbons. This was a new affectation, and it suited his dramatic persona perfectly.

"Greetings to you on this most auspicious day, Grand Sentinel!" cried Bloom as he straightened from his bow. "I trust our new Family members are all of them well and strong?"

"Very well, thank you." Torian had pored over the records the doctors had cross-loaded to him before he had even moved from his office. "But we have business of a different kind, you and I." Torian gestured toward a chair.

"Of course." Bloom perched on the edge of the seat, his hands folded on the head of his cane. "I am pleased to be able to report I have found the reason Field Coordinator Siri Baijahn is being returned to us."

Torian steepled his fingers. "And that is?"

"It seems our saints left behind quite the illicit communications network on their last visit."

"Did they?"

"Oh, yes. And much of it is still in working order. I have the Clerks mapping it now, just in case you wanted a tour before you shredded it."

Torian pursed his lips. "No, no shredding. I think it will prove very useful."

"As always, you meet my highest expectations." Bloom smiled as he cocked his head. "Will we be listening in on our pretty listener?"

"Perhaps. But we will most definitely be making use of her. Are you ready to do that?"

Bloom waved his hand noncommittally. "We were casual acquaintances. I think I amused her." His tone was brittle. "The aging party host and actor, clinging to hopes of a resurrection of his playground." He paused and Torian was forced to rein in his impatience with Bloom's inefficient, dramatic style. "I think she had some notion I might be useful in the saints' various efforts. I expect she will contact me when she settles back into her place on Dazzle. But then"— he narrowed his eyes shrewdly—"you knew that."

Torian shrugged minutely. "And we can see she pays the price for underestimating you."

"Really?" Bloom leaned forward. "How is that?"

"We have taken steps to make sure Siri Baijahn is rendered . . . susceptible to suggestion. That she is off-balance. We need her pushed over the edge as quickly as possible." He had hoped to allow the imbalance they'd manufactured to take its own course, but with Ambassador Bern removed from the equation, there was a certain probability that Field Commander Drajeske might begin to stray from the path they had laid out. She was rusty, but her actions aboard Kapa's ship proved she was not as sloppy as they had been hoping for.

"And what is the nature of this . . . push you've given Coordinator Baijahn?"

"You don't need to know that." Torian touched the wall, opening some windows for new reports. He blinked his eyes as a bead of sweat dripped off his brow. *We must work out the heat-exchange problem.*

"I beg to differ, Sentinel," said Bloom. "If I am to create an illusion, I need to know everything that has been done to her, and I need to know how it works."

Torian frowned. "I am only asking for some puffery." *Patience,* he reminded himself, but that was difficult when it felt like the side of his neck was on fire.

"No." Bloom raised one finger. "You are asking for a lie. A sophisticated one. It's easy to lie to a stable person, but one who is 'off-balance,' as you call it? Such people develop very solid views of the world and take them very seriously. If I say the wrong thing to her, I will run into a wall, and the whole thing"—he threw up his hands—"goes up in smoke."

Torian glowered at him, wishing he could read Bloom's crooked mind. But that was not yet possible. His own words about being forced to rely on independent, unpredictable beings for the prosperity of his family played back to him.

"Sentinel"—Bloom sighed—"we've both gone too far to start doubting each other now."

Torian narrowed his eyes at Bloom.

"What is it?" Bloom inquired.

"I am wondering what you want."

Bloom laid his hand on his breast and bowed humbly. "You've offered me so much, what more could I possibly want?"

"I don't know," confessed Torian. "You really are the most amazing liar I've ever met." *And yet you are the one person on Dazzle I have to trust. You can, I'm sure, appreciate the irony in this.*

"I'm an actor, my Grand Sentinel, and a very good one. But since I have demanded honesty from you, I must return it." Bloom spread his hands and looked about him as if addressing an invisible audience. "What do I want? I want to go out with a bang."

For the first time in a very long time, Torian found himself surprised. "I'm sorry?"

"The world I built and mastered is gone. Even if I left this ruined system—and believe me, I have thought about it— I'll never again do anything on the scale that caused a world to be named Dazzle." His expression grew distant, an aging man reliving his memories. "It's over. Frittered and finished. Done." He snapped his fingers. "I was going to kill myself, you know, before you came to me with your ... proposal. But then I saw it—one last illusion, the greatest ever." Bloom's whole face lit up. He lifted his hands and rose lightly to his feet. "I am working in the theater of the universe, and empires are my audience. No one has ever done that. No one ever will again. This moment is unique, and it is mine to create." He held the pose and all Torian could think was that this was a man who has looked upon his god.

Slowly, though, Bloom returned to more workaday realms. "Can you understand?" he asked.

"No," Torian admitted. "But I do believe you."

Bloom bowed again. "Thank you. Now"—he settled back into his chair and steepled his fingers—"I believe you have something to tell me."

SIXTEEN

KAPA

"Well, *Captain*?" sneered Gull. "Now what?"

Kapa faced his crew, those who were still breathing. They had all crammed themselves into the crew cabin of Amerand's shuttle and sealed off their own ship. What was left of it.

Aware he was facing five dangerous people whom he had promised wealth and freedom, Kapa struggled to think against the pain. It burned in his broken wrist. It spread out from his broken nose. He gasped and wheezed to get enough breath.

Unfortunately, the only thought that came to him was: *I'm dead.*

Either their client was going to kill him for his failure, or his crew was going to shove him out the air lock to make themselves feel better. They'd still be all in a battered can out in the middle of nowhere, but at least the fuckless wonder who'd brought them there would be dead.

Kapa understood the feeling very well. He grinned, showing all his teeth. He'd take at least one of them with him.

"Ship!" cried Isha so suddenly Kapa thought she was just cursing. But she pointed, and he pivoted. On the screen glowed a sleek silver ellipse, lights shining from its windows and its multiple scopes.

While his crew gawped, Kapa forced his boots to move. He dragged himself one-handed up into the cockpit, and fell into the pilot's chair. Someone had followed him up the ladder. He didn't turn his head to see who. Pain blurred the edges of his vision and he shook his head hard. He couldn't black out. Not yet. His good hand shook as he tapped out one of the few standard commands he remembered from the academy.

One of the shuttle's scopes zoomed in on the approaching ship.

"Fuckless," Kapa croaked. "It's the saints."

SEVENTEEN
TERESE

In the end, it took closer to seven hours for the rescue to come. I kept thinking how pathetic it would be if I had destroyed my marriage and my relationship with my children for the privilege of dying out in the vacuum. By the time they clamped onto our side and started exchanging air between the peeled core and the towing ship, we were all back in the cradles with the pressure caps closed and our masks on, watching the last bar on the emergency O_2 dissolve.

It was a very long, very uncomfortable wait, even without the drama of worrying if we were going to be able to keep breathing by the end. We were exhausted, we were battered, and more than a little frightened. The pirates who had donated their engine core to us had not followed good safety protocol and it was deficient of things like water, emergency rations, and sanitation facilities. Siri hadn't said anything during that last hour, she was so sunken in on herself, and I just had to hope her Companion was taking care of her.

I struggled not to think. I just wanted to stay alive. I could think later. I had plenty of subjects to choose from: how we were relying for emergency care on a doctor sent by the Blood Family, but known and trusted by our minder, who had just given a very clear indication he was ready to switch sides; how we'd been kidnapped by a smuggler (or a pirate, depending on your definitions), who was also a friend of that same minder.

Erasmus was not a huge system, but the coincidences were starting to pile up.

The rescue ship was only a little less spartan than the core itself, but it had air, food, water, and a functioning sanitation system. Most important, though, they *didn't* have pitch, yaw, or spin. It was another twelve hours in another tin can, but we were feeling almost human again by the time they opened the air locks onto the sloping tunnel that led to Dazzle's port yard.

Liang, Orry, and Commander Barclay were there to meet us. I hadn't liked Barclay all that well when we met, but as a med team made up of Solarans from Liang's crew surrounded us, I was prepared to revise my estimate. With our doctors came a fleet of carts with stretchers and O_2 and about everything else we could need, no matter what state we arrived in.

As soon as I was sure that Siri—grousing about being treated like an invalid for a couple of bruises and accompanying headache—was in the hands of our own people, I looked for Emiliya Varus. I wanted to thank her.

Actually, I wanted to find out where she stood.

When she wasn't actually checking on Siri, Dr. Varus had stayed in her emergency cradle, saying little. I hadn't pushed her. Siri had a concussion, and albeit more slowly than at first, was being spun and sloshed around in a way that could not have been good for her. I didn't want my unwelcome overtures making our doctor careless or reluctant.

But as I looked around the port yard, I couldn't see her. We were a crowd of Solarans, secops, and Clerks. The slim woman in her medical whites had vanished.

To say disquiet set in would be putting it very mildly. I

turned, intending to ask Amerand if he knew where she went, and almost crashed into Orry Batumbe.

"God and the Prophets, Terese!" He grabbed me by the shoulders and planted a kiss on my cheek. "I thought we'd lost you!"

"Not this time." I shook him off, but I smiled as I did. "Orry, did . . ."

He cut me off, sure what I was going to ask. "You've got two messages from your David waiting for you, and no, I didn't send anything out. I wanted to be sure what to send."

The blood drained from my face. *Messages, from David? What kind? Why?* I squeezed my eyes shut, and Orry put a hand on my arm. I'm sure he thought I was overwhelmed by emotion, which I was. He just didn't know which one.

Orry's grip on my arm tightened and I opened my eyes. One of the Clerks was gliding up to us: a pale woman with short, straight brown hair and hard, bright eyes. So hard, in fact, I wondered for a moment if they were badly made cameras.

"Field Commander Drajeske," she said, completely ignoring Orry. "I have recorded that you made an unauthorized transmission from the peeled core at 11:20:34:12:09, local time and date."

Ah. I was wondering when you'd show up.

"Yes. That was to our people stationed in Habitat 2. I wanted to see if there was any way they could reach us more quickly than the ship from Flight Control."

The Clerk didn't even blink. "And why was that?"

"Because we were going to run short on air," I answered. "I was hoping to save lives."

"It was unnecessary," said the Clerk.

"I didn't know that at the time, did I?" I answered, working to keep my voice even. That I had also told our people to get busy and find the pirate ship if at all possible was nothing this person needed to know.

The Clerk just stood there staring at me. She blinked once. "That is an acceptable explanation at this time."

I bowed. "Thank you. If I can be of further assistance, you know where I'm stationed."

The Clerk did not even nod. She just turned away and re-joined her fellows. I drew in a deep breath and let it out slowly and tried to shift my mind back to the situation at hand.

"Are they all like that?" I murmured to Orry.

He shook his head slowly. "Rumor has it they've been tightening the reins lately. Too much water smuggling, or maybe they think the OBs are going to try another break-out. Or maybe it's just for your benefit." He tried to say that last like a joke.

Or maybe Fortress got wind of Bianca's plans. My jaw worked itself back and forth. *And maybe after they killed her for it, they decided they'd be wise to keep a better eye on the rest of us.* I scanned the crowded port. Emiliya Varus was still nowhere in sight. Captain Jireu—*Amerand* (six hours in a peeled core tends to put you on a first-name basis)—on the other hand, was easy to spot. He stood to one side of the upper entrance with Commander Barclay. I couldn't hear what they said to each other, but whatever it was, Barclay eventually let Amerand walk away.

I touched Orry's shoulder. "Give me a second, will you?"

Orry followed my gaze, and when he realized who I was looking at, he raised his eyebrows significantly. "Pardon-pardon," he said in the local dialect. "I'll be with the trans-ports."

Irritation at Orry and his constantly inaccurate assumptions flashed through me, but I didn't have time to explain. I moved to intercept Amerand. There was something missing from the scene, but my fogged brain couldn't think what it was.

"What are you going to do?" I asked. Even though Amerand was standing still, he seemed to vibrate, as if he'd found the energy that had been drained from the rest of us.

"The first thing I'm going to do is check on whether Kapa's been found by the Security." He sighed, and something of that energy faded. Reminders of reality will do that, I guess. "Or whether whoever sent them got there first."

"Any ideas who did send them?"

"Could be any of a hundred." Amerand shrugged and gestured broadly. "You could be seen as valuable in any number of ways."

I managed a sour smile. "Always nice to be wanted." I chose my next words carefully. I had not forgotten for a minute what he'd said in our lifeboat. "Will you help?"

He nodded. "As I can, yes. But you need to know . . . I permitted my ship to get seized by smugglers. I may not have a commission after my next meeting with my commander."

Favor Barclay, whom Siri had pegged as a coward. "I understand. If I can help . . ."

"Thank you," he cut me off. "But probably not."

It was my turn to nod. "Either way, will you come down and find us?"

His smile was sharp, more determined than glad. "Either way, I will."

"Thank you."

He looked at me mutely, that new energy visible again. By then I thought I could put a name to it.

Hope.

Amerand Jireu saw me as someone who brought him hope. It had been a very long time since I had been on the receiving end of such a look. The reality and the responsibility of it twisted together tightly inside me.

We both turned away from each other a little too quickly, like we couldn't stand to look a moment longer. I climbed into a rattling little electric cart with Siri and Orry, and we started down through the thoroughly repurposed casino city to the home base of Common Cause Relief.

Somewhere on the way, I realized what had been wrong with the scene up in the port yard. Amerand had been there. His commander had been there.

His Clerk had not.

There had been Clerks, and there should have been one with him, following him. I'd run through hours of recordings on the flight from the Solar System. I needed to know what normal looked like in the place I was coming to. A captain of the Security should have his own Clerk standing right behind him while he was on the home station.

So where was he, or she? Who could have authorized him to go unwatched? And why?

The disquiet I'd felt before returned and redoubled. I needed to talk to Siri, but I couldn't say anything at the moment. I hung on to the bar beside my seat as Orry eased our way over the creaking bridges and poorly propped-up balconies until we were finally down on solid stone.

The Common Cause base was a dramatically curving building whose central dome helped hold up the erratically lit "sky." Greasy green flocks of parakeets shrilled and shrieked, and rose in indignant clouds at our approach. Orry had to navigate around a curving queue of people who carried jugs, buckets, and bottles. They'd hung empty containers in great clusters from their belts or from yokes balanced on their shoulders. A lucky few had pushcarts piled high with empty vessels. All of them waited for their turn at the single shiny spigot sprouting out of a shallow basin that had probably once been part of an ornamental fountain.

They had probably waited in line most of the morning, and would wait the rest of the day. One look at them was enough to make my particular set of problems seem very, very small.

Poverty does not change no matter where human beings have gone. It is hollow eyes and stained teeth and hands that will break if you take them roughly. It is scarred, and its sores are open and won't heal. It stinks of shit and sour breath. It is wary, afraid to hope, terrified to trust, but too weak to do anything else. When you arrive with your boxes of nutrient powders, your vitamin-infused rice, and your pills, it will kill you if you're not careful. Not for its own sake, but for the sake of the children, the brothers and sisters, the fathers and mothers, who are dying because they do not have what you do.

In low-gravity environments, it is also incredibly fragile. The three hundred years Erasmus had been inhabited were not enough for the human physiology to adapt. Bone and muscle loss were real problems. I could tell by looking that most of the people here were doing their best to force their bodies to be stronger by weighting their clothes. Their tattered hems were bulky with stones. Metal plates had been attached to robes and leggings. Rough mail shirts and kilts of twisted wire draped all but the youngest children, but they were all still too thin, and too small.

Even in the middle of all this, the too-small, too-thin

kids were being kids. At least a dozen had hoisted themselves up the pillars and the buildings, chasing one another in a three-dimensional game of tag. They shrieked and made spectacular leaps from one handhold to another. One child of indeterminate sex jumped carefully down from a second-story perch and ran up to their parent. I saw the white flash of eggs slung in the fold of a ragged cloak.

I thought about Fortress, sitting in the middle of an entire world of wealth and water, and my weary and sickened stomach turned over hard. In that dizzy moment I wondered if I'd judged Bianca and Bern too harshly.

"Welcome to my world," said Orry as he parked us near the grandly arched front door.

"Yeah." I climbed out. "Yeah."

Siri still had a constant headache, but the med techs had assured me six or seven times that she was in basically good shape. Even so, I ordered her into the clinic for the night, and she went without too much grumbling.

"Are you going to tell me what happened?" asked Orry as we left the clinic for the crowded lobby.

I grimaced. "Not yet. I need to stop moving for a while. I need . . ." *I need more than I can explain to you.* "Is there someplace I can crash?"

"This way," he said kindly. I knew he was burning with curiosity, but he also saw the state I was in. He led me up the stairs to one of the dim rooms on the first floor and lifted aside the piece of flexible sheeting that served as a door. The chamber beyond had been stripped down to the foundations a long time ago. The floor and walls were nothing but dusty stone. Curtains made of more grimy sheeting covered the window. The outside light leaked in a little around the edges. The only furnishing was a bed in the corner made up of a thin mattress on top of tightly tied bales of what might have been more sheeting.

It wasn't spinning, and it had a horizontal place I could lie down. Heaven.

"Thanks," I said. "Is there . . . is there a secure station you can route those messages from David through?"

"Give me your glasses." Orry held out his hand. "I'll cross-load them myself."

I pulled my glasses out of my belt pocket and handed them over.

"Anything else?" he asked as he pocketed them. I shook my head.

"Get some rest." He laid a hand on my shoulder and shook me gently, a gesture that chided me to remember I was not in this alone.

Then, to my relief, he left.

I walked over to the bed and sat down. I wrapped my arms around myself, stared at the sheeting hung in the threshold, and waited.

Slowly, set free by stillness and safety and the realization that I was not only alive but was likely to stay that way, the aftermath began. Goose pimples trembled on my arms. My skin crawled. The tremors worked their way deeper, until my muscles cramped and spasmed. Uncontrolled—and uncontrollable—shudders shook my whole body. Tears poured in rivers down my cheeks. I clamped my jaw shut with every ounce of strength I had.

Unwatched and alone, I fell apart.

I'd watched a man and a woman die. I didn't know them. I didn't know if they were good or bad, if they had family or were alone. I just knew they had been alive, and now they were not.

But worse, so much worse: Bianca was a traitor. Bianca Fayette was a traitor, and it had maybe got her killed, and I'd been kidnapped by a pirate who wanted to sell me and Siri off to . . . who knew what. Maybe because of Bianca.

She'd saved my life and maybe she'd just almost gotten me and Siri killed. We'd made it, though, by the skin of our teeth. But it almost didn't matter, because no amount of living could change what Bianca had done. It couldn't erase the attack and how we'd fought for our lives. Nothing could change anything I had done or seen, and all I could do was sit and shake until my body had purged its fear and decided to let me rest.

Eventually, the trembling did ease. Slowly, I was able to breathe without sobbing between clenched teeth, and the tears dried on my face. Slowly, I was able to stretch myself out on the shifting, lumpy bed and sleep.

EIGHTEEN

SIRI

It did not feel good to be back on Dazzle.

Dr. Gwin's ministrations cleared up the worst of Siri's headache and faded the purple-and-black bruise down to green and yellow, but Gwin wouldn't do anything about the slight queasiness from the too-light gravity and too-fast spinning of the little moon.

"You'll get used to it," Dr. Gwin announced. "You did before."

"So much for the healer's oath."

"First, do no harm," recited Dr. Gwin placidly. "Not allowing your body to make its own adjustments would leave you dependent on chemicals. Very harmful."

In the back of her mind, Siri knew Shawn was smiling at her. It did nothing for her temper.

The doctor was certainly a stubborn one, that much was certain. Nothing Siri could say to Gwin—or any of the three assistants who came and went during the clinic's night shift—could get her released. Shawn spent the time alternating between sneering at her protests of "I feel fine!" and suggesting she just make the best of it and get some rest.

I don't feel like resting, she'd told him, aware she was beginning to sound petulant. *I want to get to work.*

"It's just another couple of hours, Siri," Shawn replied. "It will wait."

It's already been too damn many hours. She didn't say that what she really wanted to do was get out of here and find Vijay.

Shawn already knew. But she needed to see Vijay, needed to make sure nothing had happened to him, and to make sure he knew nothing had happened to her, not really.

Even Shawn could not argue with that.

Somewhere into the second hour of trying to get some sleep on the narrow, sterile monitor bed the clinic staff had threatened to strap her into, Vijay walked in.

He was clutching his arm and swearing, and it took Siri a good three minutes to realize the thug with blood dripping down his wrist was Vijay. She sat up straight, mouth open. He perched on the edge of the one empty bed and didn't even look at her while he held his arm out for the clinician, who swabbed and sealed and asked what he'd done to himself.

"None of your fucking business," snarled Vijay . . . Edison. His cover name was Edison.

The clinician shrugged. "You're going to want to take it easy for a few hours while that sets, or you'll split yourself open again. The bed's free if you want it."

In response, Vijay/Edison kicked his boots off and dropped backward until he lay stretched out on the cot. He grinned over at her.

"Hey, lady, come here often?"

Siri rolled her eyes. "What century are you from?"

"You pick. I won't disappoint."

They couldn't say anything real. She hadn't swept the room yet.

"So, were you with that load of Guardians that got caught by the smugglers?" He folded his hands behind his head.

"How'd you hear about that?"

Vijay jerked his chin toward the door. "It's been big news. Everybody's got their parts in knots. There've been lockdowns, searches, bunch of arrests. The whole big security-theater spectacular."

"Yeah, well, it wasn't all that much on our end." Which wasn't true, but that was not important now. "We're all okay." *I'm okay.* She thought toward him. *I promise. And you're taking a hell of a risk with your cover.*

"Did you expect any less?" murmured Shawn.

Siri swallowed. *I didn't even think about it, but this is killing me.* She wanted to reach out to him. No. She wanted to fall into his arms and hold on for a year.

"Keep it together. Just think about what Terese will do if she hears about this."

Which effectively destroyed any urge to break cover.

"If you're okay, what're you doing in here?" Vijay wrinkled his forehead. If he'd had any eyebrows left on his scarred face, he would have been raising them.

"Failed to duck fast enough." Siri shrugged, and wished she hadn't. A wave of queasiness ran through her. "Nothing huge. But my commanding officer is paranoid and she wants me under observation."

It was clear from his expression Vijay didn't believe her, at least not completely, but what could he say?

"So, you hear any more about this Bianca Fayette thing over there?" he asked curiously. "Everybody's saying that's what your bunch is here for."

Just making conversation. Anybody would ask . . . She swallowed again around a fresh wave of nausea. Vijay knew. Aside from Terese and Misao, Vijay was the only one she'd told about her theory, that Bianca might still be alive. He was the only one who hadn't dismissed her out of hand.

How do I even begin to tell him? And what in the name of all that's sacred do we do if she is alive?

Memory assailed Siri, of Bianca on the deck of a shuttle. Bianca had gripped Siri's arm hard enough to hurt. "They don't count," she'd hissed. "Not anymore. They gave it up when they laid hands on one of mine."

Siri closed her eyes. Terese didn't want to believe Bianca could break the rules, but Siri believed it, and she knew Vijay would.

But that time had been one person. This time . . . it was a whole world. Terese had only been doing her job. Bianca had been . . . Bianca had been . . . even now she could barely think it.

"Do you want me to send a burst to Took?" Took was Vijay's Companion. Across short distances, for extremely short time frames, one Companion could send a data burst to another.

No. Too risky. Any wireless communication, no matter how brief, might be spotted.

"Well, that can't be good." Vijay rolled over on his side and propped his head on his hand. "So what is it?"

"You talk too much." Siri rolled over on her back.

"Got nothin' else to do in here, and you're a hell of a lot better-looking than that aide."

"You're a freakin' Neanderthal."

"And I bet you just love that in a guy."

Siri bit her lips in an effort to frown, remembering how she'd react if Vijay was what he seemed to be. "Shut it. I want to get some sleep."

"Oh, come on, we could be good. Guardian and gorilla."

Siri's gaze slipped sideways, and she tried to read Vijay's expression. Was he actually suggesting they put on a relationship act for the cameras? It was a risky move, but it would give them an excuse for meeting, instead of just making drops . . .

"Terese will bust you back to private for the next hundred years."

Only if you tell her.

"I'm attached," said Siri out loud.

"How attached?"

Siri rolled over on her side and let her eyes travel up and down Vijay slowly, appraisingly. "Enough that I don't have to take anything that comes along."

"Good. I hate it when they're desperate."

"Why do I get the feeling that's a lie?"

Vijay grinned at her, and underneath the scarring and the hard talk, she saw his relief. She'd shown him what he wanted most to see, that she was all right, truly.

How am I going to tell you?

"You see right through me," Vijay whispered in a tone of overly oily seduction. "And I just love that idea."

"Shut it," she said. "Before you wreck your chances." And she rolled over on her back, folded her arms, and closed her eyes.

It was a struggle, but she managed to stay that way. Somewhere, exhaustion caught up with her, and she did sleep. When she woke up in the flickering light that passed for dawn on Dazzle, he was gone.

But he'd left a folded-up scrap of sheeting beside her pillow with the name EDISON RAY scrawled on it. As she picked it up, Siri felt the slight weight of a sliver drive.

Nicely done, she thought toward Vijay, wherever he had gone, and she tucked the sheeting into her pocket and looked around for an aide to get her signed out.

Either Dr. Gwin decided she was recovered, or Siri had finally worn the clinic staff down. It didn't really matter. Gwin cleared her for release, and she marched out into the lobby, bouncing awkwardly before she remembered to adjust her gait for the lighter gravity. She didn't change her direction at all, though, she just headed straight for the door and out into the streets.

The battered, stripped-down lobby was exactly as she remembered it, as were the people who passed to and fro: the ragged Baby Ds and the bustling Solarans trying to keep their own spirits and professionalism up in the face of the poverty that they could do little about, and the constant grind of permanent servitude, which they could do nothing about at all. The air was filled with the mixed smells of dust, unwashed bodies, and, incongruously, hot fresh food. Siri's stomach rumbled painfully.

Breakfast? she thought to Shawn. It had been tough to eat the food aboard the Erasman ships, in part because it was tasteless, in part because she was pretty sure she was increasing somebody's debt levels with each bite.

"Breakfast," Shawn agreed.

Siri turned her footsteps toward the cafeteria, but stopped when she saw Liang Chen coming down the stairs with a steaming mug in one hand and an ancient datapad in the other.

She and Liang had not gotten along well the last time she was here. Back then, she'd thought it was part of his general dislike of the Guardians. But she found herself wondering what he had known about Bianca and her intentions. Vijay wouldn't have told her that the word was out that they were here about Bianca if it wasn't true. Had Liang been talking?

"Hello, Liang," said Siri quietly.

The director of the aid mission on Dazzle stopped in midstride and looked around, confused for a moment. When he saw her, he frowned.

"Siri. How are you?" Liang's tone made it clear this was courtesy, nothing more.

"Well enough that they let me out." She jerked her chin over her shoulder toward the clinic entrance. "Is my old room still there?"

"Pretty much as you left it."

"I'll bet the Clerks have been all over it."

Liang shrugged. "What'd you expect?"

They stood there for a moment, awkward, neither sure whether they should end or continue the conversation.

"How's the new boss?" Liang asked abruptly.

Siri felt her eyebrows lift. "Technically, she's the old boss. She was recalled from retirement."

"She's another of Fayette's, then?" He tried to say it casually, but it didn't take a trained listener to catch the tension underlying the question.

What do you know? "You could say so, yes. We all put in a lot of time together, back when."

Liang's answering grunt was at best noncommittal. "I suppose I'd better leave you to get to it, then."

Siri nodded. She wanted to say something to let Liang know that she knew what Bianca had been doing, that they were here to make up for it, and to clean up after it. But words would not come. It would be too much like an apology. In the face of his barely hidden hostility, she just couldn't make herself do it.

"Let us know if we can help with anything," Siri said. Liang's mouth twisted up and she practically heard him thinking, *You've got to be kidding.*

"I will, thanks." He was already walking away, sipping from his mug and thumbing his pad.

"Need to work on those interpersonal skills," said Shawn.

Me or him?

She snagged a hot roll and some tar-black tea from the cafeteria and trotted lightly up the curving central stairway to the third floor.

Last time she'd been to Dazzle, she'd been assigned Room 356, one of the few chambers in the former luxury hotel that still had a solid door. Siri pushed it open, releasing the odors of dust and mold.

Yep, she thought as she stepped inside. *Pretty much as we left it.*

It was a dump, no two ways about it. The bed was assembled from bundles of sheeting. The blankets looked clean, which was something. There was one folding stool for guests, and one chair with a broken leg held together with tape. Pipes and hoses, bits of pumps and motors, lay scattered about. Nameless rusted machines spotted with bird droppings sat next to clean spools of mustard yellow carbon fibers. It was the working space of the mechanic and all-around-fixit woman that was Siri's cover. Siri mentally congratulated Liang on his community relations as she picked her way over to the scarred cabinet beside the bed. Anywhere else on Dazzle, most of this would have been carried off already.

Siri stuffed the last bits of the roll into her mouth, set her mug down on top of a fiber spool, and pulled her glasses out of her belt pocket, hooking them into place over her ears. She also pulled out a thin cable and attached one end to the earpiece and the other to the cuff on her gloves. She tapped a command on the back of her hand, then turned in place, scanning the room.

Three red dots glowed on her lenses: one in the seam

between ceiling and wall, one on the upper corner of the cabinet, and one on the seam between wall and floor, aimed at the door. Three microcameras left behind by the Clerks.

Right. Do you think we need to be subtle about this, Shawn?

"No."

Neither do I.

She started with the one by the door, plucking it up between thumb and forefinger and squeezing until it made a soft but satisfying pop. She had to stand on the bed to get the one by the ceiling, and on the rickety chair to get the one on the cabinet.

She dusted her hands off and jumped down, landing on her tiptoes just because she could. *Next.*

Someone had brought up her duffel and her hard-sided equipment case. Siri snapped the case open. The latches were coded to her fingerprints, and, supposedly, would not open for anyone else. She didn't rely completely on that. The Erasmus Clerks were nothing if not efficient. The microcameras were just the beginning.

They pay attention around here, Siri, warned Bianca's voice from memory. *They are always paying attention here.*

Had Bianca forgotten that? she wondered as she lifted out the control unit for her station, an unadorned silver square, fifteen inches on a side and half an inch thick. Like the case's latches, it should respond only to her touch. Like the latches, she didn't rely just on that.

"She might have," answered Shawn quietly. "If she was angry enough."

Siri nodded. Bianca's temper was legendary.

But it doesn't make sense. She balanced the control unit on one hand and folded down the shelf from the station cabinet with the other. Bianca only truly lost it when it was personal.

Bianca's words came back to Siri again. *They laid their hands on one of mine.*

"Maybe it got personal. She and Bern were involved."

Maybe. But it didn't feel right. Siri laid her palm on the control unit. *All right, Shawn, fire it up.*

"On it."

There was a tiny burst of heat at her temple as her Companion sent a coded signal to her glasses, which her glasses relayed to her gloves. Siri ran her fingertips over the shelf's pitted wooden surface. Where she touched, faint mustard-yellow lines embedded in the grain of the wood glimmered briefly. Siri slid the control unit into place on top of the lines. She laid one gloved palm on the box and one on the shelf. She stood there a moment, letting the system power up and read and confirm her identity. The system needed the touch of an authorized person's gloves to work, and the gloves needed the proper pair of living hands. If anyone got the urge to go all twentieth-century on a Guardian to open up the network, they would be in for a rude surprise when the box flash-burned in front of them.

Siri slid her fingertips across the top of the box, activating the commands to open the connection between the control unit and her glasses, at the same time downloading the first set of prerecorded chatter. These were coded messages, carefully designed by teams of experts back on Earth to be puzzling and innocuous. They'd fire off at random intervals while she was at the station, providing the illusion of activity to any Clerk who happened to be listening in. In the meantime, Siri could get on with her real work.

Open it, she thought to Shawn.

Again, she got the brief burn as Shawn transmitted the code that opened the microfiber network she'd laid out with such care during her last visit. It was incomplete and in some ways primitive, but it was a start.

When the voices of Dazzle's streets filled her ears, she also knew at least some of it was still intact.

Smiling, she settled back in the chair and closed her eyes, letting her fingers wander across the control unit, getting the touch of the box again, raising and lowering voices, switching locations, filtering and focusing.

Listening.

". . . promised to have the spigot going at first light. Unless you want . . ." Liang outside giving someone hell.

". . . take this up to Shirar's corner, should be able to get twenty or so . . ."

". . . haven't got all day. I won't get the second shift if I'm not . . ."

". . . Papa! Where'd you go? . . . Papa! . . ."

"Siri, are you hearing that?" asked Shawn abruptly.

What?

"In the background. There's some interference, or something."

Siri relaxed, settling into herself, making her mind as still and quiet as possible to open her ears. Slowly, she did hear it; a kind of murmuring, almost a whispering.

She moved her fingers across the control unit, trying to focus in more closely. *Are we picking up the ventilators?*

"Maybe, but I don't think so."

We haven't had a chance to walk any of the lines yet. Something's probably broken, or degraded. It's been two years. She glanced at the diagnostics report on the back of her glove—.03 percent complete.

"That's probably it," said Shawn.

You don't sound convinced.

"I don't know . . . It just doesn't feel right."

Her Companion was in part the voice of her own subconscious, which made Siri inclined to trust him in such situations. She listened again, opening wide, diving deep. Some people strained to listen, but what you really needed to do was relax and stretch. Bianca had taught her that. Siri opened herself up to the susurrations just on the edge of hearing, letting them wash through her, following their rise and fall.

Shawn was right. It didn't sound like ventilator noise or like the random static she'd expect from a break. But what was it? Had the Clerks discovered her lines and found a way to tap them? Possible. But a tap shouldn't be letting sound in.

"It's like something's trapped in there," murmured Shawn.

Nasty idea. Siri leaned forward, stretching, focusing. But the more she tried, the more the sound seemed to slip away.

"Siri?"

Yeah?

"Visitor."

Siri lifted her glasses. Someone was knocking on the door. God, she must have been far down not to have heard that. She slotted the control unit into the holder at the back of the cabinet, folded up the shelf, and snapped the cabinet door shut.

"Come!" she called.

The door opened, and a lean little man dressed entirely in sparkling black and white waltzed in.

"Natio Bloom." Siri got to her feet and bowed.

"Field Coordinator Baijahn!" Bloom's bow was much more theatrical than hers, and she smiled to see it. "If you are still a mere coordinator. Perhaps you've received a promotion while you've been away?" He cocked his head toward her.

" 'Fraid not." She gestured toward the stool. "Please. How have you been?"

"Oh, getting by, getting by." Bloom sat and rested both his hands on his beribboned walking stick. "Our gracious *Saeos* are still pleased to give me work every now and then, and, of course, I'm glad to do what I can for my own poor world."

"If it involves lunching with the roof class and complaining about how bad things are, yeah."

"What have they got you doing this time?" asked Siri.

"The natal celebration for the most recent arrivals to the Blood Family." Bloom's grimace was as theatrical as his bow had been. "Still, it's something to do. And what brings you back here?"

Siri saw no reason not to be at least partly honest with him. Word would be getting around soon enough anyway. Besides, if she had learned anything about Bloom from the last trip, it was that he liked being in the know and would go a long way to stay there.

"We're trying to find out how and why my former commanding officer died."

"Really?" Bloom sounded surprised. "That was supposed to have been a robbery."

Siri shrugged, and waited. People in general did not like silence. Usually, they would talk too much in order to fill it.

"Ah." Bloom nodded several times. "I should have known."

"Known what?"

Bloom pursed his lips. His eyes flicked toward the door. But Siri shook her head. "It's just us here."

"Well, when I heard you in particular were returning, it did lend credence to certain . . . rumors."

Siri arched her brows, inviting him to continue. Bloom, however, chose to be coy.

"Voices have been cropping up in unexpected places, in the undercurrents, odd whispers in strange places." A smile played about his lips. "You understand, I'm sure."

Unexpectedly, Siri heard the unidentified background noise from her listening network, rushing back and forth, just exactly like whispers from another room.

She leaned closer. "And what are they saying, these unexpected voices?"

But this time, Bloom drew back. The coy smile faded, leaving behind a genuine concern Siri could never recall seeing on his face before.

"That perhaps this time *they've* gone too far," he whispered. "That they've beggared Erasmus so they can make the jump elsewhere. Maybe even go out with a bang."

"Bang?" Siri repeated softly. "What do you mean?"

But he shook his head hard. "I'm sorry," he said quickly. "I can't. I can't risk suspicion. I really only came to give you this . . ." The normally sure-handed Bloom fumbled as he reached for his jacket pocket and brought out a thin white square. "It's for your commander, but I was informed she isn't in just now."

Siri took the white oblong. It was a surprising thing, a piece of actual paper, thick and stiff as canvas with static words laid on it.

"Just an invitation to a sit-down with the Honored and Elected Citizens Council." Bloom got to his feet. "A group of nobodies doing nothing like the rest of us," he added bitterly. "But it would be good for appearances if she came."

"Bloom," said Siri softly. "If there's something you're hoping I'll find out, why not just tell me?"

But Bloom shook his head again. "Not here. I can't."

"It's safe. I promise."

"No, it isn't," he snapped. "You don't know ... you don't know what they're doing, with the Clerks and the network ..." He clamped his mouth shut. "Later. I'll tell you where."

Bloom drew himself up, suddenly every inch the suave old man he had been when he walked in, and took himself out of the room. The door shut with a loud snap.

Siri stared after him, turning the invitation over in her fingers. *Well. What do you think of that?*

"I think we'd better get to work."

Yeah. Me too.

NINETEEN

TERESE

In the end, I slept for twelve hours, despite the fact that the sheeting "door" did not keep out the sound of voices and the warped window did not keep out the sound of parakeets. I woke clearheaded and insanely hungry.

Someone had stashed my duffel in the corner of the room. I reveled in the luxury of being able to change into a clean uniform and fresh socks. I tightened the pocketed belt around my tunic and checked to make sure I had all my gear.

Orry had been back. My glasses lay beside my duffel. I picked them up and stared at them.

Two messages from David waited in there. I swallowed and stowed them away in my belt pocket again. I needed breakfast. I needed to start getting a handle on the situation.

I started making my way down the corridor before I could think the word "coward" too many times.

I went to the clinic first, but Siri wasn't there. They said they'd released her as soon as it was lights up, because if she was well enough to be that much of a pain in the ass, there wasn't a whole lot wrong with her. She had thought to leave me a note on a scrap of sheet.

If the Field Commander has time after breakfast, could she come to Room 356 to inspect the diagnostic computer?

Ah, the joys of early-morning snarkiness. Was there any better sign of a healthy subordinate? I tucked the sheet into my belt pocket and made my way to the battered dining hall. As I crossed the lobby, I found my gaze straying this way and that. It took me a moment to realize I was looking for Amerand Jireu.

Too soon, I chided myself, and turned into the dining hall at my left hand.

The place was mostly empty of diners. Liang had hired a lot of local cooks and other helpers, though, and they moved back and forth, cleaning up from breakfast and setting up for lunch. Liang himself sat at a surprisingly beautiful table made of reworked plastic and stone, carved and polished as smooth as a shell. The table was covered with platters bearing hot food. *Heaven smells like this when you arrive.*

"Good morning," said Liang. "Sit. Eat."

"Thank you."

The food was impressively good, and there was plenty of it. Congee flavored with strawberries and raspberries, soft-boiled eggs, toasted potato bread, stewed tomatoes, and smoked fish and, for a real treat, ham steak. There weren't many dry colonies that managed to raise pigs successfully. Chickens and ducks were much more the norm.

Liang nibbled a little toast to keep me company and listened while, in between bites, I told him what had happened out in the black sky.

When I finished he sighed. "Well, that didn't take long."

I squinted up, trying to look at his face and keep an eye on the tea I was pouring at the same time. "What didn't?"

"Bring back the Guardians, and we get escalation."

"You said there'd been violence, *and* a kidnapping." *And then there was Bianca . . .*

"One kidnapping, and that was a while ago. We've been able to keep things at least equitable with the local gangs. Something Captain Jireu has helped with, by the way."

I nodded, and set down the teapot. "That's good to know." I took a sip from my mug. "Wow, this is . . . really terrible."

"Get used to it," said Liang, sighing again. "It's how the locals drink it. And you're right, we've had some problems, but this is a whole different scale. The water smugglers are big business and high-level corruption. They're well above quarreling over a few boxes of supplies that we'd've let them have anyway."

"I see." I pushed the stoneware tea mug away. "And that gives us something fresh to worry about."

"The fact that someone is trying to kill you?"

"The fact that they aren't. Whoever was paying this Kapa wanted us alive and under their control. Why?"

"I will assume that's rhetorical."

"I'm afraid it's going to have to be for now." I looked down at my empty plate, as if I was surprised to find my appetite had disappeared. "What can you tell me about what happened with Bianca Fayette?"

Liang's eyes narrowed. He took a long, deliberate drink of midnight-black tea. I wondered briefly if he was just trying to prove he could do it.

"Bianca Fayette was probably a very good listener," he said. "But she was a hazard to my operation here, and whatever happened to her was more than likely her own fault."

He waited, not dropping his gaze, daring me to take offense. If I hadn't already talked to Bern, I would have. "Do you really think she was killed in a robbery?"

He shrugged, irritated. "It could have been. You saw outside." He nodded toward the courtyard. "Poverty breeds violence, and there's a real problem between the OBs and the Baby Ds, and . . ."

Liang let the sentence trail off and studied the dregs in his cup.

"Why didn't you complain?" I asked. "About Bianca?"

He set the mug down with a loud thump. "Everybody keeps asking me that. Do you have any idea how hard it is to complain about the Guardians?"

I took a deep breath to keep from snapping at him. Liang had been here for years, trying to help stabilize this place. This was a home to him. Those ragged people in the yard waiting for water were people he knew.

I focused on the important part of his statement. "Everybody's been asking about your complaining to the Guardians?"

"All right, not everybody, but you and Captain Jireu."

I frowned. "He investigated Bianca's death?"

"Not as such, but he was the one asking me about her before you came."

"Asking how?"

Liang told me about his conversation with Amerand Jireu. I found I did not like it that Amerand had been asking questions about Bianca. I did not like it that he knew both Emiliya Varus and the pirate Kapa. I did not like the feeling of being down at the center of a vortex with him.

I thought again about the hope in his eyes and found myself having to wonder just what he was hoping for. I thought about how he hadn't had a Clerk standing beside him when he got back from being abducted by a pirate both he and Emiliya Varus knew.

I rubbed my eyes. I'd been in this thoroughly-screwed-up system for barely seventy-two hours and already I was having trouble seeing straight.

Liang eyed me narrowly. "So, you've had a chance to talk with Ambassador Bern?"

"Yes, and he's resigning."

Liang froze in place. He blinked. "Okay," he said, slowly.

"You need to know, I'm not here just because of Bianca Fayette. Erasmus has been classified as an extremely active hot spot. Whatever Field Coordinator Fayette was doing . . . it may or may not have made it worse. It's one of the things I've got to find out." I got to my feet. "I need to meet with my people, then I need someone to show me where her body was found."

"Okay," Liang said again, and I left him there trying to wrap his mind around our conversation. Something in me did not want to make this easy for him, and even though I knew I wasn't being fair, I just walked away.

When I got to Room 356, the door opened to my touch and I stepped inside. Siri sat at her listening station, her hands on her knees. Her glasses covered her eyes, and a gold clip capped off her right ear. Both had black wires snaking down to a thin silver rectangle.

For several centuries, computer encryption had made interception of electronically transmitted data next to useless. Codes could be based on randomly generated, one-time-use keys 2 million characters long, and every transmission device could encrypt right at the source. The improved technology had returned spying to its basics.

Miniaturization was our ally on this one. Last time Siri had been here, she'd canvassed the city with her toolkit and her fixit skills, generally making herself useful to people who didn't have the resources to make basic repairs. Everywhere she went, she'd laid down a network of near-invisible microcables like cobwebs, connecting them up as she could, turning patchwork into a listening network.

Officially, we were allowed exactly one transmission terminal, and one hour a day to use it, and then only to call our ships out at the habitat. Other than that, we couldn't transmit anything wirelessly. The Clerks might not be able to understand what we were sending, but they could tell a transmission was happening, and, given enough time, pinpoint the originating device. They'd warned us about this. But they hadn't realized—and hopefully still didn't—that it was still possible to wire a city for sound, if you were patient. If you were good.

Siri was both. She'd learned from Bianca, and however far wrong she had gone, Bianca had still been the best.

As I crossed the threshold, Siri lifted her glasses.

"First job." I gestured toward the windows. The illumination outside flickered as if a lightning storm were passing through. "You are doing something about the light."

"On it." Siri tapped a note onto her glove. "But I'll probably have to get some kind of permission from the city authorities and all that."

"How are you feeling?" I stepped around the tables and the junk to stand next to her. A green-and-yellow bruise made a bright blot for her cheek, but she looked alert. More, she actually looked cheerful.

"I've got a headache, but I'm all right."

"I take it the network's still there."

"Amazingly enough, yes. In fact, fixing the lights will let me lay down some new cable."

I nodded. "Hear anything good this morning?"

"Not yet." She frowned. "There is something going on. It's right beneath the surface, but I can't get hold of it yet."

Her fingers brushed the comm-node box, almost as if petting a cat.

I frowned. "What kind of something?"

Siri just shook her head. "I wish I knew. It's more a feeling than anything else right now. But something's changed since last time."

"And not for the better?" I finished for her.

Siri grimaced. "'Fraid not. Sorry."

"Well, that's why we're here, isn't it?" I said casually. "We want to focus on movement, especially for any shifts in or around the habitats and the gates."

"Already on it. And you'll want this." Siri handed me a sliver drive. "Reports."

"Thanks." I tucked it into my belt pocket.

"And we had a visitor this morning."

As I raised my eyebrows, she told me of her encounter with the Master of Dazzle.

"So, it's not just a gut feeling." I ran my hand through my hair. "Move as fast as you can with him. We do not have time for a slow dance." *If Bianca had a chance to set something in motion, it might still be in motion. If it can be traced back to her, to us . . .*

"Understood," Siri was saying. "But if Bloom really does have anything, he probably won't be giving it away for free."

"We've got a budget. Use your discretion. If he wants out of here, we'll arrange it."

"Yes'm." Siri dropped her glasses back down over her eyes and settled back, listening, following the gossip lines, the power lines. I had already ceased to exist for her.

The sliver of reports burned in my pocket while I made my rounds. I had the rest of my people to check in on. Everybody, admirably, had thrown themselves into their work, getting things set up for when we got back, or for whoever would be sent after us. Jasmina and Dosh were already deep into it with Liang's accountants, setting up the funds-distribution systems, deciding what to track and what to discreetly overlook. Dr. Gwin looked ready to expire from old-fashioned apoplexy because the Erasmans were giving her so much grief about getting supplies down from the ships parked at the habitats. I recommended she go to Jasmina and get an "incidentals disbursement." Liang would know which wheels to grease, or Amerand might.

It was 11:00 local time, and Amerand had not shown up yet. I made myself put off worrying about him. I had one more of my people to check on.

I went back to my room. It was stifling hot in there, and there was a smell I didn't want to think about, but I didn't open the window. I shoved the bed up against the threshold. It was a lousy barricade, but it was all I had.

I sat on the floor and rested my back against the wall. I pulled my glasses out of my pocket and slotted the drive into place on the earpiece.

On a normal mission, Vijay would have just sent me a coded message, but he couldn't in the Erasmus System. The Clerks would be too likely to spot and trace the unauthorized signal. Probably Siri and Vijay had not even met to hand off this sliver. Probably they had made use of their local knowledge and arranged a drop site so as not to be seen together too often, or to have Vijay risk blowing his cover completely by being seen with me. But perhaps they had met, just long enough to exchange a glance, a swift touch of hands. Just a moment to see each other and to know that all was right.

This obsession with your subordinates' love life is unhealthy, Terese.

I tapped twice on the earpiece to activate the sliver. The world in front of my eyes went dark. Then, slowly, light and color unfurled until I was standing under Dazzle's uncertain lights. Here they were too bright and too yellow. I was too tall, my arms were too big, too masculine, and covered in crude red tattoos that bunched and swirled on my skin.

I was Vijay Kochinski and I was setting out to announce my reputation as a bad guy among a group of people known locally as "saints" as quickly as possible.

What followed was more or less a highlights version of Vijay's time on Dazzle. They were short clips, just setting the scene, giving me some faces, a few names, letting me know whom he was making contact with and how. I watched through Vijay's eyes as he stood watch over pallets of supplies. I stood sullenly through a chewing-out by the aid foreman on the first shift of the first day. That night, I cruised through the city on my off-shift, scoping out the bars and the dives, mostly on the base streets. I avoided one fight and failed to avoid another and was rattled and shaken and knocked to the ground while the man I'd been drinking with just a minute before watched with a slick grin on his face.

Then the scene shifted again. I lounged against a wall, or maybe a stack of crates (there were plenty of those around), watching two men approach. Both of them were well dressed in ways that spoke of pride in their wealth rather than comfort with it. Their stride was purposeful and Vijay straightened up slowly.

"Pardon-pardon," Vijay said as they stopped in front of him. "I can't let you past here unless you've got a business warrant."

The first man was well into his fourth hard decade. He had pale brown skin and hair that fell in corkscrew curls held back by a band of woven copper wire. Silver scales covered his scarlet coat, turning it into an extremely fashionable piece of armor. He shook his head at Vijay.

"And here we were such friends just a day ago," he said, his face becoming a picture of regret.

Vijay squinted at him. "Is that you, Meek? Sorry, didn't recognize you in the good light."

"Meek's" smile was not amused. "It's me. And this is my *patri*, Papa Dare. You remember we talked about him?"

"That I do remember." Vijay's eyes flickered up and down, sizing up Papa Dare carefully. Dare was not an imposing man. He was on the small side, and he was fat. The heat brought out perspiration on his pale, slab-cheeked, full-bearded face. He wore a rich purple coat, sewn over with silver scales, that was probably hot as the very hinges, but would turn a knife like the pair he wore openly on his gold chain-link belt, and might at least slow down a projectile from a weapon similar to the handgun holstered over his shoulder.

"And what has you gentlemen out to our transit depot so late?" Vijay asked warily.

There are some things that do not change. Where there are valuable goods, there will be thieves. Where there are thieves, there will be people who organize them—and take most of the profits.

Sometimes, if you're careful, you can make good use of this facet of human nature. But you must be *exceedingly* careful.

Papa Dare's smile was even less amused than Meek's had been. "I think we need to talk, you and me, Edison."

"What would I need to talk to you about?" Vijay dropped his arms and shifted his stance ever so slightly.

Getting ready to fight.

"Now, now," chided Meek. "I'd be very polite if I were you. Not a lot of places to run away to in our city."

Vijay considered this, especially the emphasis on "our." "And I'm going to need to run, why?"

"Because maybe you're not very smart."

"Uh-huh." Vijay's eyes narrowed. "I'm smart enough to know I don't like the way this is going."

"Ah. Good." Meek flashed a wide white smile. "I told you we could talk to Edison, didn't I, Papa Dare? Maybe he just doesn't know. He's a visitor after all. Maybe nobody told him that if he wants to do business here, it's our family he talks to."

"Your family?"

Dare's smile grew sharp. "You don't think the Blood is the only family in the Vault? You do not even know how many I got in my particular family."

As threats went, it was not subtle, nor was it original. But it was one of those things that had stayed around because it tended to work.

You'd certainly have thought it did this time from the loud swallow Vijay gave, and the weak-water sound to his voice. "Silly me."

"That's right." Dare reached out and patted Vijay on the arm. "That's very good, Eddy. Silly you. And what are you going to do about being so silly?"

Vijay sighed. "I'd say I'm going to give you this." He reached inside his shirt and brought out a flex screen. He unfolded it, an odd gesture, but it was to give me, or whoever experienced this XP, a look at it.

It was a manifest, with pallet numbers, and the access codes to go with them. If they showed it to Liang's people, these two could take possession of one of the charity shipments. The codes told me they'd get medical supplies mostly, but also several cases of perma-ice, which I was willing to bet sold for quite the price on the local black market.

Dare received the manifest with a nod and handed it to Meek. Meek looked it over carefully before slipping it into his own jacket pocket. "There. Didn't I say, Papa? Reasonable, civilized people, the Solarans. Positively refreshing to deal with."

Papa Dare nodded. "You keep yourself clean, Eddy," he said to Vijay. "I don't like having to make second trips."

"I will," said Vijay. "Unless."

Meek went very still. "Unless?" he repeated.

"Unless you and I can maybe do a deal."

Dare looked down his pug nose at Vijay, which, considering the height difference was a good trick. "What kind of deal would a reasonable, civilized Solaran want to do with us?"

Vijay shrugged. "So, I'm this reasonable, civilized Solaran, and I'm stuck in this shit job working off my time for unsociable behavior because I don't like my own face or anybody else's very much. Maybe I'd like to find a way out of it, except jumping ship without any exchange is a really dumb idea."

Dare's eyebrows lifted, creating deep wrinkles in his brow. "You surprise me, Edison. I thought your kind all got your balls cut off at birth."

Vijay snickered. I had never heard him produce such a nasty sound. "A lot of us do, yeah."

"Well." Dare nodded to Vijay. "Well." He nodded to Meek, who nodded back, and I could practically see the thought of profit shining in his eyes. There was shakedown potential here, and he could smell it. "I'll have to think about this. As it happens, there are some new markets opening up, and we might need some new hands." Dare patted Vijay's arm again. "You sit nice and quiet, and if a job comes along I think would be right for you, Meek will let you know."

"Thanks."

"Nice and quiet, Eddy." Dare shook a finger at him. "No more business."

Vijay bowed, hands folded, the picture of dignified submission. "No more, Seño Dare, unless you clear it."

Dare beamed. "Reasonable. Civilized. This is what I like about you saints. No fuss. No bragging and wasting time or pardon-pardon. Just get it done."

Dare and Meek strode away through the twists and turns of the transit depot, unhesitating and unafraid. Behind them, Vijay let out a long, long breath and slumped back against the wall.

I removed my glasses. Vijay was in the thick of it already. Good for him. Now it was just a question of how quickly he could move up the ladder. I looked at my watch. I'd been viewing a little over two hours, undisturbed.

Amerand still hadn't shown up. I looked toward the door. I looked at my glasses. I bit my lip and slid them back into place and opened the connection again.

The room darkened, then brightened and I was home. I was in David's study with the tarnished November sunlight streaming in through the window, lighting up his angled desk and his shelves full of antique books and ledgers, and David himself.

A sweet pain flooded me and my hand lifted to reach for him before I could stop it.

"Hello, Terese," he said softly.

"Hello," I whispered to the recording, which could not hear me.

"I wasn't going to do this. Not until . . . until I knew for certain what to say. But now I don't think I ever am . . . going to know for certain that is . . ." He stopped and looked away toward the window. Snow clung to the rocks by the shoreline and the grey water shifted sluggishly.

I could barely breathe. *You're going to leave me. You're going to leave me and I can't blame you because I've already left.*

"I haven't made any grand decisions, if that's what you're worrying about right now," David went on. "I keep trying, and nothing comes. One day I think I'll just cut it off, do a Turnover, and let you get on with . . . with whatever it is you need to do out there. The next I think I'm going to come charging out after you."

He chuckled softly but didn't smile. "Stupid, isn't it? Going through all this to get you a message just to say I don't yet know what I want." He faced the camera again. "But I do miss you, Terese."

He touched the edge of his desk and faded away.

I miss you too, David. I do. My cheeks were wet. I wiped them.

Because I gave no other command, my view brightened, signaling the start of the second message.

David sitting in his study again. It was night, and he had only one light on. Behind him the windows were solid, glimmering sheets of black.

"Got your message today, Terese," he told me. Hope flared painfully in me. "God and all the Prophets, I really, *really* wish you'd said something different. Because, you know, we don't have a really good track record with you and promises."

I winced and closed my eyes, but I couldn't shut out his voice.

"I'm taking leave and going out to Berlin. Spend some time with the kids. You might look for me there first when you do get back." There came a pause that stretched out so long I almost thought the message was over. I almost opened my eyes.

"Was it even real to you, Terese?" David whispered. "Was any of our life together real to you?"

There was a click, and silence. If I opened my eyes, I'd be alone in the dark.

I tore my glasses off. *What the hell were you* thinking, *sending that?* I demanded, not sure if I wanted an answer from myself, or from David wherever he was. I knew I wanted to be angry at him for sending these asinine, spineless messages—for making me cry, for making me afraid, in the middle of a mission. I never thought about home when I was active. I never thought about anything but the job.

I'd never had anything but the job before. I'd never really wanted anything else. But I'd had Dylan then, and Bianca, and the knowledge I was good at what I did.

Now . . . now I had an empty room and a heartful of dust, and Bianca was a traitor and I didn't know whom to trust, and David didn't even know if he was leaving me or not.

All at once, I couldn't sit still. I couldn't think about this, I couldn't be this other person. I had to be the Field Com-

mander. I had to get out of here, to find Amerand Jireu
and work out who he was, what he was doing. I had to find
Emiliya Varus. I had to find my way from what had happened
here to what was happening on Fortress and *why* it was all
happening.

I crammed my glasses back into their pocket, kicked my
makeshift bed back against the wall so hard it bounced, and
headed downstairs to the lobby.

Locals and aid workers performed triage in the middle of
the babble of voices and the smell of humans who didn't
have access to adequate water and sanitation. Feeling petty,
I moved over to the man stationed at the door as a sort of re-
ceptionist and asked if Captain Jireu had been by and left
me a message.

He blinked up at me, as if trying to understand, but before he could say anything, we were interrupted.

"Pardon-pardon, Seña?" An old man with leathery skin
and hollow cheeks stepped up to me. He was bald and pale,
but the muscles that showed in his forearms beneath his
neatly mended blue coat were still wiry. "You are looking
for Captain Jireu? I think I am looking for you."

I bowed. "Pardon-pardon, Seño," I answered. "I do not
think I know you."

"I am Finn Amerand Jireu. Captain Jireu is my son."

I confess I stared at the wizened man. The years had been
hard on him, but I could see the family resemblance in the
shape of his face and the intensity deep behind his eyes.

I dug around in my memory for class-appropriate formality and found it. "I am grateful to meet the father of my
friend."

He bowed. "I am sent to find you."

"Do you have a message?" Why would Amerand be

sending his father to run such an errand? Well, it was pretty clear trust was not something they had a lot of in the Erasmus Security.

"No, pardon-pardon. But news." Finn Jireu straightened up. "My son is being questioned. His Clerk is dead."

TWENTY

AMERAND

The first thing I did when we stepped from the peeled core to the port yard was breathe deeply.

The second thing I did was look to see who had come to meet us.

I almost had to jump back from the crowd of saints who swarmed up to surround Terese and Coordinator Baijahn. At first glance, it looked like Liang had brought half his staff with him—and all the doctors. I heard Captain Baijahn first protest, then swear as they sat her down on the nearest crate for a good going-over.

Terese rolled her eyes at me, then turned her back. I didn't even allow myself to nod. I had to face Commander Barclay, and with him, a half dozen Clerks, none of whom was Hamahd. Fear settled into my empty stomach.

Without a pause even to look at me, four of the Clerks hurried toward the peeled core. Commander Barclay folded his hands behind his back, and I had the distinct feeling those hands were clenched. His jaw most definitely was.

I was bone weary. Behind me I heard the saints swearing and laughing and asking endless variations on a single question: "Are you sure you're all right?"

I could have choked on my envy. As it was, I didn't even dare glance toward them.

"I need your report," Commander Barclay told me. "Take a moment to get yourself together and come straight to my office."

I bowed. "Yes, Commander."

I turned from him and found myself facing Terese Dra-jeske. Commander Barclay bowed to her and she to him, and the commander left to consult with the Clerks, but I suspect he did not go too far. Terese's gaze kept flickering over my shoulder.

"What are you going to do?" she asked.

I sighed. Even having to stop to think about it brought a wave of weariness over me, but we were on the ground, and there were Clerks surrounding us, and Barclay was behind me. That precious moment in the black sky was gone for good.

"The first thing I'm going to do is check on whether Kapa's been found by the Security." I grimaced. "Or whether whoever sent them got there first." *We might be able to bring Kapa back alive.* I remember thinking, *They don't get to finish him. That's my job.* He could do what he liked to the Blood Family, but he'd turned on me—on Emiliya—and that betrayal burned a stark, ashen line through my thoughts.

"Any ideas who did send them?"

I shrugged. "Could be any of a hundred." I saw the city stretched out beyond the viewing platform; the broken, decaying city that had looked like an endless palace to me when I first blinked in its fading lights. "You could be seen as valuable in any number of ways."

Her smile was mirthless. "Always nice to be wanted." She hesitated. She was trying to decide how to proceed, trying to keep track of all the ears and all the potential harm she could do by speaking. It was odd to watch someone struggle with something I did as easily as breathing.

In the end, all she said was, "Will you help?"

I nodded. "As I can, yes. But you need to know . . ." I licked my lips. Here was what I had not allowed myself to think about. "I permitted my ship to get seized by smugglers. I may not have a commission after my next meeting with my commander." *I may be dropped into peonage, and never let go. I'll have to find a way to tell her, or to tell Emiliya . . .*

Where is Emiliya?

"I understand," Terese was saying. "If I can help . . ."

"Thank you." I cut her off, craning my neck through the crowd of saints, guards, and Clerks, looking for the flash of white. But I couldn't see anything. Emiliya had vanished. "But probably not."

"Either way, will you come down and find us?"

I nodded. "Either way, I will."

"Thank you."

Terese turned away from me, and I turned away from her, both of us switching the other off from our awareness. My whole business was now to cross the dusty expanse of the port yard with the darkness yawning overhead, letting the reflected light from Fortress and the shining worlds pound down on the back of my neck.

Letting two Clerks fall into step behind me without letting myself be seen to care.

I still didn't see Emiliya anywhere. It was as if she had vanished, or been spirited away. *No.* She was working for the Blood Family, for the Grand Sentinel. They wouldn't have just taken her.

She was working for the Grand Sentinel and she had heard every word I had said to Terese Drajeske.

No, I thought again. Emiliya would not betray me. Not like that. It was impossible. It was not how we treated one another. I had done my best by her, and she had done her best by me, and if that hadn't been quite enough on either side, it still wasn't reason enough for her to turn me over.

She was not like Kapa.

There were toilet rooms on the far side of the yard. I passed a battered piece of scrip to the ancient man who stood sentinel there and went inside, with the Clerks following close behind.

I relieved myself into the filter toilet. I rubbed hands, neck, and face over with cleaner and scraped it off and felt no better. The Clerks watched me in silence. They were both men. One was slim and delicate, the kind who'd grown up malnourished as a child and never recovered from it. The second was solid muscle from boots to bald, pale head. Their eyes were alert, engaged, darting back and forth as if they could see—or hear—more than I could. I thought about the rumors about their network again. Were they getting reports through the bones of their ears? It was certainly possible. The idea made me itch. I tossed the scraper and towel into the bin for the old man to clean.

"Where's Hamahd?" I asked.

The thin, delicate one actually jumped. I watched him struggle to focus down on me.

"He has temporary duty elsewhere." His voice was light, breathy. "He is expected to return to assignment here."

"Are you his replacements?"

The block Clerk blinked rapidly. "That has yet to be determined. Are you finished, Captain Jireu?"

"Yes." I turned toward the door. Hamahd had been "temporarily assigned" elsewhere before. Clerks, like the rest of us, needed to be debriefed, retrained, and reminded of all the different kinds of strings that held them in place. After the first few times, I managed, mostly, not to let it bother me.

But this time was different. This time I really had done something.

Of course they hadn't heard. They couldn't have heard. There was no possible way Kapa would have disabled the flight safeties only to have the cameras on.

No possible way they could have heard unless Emiliya told them.

But even as my mind filled with thoughts of Emiliya, part of it was busy trying to calculate what the cost of maintaining two Clerks was going to do to my debt levels. This was what ten years in the Security had done to me.

By the time I reached Upsky Station, perspiration was trickling down my back. I walked down the shabby corridors toward Commander Barclay's office. We passed the Clerks' hive with its busy silence. I glanced toward them as frequently as I dared, searching for Hamahd's form and wondering how bad things had gotten that even he would be a comforting presence.

When my new Clerks and I entered his office, we found Commander Barclay alone and standing by the window overlooking the Upsky park. The light outside flickered strongly at that moment. He waved me to a chair with a table and a full welcome jar beside it. I drank off two cups of the water far too fast for courtesy, but my throat burned and I wasn't going to waste the chance.

Barclay watched me without comment until I set the cup down.

"What happened?" he asked simply.

I felt the Clerks at my back. I swear I could sense their gazes as they swept back and forth. I set that aside and gave as bland and factual an account as I could of how we had spotted Kapa's ship, how we had given chase and taken hold, and how everything had gone wrong.

Barclay listened, frowning, his dark brows drawn low over his eyes.

"He was known to you?"

Here it came. I had known it would. It had to. "We grew up together on Oblivion, and we were in the Breakout together."

"And then the academy."

"Yes." *Keep it calm*, I ordered myself. *Keep it down. Let them ask the questions. Do not say anything you do not have to.*

"He resurfaced again just a few days ago."

Of course. Of course. I kept my face calm. "Yes."

"And you did not think this was worth bringing to anyone's attention." My commander glowered at me. I could feel he was trying to tell me something. It was beating against my mind, but I couldn't understand it. He and I had never had any rapport. We had never wanted one.

"He said that he was paid up and legal. I believed him. I was wrong." I was so tired. I wanted to go home. Did Father even know anything was wrong? *Where is Emiliya?*

Barclay just looked out the window for a long time, not caring now if I saw his clenched fist behind his back.

"Your assistance will be required with the salvaged engine compartment," he said. "The Clerks want to give the core a thorough going-over, to see what the pirates are up to in terms of beating the security protocols. If you've altered the commands at all, you are going to have to show them what you've done."

"With respect, Commander," I said. "It's going to be difficult to shuttle out to Habitat 1 and still be on duty for the saints."

"The core will remain docked with us for a while."

I met and matched Barclay's bland gaze. A peeled core—a working internal drive—was an incredible prize. It would be classified as Highly Dangerous under the Flight Guidelines, but if one handled the circumstances carefully—if one knew the right people to ask, the right records to tweak and send—it could potentially be sold for more than the average year's debt. Especially if one had access to the right people inside the Clerks.

"Yes, Commander," I said.

I found myself wondering afresh exactly where Hamahd had gotten to. Barclay might press a favor out of him in order to let him keep his easy posting here.

I bowed my head briefly in acknowledgment. If Barclay wanted to engage in an auction for the core, it didn't matter to me. If Hamahd was in on it with him, it was none of my business. What I wanted to know was where the hell Kapa had gotten his hands on it in the first place.

Barclay's glower had returned, trying one more time to force me to understand the meaning of his silence. I just looked back. *I'm tired. I'm hungry. Let me go home.*

"Dismissed. You have the night off, unless the Clerks need you."

"Thank you, Commander." I made my formal bow, received my dismissive nod, and left, my new pair of Clerks behind me.

I should have been suspicious when they didn't demote me. I wasn't. I assumed Commander Barclay had no one he liked better to replace me. All those years of not making trouble, of following orders and keeping the OBs from making more than the acceptable amount of trouble, were showing dividends.

This is what hope does to you when you're not used to it. It is very like being drunk. You don't realize how badly you're impaired until you see the results of your spree.

I wanted to find Emiliya. It must have been brutal, having Kapa turn on her like that. I needed to make sure she was all right. But I had reached my limit. I had to rest, I had to eat. I had to let Father know what had happened.

I had to find a way to let him know I had thrown my lot in with Terese and the saints. I tried to picture what he would say, and I couldn't. I could not even begin to formulate the thought.

And I had to find out what the secops on my station had been up to behind my back. They weren't any more corrupt than usual, but there was more than one of them who would have the knives out if they thought a better place had opened up, and everybody's back would be a target.

And we had not just one place vacant now, but two. The image flashed through me of Leda and Ceshame crumpled on the deck, the last of their life oozing out with their blood.

It was too much. I knuckled my eyes and tried to think. I turned to my new Clerks.

"Could either of you tell me . . ."

But neither of them was looking at me. They had both turned to stare up. I tracked their gaze. At first, all I saw was a figure in black, tearing along the upper walkway, dodging the other pedestrians, forcing his way through the crowds, and he glanced down and saw me staring up.

Hamahd. Hamahd racing across the bridge like a madman.

"Captain!" he shouted. "Captain!"

I didn't know what to do. I was watching an impossibility: a Clerk, my Clerk, in a blind panic. By the time I remembered it was possible to move, the pair behind me were already running ahead, swarming up the ladders, storming across the rapidly clearing bridges. No one wanted to see this. No one wanted to be anywhere near it.

Hamahd saw them coming. He started backward, away from his own kind.

He looked down at me standing there gaping up at him. They were almost on him, moving smooth as machines.

Hamahd stood there for a moment, watching them come on. Then he swung himself over the rail and he jumped, diving headfirst toward me. His coat billowed in the wind as he fell down, arms outstretched, a great black bird diving down on its prey.

"Hold him!" shouted someone. I leaned out and snatched at the air, and somehow, grabbed his hand. Even in our light gravity, I about wrenched my arm out of its socket, and the rail bashed against my ribs and wobbled—it held. Pain blinded me for an instant, but I hung on.

"Captain," Hamahd gasped. "They're using you."

"Hamahd, get up here, have you lost your mind?" The Clerks had changed directions, they were running toward us. I saw them and so did Hamahd.

"They're going to use you to finalize the new network." He curled his free hand around the railing. It was buckling. It was going to give. "Get out. The saints could still get you out."

They were almost on us. Hamahd braced his feet against the balcony. I made to haul him up. But he arched his back, yanked his hand free, and fell.

Light gravity or not, the laws of momentum and the stone beneath were too much for his human body, and his head broke open with a sickening crack. People screamed, then I could move, because it was a dead body down there and suddenly it was my job.

It was my Clerk.

I made it down ahead of the two newcomers. I knelt beside Hamahd. His skull had flattened against the street and blood and brains glimmered around him. His hand stretched out, naked and empty in the gory puddle. His eyes fluttered closed, then open, then closed again.

In the next heartbeat, I was shoved back on my ass and my view was blocked by not just the two new Clerks, but a host of others, ten, perhaps more. They surrounded Hamahd's body, a living wall of solid black. I heard them murmuring. I saw one, the slim one who had begun following me, lift his head, looking for all the world like a snake taking a scent. He swiveled his head, and his gaze fastened on me.

He pulled himself free from the dark clot made by his fellows and walked over to me, where I sat in an undignified position on my rump, still too stunned to move. The Clerk held out his long, fine-boned hand. I swallowed. I grabbed it. I let myself be pulled onto my feet.

I was an inch from him and looking into his eyes. They were fully focused on me, and horribly bright. A human being should not be that awake and alert, that tightly concentrated on every detail in front of them. There was a manic look in those gleaming eyes, for all his face remained utterly expressionless.

They're using you . . . Get out. The saints could still get you out.

"If you speak a word of this, it will be known," he said flatly, turning away. Together, the Clerks lifted Hamahd's broken body and carried him off.

As they passed, the people turned away, doing their best not to see.

TWENTY-ONE

SIRI

The Luxe towered over Siri like the cup of a gigantic stone flower. Its roof spread out far broader than its foundation and its shadow darkened the streets for several blocks around. It was the remains of excess on a magnificent scale, like the corpse of a great king.

The pedestrians pushing past her were a mix—not the bottom of Dazzle's population, but definitely not the top either—and they eyed her uneasily. Siri had worn her uniform and brought her gun, so she stood out more than a little. They didn't know who she was, or didn't like who she was, or couldn't work out how to exploit who she was. The back of Siri's neck began to itch.

Good thing we brought the gun.

"Yeah."

If there had ever been doors facing the street, they were long gone. The empty threshold had been crudely enlarged—hacked open, in fact.

Was that to get something out, or let something in? Siri wondered, running her fingertips over the broken stone.

"A little of both, I expect."

Once past the foyer, the lobby of the Luxe opened out in all directions. The blossom proved to be only the top of an hourglass with walls curving away both above and below. Screens might have once provided the illusion of windows, but now they just sputtered and flickered, giving the place the strobe effect so disconcertingly common in many sections of Dazzle. High above her, Siri glimpsed the black sky and the brilliantly shaded sphere of Reesethree, with Moonthree just coming into view. She looked down a series of sweeping staircases that would have looked at home in Versailles to see the wasted remains of a formal garden. Dead light poles stood sentinel over ancient piles of twigs and brushwood. It was dry as dust. Dry as death.

Why the hell did Bloom want to meet us here? Siri coughed and tried to breathe shallowly through her nose. *If we're walking into an ambush, Terese is going to kill me.*

"Then she should have been on station to order us to bring backup," Shawn said, echoing the words Siri had uttered on her way out the base door. She didn't bother to answer him. She'd also been ordered to follow up with Bloom, and Bloom had asked for a meeting.

She had to admit she was relieved to get away from her listening post, and the whispering she'd been hearing on the network. It was maddening. It was voices, she was sure it was voices, but she couldn't focus on them, and what was even more strange, she couldn't filter them out. No matter what she tried, she still heard them.

Halfway to the Luxe it seemed as if she could still hear them, whispering under the voices and city noises around her. She'd tried to tell herself it was ridiculous, but the idea wouldn't leave her.

The problem was, Shawn heard them, too.

That didn't make any sense at all—not to her, not to him—and she felt his confusion snaking out into her mind, which made everything worse.

A faint pathway had been worn in the dust, and Siri followed it where it led off to the left. The spot between her shoulder blades, right under her weapon, twitched.

"It's all right," said Shawn from the back of her mind, sounding almost normal. "We're together in this."

So why aren't we together in getting out of this? There's got to be a way in around the outside. They stopped in front of a silver pillar breached by a pair of doors embossed with the symbols for "Elevator" in about fifty writing systems, all of them shining with a friendly blue light.

"It's not so bad. There's some power, and that elevator's in working order."

Bloom had specified floor 27. Siri glanced around the cavernous ruin. If there was a stairway, she would have to search for it, and probably waste a lot of time, given the scale of the place.

As if sensing her thought, the elevator doors opened, showing her a blessedly dust-free car. Siri stepped inside. The doors closed. The car shuddered, dropped a sickening half inch, then slowly started to rise. When it ground to a stop, it dropped again, a good half foot this time before it jerked back up. The doors opened, and Siri dove out onto the tiled elevator bank.

A red carpet, flanked by red-velvet ropes as miraculously clean as the elevator car, stretched out in front of her.

Where've I seen this before?

"If you have, it was before my time."

She swung her weapon down around to the ready position and followed the carpet to an arched doorway hung with more red velvet. Siri pushed this aside and instantly recognized the place in front of her.

It was a theater. An ancient but perfectly maintained proscenium arch stage, complete with heavy velvet curtains and footlights, filled the space in front of her. Painted frescoes soared overhead, and gilded curlicues glistened on scarlet walls. Siri stared as she walked forward but did not take her hand off her weapon.

"Behold!" cried Bloom's voice from the darkness. "The greatest of palaces!"

The footlights flashed, blinding her momentarily. When her vision cleared, Bloom trotted out of the wings and down the stairs.

"Coordinator Baijahn." He met her halfway up the aisle and grasped her hands. His own were neatly gloved in white. "Thank you so much for coming."

"Glad I could, although . . ." She gestured at the cavernous space around them. "A bit much, don't you think?"

He chuckled and rubbed his hands together. They gleamed very white in the theater's shadows. "I suppose it might seem that way." His gaze traveled lovingly across the painted ceiling and down to the stage. "But this was the first space I ever managed and since then I've kept it as sort of a pet project." Bloom paused. "It's never gone away, the living theater," he said softly. "Not even with the XPs and the other everyday miracles. We've never been able to quite make the human brain believe utterly in electronic illusion, you see. A disconnect, a distance, remains. But when there's another human involved, the disconnect goes away. With a human, you believe."

He looked intently into her eyes as he spoke those last words, and it seemed to Siri he was trying to tell her something or giving her a chance at understanding something. But although she tried to listen, all she heard beneath his words were echoes of the never-ending whispers she'd been tracking since she'd turned her network on.

Am I going deaf? Am I losing my mind?

"No. Neither. Something is happening. Something real."

Bloom turned to face the stage, but not before she saw his expression fall into disappointment.

"It is also," Bloom went on, "the one place on Dazzle where I am the one who controls all the cameras. Thus, we can talk here without the Clerks' interference." He gestured toward the rows of velvet-upholstered chairs, indicating she should sit. Siri looked at the nearest seat, thought about how long it would take her to get out of the thing if she had to, and opted for just leaning against the arm.

Bloom shrugged. "I never intended to be speaking with you about this. I thought I would finally find a way to use my skills to regain something of my former position and power. But, when Dazzle fell, she took us all with her." His expression hardened. "They had no right to do as they did. No right."

Is he talking about the OBs or the Blood Family?

"Maybe both."

"When you left us, and your superior stayed, I understood that something was changing, something major, or your people never would have bothered to leave a Guardian with us. So I started doing a little investigating on my own." He gazed modestly down at his fingertips. "I am still allowed to travel as freely as any of us are, for my work. It means I can see and hear a fair amount if I put my mind to it."

He paused again, waiting for her to deliver some compliment. "Something else you excel at, I'm sure," she said. *Oh God, has he been to Hospital? Has he seen Bianca there?*

His gesture was noncommittal, but Siri had the odd feeling he thought that she could have done better than that, but her heart was in her mouth. It was all she could do to keep quiet and keep listening.

The whispers seemed to gather close around Bloom.

"What I saw was that the Clerks were spending an inordinate amount of time traveling back and forth to Hospital."

"Hospital?" Her voice was tight and strained. He had to know by now something was up with her. But she couldn't say anything. She didn't dare.

Bloom nodded. "It was terribly strange. Hospital is its own sealed system. Its Clerks are almost a separate branch of the Security. I thought at first it might just be some kind of new audit. But soon I realized it was something much more than that."

A spasm of pain shot up Siri's arm. It was only then she realized how tightly she'd been clutching the chair arm. "What did you find?" *Bianca. I knew it. I knew it . . .*

Bloom's gaze slid sideways. Siri bit down to stifle a scream. The whispers seemed to grow louder, almost becoming intelligible, as if they were trying to tell her something.

Or tell Bloom something.

"Have you heard anything about the Clerks' network?" he asked.

It was as if the floor had dropped out from under her and Siri had to struggle to respond. "We've been hearing rumors of something new . . ."

"They're not rumors," said Bloom. "It's real, and it's vast."

"All right. All right. Not what we hoped for, but we've got to follow up."

"So what *is* the new network? How does it function?"

"I don't know," Bloom admitted, anger plain in his voice and on his face. "I've tried to find out. I've given it everything I've got, and believe me, my tech is as good as you can get, in this system anyway. I still don't know. What I do know is that it has something to do with direct connections between human beings, with the sharing of knowledge, mind to mind."

"You're talking about telepathy," said Siri. "Automated telepathy?"

But Bloom shook his head slowly. "Oh no, something far more obscene than that." His voice trembled with emotion. "I'm talking about the Clerks' victims. All the ones they've killed or made to disappear."

"What?" cried Siri, starting to her feet.

"What?"

"It's been a rumor for years," Bloom said. "That the Clerks have developed a way of . . . sucking the person out of a person. Siphoning, they call it. They distill the spirit, the essence, the voice, the *you*. They secure it in their network, trapping their victims, turning them into nothing but voices streaming back and forth through the ether from Clerk to Clerk."

"Impossible," Siri said, but her voice had no force. *What about the whispers? The whispers in the network.* "Ridiculous."

"I knew it," said Shawn. "I knew they were voices. I can still hear them. It's not illusion."

Stop.

But Shawn didn't stop. "Voices," he said again. "I was right. Siri, you hear them too. You hear them through me."

Shawn, stop it, please. It's impossible. It's got to be.

"Back and forth, back and forth. All those voices," said Bloom, his voice low, almost singsong. "The lost, the trapped, the enslaved. This is what they do in their secret wing on Hospital."

Siri struggled to breathe, to think. But that endless whispering just on the edge of hearing filled her mind. She wasn't imagining it. It was real, she could feel it resonating in the bones of her ears.

"Yes. That's it. That's got to be it. We have been hearing Bianca. They've got her trapped in there. If we could pin it down, find the frequency, we could break it open, let her out . . ."

"Stop it. Slow down!"

Bloom's eyebrows lifted. "I'm sorry, Coordinator?"

"Sorry." Siri shook her head. Fortunately, Shawn had subsided and she could focus on the man in front of her. "It's a lot to take in."

"I know, and I've had years. But . . . you do believe me?"

"I believe him, Siri. It makes perfect sense."

"I don't know," she said to Bloom, and to Shawn. "You haven't given me much proof."

"But you *feel* it. I know you do."

"I don't know," she said again, but the words were weak.

"Will you at least promise me you'll look into it?" Bloom reached out and took her hand. "I can't do anything outside of this space. They're watching me. They're watching all of us. Everyone thinks the cameras are in the cleaning drones, but I think they've really set the essences, the voices, to watch us."

"I will do what I can." Siri rubbed her forehead. Shawn was restless in the back of her mind, almost as if he wanted to break out of her skull and fly free, looking for the voices on the wind.

After all, what was Shawn but a voice in her head?

"Thank you." Bloom released her hand. He smiled, wistful and tired. "We probably shouldn't prolong this. They'll be watching us both now. I'll show you out."

He took her down the elevator. Walking through the

mausoleum of grandeur was excruciating. Siri breathed in the dust and thought about the voices, the essences, trapped and transmitted across whatever frequency the Clerks had claimed for themselves.

It can't be possible. It can't be true.

"I don't want it to be, but I feel it."

I know. But . . . how?

"That's what we need to find out, Siri. If they've trapped Bianca's essence somehow . . ."

She was so lost in her inner conversation, she almost failed to realize that they had reached the main doors.

"Thank you for listening to me, Siri." Natio Bloom pressed her hand once more. "I hope we will be able to speak again soon. But I urge you to take care. The Clerks are not to be trifled with, even, I think, by the Pax Solaris."

Siri nodded and turned away, walking down the base streets, into the flickering shadows.

When Siri Baijahn was out of sight, Bloom returned to the theater. He mounted the stage slowly, stepping on the pair of switches that killed the vibrations running beneath the floor.

He reached up to the proscenium and touched a switch.

The houselights came up and much of the room vanished: the balconies and frescoes, the velvet curtains, the scarlet-and-gilt paint. What remained was a scuffed white cavern with rows of incongruous red-velvet seats, all facing a featureless white stage.

"And there you have it," said Bloom to whoever might be listening. "Very simple really. Take someone away from the familiar, put them in a situation already resonant with emotional meaning, and tell them your tale. A very ordinary illusion, really." He tried to keep the disappointment out of his voice, but did not entirely succeed. "Now she has a shape for her delusions, and she'll fall as quickly as you could wish."

He walked to center stage, spread his hands, and Natio Bloom bowed deeply to his empty space.

TWENTY-TWO

KAPA

Kapa Lu sat in a comfortable private cabin aboard the saints' sprawling city ship. The rescue shuttle took two jumps to get them there, and he had no idea where that was, except that it couldn't be the actual Solar System, because that would have taken four jumps from where they had been.

The illumination for the room was the best simulated daylight he'd ever seen. There was also a long, narrow strip of window that showed the black sky and a single yellow star shining in the far distance. The carpet was soft and whole and clean. So were the blue shirt and black trousers he'd been given to wear. The bed had swaddled him comfortably for the ten hours he slept. The chairs adjusted to fit his contours. He had been extremely well fed, and for the first time in more years than he could remember, he was not thirsty. Their gravity was too heavy for him and he ached from it, but he was adjusting.

Emiliya, you should have come with me. You'd love this place. He tried to ignore the way his good fist tightened at the thought. He'd figured her for smarter than that. He'd loved her. She'd loved him—he knew it. How could she not see that the shadows were the only place for someone who wasn't in the Blood Family? He wasn't free, but at least he had a shot. He would have gotten her the same shot if she'd just remembered how good they used to be . . .

If he ever saw Amerand again, he was going to stomp him into the deck for stealing all Emiliya's nerve. But Jireu always had been a fuckless coward, even back in the tunnels, always hiding from every fight. Always trying to play it safe. How the hell could an OB believe *anything* was safe?

Kapa's wrist itched under its beige stabilizing cast. The saints' doctors told him that was a side effect of speed-healing the bone. The gook they spread on his chest and stomach had already taken away the pain there, and the bruises. His nose also itched under the form they secured over it, which was somehow more annoying. He'd been told the itch would fade in six more hours and that he should touch the red circle shining on the top of the broad desk if it didn't. That would open an active pane directly to his doctor in the ship's clinic.

They also told him the green and blue lights would open panes so he could talk with his crew. He hadn't touched those.

He had been further informed that the door would be unlocked as soon as his debriefing was completed, then he could have the run of the ship, anywhere that was not crew-only access.

Kapa found himself utterly and truly stunned at these calm declarations.

Do you even realize I tried to kidnap, then kill, two of your own? he thought as his guard asked if he had any questions. *Don't you care?*

The arched doorway lit up green, the signal that someone was about to enter. Kapa turned away from the window. His good hand flexed automatically, but he had nothing to grab hold of. The portal swung open a split second later and a single man entered. He was about Kapa's height with black hair and startling, pale green eyes. His uniform was very like the ones the saints had worn.

"Seño Kapa Lu?" the man inquired. "I am Marshal-Steward Misao Smith." He bowed slightly. "I'm here to ask you a few questions."

Kapa shrugged.

"Shall we sit down?"

Kapa shrugged again, and sat in one of the chairs beside the active desk. The saint, Marshal-Steward Misao Smith, sat across from him. The desktop lit up at the touch of Smith's gloved fingertips. Several panes opened immediately. As Smith shuffled them, Kapa's gaze flickered from the man to his work, trying to find a hint as to what was coming. But Misao Smith's face gave nothing away, and the displays he sorted might have been written in hieroglyphs for all Kapa could read them.

"Now." Misao folded his hands. "The first thing you need to know is that you have currently broken no laws within the boundaries of the Pax Solaris. Therefore, if you now wish to request asylum, it will be granted to you."

Kapa crossed his arms over his chest, a little awkwardly because of the cast. "So what if I did?"

"You will be given the status of legal refugee. You will be assigned a living space, a stipend, and enculturation assistance. You will also become subject to the laws and regulations of the Pax Solaris."

"Uh-huh." His nose itched like hell. Kapa tucked his good hand under his armpit to keep from rubbing the healing frame. That just seemed to make it worse. "And if I don't ask for asylum?"

Now it was Smith's turn to shrug. "It is your decision. If you do not wish to receive refugee status, we will provide you with transportation to the destination of your choosing, outside the Pax Solaris, as soon as it can be arranged."

Kapa narrowed his eyes. *What're you hiding under those words?* "I'd have to think about it."

"Of course," agreed Misao Smith easily. "Now, we are first of all interested in why you led a kidnapping attempt on Field Commander Terese Drajeske and her escort."

Kapa settled back, resting his cast on his thigh. "Suppose I don't feel like telling you?"

Smith didn't even blink. "That also is your decision." He moved a couple of the panes around on the desk and studied the new one that came up. He said nothing. He did not look up. He sat there, apparently engrossed in his work, and the silence stretched out.

Kapa's heel started to tap.

"Is that it?" he asked.

Smith looked up. "I'm sorry?"

"I said is that it? Is that all?"

"What else would there be?"

"I don't know." Kapa could not keep the irritation out of his voice. "You guys are in charge here."

"Yes. But if you decline to answer my first question, I cannot continue."

"And you're just going to sit there?"

"I am not going to *just* sit. As you see, I have a great deal of work to do." Smith gestured at the desktop. "Field Commander Drajeske and Field Coordinator Baijahn are my direct subordinates. I have a particular interest in this mission, and there is a lot of follow-up to do. I do not normally come out into the field anymore, which has put me behind on a number of fronts." He pulled a stylus out of the holder at the desk's edge and began making notes on one of the panes, tapping keys with his free hand.

Kapa stared.

Okay. Whatever. The saint wants to sit there and push his buttons, who cares? Kapa got up from his chair and wandered over to the window. He watched the single star for a while. He turned back. The saint did not shift position at all. Kapa paced to the end of the cabin and back again. Smith did not look up.

Well, if you're going to be that stupid . . .

The carpet was soft, and his movements soundless. He slipped up behind Smith, angling his approach so his shadow did not give him away. He raised his good arm to bring it down around the saint's neck.

The room spun and pain shot from his wrist to his shoulder. When he could see straight again, Kapa was on his knees, and Misao Smith had locked his arm behind his back.

"You really are a very slow learner, Seño Lu," Smith remarked as calmly as if he were still sitting at his desk.

"All right, all right!" shouted Kapa. "It was worth a try. Lemme go."

Somewhat to his surprise, the saint did let go and stood back. Kapa rubbed his sore wrist. He glowered at Smith, who sat back down behind the desk.

"Why did you attempt to kidnap Terese Drajeske and her escort?"

Kapa got to his feet awkwardly, not wanting to use either of his hands. His healing fingers didn't have a lot of strength and his formerly good hand was now a mass of pins and needles. He dropped into the chair. "I was offered an internal drive ship if I could bring your people in alive."

"Who made the offer?"

Kapa considered for a moment. *Either you mean it about the legals and I'm free now, or you're a fuckless liar and I'm screwed.*

But the worst way you can screw me is to send me back, and I bet you know that.

"An old guy named Nikko Donnelly," said Kapa. "He's in charge of Habitat 3."

"And how did Seño Donnelly have an internal drive ship to give you?"

"He's Blood. Diluted, but in there, and he's connected into the shipyard."

Smith made a note. "He was able to purchase this ship?"

Kapa snorted. "Not likely. He's on probation with them. Did something naughty-naughty back in the day. Never heard what, but it got his allowance cut off."

Smith made another note. "Why did he give you an ID ship before you had completed your task? You might have simply stolen it."

"He'd junked the codes. Scrambled them. The ship could only jump between Erasmus and the spot you found us. He was going to hand over the good codes when we handed over your saints."

"So Donnelly had access to not one ID ship, but two. One for you to use in the kidnapping and one to go out to meet you."

"I guess."

Smith read over his notes. "Given the level of security surrounding internal drives in the Erasmus System, that seems most extraordinary." He frowned. "Was Nikko Donnelly acting as an official representative of the Blood Family when he contacted you?"

"How the hell would I know?" sneered Kapa. "If I had to guess, I'd bet somebody closer to the best Blood gave it to him and told him what to do with it. Probably told him he'd get back in the good books if he did."

"But you didn't ask?"

"He had a job and a price beyond anything I'd dreamed of. That was the beginning and the end of what I wanted to know about him."

"I see." Smith made yet another note, selected another pane, and dragged it in front of him. "Very well. Thank you, Seño Lu, for your cooperation. Now, I am going to ask you again, do you wish to accept asylum in the Pax Solaris?"

Kapa's jaw worked itself back and forth. What if he did? What if he made this little fuckless saint let him go inside the precious Pax, made Smith have to deliver him safe into one of their tidy little worlds, *pay* him a salary for fuck's sake, and do everything but wipe his poor little refugee ass?

Serve the smug little bastard right.

"Okay. Yes. I accept asylum in the Pax Solaris."

"Very well." Misao made yet another note. "Your official acceptance of refugee status is hereby recorded and sealed." He stood up. "As is my filing of an official complaint of attempted assault on a serving officer of the Solaris Guardians. An appointed legal representative will visit you as soon as you are transferred to port to explain your options and obligations."

Kapa's jaw dropped. Smith walked out of the room and let the door close behind him.

TWENTY-THREE

EMILIYA

Emiliya Varus's interrogation by the Clerks lasted approximately seven hours. She must have done fairly well, because at the end of it they allowed her to sleep on a cot in the interrogation room. There was even a toilet she could use, and a meal of ham, fresh bread, and black tea before they let her walk out into the streets.

There were clearly advantages to being in the pay of the Grand Sentinel. She'd never been fed by the Clerks before.

The Grand Sentinel. Emiliya blinked in the flickering light. What was he doing while she was being questioned by the hard-eyed Clerk in that windowless room? What had he been doing to her mother?

I did everything he asked. I told the absolute truth, about everything that matters to them. All right, she'd left out a couple of things about Amerand . . . But if they'd caught that, they'd have said so while she was still in the room. They'd never have let her go.

Emiliya swung around the curve of a copper-sided dome and took off across the rooftops at a run.

Home. She had to get home. She had to tell her mother what she'd done. She had to see her siblings. She had to make sure they were all right, and that the Grand Sentinel wasn't lying.

She had to be sure they were really free.

Her breath came short and painful. She stumbled and staggered, but she didn't stop.

In the section of Dazzle where her family lived, how much room you got was largely a function of how much room you could hold on to. Andera Varus and her oldest son Parisch made a formidable combination. They took and they held an entire suite, midlevel, outer east wall, in the Erasmus Tables building.

Emiliya made it to the Tables' roof and threaded her way across, avoiding the ducts that were nests for snakes. The access door was long gone and she charged down the stairs, swinging herself over the rail, dropping down a full floor at a time, landing sure and steady on both feet.

When she emerged into the gloomy, dusty hall, it was empty. She remembered vaguely that it was water-market day. No one would have any time to be hanging around in here.

Which meant there was no one to greet her. It also meant there was no one to block her view of the open door.

It's not ours, she told herself as she walked down the corridor toward it. Her shoes had soft soles and made no sound on the bare floor. *It's not ours.*

She repeated that mantra until she was standing in the doorway and staring into the suite of rooms that was her mother's home.

No one was there. Emiliya tried to tell herself that her family had just gone to the water market. She stumbled from room to room. The last room, in the far back of the suite, was her mother's. Her entrance disturbed a snake on a window ledge and it slithered under the bed. The rustling patchwork blankets were still on the bed, but the clock was gone from the shelf. So was the only-semilegal active screen that Parisch had stitched together and kept working by sheer force of will.

Maybe it's temporary, she thought desperately. Hers wouldn't be the first OB family to clear out on short notice to hide from the Security or one of the gangs. Parisch thought he was a tough. He could easily have offended some *patri.*

Emiliya scanned the rusted shelves, looking for some hint as to where they had gone. But there was nothing.

"They wouldn't leave without telling me," she murmured. "Their account can't have been cleared *that* fast. They wouldn't go without me."

But she'd been out in the black sky for at least a day, and then there was her interrogation, then she slept. She ate. All that time, with no one knowing where she was or if she would ever come back. Two days can be a very long time to wait when you're trying to keep ahead of the Blood Family.

They must have left recently, because otherwise the place would have been stripped down to the stone by the neighbors. They hadn't been taken by the Clerks. There would have been a secops on station here to greet her and tell her that her family was in custody.

Biting her lip, Emiliya lifted the lid of the clothes chest at the foot of the bed. Empty. She held the lid with one hand and with the other she picked at the corner of the bottom with two fingers. It was a hard scrabble, but she got it, and the chest's seamless liner peeled back and lifted up. That was where the family kept its precious store of scrip and promissory cards. Little bits of positive balance hoarded like water ice.

Her arm trembled and she had to blink several times because her vision was beginning to fail her.

The space was empty, and Emiliya was forced to believe. Then she noticed the wadded-up bit of writing sheet jammed in the back corner. Emiliya retrieved it and let the false bottom settle back in place. She lowered the lid and sat on the chest. Carefully, because the thing had been used so many times it had grown fragile, she smoothed out the sheet.

There, scraped out in her mother's sprawling, unpracticed writing, were two words.

THANK YOU

Emiliya stared. She blinked. She read the words again.

THANK YOU

There was a strange noise coming from somewhere, and she realized it was her, choking on her own breath. She pressed her hand against her mouth, then against her eyes.

They'd left her. Her family, with her mother no doubt in the lead, had left her. This was no spur-of-the-moment thing, either. It was too clean, too accomplished. Her mother had *planned* it. The second their accounts were clear. The second they had a positive balance. She might even have kept the bags packed from the moment Emiliya had gotten into the medical academy.

How could she do this to me? After I fought and I starved myself trying to get a positive balance for her. After what I did . . . after everything I did . . .

THANK YOU

Inside, Emiliya raged and screamed. It wasn't reasonable. After all, her debts weren't cleared. She couldn't have gone with them in any case, but *they* hadn't known that. Her mother hadn't known that. She hadn't waited for Emiliya, the one who freed her, to make it home. She'd just taken what she had and left, leaving Emiliya to fend for herself.

In her mind, Emiliya ran through the suite, smashing and tearing anything that would give beneath the force of her hands. She wept and howled and banged her fists bloody against stone and metal.

But if anyone had been there, they would have only seen her wipe her eyes and carefully fold up the ragged, wrinkled note to tuck away in the pocket of her medical whites.

A knock sounded, someone's knuckles on the threshold. Emiliya jumped. *Did I leave the door open?* She couldn't remember. She rounded the corner slowly, afraid to see who or what had come to her empty home.

Standing in the corridor threshold was Field Commander Terese Drajeske. Emiliya stared for a moment.

"Field Commander."

"Dr. Varus. May I come in?" Terese Drajeske stepped in without waiting for an answer.

"How did you find . . . this place?"

Terese smiled, abashed. "Orry Batumbe said he knew several Varuses in the city. I've been going door to door."

"Oh." Emiliya gestured a little helplessly at the front room. "Won't you sit down?"

"Thank you." The Field Commander settled gingerly onto one of the chairs made of disassembled crates. "I just wanted to make sure you were all right."

"I'm fine, thank you." Emiliya couldn't tell whether the Field Commander recognized the lie for what it was. Most saints wore their emotions out in the open, but this one was different.

"I'm glad," Drajeske said seriously. "Because you saved

my life, and my second's life. I'd hate to find out you got
pinged for it."

"No, I'm fine." *What is this woman really doing here? Does she
know what I did to her second? No, the saints don't think like that.
They've never had to. She trusts Amerand and Amerand trusts me.*

"That's good." The Field Commander nodded.

Emiliya folded her hands. Maybe she'd be lucky. Maybe
the woman would leave, and she could start working out
what she was going to do next.

But the Field Commander didn't budge. "May I ask you
something?"

"Certainly," Emiliya answered reflexively. She'd learned
long ago never to appear to be reluctant to answer a question. It made people suspicious.

"If I wanted to get to Hospital, how would I go about it?"

Emiliya's throat tightened and she regretted her agreement, but it was too late to withdraw. It was all right. She
knew how to work an interrogation. Say as little as possible.
Stick to the truth, but leave out the meaning.

She faced the Field Commander as if she were a casual
stranger. Emiliya was used to people vanishing suddenly
from her life. Her lover had vanished into the Security, then
into the shadows. She set it aside. Her mother, her whole
family, was gone in an eyeblink. She had already begun to
set them aside. If she could do that, she could surely set aside
a few hours spent with a woman pretending to fight for her
life.

Or was I really fighting for my life? I wonder if I won or lost?

I'm drifting. Not good. The Field Commander was looking
at her with a sympathy that veiled a great deal. *What did she
want to know? Oh, yeah. She wants to go to Hospital.*

"I'm afraid I'm too far down the chain to help you with

that, Field Commander. You need to ask Commander Barclay or the Grand Sentinel. They're the ones who can arrange the permissions."

Saints are truthful. Saints are open. No saint can find out anything one of us wants to keep hidden.

Terese Drajeske sighed. "I thought so. But I thought I'd ask, because there doesn't seem to be any regular traffic between here and there."

"No," replied Emiliya politely. "Not really."

"Which is odd, because there's also not a lot of traffic out-system from Hospital; but according to all our records, it's Hospital that's helping finance the system."

Emiliya tried to look abashed, but it was hard. "Sorry," she said. "I really wouldn't know."

The Field Commander nodded as if she understood. Anger surged through Emiliya. How dare this person, this *saint*, this *alien creature*, even pretend to be able to understand what was happening here?

If she's such a naive fool she can't even take care of her own people, maybe they deserve whatever they get.

"So," the Field Commander went on pleasantly, "how is it that you and Amerand and Kapa all know each other?"

The change of subject caught Emiliya off guard. *How did she know . . . never mind, never mind. Just answer the question.* "We were . . . we were neighbors on Oblivion and shared a ship during the Breakout."

"Was it your idea to put Amerand on our watch?"

It was too much. Emiliya burst out laughing. The Field Commander pulled back, looking mildly offended. "I'm sorry," gasped Emiliya, "but you really have no idea how far down the chain I am, do you?"

Go away. Why won't she go away? What's she after? She can't know. She can't have found out. There is no way the Grand Sentinel would give me a dose the saints could trace. Unless he wanted them to catch me instead of him . . .

Stop it. She's a saint. She's after what she says she is.

"The chain of command is proving extremely difficult to track here," Terese Drajeske replied. "The Grand Sentinel, for instance. I'm having a very hard time arranging to talk with him." She cocked her head. "But you knew he would help you."

Which did not sit well with her previous claim of being far down the chain. *Mistake.* "He vetted me for the biosecurity team," she said, and hoped it would be enough.

"And he told you what you'd be doing?"

Emiliya looked quickly away and ran her tongue across her bottom teeth. "We all of us just follow orders," she said. "I was ordered to do your scans. Amerand was ordered to take your watch."

"And Kapa?" asked the Field Commander.

Kapa. Skinny little boy who ran the tracks between the dead trains with the rats and the gangs on his heels. Kapa, who could jump farther and fly higher than any of them. Kapa's skin and hands against hers. Kapa pushing her up against the wall, and her arms and her legs wrapping around him . . . all so very long ago. She'd followed him and fallen for him for the same reasons Amerand had—because they were afraid and he wasn't, and they'd hoped that somehow he would take them with him when he finally flew away.

Kapa, who'd sworn he'd come back for her when he went into the academy, but then melted into the shadows and left her behind as easily as he had left Amerand.

Kapa.

"Kapa was in the shadows," she said. "If he was following

orders . . . I wouldn't know about that." She shifted quickly, aware she had made another mistake. Not that it mattered. This woman didn't matter. *What's she going to do, report me to the Clerks?*

The Field Commander stood and bowed formally. *She recognizes a stonewall at least,* thought Emiliya with a kind of desperate gratitude.

"Thank you for your time, Dr. Varus. I won't take up any more of it. I don't want to get either of us in trouble." Drajeske smiled with a casual mischief that made Emiliya's blood burn. "I seem to be wandering about without my keeper. I'm sure they'll catch up with me for that sooner or later."

"Field Commander?"

"Terese," the Field Commander reminded her. They had gone onto a first-name basis when Terese had helped glue her to the ceiling. *Glued me to the ceiling! Kapa would have laughed so hard.*

"Did," Emiliya licked her lips and tried to change her mind, but she had started the question and couldn't think fast enough to come up with a plausible replacement. "Did Amerand send you?"

"No. I haven't seen him since we got back." The commander's gaze was too sharp, too obvious. She believed she was about to hear something meaningful.

"Neither have I."

The Field Commander blew out a sigh that ruffled the curls falling across her forehead. "Interesting. Well." She paused once more. "You know where our base is, I think?"

"Yes, I think so."

"Amerand is likely to have to take up his station with us again right away, especially since I've been on the loose, so if you want to see him before you head back to Hospital, or if you want to leave a message for him . . ."

"I see. Thank you."

"Good-bye, Dr. Varus." Terese bowed again. This time there was a hint of acknowledgment in the gesture and the look. She knew she'd been beaten, that she would come away with nothing.

"Good-bye," said Emiliya.

The Field Commander turned and left without looking back.

It was almost too much to stand. Almost, but not quite. Emiliya was a child of Oblivion. She would keep going. She felt her mother's rough hand over her heart. *This is still beating,* Mother said, after one of the riots, the first time a friend didn't come back. *As long as this is still beating, you can keep on going.*

Thinking on her mother's words, it occurred to Emiliya, oddly and belatedly, that she was free. Her family had been her hostages. They were gone now, probably beyond the reach of the Security and the Clerks. There were those who said the black sky wasn't that big, but Emiliya didn't believe that. Her mother would not have started a run she couldn't finish. She was very thorough like that. So, they were gone, and if she did wrong, if she made a mistake, there would be no one else to suffer. No one to arrest or imprison. No one to execute for the crime of having a rebellious relative.

It touched Emiliya like a faint reflected light. That was what her mother had been thinking. That was why she'd run so fast. Her mother had made sure Emiliya would have the one set of skills that was known to have use and worth beyond Erasmus, and set her free.

THANK YOU

Free, Emiliya Varus walked down the stairs and into the street. Free, she didn't know what to do or where to go.

She had no money. She had nothing with her but her medical whites and her depleted doctor's kit. And freedom. It wasn't much, but she'd worked with less.

Emiliya Varus turned her footsteps toward the port yard.

It wasn't really a bad walk. It was a long way up, but Emiliya walked farther almost every day in the Hospital complex. Some of the bridges were in bad shape, but she knew how to judge her risks.

The area around the port yard was in fairly good shape. Trade from those shipping, warehousing, and related enterprises brought in the money and paid for repair. No one bothered her as she walked down the well-ventilated corridors, although some looked on her medical whites with envy. It had been a long time, but Emiliya still recognized the order of doorways, the graffiti and other signs, some of them subtle, some not subtle at all.

She knocked on the sixth door from the south stair. An old woman opened the door. She had bones like a starved bird and a dowager's hump that lifted her shoulders permanently around her ears. She and Emiliya stared at each other for a long time. Emiliya managed a watery smile, and the old woman's sparse eyebrows shot up in surprise.

"You're Andera's girl, yes?"

Emiliya nodded.

"Andera's and . . . that man, what was his name?"

Emiliya didn't think for a moment the old woman had really forgotten. "Nikko Donnelly."

"Nikko, Nikko Donnelly, that was it. Long time ago." The old woman shook her head.

"Got a chair for a sister OB?"

The old woman pursed her sunken mouth. "I think that's going to depend on what *he* has to say." She nodded, and Emiliya turned.

Behind her stood a Clerk, tall and composed in his plain black coat. Cold fear shot through Emiliya and she froze before she remembered she was now on the side of—in the pay of—Fortress itself.

I have already been cleared.

The old woman slipped backward and bolted the door so softly Emiliya barely heard her. She just felt the breeze. Somewhere, Emiliya heard the parakeets chattering, but other than that, the corridor was silent. All human sounds had died away.

Emiliya straightened herself. "Is there something I can do for you, Seño?"

The Clerk stepped right up to her, standing less than six inches away. His breath was warm and smelled of nothing at all. "I have you identified as Emiliya Varus," he said.

"Yes, Seño?" She resisted the urge to step back. *Have they got you people on drugs now?* It was possible. His pupils didn't look right even though his eyes sparkled with awareness.

He nodded once. His expression was intense, involved, with her but not with her. "You will return to Hospital and resume your duties."

Emiliya's heart stopped, but she managed to work a note of mild surprise into her voice. "Of course."

The Clerk's eyes snapped into focus so quickly, she could practically hear the click. "No, I think you do not understand me. You will do this because otherwise we will find it necessary to refine the questioning of Amerand Jireu."

The last of the blood drained from Emiliya's face and her ability to dissemble went with it. "What?"

The Clerk's focus faded, and snapped back again. "Captain Jireu is needed for other duties, but the law and public vigilance cannot be overlooked, no matter how inconvenient. If he is involved in a conspiracy against orderly trade and the public peace, it will be discovered."

Amerand? They are holding something on Amerand? Why would they tell me?

Because they knew she was his friend. Because they knew that she had tried to love him even if Amerand didn't know it.

She was wrong when she'd thought they had no hostages anymore.

The Clerk watched her with his alert, intense, unfocused eyes. "You are authorized to return on the *Argos*, leaving from Bay 12 in four hours. Your access numbers have already been verified. You will need only your personal identification and Hospital residency codes."

"Thank you, Seño." Emiliya bowed, because there was nothing else she could do.

The Clerk turned on his heel and strode away before she straightened up.

Two hours. I was free for about two hours. A little less. One hour and fifty-two minutes. One hour and fifty-three minutes, maybe.

Does Amerand know this is happening? She could never tell what he knew. He only used his Security connections when there was no other way. It was as if he didn't use his power, he didn't have to admit having it. He didn't have to really be in the Security, not all the way.

Amerand never truly committed himself to anything— not to jump from one ledge to the next, not to the Security, not to her, not anything. Not like Kapa, who never did it any other way. That, more than Kapa's shadow, was why they had never come together. Amerand probably thought he was sparing her, but he was sparing himself and pretending to leave them both free.

But even as she thought this she remembered how Amerand looked at the Field Commander, the new notes in his voice as he promised her help. There was something in that moment so far beyond the shabby loyalties she had known that she didn't even have a name for it.

Does the Field Commander know the Clerks have special plans for Amerand? Why didn't she say anything? Emiliya covered her mouth. *Because she wanted to find out if I knew. She wanted to try to see if I had anything to do with this.*

I've been played by a saint!

Alone in the corridor, Emiliya Varus began to laugh. She laughed until the tears ran down her cheeks and she couldn't tell whether she was still laughing or weeping. In the end, she straightened up, smoothed down her jacket, and began the walk to the port yard.

TWENTY-FOUR

SIRI

Siri stood at the base of a rickety ladder that had been bolted up the side of a building as an afterthought. Around her, the people of Dazzle formed a churning, boiling mass. There was no restriction by class here. The rich in their gleaming finery, the poor in their rust and rags, surged up and down the streets. Carts pulled by hand or creaking along with sputtering electric motors eased their way through the foot traffic. It was the only place Siri had seen in the broken-down city that was genuinely crowded, and everyone carried containers: jugs, crocks, skins, canteens. In the light gravity the pyramids and bundles could be of eye-popping size. Everyone was shouting. It was like a hundred auctions all happening at once. "Water I got!" "Start it at ten! You got ten? No?" "You! You! What'll you say?"

"Water I got!"

Crowds formed shifting walls around the water sellers. The Security, dressed in full-body armor, stood on platforms and balconies with their guns cradled in their arms. Some of them looked hard at Siri, but not for long. She'd left her uniform back at base and was dressed in plain work clothes. To them, she appeared to be just another of the garden-variety saints you saw down in the base streets. Probably they thought she was out on some pointless charitable errand. Nothing for *them* to be concerned about.

Another time she might have enjoyed being here. Unlike the rest of Dazzle, this place had life. It was still part of the same messed-up system, but it was brimming with people doing their level best to carve out lives for themselves and there was an energy, a vitality, in that.

But she kept feeling distracted. The whispering wouldn't leave her alone. It was as if, now that Bloom had made her aware of its presence, she couldn't shut it off. She wanted to be back at base working her listening station, searching for the hidden frequency. It had seemed so implausible when Bloom had told her about it, and yet . . . Shawn was so certain. She couldn't ignore it. She had to prove it one way or another.

And if it was real, he was right—they had to find it, had to open it up. Even if it was just some kind of electronic ghost of Bianca in there, they couldn't leave her. Even Terese would see that. But Terese would have to be shown, especially after Siri had tried to convince her Bianca might still be alive.

"She might still be," murmured Shawn. "We don't know. We won't know until we find the network."

I know. I know. But we can't miss the meet with Vijay. Guilt surged through her. She wanted to see him. She needed to know he was still okay.

Maybe she could find a way to tell Vijay about the network. Vijay would believe her even if Terese wouldn't. Vijay had always trusted her.

Where is he? She shifted the jug a little and pushed herself up on her tiptoes, craning her neck above the crowd.

"There."

As soon as Shawn said it, Siri spotted him. She hated what they'd done to him, even though it made for an excellent disguise. Vijay shouldn't have looked like he couldn't stand his own life. It was the opposite of everything he was.

Vijay waded through the crowd, making good use of his height to pick out a path. Siri waved her free hand and he elbowed his way across to her, earning more than a few curses as he did. He swept her in close with one arm and gave her a long, open kiss.

A Solaran thug meeting his woman. She could feel the secops sneer as they looked down, but that didn't matter, so long as they were only seeing the show.

"Hey, lover," he murmured, and with his arm still wrapped tight around her waist they strolled up the street. They casually skirted the edge of the thickest crowds, where the shouting would cover conversation and the shifting sea of human beings would keep them from standing out.

"Any news?" asked Siri quietly.

A sly smile spread across Vijay's face. "Oh, yeah. Your kidnapping seems to have had an unintended consequence." She felt him slide the sliver drive into her side pocket.

"What?" There were rules about the kind of information that could be passed in crowded places. She and Vijay long ago decided these should be considered as guidelines rather than absolutes.

"Seems Kapa Lu was making fairly regular runs for a smuggling outfit. Out to Habitat 3," he added quietly.

"Really?" murmured Siri.

"Really," Vijay repeated. He nodded toward a door marked with a green spiral, the sign for a public restaurant. Siri shook her head. "And my would-be employer showed up today spitting mad and badly shorthanded. Wanted to know if I could work cargo and keep my mouth shut."

"Did you find out where the cargo was bound for?" Siri pointed toward a tiny cart where a woman swirled a wok made of hand-beaten metal over a small heating-coil stove. Vijay shrugged.

"I'm a genius, I am. And he was really pissed. I bought him a few drinks and let him rant. Do you have any idea how god-awful the local moonshine is when you mix it with the local tea?" He grimaced.

"Sounds like a very macho combination." Siri broke off as she approached the woman with the wok. She was swirling peanuts in hot oil and chili powder. After a little dickering Siri exchanged a couple of battered sheets of scrip for two patchwork bags of very hot nuts.

"And I am not man enough." Vijay chuckled and bent down so Siri could pop a peanut into his mouth. He chewed thoughtfully. "Hey, these are good."

"Found her yesterday when I was out and about," Siri mumbled around her own spicy mouthful.

They moved on so the woman could serve other customers, and Vijay reached across to fish another peanut out of the bag. "So, what's the word on your end?"

Siri bit her lip, considering. "There's something you should know," she said softly. "But it's 'out there.'"

"Everything about this place is 'out there.'" They moved into the shadow of a sagging building. "Today I broke up a fight between two guys over a string of dead rats. Seems the person who brought back the most was going to get the extermination contract." He made a face and popped another peanut. "What have you got?"

She turned to Vijay. She shivered. *Shawn?*

"It's up to you, but be careful."

Okay.

Moving close, leaning on his shoulder, as if she were

only a woman whispering suggestions into her lover's ear, Siri told Vijay what she had learned from her encounter with Natio Bloom.

To her utter shock, Vijay burst out laughing.

"Okay, okay," she murmured. "Enough for the witnesses."

"Buddha wept, Siri. You had me going for a minute."

"You don't believe me."

He looked at her, opened his mouth, and looked again. "Siri, what's the punch line?"

"You don't believe me." She backed up a step. *Shawn, something's wrong.*

"I can't hear. They're too loud. Siri, they're too loud!"

I don't understand!

"Talk to me," whispered Vijay. "What's going on?"

She felt herself staring. She felt herself shaking. In the back of her head, Shawn struggled as if against chains. "Too loud, Siri. It's the voices. They're here. Here now!"

Something was wrong. Something was wrong and it was coming from Vijay. And she'd just told him everything she knew.

She forced a smile. "Some joke, isn't it?" she says. "Bloom's quite the character. Siphoned voices. I won't need to go on the ghost tour now."

"I guess not." Vijay pulled her into a hug and kissed the top of her head. "But no more of that, okay? I'm too wound up for that kind of joke."

"Okay," she murmured to his chest and tried not to shudder as he stroked her back. "Okay."

After she left Vijay, there was only one place Siri could go, one place that remained safe. She made her way down the foundation streets to one particular subway entrance. She looked around carefully before she descended the skeleton of the spiral staircase. It creaked badly under her boots.

When she reached the bottom, Siri stood still, facing the shaft of light that came from the hole above. Dust motes drifted like tiny stars. She set her back to the wall so nothing could sneak up behind her and slid down until she sat on the cracked concrete, her knees drawn up to her chest.

He didn't believe me. Siri gripped her hair with both hands. *He laughed at me. Why would Vijay laugh at me?*

"Vijay wouldn't," Shawn answered softly.

But he did.

"That wasn't Vijay."

Shawn?

"We only saw him postsurgery the once before he went under, and it was dark . . ."

Siri wrapped her arms tight around her legs. *If . . . if they can siphon a person's voice out and keep it in the network . . . could they put it into somebody different?*

"Hospital the size of a planet," said Shawn bleakly. "They might be able to build the body just for the purpose. If they've collected all those voices, all those essences. If they could load them into constructed bodies, they'd make the perfect spies."

But we don't know yet. We've got no proof! We don't know anything!

"I know, Siri, and you do, too."

Siri sat there, paralyzed. She didn't know. She didn't *want* to know. It was too much. It was too terrible. But she couldn't doubt Shawn. He was her Companion. She had to trust him, that was what he was there for, to be the one voice she could trust no matter what.

Siri bowed her head. *Vijay!* She screamed his name in her

thoughts, half-enraged, half-horrified. She had to press both hands to her mouth to keep from crying out loud. *They got Vijay too. And I told him everything!*

"We need to tell Terese," whispered Shawn.

Siri shook her head violently. *What if Terese doesn't believe me? She didn't believe me about the thing everybody thought was Bianca's body. What if this time she thinks I'm crazy? She'll ship me back home.*

She couldn't breathe. She wondered if there were nanos in the dust. There could be. Nanos in the dust getting into her blood, isolating her essence, separating it out, getting it ready for siphoning.

No, no, don't think like that. Work the problem. She bit her lip, pulling herself back together.

"What do we do, Siri?"

If they've . . . if they've constructed a living body and stored his voice in it, it will have to be seated in the construct somewhere. If we dissect it, that will give us a clue as to how their network functions.

She felt Shawn nodding. He understood without her saying it why they truly couldn't tell Terese what was happening. This thing, this construct, that held Vijay's voice might not properly be a live person, but she didn't have time to waste convincing her commander of that. Terese would probably have to take it up the line, and by the time clearance came back down to take it apart, it would be too late.

She'd have to bring Terese definite proof. When she opened up the construct and exposed its workings, Terese, and Misao and the whole chain of command, would see she was right. They'd be able to refocus the mission, and Vijay and Bianca would be freed.

Siri straightened herself up and smoothed down her tunic. She'd have to play this very carefully. But she was trained and she was practiced. Nobody would see anything was wrong. Nobody.

Siri climbed lightly up the spiral stair and turned her face toward the base. She strode purposefully through the empty streets.

She did not see Vijay emerge from the doorway and stare after her.

TWENTY-FIVE
TERESE

From a shadowed doorway, I watched the Clerk take his leave of Emiliya.

Of course I followed her. That was why I found her and had that conversation. I already knew she wasn't going to tell me anything voluntarily. When you've spent upward of sixteen hours in a confined space with a person, the fact that they want nothing to do with you becomes fairly obvious.

But I needed to see what she'd do next. I needed to know if the conspiracy she was involved in was official or illicit.

She'd left her mother's home and gone straight to the Clerks.

Official, then. She was a link in the chain that led to the war, no matter how far down she claimed to be.

And the invisible Grand Sentinel Torian Erasmus was on the other end. I should have known, but he'd covered his tracks well. We'd gone over what data we had again and again. Looked at one way, he was an actual player. Looked at another, he was just another of the Bloods picking over the leavings of Jasper and Felice Erasmus's system to see what he could get out of it.

Now that the Clerk was gone, Emiliya Varus, who had heard Amerand promise to help us, was dissolving into hysterical laughter. I made myself stand and watch, although my feelings bled for her. Whatever she had done, it was not going well, or easily.

Did you murder Amerand's Clerk? Was it possible the Clerk had come to tell her they would not let her get away with it, no matter what the orders?

Which led to the question: If she'd killed the Clerk, and Torian was pulling her strings, why did Torian want Amerand's Clerk dead?

Eventually, Dr. Varus straightened herself and walked rapidly down the corridor, finally banging through the door at the end that led, I knew, to the crumbling, much-mended staircase.

I was worried. No, that's not right. I had been worried before—now I was frightened. For myself, for her, and most of all for Amerand Jireu.

The problem was, there was next to nothing I could do. Amerand, already under suspicion for murder, would probably have treason added to the charges. If I barged in demanding his release—assuming I could even find him—I'd only confirm that he was working with us.

The lights dimmed for me. I felt stone under my hands. I tasted old blood in my mouth.

Nothing was going the way it was supposed to. I had next to no time before I had to head back to Fortress into whatever cage they had waiting for me there, and I hadn't even scraped the surface of what was happening on Dazzle. Siri had come back from her meeting with Natio Bloom subdued and said she'd have to verify the info he'd given her before she knew what kind of source he'd turn out to be. I was supposed to put on a public face and make nice with the citizens council, who'd sent their invitation via Bloom. I was supposed to help Siri sort through our fragmented and barely coherent data about the real power structures of the Erasmus System. I was supposed to find out who'd killed

Bianca and how these people were going to make war against us.

But I couldn't leave Amerand without at least trying. If for no other reason than that he was my only connection to Emiliya Varus, and she was my only connection to the Grand Sentinel. It was a slender thread, but a whole lot was hanging on it.

Around me, doors began to open. People emerged cautiously, as if in response to an all-clear signal I couldn't plug into. I didn't wait any longer. I headed for the stairs to make my way back to the Common Cause house.

Liang didn't like me or the Guardians. That was all right. But he did like Amerand. He wouldn't leave him to the Clerks' tender mercies.

I threaded my way through the people queuing at the single tap in the base courtyard. I opened the door for the lobby and saw Liang standing at the base of the curving stair, one still figure in the midst of noise and bustle.

Waiting for me.

"My office," he snapped. He marched away before I could say anything, and the force of his anger almost lifted him off the ground with each step.

I didn't try to talk. I just followed him down a flight of stairs, then through a whole series of aesthetically curved, time-stained hallways, and into a room about the size of a storage closet. He had to jiggle the door to get it to shut all the way. When it was shut, Liang snicked the latch closed. The light panel in the ceiling buzzed erratically as it worked its way up to full brightness.

Liang faced me.

"What have you been saying to Amerand Jireu?" he demanded. "What did you promise him?"

"Nothing," I replied. "He offered to help us. I hadn't had time to make any kind of response."

"It doesn't look that way." Liang folded his arms. "Captain Amerand Jireu gets back from being kidnapped by smugglers and spending sixteen hours cooped up with you, and his Clerk either falls or is pushed to his death from the rooftops." He paused, and added, "It takes a hell of a long fall to kill someone in this gravity."

"You do not believe Amerand Jireu killed his Clerk," I replied evenly.

"I don't know." Liang's admission was both brutal and bitter. "The Clerk is dead. No one wants to talk about it, but the word is out there. I'm asking again: What did you say to Jireu?"

"As if I'd tell you that I urged him to commit murder in direct contravention of my service oath."

Liang didn't even blink. His steady gaze was just one goad too many. I moved forward, right into his space. "I don't know what Bianca Fayette did that's got you so mad at the Guardians," I said evenly, "and I don't know what kind of frame the Security is trying to build around Amerand Jireu, but neither I nor mine did this thing." I drew myself up to my full height. "You either tell me what this is really about, or you get the hell out of my way, Seño Chen."

For a long moment, we stood like that, both of us stretched to our breaking points. I watched a vein in Liang's temple throb unsteadily as he tried to find words strong enough for the emotions dammed up inside him.

"You've seen what we're up against here." He swept his hands out. "Field *Coordinator* Fayette comes on the Tour. She's supposed to conduct a full evaluation, start getting us resource coordination, help us work out what's really going on so we can make substantive change. What does she do? She sends her entire crew off and stays behind partying with the ambassador and the smugglers."

He leaned forward so I could not mistake what he said. I had brought myself into his space, and now he would not let me go. "Now you turn up, and *you* are taken off by those smugglers, and one of the few genuinely good people I've met in this system goes over the edge." Rage shook his frame.

I made myself focus on the important words. "Bianca Fayette had contacts with the water smugglers?"

"You better believe she did. Here, and on Fortress. She probably could have given a full list to the Blood Family if she'd felt like it. I take it this is something else your superiors didn't know about."

I had no answer for that. Instead I asked, "Do you know how much time she spent with Torian Erasmus?"

"She practically had a standing engagement whenever he was over here." Liang cocked his head. "What I'm really trying to figure out is whether you're here to cover up what Fayette was doing or keep on with it."

For a moment I couldn't even breathe. When I was finally able to make myself speak, I said, "I am leaving this room now. I am going to continue my operation and I will expect your cooperation. I will be making a full report of this conversation to the Marshal-Steward. If I have even the first inkling that you are undermining me, I will have you removed."

"You do that," he said. "You do all of that. If you're so starry-clean, you go ahead."

"I've heard you," I said, and walked to the door. I opened the lock and left him there.

I walked across the lobby with no real destination in my

head. I couldn't even see straight. Eventually, I found myself in the dining hall. This time it was almost half-full, mostly with Erasmans, sitting on the long benches, drinking from bowls, tearing apart loaves of bread and sharing them out with their families.

I sat down on an empty bench.

What am I going to do? I stared at the ceiling. I should not have come back into the Guardians. I should not have even tried. This whole situation had gone completely pear-shaped, and I had no idea how to straighten it out. And for the cherry on top, I might become responsible for the death of Amerand Jireu.

I should have known better than to listen to him. I should have cut him off before he'd spoken a word.

My head started to ache. I folded my arms on the table and rested my forehead on them.

I thought I was used to the blows from Bianca's secrets, but this one had caught me off guard. We'd combed through all Bianca's reports and Jerimiah's fragmented memories. There was next to nothing about the Grand Sentinel. That was one of the reasons we hadn't been sure if he worked any real power. If he had, Bianca would have known. Bianca always knew where the real power was. It was what made her so good.

I thought about Jerimiah and his fragmented memories. I thought about Liang's telling me Bianca partied with the smugglers and spent time with Torian Erasmus that she didn't report. I thought about Siri, sitting in my room at the Palmer House and telling me Bianca was still alive.

I thought about how there were very few ways a person alone could work a genuine takedown. I thought of all the ways you could betray an oath, about human greed and weakness, and how those who lived too long served too many masters.

I thought about what it would take to cut out your own Companion so it could never betray you. So the Guardians would truly believe you were dead and never seriously come looking for you. Bianca was one of the few Guardians who knew the loss was survivable because she knew me.

I missed Dylan. I missed David. I hated being alone. I hated myself for being fool enough to walk into this morass. I wanted to go home. Now. Even if David had left me for good. Even then, it couldn't be worse than this. I squeezed my eyes shut. No. That idea was just making this mess worse because that was the pain that wouldn't leave.

"I see our chief has had his little chat with you."

I lifted my head. Orry was standing there holding a bowl and a cup of something that steamed. "Here, eat this." He set them down in front of me.

"I can't . . ."

"Eat." He produced a spoon, lifted my hand, and wrapped my fingers around it. "I'll feed you if I have to. Starved, you do no one any good."

I spooned some porridge into my mouth. It was bland, but it was hot, and after a few mouthfuls I found myself eating steadily until my spoon scraped the bottom.

"Better?"

I nodded and pushed the bowl away. "Have you got a Bianca story to tell me, too?"

He shook his head. "Not me. I just work here."

"I'm starting to get the idea nobody 'just' works here."

He shrugged. "Maybe not, but I do my best."

"Why? You're supposed to be here making things better."

He grimaced. "I've come to the conclusion that that's the

first mistake. This place is rotten to the core. Trying to make it better just gets the rotten on you."

"And you think that's what happened to Bianca?"

"And Bern and Liang." His smile was crooked and more than a little sad. "It's probably happening to you too, only you haven't noticed it yet."

"And what about Amerand Jireu?"

Orry sighed. "You need to be really careful around Amerand . . . did you know Liang's been helping him look for his mother for the last four years?"

"No." Something else I didn't know. *Misao had it so right. We went in on this one blind.* "Is she . . . a hostage?"

"Yes and no." Orry waggled his hand. "She and his father sold themselves into debt slavery to buy him his slot in the Security. This was after they risked everything to pull all three of their kids off Oblivion in the Breakout."

"So he's got more family?" I thought about Finn Jireu— thin, dried-out, and tough as leather despite his obsequious pardon-pardon.

"He *had* more family," Orry corrected me. "His oldest brother was killed in the riots that came after Oblivion's children landed on Dazzle. His younger brother was killed in the riots that came after Oblivion died. After that, his parents decided they had to get him somewhere safe, and the only safe place was the Security, and the only way in for an OB was to pay the fees, and the only way to pay the fees was peonage."

"Amerand told you all this?"

"Liang did. In bits and pieces over the years. Amerand's parents were swallowed into the peonage workforce. Eventually, he was able to find his father and get him swapped out by claiming him as a servant." We looked at each other, silently acknowledging the obscenity of that. "But his mother vanished. She might be farmed out on a diaspora world somewhere. Or not." Orry shrugged once more. "The point here is that if there's anyone who might be ready to do a personal takedown of the Blood Family, it's Amerand. He might just decide to push things if he thinks we're bringing about the end times."

Unfortunately, this squared very neatly with the Amerand I had seen: the young man who moved with a kind of forced poise. He was trained to violence, raised in a place where finding the right level of corruption was a survival trait. Had my half promises been the final straw? My throat tightened. They could have been.

"Would Amerand kill his Clerk?"

"If he thought the Clerk had hurt a friend or family, he might. Loyalties get very personal here. There's nothing else to trust but the person next to you or, better, the person who shares your blood."

My hand tightened around the cup. I thought about the dead I'd left behind on the ship. Wasted lives I'd had no time to mourn, blood I'd had no chance to come to terms with.

Then I thought about Emiliya Varus and her meeting with the Clerk. I thought again about the tangled chain of war and murder. It was not only loyalties that were personal here, it was command. There was nothing objective and very little exterior. Your power on Dazzle depended on whom you knew—and whom you frightened.

"Why are you still here, Orry?" I asked suddenly.

Orry stared at my empty bowl. "Because while I'm here to help, maybe one of those kids out there doesn't get sold into slavery."

I nodded. We just sat for a while, letting all that had been said settle down further. Then a new thought dropped like a pebble into the back of my mind.

"Orry," I said. "If Amerand Jireu is accused of murder, why haven't they picked up his father? His father is hostage to his good behavior, right? If Amerand does something wrong, his father gets punished too."

Orry stared at me. He opened his mouth. Then he closed it.

"I don't know. That should have been done as soon as the accusation went through."

"But it was his father who came to tell me Amerand was in custody." We stared at each other. "Something is very wrong here."

"And in a new way," said Orry, with something like wonder in his voice. "Congratulations, Terese. I didn't think it was possible."

There were a thousand things I should have been doing at that moment, but understanding was more urgent than anything else. I had to know why Kapa and Emiliya Varus and Amerand Jireu had all been tossed into my path. I had to find out which side Amerand was really on and what it meant that Emiliya Varus was on speaking terms with Grand Sentinel Torian. Until I understood that much, I would remain caught in that spinning wheel.

"Orry, I need a favor."

"What's that?"

"I need you to get a message to Finn Jireu for me."

He turned his head so he looked at me sideways. "What kind of message?"

"I need you to say that if anyone needs to talk to me for the next two hours, I'll be conducting an investigation of the place where Bianca Fayette was found. But you'll have to show me where it is." I hadn't even been able to do that much yet.

Orry narrowed his eyes. "All right. Bring that big-ass gun of yours and we'll go."

Five minutes later, with my weapon slung on my back, Orry and I went down into the street. The crowds were thin this morning. People watched us from doorways and alleys, but hurried about their business as soon as we caught them looking. The parakeets rose in lemon-lime flocks from the trash heaps and the snakes warmed themselves on the ledges.

I was able to walk with Orry around three corners, and across a bridge over a ragged gap where a tunnel roof had fallen in. We parted ways at the base of a huge stone tree. Orry turned left, and I kept straight on, going slow, trying to follow the landmarks he'd recited for me.

At last, I stopped by a subway entrance that was now no more than a circular hole in the street. The skeleton of a spiral staircase led down into the dark.

I paused, looking into that hole and steadying myself. I could feel Bianca's eyes on me, waiting with infinite patience as she could once she'd really hunkered down. When all that patience was directed at you, it could drive you faster and harder than the worst threat because you knew no matter what you did, she'd still be there when you were done, just where you'd left her. Waiting.

Naked struts juddered under my boots as I carefully climbed down. Stone muffled the noises from overhead but magnified the joints' rusted creaking. The smell was of stagnation. If the vents were functioning, they were clogged. It was hot and close and still. There was dust and fermenting waste somewhere, and a lot of feces. I choked once and coughed, telling myself to get over it, I'd smelled worse.

It worked, mostly.

Finally, my boots touched the floor again. Thick shadows and too many rustling sounds filled the tunnels, reminding me that the lost, the hidden, the rats—and whatever hunted them—all waited down here with me. Something big moved and I turned on my heel, bringing my gun around. Footsteps moved through the darkness, fleeing. I relaxed just a little and pushed my weapon back, but I flexed my hands in their armored gloves and my mind settled into its fighting stance.

The space under the stairs was black. A single grey beam of illumination shone from the top of the stairs like a spotlight. My back was on high alert, stiff and prickling. I shouldn't have done this. I should have picked a different meeting spot. I shouldn't have climbed down into Bianca's tomb alone.

But I wasn't alone. She was behind me. I could feel her breath. I could hear its echo in my own harsh breathing.

I adjusted my uniform cuffs and brought my right hand-light up so I could shine it into the space under the stairs.

The space was mostly bare stone. A little dirt had drifted into the corners, but not a lot of refuse. The residents of Dazzle scoured their home for any scrap that could be turned into something else and carried it away.

The stone was stained with age, maybe shit, maybe blood.

I switched off my light.

The darkness was immediate. My throat closed. My heart sped up. My breath rang in my ears, too loud and too hard. All at once, I was sweating bullets inside my gloves and under my armor. It was all too heavy, and yet I was too exposed. Darkness can see you. Darkness creeps under your skin and into your head. Daylight thinks it sees, but darkness knows. Darkness is what you carry in a hole in your head. It's already inside you, waiting to find that little crack, that break so it can leak into your brain and fill you up.

I didn't see anything. Of course I didn't. I hadn't expected to. I just wanted to be there, where they found her, to try to understand what she'd been *doing* here. That this was a probable blind spot in the Clerks' network where I could reasonably be expected to be spending time was a bonus. I could wait for Amerand here, and maybe at the same time find some lost last part of Bianca in myself. I could say the prayers and swear the oaths that I held dear and begin to come to terms with wasted blood and wasted life.

Then, in a flash, I saw Bianca lying at my feet. Rigor mortis had come and gone. She sagged, almost melted onto the stone. Her deformed head was twisted at an angle you never see on a living human, but it covered up the horrible wound over her right eye and allowed her cloudy left eye to stare up at me. Her arms were bare and bruised. Her flesh hung loose on her broken bones. Black blood crusted her lips and her fingers. If I lifted her head, if I touched her hand, it would be impossibly soft and horribly cold.

Then it was gone.

I knew what it was. It was a hallucination, dug up out of my black hole, tied in with my old training. I had come here wanting to see Bianca, and my tortured subconscious had provided a vision. If it was not the one I wanted, whom did I have to blame?

But the worst part was, seeing her so bitterly, terribly dead was still better than if I'd seen her whole and alive. I wanted her dead. I didn't want her alive. Alive now would have been so much worse.

"Field Commander?"

I jumped and spun, coming down in a ready crouch, my hand on the stock of my weapon to bring it around.

Amerand Jireu walked into the thin grey light that trickled down from above, his hands up and open.

Stunned and shaking with relief, I rushed forward and embraced him. Slowly, his hands closed across my back. For a heartbeat we stood like that, before I remembered that this was not a son, not a friend—not even a Solaran—and I stepped away.

It was then I realized he wasn't wearing his uniform—just a stained tunic and loose trousers, with old, well-worn boots.

"Are you all right?" I asked. In the back of my mind, I started working up the chain of requests it would take to get him off world.

"I don't know," Amerand whispered hoarsely. "They never took me in." He said it like a man who had witnessed a miracle, a terrible Old Testament sort of miracle.

"Why'd you send your father to say they had?"

"I was hoping you'd work out what it meant. I . . . Something's going on, Terese. I don't know what it is. But neither one of us should still be walking around free."

He told me what had happened, how he had witnessed his Clerk's suicide, what Hamahd had said, and how he had been warned to keep his mouth closed. He'd walked back to his station, expecting to be taken into custody at each step. But nothing had happened. Nothing at all.

"I wanted to make people think I'd been arrested." He spread his empty hands. "If I wasn't even questioned, everyone would wonder why. Everyone would believe I'd finally given over, crossed the lines. I'd be . . . shunned. My network would disintegrate. I wouldn't be any good to anyone. I wouldn't even be able to protect my father."

I nodded. *You couldn't look like you were connected to the Blood Family, which is the only comprehensible way you could be free after your Clerk died.*

"If I disappeared for a day or two, and just . . . came back. It would look like I'd been questioned and cleared. I think. I hope. My father's waiting for the Clerks to come to our house. If they don't in the next couple of hours, he's going to disappear for a little too . . ." He stared at me, genuinely afraid. "Hamahd said they were using me, Terese. To finish their new network. What the hell does that mean?"

"I don't know," I answered honestly. One more piece in the puzzle. One more piece and I couldn't see how any of them fit. "I wish I did."

"But it doesn't make *sense*." He whispered the words. A man who had lived his life being overheard wouldn't shout. "They know I'm running around loose. If they're using me, why haven't they even given me a new minder? Why haven't they come after me?"

"I don't know," I said again. "Unless . . ."

"Unless, what?"

"Unless we really are at the end of something. Unless whoever is running the game thinks you've been compromised by what Hamahd said, or that they can afford not to care about us." *Or unless you really are their spy.*

Or unless "they" just want us to think that. But if Amerand is spying for them, why would Dr. Varus be reporting on him? My stomach turned over. That's the problem with having an agent—you need another agent to check up on them.

Or is she just in trouble with the Clerks for murdering one of their own?

Unless they just want us to think that.

Paranoia is infectious. It's also an incredibly useful tool. If you can make people afraid enough, uncertain enough, they will simply stop moving.

I had thought the Erasmus *Saeos* had my cage waiting for me on Fortress. Perhaps I was mistaken. Perhaps they had built it for me right here. The triangle of Varus, Jireu, and Kapa had certainly managed to keep me thoroughly distracted since I got here. Look at me. I was here with him, worrying about what he was doing and what Dr. Varus was doing instead of what had been going on between Bianca and the Blood Family.

"He said to let you get me out of here," whispered Amerand.

That halted every thought careening through my mind. "Who did?"

"Hamahd, before he pulled away. He said to let the saints . . . let you get me out of here."

"Do you want me to?" *Say yes, Amerand. Just say it, and I can pull you out of here immediately. I can get you safe where they can't overhear you and we can find out what you really know.*

"What about my father?"

"Him too, if he asks." I touched Amerand's arm. He was far too young for all he had been through. "You don't have to stay here, Amerand. All you have to do is ask and I am required by the Common Cause Covenant to grant you asylum."

He looked at my hand on his sleeve, and I found I could not read his expression at all. "And my mother?"

I drew back. "I'll do everything I can to help find her."

Which was probably very close to what Liang had promised him four years ago. Amerand turned away from me, and faced the shadows. His fingertips rubbed together as if he were trying to scrape something off them.

"What about Emiliya?" he asked softly. "Her too? If she asks?"

Now it was my turn to hesitate. "There's something you need to hear."

I told him about finding Emiliya in her empty home, our "pointless" conversation, about how I followed her.

About how I saw her meet with a Clerk.

"No," he said flatly.

"I'm sorry, Amerand. I saw . . ."

"No," he said again, holding up his hand, blocking the words. "You may have seen a Clerk speak to her, but he did not *meet* with her."

"She went straight from talking with me, to . . ."

"No," he repeated. "I don't know what happened. Maybe the Clerks took her family in. They might be holding her people against her good behavior." He looked sick at the thought and like he wanted to bolt immediately.

"Then why didn't she go with the Clerk? Why didn't they take her in? She wouldn't have simply left if they were holding her mother . . ."

"I said, no!" His fists clenched, and for one sick moment, I thought he might actually raise one to me.

He seemed to think so too. He backed away. He turned, shaking, trying to catch his breath. He ran one hand through his tightly curled hair. When at last he turned back to me, he seemed unable to speak above a whisper.

"You don't know her. You don't know . . . Do you even know what happened to us? To Oblivion?"

I didn't understand where he was going with this, but I

was going to have to follow. "I know Oblivion died," I said carefully.

"It was left to die. Our punishment for rebelling. Our punishment for deciding we didn't want to be a prison anymore.

"When the system really started to fall apart, the prisoners began attacking the guards, more or less to see what would happen. I was five when I saw my first murder. It was a guard, and it was the first time I saw that they were human, that they could bleed. I cheered.

"After that, the guards started leaving, and we prisoners started helping them along. We even let some of them take whole ships."

He waited for me to be shocked. I wasn't. He was a child, a child of prison and violence, how could he not join in a rebellion? It was only human.

"We declared our independence. We thought . . . my parents thought that Fortress would need us. They needed us to work, to send out to work, to bring work in. That was what they had always used us for, after all. We could force them to negotiate.

"But they didn't. They were smarter than that. They said fine, you be independent, and they left us alone.

"At first, everyone was ecstatic. We were *free*. But pretty soon, things started to go wrong. You see, unlike Dazzle, Oblivion didn't grow enough food to support itself. The farm caverns were more for oxygen production than food production. They tried to get some kind of government together, some kind of rationing . . . but we'd been prisoners too long. Before long, it was all strong men and staking out territory, and when you drink up the water the plants don't grow, and when the plants don't grow . . ." He waved his hand at the air around us.

"My parents and some others saw it coming. They organized the Breakout. They ran for their lives, and they left Oblivion behind."

"And they came to Dazzle, and no one wanted them here, and they had to take what they needed," I finished it for him.

"Which made Dazzle open itself back up to Fortress, which it had shoved out much more successfully than we had. They had the advantage of starting out with a working economy and a city actually designed for people to live and communicate comfortably in.

"And while we were forced back down into submission here, Oblivion died. Fortress didn't have to do anything. They just had to leave it alone. No water, no plants. No plants, no air."

Amerand flexed his hands. "So we do what it takes to stay alive. We bow and we scrape and we sell off our children just like Baby Ds do, but we do *not* give each other over to the Blood Family or their Clerks. No matter what. We are the last of Oblivion's children. We do not forget how the lights went out."

He needed to believe it. The alternative was too painful.

Oh, Amerand, I am so sorry.

"They're using me," he said. "I don't know what for, but I can't just run away into the shadows, or even into asylum. How do I ever come back if I run away now?"

I'm the last person in the universe who can answer that question, Amerand.

"It's up to you," I said.

He nodded, and he straightened, his military bearing coming back into play despite his worn civilian clothes. "I'm going to come back and take up my station with you tomorrow. I am going to wait and watch to see who notices and what they do."

I nodded. "Good plan." In fact, if he was going to stay, it was the only one. "Now, listen to me very carefully, Amerand. I want us to be clear. Did you mean what you said before? That you want to help us?"

He nodded slowly; his gaze did not flicker.

"I need a way into the Security's network," I said. "I need a way into whatever archives there are about movement permits, and I need records from the 'scopes." *And if they're using you to work over the system in some way, I need your identity to check it out.*

Amerand shook his head. "We only have records going six months back, and I don't have access to all of those. The Clerks have the whole picture if anyone does."

"It doesn't matter. Even a slice will help."

He pursed his lips, hesitating. Then he said, "Can you take down a code?"

I activated the screen on the back of my glove. "Go."

Amerand gave out several long strings of letters and numbers. I tapped them in, encrypted them, and stored them.

There's one more thing I need from you, Amerand.

Slowly, I pulled off my glove. I stepped up to him and laid my naked right hand against his temple. It was an intimate gesture, suitable for lovers. His eyes were wide and deep and painfully young. His skin was warm under my palm, and I could feel the scrape of his sprouting whiskers. Slowly, I felt an unwelcome but real tide of yearning rise in me.

"Look out for yourself," I said. "If it gets out of control, come to us. We will help you, I swear it."

Hope shone in Amerand's eyes, coming out of a sorrow so deep I couldn't see the bottom of it. "Thank you," he whispered, and he turned away and took off running, lightly, swiftly down the tunnel into the dark. Carrying my spot camera right beneath his hairline.

I stood and watched until I couldn't tell him from the other shadows.

TWENTY-SIX

TORIAN

Torian sat behind a curving table in his clean, efficiently appointed, private-passenger cabin. He stared angrily at the active pane in front of him. Through it, he glowered at a man in a Clerk's coat, his ruddy complexion gone pale with fear and guilt.

Good. Torian's skin burned red with the effort of his concentration.

The man had almost ruined more things than even Torian could easily name. This did nothing for his temper.

"How was this permitted to happen, Master Kane?" demanded Torian. *You know what you did. You know the damage you nearly caused. You feel it.* Perspiration rolled heavily down Torian's face and the side of his neck still burned despite the recent adjustment to his modifications.

The Master Clerk, Hagen Kane, bowed and trembled. For a moment, Torian thought Kane would drop to his knees. He almost hoped it would happen. It would show how well the emotive aspects of the new network functioned and how fully the Master Clerk accepted them as his own.

"I don't know, Sentinel," Kane whispered. "Hamahd had been received into the network. The commands were introduced. There should not have been a disconnect."

He should have brought Kane to Dazzle. He should have brought him close enough to synch up the network fully. He never should have let Kane out of his range.

"You permitted Hamahd to return to duty before he was fully accepting," Torian said flatly.

"No, Sentinel!" cried the Clerk, aghast. "He gave all the proper responses."

"Then he lied to you."

A visible shudder of revulsion ran through the Clerk. "That is not possible."

"It is one or the other, Master." Torian's eyes narrowed. *Which will you decide is worse?*

Kane's face fell into abject misery. "I don't know, Sentinel." Tears shimmered in his eyes.

Torian regarded the Master Clerk. Except for Torian himself, Kane had been the final overseer of all the Clerks in the system. Before he had accepted the network, he had been a cold, calculating man and Torian had respected his steady professionalism. That was why he had wanted Kane as the linchpin of the network. But now Torian watched the uncontrolled fear and guilt possess the dedicated and previously rational man, even without the full synchronization.

It can be fine-tuned, Torian reminded himself firmly. *We will have time to get the balance right after the move.*

But at this time, a heavy hand was advisable. Torian leaned closer to the screen.

"I have offered you survival, Master Clerk," Torian said softly, with a note of regret in his voice. "Neither Moontwo nor Moonfour will last long once we withdraw, but your people will not even last long enough to see the lights go out."

"I know, Sentinel." Kane hunched his shoulders miserably. "But we are having to move so quickly . . ."

"If you cannot safely receive all your people into the network, then you will have to become selective."

Slowly, Kane lifted his horrified gaze. Slowly, he shook his head. "Do not ask that of me."

"I am not asking anything I am not prepared to do myself," Torian told him grimly. "Do you know how many of my blood, my *blood*, Master Clerk, not just colleagues, I am sacrificing?"

The Master Clerk bowed, his hands clutched tightly at his breast. "I hear, I hear."

"Yes, you do. I know." Torian let his voice soften, though he felt anything but sympathetic. *Bloom would be so proud of me.*

Kane did not straighten. A tear dropped down onto the shining floor. "I will do as I must," said the Clerk.

"Good." Torian nodded. "Take heart, then."

"Yes, Sentinel." The Clerk did not raise his eyes. "Thank you."

Torian touched the active pane and let it go dark. He was certain Kane would do as he promised, but this had only advanced the timetable. Any delay meant that the Clerks who remained outside the network might come to realize there were now haves and have-nots, or, more accurately, survivors and victims.

Torian sat where he was, and for a long moment he simply let himself be exhausted. *This has to be finished soon.* He could not keep on much longer. Even he had his limits. He'd come dangerously close to a mistake when he trusted Kane to assemble the second tier of the network. Fortunately, it was Amerand Jireu's Clerk who had failed to integrate. Amerand was now so firmly attached to the machinations of the Solarans that he would be thoroughly blinkered, both by the Solarans' worldview and his own desire for revenge.

Was it a coincidence that it was Hamahd who had failed to accept? Or was he affected by too much proximity to a rebellious individual like Amerand? That was something he would need to examine. A network built upon the human mind was sensitive to emotional and environmental influence. Details such as this were important, at least until the whole net was connected and stabilized.

Torian rubbed his eyes. It was almost time for launch and he needed to complete his interview with Emiliya Varus before then. That idea only weighed him down further.

Perhaps we don't need her. Perhaps it's only an additional risk.

No. Torian scrubbed his whole face, trying to recover his rational detachment. Now was not the time to reevaluate the plan. He was too tired and his head ached too badly. It was too close to the end. If he started changing his mind, he would never stop.

He pictured the infant, Indun, in Mai's arms. He saw her red newborn face and her rosy little hands. *I've built you a whole world, Indun, for you and your siblings. I will not fail to deliver. Not this time.*

But he longed to sit still, if only for a moment. He never thought he would come to regret the distributed system that he had helped develop for Erasmus, but the extended hours of travel from moon to moon were more wearying than any other aspect of the long plan.

Torian shoved his self-pity firmly aside and leaned back in his chair. He pressed his fingertips together to trigger the proper level of concentration.

Bring me Emiliya Varus. Torian shaped the words clearly inside his mind.

A sensation of presence came over him, of some other entity just out of sight. "As required," it said, and was gone.

By the time Emiliya arrived at his cabin, Torian had eaten a small meal of tea and samosas. He washed his face with real water and checked the latest genetic scans of the new children. The news was all good, and he felt distinctly refreshed.

Emiliya did not look half so well. The strains of the past few days were telling on her. Her hair trailed loose around her shoulders and, unpardonably in a doctor, her ragged fingernails were dirty. She bowed low and correctly before him, and Torian allowed himself a moment of empathy. *I also know what it's like to feel at the end of your resources.*

Torian gestured toward one of the cabin's comfortable chairs. Emiliya accepted with the air of someone who had no choice.

"How can I help you, Grand Sentinel?" she asked.

"I am going to make you an offer, Emiliya."

She looked down at her dirty fingertips. "Another one?"

"I did not make you any offer last time," he reminded her, trying to do it gently. "You were the one who came to me."

She twisted her hands together.

"It was not something I'd forget," he continued. "You came because your family meant more to you than your own freedom. That is a great thing indeed. It impressed me very much. As did your actions throughout the whole of your assignment." He had paid close attention during her last interrogation. It was true she did not inform them of Amerand Jireu's betrayal. However, taken in the balance with all her other actions, that was a minor blot and easily correctable with the proper level of networking.

She looked up at him. "I should say thank you, Sentinel, but I am falling short on courtesy."

He nodded briefly. "I understand. It has been a difficult time, but you have been strong and you have persevered."

She licked her chapped lips. Courage, coming from his compliments, or from her own feeling of having reached the end, made her speak. "Where is my mother?"

"Gone to the black sky, and your siblings with her," he said. "Their fate is in their own hands now."

Emiliya swallowed. Wary hope flickered across her features. "And you have an offer for me?"

"A share of what the Family is so jealously guarding from the Pax Solaris."

Emiliya's face went absolutely still for a long moment. Torian recognized the behavior. It was the natural consequence of living an observed life. She did not want him to see what she was thinking.

"Are you going to tell me what it is?" asked Emiliya at last.

"Immortality."

Emiliya looked away, the first quick movement she'd made since she entered the cabin. "The Solarans already have immortality. They've had it for centuries."

Torian dismissed this with a wave. "I am not talking about their chained, restricted immortality that has to be so painfully renewed every twenty years and relicensed every hundred. I am talking about genuine immortality. One treatment, one set of genetic switches inserted, another few reset, and it is done. It is yours, and your children's as well."

"That is not possible."

"It has already been done." Her eyes widened. "Mai. Shora. Tamarra. Effes. They have already gone through the process."

He watched her turn the names over in her mind, and

assign the titles to them. *Saeo* Mai, Grand Matron Tamarra, Master Treasurer Effes. The highest-ranked women of the Blood Family. All of whom . . .

"They all gave birth recently."

"Yes." Torian did not fight the smile spreading across his face. "And their children have all the necessary genetic markers, inherited from both mother and father. Those genes are dormant at the moment, of course, but they will begin to switch over with adolescence." He leaned forward. "Think on it, Emiliya: Death and time are gone from us."

"Forgive me, Grand Sentinel, but why should I care that the Blood Family are to become immortal?"

"Because you are one of us."

Emiliya blinked. "What?"

He sighed and attempted to remain charitable. She was having to absorb a lot of new information, and in some ways, what came next would be the most shocking. "Who is your father?"

"Nikko Donnelly," she answered promptly.

"Nikko Plaice *Erasmus* Donnelly," Torian corrected her. "He was a supervisor on Oblivion, once upon a time, but lost his discretion to a very young, very beautiful woman who was there finishing her own mother's sentence for murder-for-profit.

"We do not like bastards, Emiliya. Too many of them salted around is dangerous to the cohesion of the Blood Family. Your father was duly exiled for his crime. He has begun his atonement, however, and may in time be permitted to return to the family ranks—although, I should warn you, he will never rise very high.

"Through Nikko Plaice Erasmus Donnelly, you are

Blooded, and your mother knew it, although it now seems she never told you."

Emiliya stared at him for a long time, her expression surprisingly transparent. He could see her thoughts darting back and forth. Years of memories were rearranging inside her, fragments that made no sense before dropped into place as understanding crystallized.

"Is that why I was allowed into the Medical?" she asked.

"In part. It was my decision. I wanted to be able to keep an eye on you, to see which loyalties had come out most strongly in your character."

"You wanted to see if I would make a good dupe," she snapped, and instantly pressed her white-knuckled hand against her mouth.

"And if that was all you had proved to be, that would have been how I used you," Torian replied calmly. "But you have turned out to be much more than that. You carried out your mission in the face of physical and emotional conflict. You held tight to family loyalty over loyalty to friends and lovers. This is strength the Family will need in the days to come."

Emiliya pushed back a strand of hair that had drifted over her forehead. She looked directly at him, a hard stare that she clearly hoped would go right through him. Torian did not blink but let her look her fill.

"Why?" she asked. "Why me?"

This was the one question Torian had been certain she would ask. "I love my family, Emiliya. I love what is to come for them, but we must see to our next founding very, very carefully." *We have made too many mistakes over the years, and I let them happen. I let Jasper and Felice begin this ridiculous system of slavery and peonage. I should have argued harder. So much waste.*

I should have made them see . . . "We must provide in all ways possible for our future and this includes providing for our own balance, most especially in terms of genetics." *I wish I could apologize to your father. I truly did not realize that our by-blows would become such a valuable resource.*

"I turned on my colleagues," Emiliya murmured, her hands twisting back and forth as if she wished she could pull off her own fingers. "What if I turn on you? I could go to the saints, tell them you're going to make the Family immortal."

Torian spread his hands. "And what are they going to do? Kill us? Sterilize or destroy the children who have done nothing but be born? Even if they have the strength left after we are finished with them, undoing us is against their own laws."

"Even if they have the strength left?" she repeated.

"Solaris is only a minor consideration at this point, and that is thanks to you."

Stillness again. Torian shifted in his chair. She must understand the implications by now. It was time for her to make her decision.

"I want proof," she blurted the words out.

"Proof?"

"That you've done what you say." Her voice hardened, showing some authority for the first time since she entered the cabin. "You lie a great deal, Grand Sentinel. You might be lying now."

Torian pursed his mouth, acknowledging the justice of this remark. "I might, it's true. It happens I'm not. However, I will give you access to my personal system. You can spend the rest of the flight perusing the information at your leisure."

"No. I'll do it back on Hospital."

"Why?"

"Because you could have a whole fake data set here. It will be harder to fake it on Hospital when I can make cross-references under my own clearances."

"Harder, but not impossible," he pointed out.

Emiliya shrugged. "At least I'll have a fighting chance."

"Very good," said Torian, and he meant it. He got to his feet. "I am glad I decided to bring you in, Dr. Varus. You have a great deal to contribute to the future of your family." He bowed.

Emiliya remained straight-backed and expressionless. She believed what he told her, Torian was certain of that, but she did not yet know what to think of it. Impatience welled up, but he reminded himself she had not been raised to expect beneficence or miracles. He'd like to give her more time, but there was none. She must either accept or be discarded with the rest.

"You chose Kapa on purpose, didn't you?" she asked softly.

"But not his ending. For that, I am sorry." The ship was found in pieces. It seemed that the corruption Donnelly had worked on the code had been too much, and when the engine compartment separated from the rest of the modules, the hatches had failed to close properly. It was a shame. Kapa Lu *had* been a useful dupe and distraction.

"I see." Emiliya glanced down at her hands, walked to the door, turned, and bowed deeply. Torian accepted the gesture and remained standing as she cranked open the door and closed it behind herself.

Welcome, Emiliya, he said silently. *Welcome her to our eternity.*

"Welcome, Emiliya," the voices responded. "We will welcome her to our eternity."

His eyes unfocused from the room in front of him and he watched Emiliya Varus from a dozen different angles as she walked through the ship's compartments, and all the Clerks bowed before her.

TWENTY-SEVEN

AMERAND

I ran away from Terese. I ran until my lungs burned and my guts ached. I ran into the dark, until I had to stop and lean against the tunnel wall, to catch my breath and find my bearings.

How could she call Emiliya a traitor? How did she *dare*! I'd offered to help her. I'd risked everything for her! And she came back at me with this.

It was not true. It could not be true. The whole world might crack apart, the Clerks might sprout parakeet wings and fly, but Emiliya would not betray me to the Clerks.

Field Commander Drajeske did not know half of what was going on.

I ground the heel of my hand into my side, trying to ease the cramp. It was my fault. Mine. I had not been paying enough attention. I had seen Emiliya working with the Blood Family, and I hadn't even stopped to think it might be because they had her family. I was an ass. An idiot. How could I have not thought of it?

Because I was too busy thinking about Kapa and Emiliya.

She thought I didn't know, but I did. I knew she was waiting for him to come back. I'd known for years. That was the real reason we had never come together. That and because we were too afraid. I was too afraid.

I had to get to her. There had to be something I could do. Even if there wasn't, I couldn't let her think I'd abandoned her, or worse, have her think I had turned on her.

But what if I just made things worse for her?

They're using you. Hamahd's voice grated in my memory. *They're using you to finish the new system.*

Using me? How in all the hells ever imagined could the Blood Family or their Clerks be using *me*? I was nothing. I was nobody. A secops captain, I barely rated my own Clerk. I didn't make trouble. I didn't want anything except my parents back. What did they want with me?

I didn't know yet. I'd find out. I would. I was onto them now. They'd trained me to watch and to listen and to find things that were hidden. Maybe not with all those drills and obedience vids at the academy, but with the surveillance that was as much a part of our lives as breathing.

I would find Emiliya. I had to go back to her. I couldn't let her think when it came down to it that I was like Kapa.

It took me hours to find her. Any other day, I would have tapped into the Security's system, or simply asked the people on watch around the port yard and similar posts. But I was supposed to be in custody. I couldn't be seen, so I had to walk the streets like just another OB trying to get through the day.

The OBs existed on sufferance in clusters here and there. They generally took one of two routes to survival: Either they kept their heads down, working with and for each other and such Dazzle natives as would tolerate them, or they mobbed up to take what they could. I started my search near the port yard, gradually slouching down to the base streets, keeping to the fringes and the edges, looking, I hoped, like someone you didn't need to pay attention to.

I almost didn't see her in the back of an OB shop, bargaining hard with an angular woman for a bunch of small, sour green grapes.

Cautiously, keeping near the front door, I stepped into Emiliya's field of vision. The movement caught her eye, and she looked up. She went white and the bunch of grapes fell from her hand back onto the pile of battered fruits. Without a word, she turned away, striding out the back door.

I dodged out the front and around the corner. I knew where she was going, and I caught up with her just as she reached the threshold to the interior staircase.

She must have heard my footsteps coming up behind her but didn't stop until I reached out to touch her shoulder.

"Emiliya."

She didn't turn. She just jerked her shoulder out of my hand. The reminder of Hamahd's hand jerking out of my grasp was almost too much to stand, but it wasn't as hard as her words.

"Get away from me."

My jaw dropped, but I rallied. I had to. "No. Listen to me. Please."

"I can't." She turned her head, just a little, just enough for me to see the desperation shining in one dark-ringed eye. "They're paying attention to me. Get away."

I took her hands. Her nails were dirty. Emiliya was a doctor. She never let her nails get dirty. If I needed a sign that they'd taken her family, this was it. Nothing else could hit her this hard. "Emiliya, I've got a way out for you."

"What?"

"The Solarans. I've spoken with Terese. They'll take you out of here if you ask them to."

She stared at me, then she laughed, a harsh, terrible sound. "You want *me* to go to the Solarans."

I didn't know what to do. I'd known she would be on the edge, but I didn't expect her to be this far gone. "Yes," I said softly. "Emiliya, now's your chance. I'm telling you. We can both pull our families out." *Tell me what's happened, Emiliya. Tell me they've taken your people. I'll help. I swear, I swear, but you've got to talk to me.*

She stared, letting the weight of my statement sink slowly through her. I was hoping to see that her heart swelled, that she felt some measure of the hope I did.

But Emiliya remained closed, dark. Dead. "I can't go to the Solarans, Amerand."

"Why?"

She just shook her head. "It's too late."

"Why?" I wanted her to admit it. I wanted us for once to speak openly to each other. I wanted that sign of how much things had already changed.

But she didn't. She just hung her head. "What do you care? You're not here because of me. You're here because of the Field Commander." She spat the last words.

Unwelcome understanding came over me. "Emiliya, are you *jealous*?"

"Are you *deluded*?" Her pale face flushed crimson. "You help a couple of saints get away from a fuckless crew of smugglers and suddenly you think they can save our worthless asses and you think I don't want to get in on it with you because I'm *jealous*! Get your head out of it, Amerand! This is not about you! Maybe your parents gave everything for you, but the rest of us are out for ourselves. Nothing changes for us! There is no way out and there's never going to be!"

And she started down the stairs, at speed. She didn't look back and she didn't look up, and I stood there and watched her go.

I knew I should follow her. I should tell her she was right. The saints would flail about like they always did, and they'd go home, like they always did, and someone would replace Terese Drajeske, and Emiliya and I would still be here, and so would the Blood Family.

But I couldn't do it.

I couldn't retreat. I had tasted hope. I had seen not only honest action but the fiery joy in it. It was freedom. It was what my parents had been searching for all their lives. It was what my brothers both died trying to hold on to. I was not going to lock myself back in my cage again.

But I also wouldn't leave Emiliya alone in here. I would do for her what I had failed to do for myself. I would find her mother. When her family was safe under the Solarans' asylum, she could go with them.

I will get you out of here, I swore to the place where she had stood. *If I do nothing else right, I will do this.*

TWENTY-EIGHT

TERESE

One of the great advantages of a fragmented network is that it becomes extremely difficult to reach people who do not want to be reached. I was in no doubt that this was done on purpose.

The luncheon with the "citizens council" was beyond pointless. They were nothing but a group of city nobility hinting genteelly at all the things I could do to help bring their city back to its fallen glory. I smiled. I nodded in sympathy. I ate the excellent food served to me by men and women whose hands were so fragile I was surprised they didn't break under the weight of the plates.

The only reason I had come at all was that the Grand Sentinel was also supposed to be there. But shortly after I arrived, I was informed he had returned to Fortress to celebrate the birth of the latest members of the Blood Family. I was told he expressed his regrets and that he had left word that he looked forward to talking to me when I came to Fortress.

This might even have been true. I'd spent the last twelve hours poring over the records Amerand had gotten me access to, and I'd learned a great deal. Movement was so tightly controlled here that it was a mark of power. The Grand Sentinel's ships came and went with a frequency unmatched by anyone else in the system. At the same time, I had the feeling there were gaps, big ones, as if the records were tampered with. I shot everything I had to our ships at the habitat, tagged for relay to Misao and the other analysts on the team. I could feel the patterns there, but I couldn't see them. There was too much else clamoring for my attention.

Like the feeling that the Grand Sentinel did not give a damn about me, and by extension, the Guardians of the Pax Solaris.

When I was finally able to make my final bow to the showboat citizens council, I picked my way across the rooftops, past the gardens, the fences, and the secops to Up-sky Station. If I couldn't question one of the major power players on Dazzle, I'd have to settle for his second. I had no intention of going to Fortress any sooner than I had to.

Reesethree shone down on me as I ducked beneath the reinforced dome of the foyer and into the heart of the Security outpost, finding a Clerk on reception duty.

"Field Commander Terese Drajeske to see Commander Favor Barclay." The Grand Sentinel might have perpetual privileges for flying between the moons, but Barclay was bound to Dazzle, at least according to the records I'd seen.

The Clerk's eyes gleamed and he opened his mouth, but I held up my hand. "If he is not here, tell me where he is, and give me specific directions on how to reach him."

It's like dealing with an avatar, I thought exasperatedly. But it worked. "He is at his home," the Clerk told me, and he did in fact give me the directions I needed.

I bowed politely. The Clerk did not.

I turned to head for the door, when it struck me something was missing. I laid my hand on the knob and glanced left, then right. Clerks moved back and forth, attending to their business in their large open workspace.

But I didn't see any other uniforms. I was in a Security station with no secops in it.

I almost turned around, but didn't. There was no reason

a Clerk would tell me the truth. If something had happened to this piece of the power structure, I was much more likely to get an answer from Favor Barclay.

Favor Barclay's home was a flat that could only be entered from the walled rooftop garden. Uniformed secops at the door confirmed my ID code and let me in. The stairs were broad and clean. The light was good enough that the series of potted trees on the landings and lining the corridor was lush and verdant. I passed a young woman trimming branches, a baby in a sling on her back.

Favor Barclay stood at his door, waiting for me. He had dark rings under his bloodshot eyes, and his cheeks were sunken in. Everything I thought I had been coming to learn flew straight out of my head.

"Please, Commander." He bowed and stood back, gesturing for me to enter.

The rooms beyond were spacious, and the first place I had seen on Dazzle where the decorations were intact. Plasterwork rosettes surrounded the bright chandeliers. Gilt trimmed the picture rails and the floorboards. The faux-wood floor was an excellent imitation of the real thing and might even have been artisan-pressed. The furniture was the elegant polished stone and inlaid metal that Dazzle craftwork produced.

"You must forgive me, Field Commander," Barclay said, ushering me into the sitting room. He was wearing civilian clothes rather than his uniform, and they were rumpled. "I am the only one here to make you welcome. My wife and the children are . . . not home." He picked up a red-and-orange stoneware jug and poured liquid into a matching cup, handing it to me.

The fumes hit me as I raised the cup. This wasn't the traditional gift of water. It was moonshine whiskey. I eyed Barclay over the rim. "Has something happened, Commander?"

He did not look at me. "Yes. Yes, it has."

I set the cup down without drinking. "Is there anything I can do?"

"No, thank you. It's my problem. My fault, actually." He wiped his palms against his black trousers. "But I expect you did not come here to find out about my troubles."

"No," I said softly. *What have you done?* "I am trying to find out what's happened to Captain Amerand Jireu." The fact that I knew was immaterial. If I didn't look for him, it would seem strange. After all, if I was an honest actor, I would want to be working with my assigned liaison.

"I don't know," said Barclay.

I raised my eyebrows. "I find that surprising."

"Yes, I rather imagine you do." Then he added very softly, "You've never been in a situation where it was better not to see what is going on around you."

"Will I be assigned a new liaison, then?" I asked, pretending not to hear.

"I imagine that will be taken care of." He continued to stare at his fingers where they rested on the tabletop. The look he gave me was supposed to be one of sympathy—as one person caught in the bureaucracy to another—but it was far too hollow-eyed to achieve its intended effect.

"Where's your family, Favor?" I asked.

The corner of his mouth twitched, and he lifted his head. "Shall I tell you a secret, Field Commander?"

"If you want."

He leaned close in a cold parody of intimacy. I smelled the sour moonshine on his breath. "The Security is currently undergoing a reorganization. It happens now and again. Especially when the water smugglers pull off a coup."

"And *have* the smugglers pulled off a coup?"

He lifted his cup. "Your near kidnapping."

It made sense. I didn't believe a word of it.

"You may have noticed we have been removed from Upsky Station," he went on. "We are being redistributed about the city as we are cleared of corruption charges."

"And have you been cleared?" I asked.

He shrugged. "Why else would I be able to speak so freely?" He gestured around him, and I saw what else wasn't there. There was no Clerk.

Another man with no minder. Another piece that had become irrelevant in the power play. He knew it too. This was the reason for his despair.

This was bad. This was very bad. But it did mean I could be direct.

"Tell me who Amerand Jireu is, Commander Barclay," I said. "Tell me why the Clerks are using him."

Barclay's hand jerked back, and the cup dropped toward the floor, spilling out its contents in thick, sparkling arcs. I swooped my hand out and caught the cup before it hit the floor.

"Thank you," he murmured as I handed the cup back to him. His hand shook as he set it down. Stone rattled against stone.

"I am sorry, Field Commander," he said. "There's nothing I can do for you until I have been confirmed in my new position. Whatever it is to be," he said bleakly to the tabletop.

"I see," I said out loud. "Can I ask one more question?"

"If you must." He made a small gesture with his hand.

"Why are you still here?"

Barclay stood very still for a moment, but I could tell he was taking a second look at me and making a decision.

He poured a fresh measure of whiskey into his stoneware cup and shot it down with a shudder.

"I needed to be able to cover my own family's retreat, just in case," he said.

I nodded as if I understood. "Thank you."

I bowed to him and he bowed to me. He walked me to the door and closed it behind me. As I walked back up the corridor, past the woman and her baby, the snip-snip of her handmade scissors made a counterpoint to the clack of my bootheels on the floor.

I made my way back through the city without remembering much of what I passed. I was too far inside myself.

I arrived back at the Common Cause house as the lights were sputtering their way toward twilight. The courtyard was empty except for the birds and the snakes, and one hopeful, mangy cat. Even sunk in my own increasingly frustrated thoughts as I was, I couldn't miss the sight of the tall, scarred man slouched next to the main doors.

I was so startled, I stopped and stared, forgetting to dissemble. Fortunately, Vijay didn't. He straightened up.

"I know, I know," he sneered. "I've got it coming. Are we going to do this in the street, or you wanna keep our business private?"

In keeping with his thug persona, he didn't wait for my answer, just shoved his hands in his pockets and storkwalked through the door on his long legs.

I followed, mouth agape. He was not supposed to be here. We were not supposed to have any contact at all. Vijay paused at the foot of the stairs and gave me a snide, quizzical look.

There were only two private rooms in the place: Liang's office and Siri's listening room. I opted for Siri's room and strode inside. Fortunately, she wasn't there. She'd said she'd set up a meet with some engineers to try to get a team together to work on the lights. I didn't want to have to dress Vijay down in front of her.

I slammed the door shut and shot the bolt home.

"What are you doing here!" I demanded.

The thug mannerisms vanished, and I was facing Vijay Kochinski. The scars, the bald head, and the skin color ceased to matter. I recognized his stance, his eyes, his voice.

"Something's wrong with Siri," he said.

I swallowed my first plan, which was to chew him out, then write him up for breach of protocol. With everything that was going on, I couldn't blame him for being as close to the edge as I was. "She's wound pretty tight . . ."

"Pretty tight!" he cried. "Are you blind?"

"Watch your mouth, Captain," I snapped.

His shoulders jerked to attention. "I'm sorry, Field Commander. I'm sorry. I'm just . . . something's really gone wrong with Siri."

A cold knot settled into the bottom of my stomach. "Tell me."

I listened as Vijay described what Siri had told him—and how badly she'd tried to make a joke of it—how he'd followed her, just to make sure she was all right, and watched her walk down into the space under the stairs.

Abruptly I remembered how I had gone down there and heard someone run from me. Could that have been Siri?

The knot tightened. This was not possible. It couldn't be what it seemed. Siri could not be losing her mind.

"I know what you're thinking," he said. "Her Companion should be keeping her balanced, right?"

I nodded.

"Took's been reminding me of that at least twice an hour since the meet, but I'm telling you, I know when she's being serious, and she was dead-cold serious—at least until she tried to tell me it was a joke."

"So, what are you thinking?"

He gestured helplessly. "Is it possible something's gone wrong with the balance between her and Shawn? Like, I don't know, some local infection that's gotten in and is changing her responses to her Companion?"

The Companion balance was a sturdy thing, but it did respond to its environment, just like the rest of the brain architecture. I thought about the particolored funguses around us, and the badly ventilated air full of spores and dust. Dr. Gwin had said one of their main health problems was a local variant of hantavirus spread by the mice and the rats. Who knew what else we were all breathing in? There might even have been some damage from the head injury Siri took.

"I've never heard of anything like that. I suppose it's possible . . ."

The bolt rattled, and slid open. We turned together in time to see Siri open the door and walk in. She looked from Vijay to me, to Vijay again.

"What's going on?" she asked.

I decided to be straight with her. I'd had enough of being forced into contortions by Erasmus.

"Vijay was telling me about your last meet."

Whatever I had been expecting, it was not for Siri to sigh impatiently and whack Vijay on the arm.

"You idiot! I *told* you! That was for the Clerks."

Vijay stared and she sighed again. "I do *not* believe this," she said to me. "So I'm trying to make the Clerks think I'm buying the shine-and-shoot Natio Bloom is selling, and this one." She shoved her palm against Vijay's chest. "This one believes me and compromises every procedure in the book to come running to you. What has this place done to you?" she said to him, real anger heating her voice. "Huh? What?"

"Look, Siri . . ." began Vijay.

She didn't let him get any further. "Did you even get around to telling her the important part? That you've got a berth on a smuggling ship and it's heading out to the habitats?"

Now it was my turn to be surprised. "You do?"

"Yes," Vijay said to me, but his attention was on Siri.

"When do you go?"

Vijay's jaw worked itself back and forth. His scars stood out ghostly white against his darkened skin. "Tomorrow. First thing."

I nodded. "Okay, then. You'd better get yourself out of here. We don't want your new employers to think this was anything but a dressing-down."

"No. I guess not." He turned around, his shoulders slumped, not in his thug walk, but in defeat.

"Vijay?"

He turned back toward me.

"Take care of yourself, okay?" *I've heard you,* I tried to tell him. *Believe me, I did hear you.*

"Yes'm." His shoulders straightened minutely, and I knew I'd gotten through.

He paused next to Siri. She looked up at him and smacked his arm again. "Get!" she said. "Go on!"

And he went. He walked out the door, hauling it shut behind him. The thud reverberated through the room.

Siri sighed and shrugged. "What're you gonna do? Clearly, my acting skills have improved." She dropped into her lopsided chair and pulled her glasses out of her pocket. "Was there something else, Field Commander?"

"No," I said. "I've just got to do the rounds and try to get this investigation onto some kind of coherent track."

"Good luck." She waved at me with one hand and slid her glasses into place with the other.

I watched her as she plugged in and slid into her own world. I left, and hard as it was, I closed the door tightly behind me. I kept on walking, down the stairs and out the lobby.

Orry, his timing perfect as ever, was there to meet me, leaning against the banister at the bottom of the stairs.

The paranoia that had been lurking just beneath the surface of my thoughts rose in a mighty wave. I strode up to my friend and looked him right in the eye.

"So," I said. "Is Liang asking you to keep watch on me, or is it your own idea?"

Orry opened his mouth, closed it as he considered lying to me, and changed his mind.

"I told him I wasn't very good at this." He smiled sadly. "Sorry."

I ran my hand through my hair. "It's all right." I couldn't decide whom to trust, why should Liang be doing any better? I needed to move, I needed to get out of there. I needed to be able to pretend I was out of doors, away from doors. I needed to find some way to think straight and I didn't know how. "Since you're keeping an eye on things, keep an eye on Siri for me, will you? If she tries to go anywhere, tell her I asked for her to wait. We need to go back over some of the old reports."

"Will do," said Orry, and I all but ran out of the lobby.

I was four of Dazzle's haphazard blocks away and three levels up when I ran out of steam and slumped against the wall. Dark was falling. Reesethree was just a burnished sliver at the edge of a patch of black sky far above.

My head was so full I couldn't shift a single one of my thoughts. I stood there and watched the people of Dazzle pass by me.

There were too many threads. I couldn't hold on to them all.

I had come here to work out if and how the descendants of Jasper and Felice Erasmus might be using the old jump gates as a means of attack on the Pax Solaris. I had come expecting to find that Bianca Fayette's death was connected to her discovery that Erasmus was a hot spot.

Now I knew Bianca had decided to single-handedly take Erasmus apart. Why? What had driven her to it? It was bad here. It was foul. But we'd seen worse. All right, we'd seen at least as bad. What had driven her over the edge? Bern said he didn't know. If Liang knew, he wasn't interested in telling me.

She had been hanging out with smugglers. Was that because she was going to use them to take the place down or because she wanted to know about the runs to Oblivion and the habitats? Had she been trying to find the war or arrange the takedown, or both?

She'd said nothing at all about her time with the Grand Sentinel. Any mention of Torian was missing from the tattered remains of Jerimiah's memory.

In the meantime, someone had risked a hell of a lot to arrange for me and Siri to be kidnapped. I'd gotten the briefing in the last burst from Misao. Kapa Lu's employer, or at least his contact, was Nikko Donnelly, a disgraced member of the Blood Family. Had Donnelly meant to hand us over to the Blood Family? What for? What could he hope to gain by risking open hostilities with the Pax Solaris?

Donnelly, Misao said, was commander of Habitat 3. Vijay's smuggling run was supposedly out to the habitats. Was Donnelly involved with the smugglers? Was he trying to kidnap us so the operation wouldn't be discovered? If that was so, why not just have Kapa Lu kill us?

Kapa said he didn't know what Donnelly was up to, and Misao believed that. So did I. Kapa had gotten in on the game because he was given freedom, or at least an internal drive ship, which was as good as freedom. With that as a prize, he would not question his employer's motives.

And out in the middle of the black sky sat the Blood Family in their fortified palaces. According to the permission records and shots from the telescopes, not one of them took a step outside to actually oversee the system they supposedly governed. Except, that is, for the Grand Sentinel Torian Erasmus, who on the surface looked as disconnected from any business of actual governing as the rest of them.

What am I missing? I demanded of the darkness where Dylan used to be. *What am I forgetting?*

Forgetting.

Forgotten.

When something is forgotten, it is consigned to oblivion.

Oblivion was dead.

Why had the Blood Family let Oblivion die?

It was a dreadful waste. Even if you didn't give an extra goddamn about the people, why let them die? You could let them get to the edge, sample death, then go in and offer them air in return for servitude. A lot of them would take you up on it.

And if you were going to let them die anyway, why waste an entire world? For almost a century, the prison had been highly successful and very profitable. I'd been elbow deep in the accounts when I was doing the historical analysis. The prison and prison labor from Moonfive had been almost as profitable for Erasmus as Hospital. Why not just go in, shovel out the old corpses, and restart the place? The infrastructure was all there. The ecosystem could be restored in five years or so.

And it wasn't just Oblivion they were wasting. I looked around me with fresh eyes. This place, too. All these people, who were struggling to survive. If they were put to work, not just in a random press-gang style, but concentrated as a workforce, they could be the basis of rebuilding the Blood Family's fortunes. Diaspora worlds always needed more hands than they thought they did. But they were letting it rot. Oh, they had Clerks and secops all over the place to keep anybody from getting ideas—and to snatch up whomever they needed—but there was no mechanism for governing, no chain of command between the people and the Blood Family.

Favor Barclay, the highest-ranking Security official on Erasmus, had been shoved out of his station. Amerand Jireu's personal Clerk jumped to its death. The cover-up was clumsy and amateurish, and the network did not even bother to act like it was going to blame Amerand Jireu. In fact, his Clerk told him he was going to be used to finish the system, and if he knew what that meant, he was a better actor than any I'd ever seen.

And maybe the real culprit for Clerk Hamahd's death was Dr. Varus.

But Dr. Varus was from Hospital, and whatever the hell it was they were doing on Hospital, it wasn't selling services to the diaspora worlds. In the past six months, there'd only been in-system flight from Hospital to Dazzle, or to Fortress. Unless they'd all been erased, no flights at all had come into or out of the system. But why erase the kind of flights that had been so common up to a couple of years ago?

Dr. Varus had also treated Siri, briefly, but she *had* treated her, before Siri had started acting erratically. Before she'd told Vijay a story about the Clerks' network and voices siphoned from people's bodies. But not before she'd decided that Bianca could still be alive, and on Hospital.

"Oh, *fuckless!*" I shot straight up. The heads of passersby turned and just as quickly turned away.

I took off running.

When I made it back to the base house, I bounded up the stairs four at a time to the third floor and all but flew down the corridor to 356. The door was partway open, and Siri sat there in her favorite listening position, one hand on her knee, one hand on her control unit. I shot forward with my hand out, slamming into the closed door hard enough to jolt my arm up to my shoulder.

Hologram.

I staggered backward. In front of me, through the partly open door, Siri sat in her room, in her favorite listening posture, one hand on her knee, one hand on her control unit.

Swearing, I fumbled in my belt pocket for my glasses and jammed them on. Now I saw the date and time stamp on the hologram, and the shimmering edges of the flex screen she'd laid over the door.

On a Pax world, this would have never worked. But here, the datasphere was so fragmented and those fragments were so tightly controlled, no one bothered to walk around with their sets or their implants switched on. I didn't even know if Orry *had* implants.

I shoved the flex screen aside and twisted the lock. It recognized my touch and snicked open a split second before I shoved my way through the door.

And Siri was gone.

I stood panting in the empty room, the blood draining to my feet.

My knees wanted to crumple, but I couldn't let them. I walked back into the listening room, pulling my set out of my belt pocket. I clipped the set to my ear, connected it to my glasses, and plugged in the lead to the comm node. If I could get a bead on what Siri had been listening to, maybe I could work out where she'd gone.

I plugged the other end of the lead into my set, and listened.

I heard silence, cold and absolute, without even any static. I pulled the set off and checked the connections. They were solid. I checked the power indicator on the back of the comm node. It was there. I clipped my set back to my ear and moved my hand across the node, seeking another frequency, another signal.

Nothing. Silence. All silence.

For days, Siri had been in here listening. She said she was amazed at how clearly the voices were coming to her, that she was even getting something new underneath the usual unfiltered voices.

I got nothing but silence.

I unclipped my set and tucked it carefully back inside my belt pocket. Siri was gone. She had been hearing voices, and she had followed them out into the city of Dazzle.

And I had no idea where.

Stop. Think. I pinched the bridge of my nose.

Siri had told Vijay that the Clerks' network was running on human voices, essences stolen from living people.

Vijay said she was serious. Assume he was right. Vijay told me. Siri found out he did. What would she do next?

My hand dropped. Siri would assume Vijay had betrayed her. Siri might assume Vijay was working for the enemy.

Vijay was out at the port, with the smugglers. And Siri knew that.

I ran out of the room, bellowing for Dr. Gwin.

TWENTY-NINE

EMILIYA

Because she was staff, Emiliya arrived back on Hospital at one of the private ports. These were little more than cargo bays, kept cleaned and polished by the ever-present drones. In a state of numbness, she submitted to the various searches, scans, and debriefings, aware the whole time that if she let herself, she would start screaming.

Amerand is wrong. The Blood Family will not permit the Erasmus System to come to an end.

I am one of them. My father is Nikko Erasmus Donnelly, and I am a member of the Blood Family.

Her mother had known that, and that was the real reason she'd left. She thought Emiliya was in good hands, and she had to get her other children, who were . . . less well connected, out of the way.

Because there was never going to be an end to the Erasmus System.

That phrase kept replaying in her head as Emiliya walked down the corridor to her dorm room.

Her door was unlocked. She went inside. It was almost exactly as she had left it. It had been cleaned and searched, but that was standard practice. Plus, of course, the Grand Sentinel would want to make sure she had no lingering secrets.

She would have done the same.

Emiliya sat down on her hard chair and swiveled her desktop toward her. She couldn't see straight. She should get some sleep, some food. She barely ate anything on the trip back, and she certainly didn't sleep.

But she unfolded the screen from the desktop, slid the cover back on the keypad, and began typing. She entered all her codes, old and new, and watched the world unfurl before her.

Reports. Requisitions. Experimental write-ups. Years' worth of information, decades' worth, flitted past. Experiments on cells, on embryos, on full-grown animals of increasing complexity, and, starting five years ago, on humans. The list of subject numbers was four columns long.

Emiliya skimmed through the reports, picking random experimental results and skipping down to the summaries. The frustrations and setbacks of seeking "true" immortality flashed before her eyes. Bellicose arguments shot back and forth. Theories were built up and torn down. It was the whole tangled mess of scientific and technological progress. It was impossible to fake such a mess. The fakes were invariably too tidy and didn't involve anything like enough people—or enough failures.

She flicked forward and backward, jumping randomly through time, tracking not by chronology but by the names of experimenters. She followed individual progress. She connected requisitions to personnel records, to names she vaguely recognized as having been dropped by friends of friends.

The final breakthrough seemed to have come about two years ago. A new subject entered the experiment. After that, the fetal trials began to succeed. The babies started maturing, instead of growing tumors and expiring in the womb. The new subject got the tag: IDFM40981A.

Emiliya's fingers ached. Her eyes blurred, but she didn't

stop. She activated another cross-check, flicked through another set of reports, looking for a name and an origin point. Where had IDFM40981A come from? If there was falsification in all this, that might be it.

At last, an initial health report opened. Human subjects all had to be scanned and examined when they came in. Variables had to be recorded and accounted for, including names and worlds of origin, even if they were never mentioned again.

Emiliya read the report.

I should have known, she thought. *I really should have guessed.*

Of course IDFM40981A was Bianca Fayette. The missing saint. The Solarans sent an immortal into the Erasmus System, and the system took her apart to see how she ticked.

Emiliya's hands fell into her lap. *So that's it. It is real. The Blood Family, or at least select members of the Blood Family, are going to live forever.*

And she really did have to choose whether to join them.

Or maybe she'd already made her decision. Her heart thumped hard against her ribs. She stood. She could barely feel the ground under her feet as she walked down the corridor to Piata's room.

The door was open. The room had been stripped. All traces of personal occupancy had been removed. Only the basic furniture everyone was issued when they came to Hospital remained.

Emiliya drifted inside. She stood in the middle and tried to keep breathing. It was far too like her mother's empty suite.

"He's gone," said someone from the hall.

Emiliya jerked around. Stash Madison—another member of her cohort who had only attained mediocrity—leaned against the threshold, his arms folded.

"I don't know what they finally caught him at, but it must have been pretty big, because the Clerks walked him out, then five minutes later they came back and yanked out all his stuff, too."

So. She already was Blood Family. She'd turned Piata over to them and hadn't thought twice about it. Piata had asked for it. It was his own fault this had happened to him. He'd gotten clever, gotten greedy.

She'd won, really. She could keep on winning.

"Maybe you should get out of there," suggested Stash.

"Yeah." Stash looked worried, but a cleaning drone polished the floor behind them.

"I'm tired," she said, just in case he was wondering how she was. "I'm going to bed. You on first shift tomorrow?"

"Yep. Seein' you then?"

"We go where we're needed."

She drifted back to her room. She shut and locked the door, not that it meant anything. *They can get in whenever they choose.*

It's all right. Nothing unexpected, and besides, what have I got to be afraid of now?

She had turned Piata in. She'd been living with that for days. The fact that she was Erasmus, as opposed to just Erasman, shouldn't make any difference. There was no reason for it to.

Except it did. It made all the difference under the whole black sky.

Emiliya smoothed her hair back, wondering what she should do. She probably didn't have a whole lot of time. The Grand Sentinel didn't seem like he was willing to wait forever. Maybe she should get a good dinner, gorge herself on meat and cake and fresh vegetables. Things she hadn't tasted in years. Of course, now she was going to have that forever. She was Erasmus. *Blood*. Surely whatever was going to happen next was going to have a life of luxury as part of it.

How am I going to tell Amerand?

She squeezed her eyes shut. It would serve him right if she just vanished. If he'd talked to her—if he'd tried to find a way while they were free for that moment in the peeled core—she could have told him . . . she could have told him so much.

Another thought came to her, tugging her mind from Amerand to the four columns of patient IDs. All the IDs that did not belong to Bianca Fayette.

She moved back to her desk. She was lighter than a feather. Lighter than air. All her new knowledge had dissolved her from the inside out, and only her ghost remained.

She found the list of human subjects. She made her connections and got her admission data. She sorted for sex, she sorted for age, she sorted for arrival time. She sorted for world of origin. The results gave her all the women from Oblivion. There were a dozen. She flicked through them.

Barai Rhu Amos was the fifth. Amerand's mother, whom he had been searching for through the diaspora worlds, hoping against hope that she was still alive somewhere, had been taken to Hospital.

She died after delivering the tenth fetal experiment implanted in her.

Emiliya looked at her closed door. They could be out there right now, waiting for her to make her decision. Or they could be on the other end of the line, waiting for her next message.

Waiting to see, for instance, whether that message went to the Grand Sentinel, or Amerand.

Waiting to see if they would have to kill her.

"No," she whispered to the screen and the empty room. "No, I don't think so."

She lifted her hands and laid them on the keys. She flicked through the records a few more times, making notations, marking the most important, double-checking the codes and keying them to the proper personnel records. Just in case anyone needed to refer to this data again. Organization was important. They always stressed that in the academy. Emiliya had organized and cross-filed her own reports for years. She was very good at it.

If anyone came looking, she wanted to be sure they found the correct information.

Emiliya checked over her work and made sure it was properly stored. She stood and crossed her room. She sat on the edge of her bed. Random thoughts filled her—blurts and strings of memory. Hope burned and choked and sputtered out, because it wasn't real. She wasn't Amerand, and she had no Terese Drajeske to make her believe.

She lay down and drew up the covers. She fumbled inside her jacket pocket and brought out one of the scalpels she was authorized to carry because of her medical specialty. She was efficient. She knew just what to do and what order to do it in.

By the time the sensor on the floor registered blood and alerted the emergency team that had the authorization to override the door lock, Emiliya had almost bled out. It was decided not to try for revival as they could do more with the parts.

THIRTY

TORIAN

Torian sighed and closed the active pane.

"I am sorry, Emiliya," he whispered, running his fingers down the edge of the black square.

"Sentinel?" The warm voice rose from the back of his mind.

Torian steepled his fingers. The office faded around him, and forms took shape in front of his mind's eye. He now stood in the middle of the Clerks' hive in the new governing palace.

Hagen Kane bowed to him.

"You should know Terese Drajeske is sending an out-system transmission."

Is she? From the authorized station?

"Yes, but this is not the approved hour."

No, it is not. Well. With that, I would say our time has come. We will simply have to work with what we have. The heat burned on his neck and the back of his scalp. *Are we following Amerand Jireu?*

"We are."

Good. Alert me as soon as his course becomes clear. We need time to activate the backup in case he fails to follow through.

"It will be done."

The Master Clerk bowed again and Torian moved his fingertips apart. Regretfully, he turned his back on his desk. He had thought they would have a few days yet.

All the important pieces are in place. They will fall in order. And even if one or two get out of arrangement, there is still time to make adjustments. After all, now that we have neutralized the Solarans, who is there to interfere?

Torian left his private office. Beyond his doors, in the central palace, the celebrations were in full cry. Eight hundred members of the Blood Family filled the great room and spread out into the side chambers. The servants moved through the glittering crowd as smoothly as trained dancers, offering food and drink, which also overflowed the tables set by the door of each chamber.

Everyone was in their finest: gold and silver, and genuine Old Earth gems—not the native analogs—shone like fragments of rainbow on gowns and robes. Security was much in evidence too, in its most formal uniform, accompanied by gilded but highly functional swords and daggers, as well as stark black projectile weapons.

It was just warm enough. The air was filled with perfumes designed to heighten sense and sensation. It was loud and glittering now, and would grow increasingly raucous as the night went on. Dancers—clothed and nude—whirled and kicked, glided and soared on stages of various sizes. Elsewhere there were illusionists, light-painters, and musicians. Fully interactive games played out on the screens, and people cheered at fencing matches, aerial battles, even a poetry competition.

Torian craned his neck, searching for a figure in black and white.

It did not take him long to pick Bloom out from the crowd. The Master of Dazzle stood in the middle of a crowd of young cousins, saying something that had them all laughing out loud. Bloom glanced toward him, and Torian nodded. In answer, Bloom bowed to his little audience and moved gracefully aside to stand next to Torian.

"You have done extremely well," said Torian softly. "How long can you maintain the festivities?"

Bloom surveyed the gathering like a master engineer, judging its level, brightness, and flow. "Three days, perhaps four, if that becomes necessary."

"I do not think it will." Torian paused. "The offer still stands, Bloom. You have earned a place with us."

Bloom faced Torian. He bowed, and Torian sensed that for once the gesture was sincere. "I do thank you, Grand Sentinel, but no. I shall watch my final great illusion play out, then I shall . . . fade away." He smiled at Torian's blank expression. "And once again, you do not understand me."

"I admit I do not."

"That is because, Sentinel, you have never been taught the absolute necessity of a well-timed exit."

"That's not what I'm doing now?"

"You know it isn't. Still, I wish you luck in your new venture. Your time will not be dull."

Torian offered his hand, and Bloom took it with a grip that was much more firm than the Grand Sentinel expected. "I will miss you."

Once more Bloom bowed, the grand, sweeping gesture that Torian expected from him. Then the Master of Dazzle turned away and slid easily into the currents of the party he had created. Torian felt a small shiver run inexplicably up the back of his neck as he watched Bloom depart.

Let him go, he counseled himself. *He would never accept the network, and how could he serve in the new system without it?*

Torian continued to make his own way through the crowds, pausing frequently to exchange greetings and compliments with the third- and fourth-degree family members. He skirted past the children, who were, of course, finding their own amusements around and between the adults and in general ignoring the ones created for them. A melancholy stained his mood, the closest he had come to regret down the long years of planning for this moment.

It is only change, the last change. Better it should be over and done with soon.

At the far end of the Grand Hall Mai Erasmus held court from her high-backed chair, cradling her daughter Indun in her arms. The other infants lay in specially designed bassinets that allowed them freedom to wriggle and coo—and also monitored every one of their vital signs.

Torian laid his hand on Mai's shoulder. She glanced up from the baby. He leaned over and poked his finger into Indun's pudgy fist. Indun grasped it and immediately tried to yank it into her mouth.

"She's hungry again." Mai sighed. "I'm beginning to think I won't be able to keep up."

"You'll do fine," murmured Torian. "And you'll have help. It's time to go, Mai."

She met his gaze and nodded once. She stood, gathering her shining skirts with her free hand. Her well-trained waiting maids lined up instantly behind her. Indun, she declared, was getting fussy. Mai glided through the party, explaining that the noise and the heat were "just too much." Indun obligingly set up a loud wail and everyone smiled to see what a dedicated mother *Saeo* Mai Erasmus was proving to be. Torian caught Estev's eye with a nod and a tiny flickering movement of his fingers. Estev bowed and smiled and said he'd better make certain his wife and daughter did not want anything, and he followed Mai out.

Torian resumed his slow circuit of the rooms: exchanging greetings, asking after health and business, hearing concerns and making promises that shortly "everything will be taken care of."

"The plan is in order," he assured everyone who asked. "The first wave will be leaving soon. Enjoy the festivities until you are called."

They all knew of the triumphs on Hospital, of the heritable immortality and the living network that would ensure the permanence of the Erasmus System and the Blood Family.

What most of them did not know was that immortality would be given only to certain, selected members of the Blood, and that these were the only ones who would be taken into hiding until such time as any fallout from their dealings with the Pax Solaris had cleared.

Those who remained behind did not, of course, know he had planned for their ending as carefully as he planned for the others' continuation. Bloom's party would keep them amused and distracted for the few hours remaining to them.

That he'd lied to the majority of the family did not trouble Torian much. He had been lying to Felice and Jasper's children for centuries.

Eventually, he reached the main doors. He passed through them into the relatively empty corridors. All around him, the motif of the family tree was repeated: in etched glass, in beaten bronze, in inlaid marbles and delicate paints. Torian drew a deep breath and walked purposefully down the avenues that would take him to the port yard.

Behind him, the celebrations continued.

THIRTY-ONE

VIJAY

One of the larger ironies of the Erasmus System, thought Vijay Kochinski, is that it is not illegal to remove water from Dazzle.

It was highly illegal to take water off Fortress without permission. It was a death sentence to be out in a ship on a course or at a time that had not been thoroughly approved and reapproved by Flight Control. But it simply never seemed to have occurred to anybody that someone might remove water from a world that was struggling to keep itself hydrated.

As a result, one major part of Papa Dare's operation was perfectly legal. He bought up water at the markets with the considerable credit and scrip he had at his disposal, and he either turned it around for resale or hoarded it in very heavily secured warehouses.

That, supposedly, was what was going on today. As a result, Vijay—along with Meek and the other four strongarms Meek had rounded up for this job—was able to walk into the port yard without any hassle from the few listless secops. Vijay wouldn't have thought much of it, except for Meek's half-drunken revelations: The cargoes weren't going to the normal ports on Market. Oh no, these were being stuffed into Habitat 3, until the thing had become a damn floating *ocean*. The *patri* was coming down hard on everyone, then that fuckless fool Kapa vanished, taking an entire registered ship with him, which meant the whole run was in danger of being postponed. The permissions had been set for nearly a month, and Papa Dare did *not* like to have to rearrange his schedule. There were dozens of people in the fragmented, shifting morass that oversaw Dazzle's port, and all of them had to be kept properly bribed, flattered, and fed. It took intense dedication to forge a chain that worked even once. Having to rearrange it would cause serious, and maybe permanent, delays.

Papa Dare evidently felt that time was an issue. Which made Vijay wonder what they were really loading into the ship today. You could stash all kinds of lethal items in a watertight container. If you filled a habitat with poison or disease, then dropped that habitat through a jump gate and into an inhabited system . . .

Papa Dare paid extra so his cargo was at least nominally secured behind one of the yard's few walls. Vijay hung back as Meek presented the promissory and manifest to the hard-eyed Clerk, one of a half dozen or so prowling the port's interior. Vijay was the most visibly scarred, and the tallest of the strongarms. No point in presenting himself for closer inspection.

But the Clerk wasn't interested in any of them yet. She ran her fingertips over the manifest as if checking for holes in the sheeting and handed it back to Meek with a nod.

Meek jerked his chin for his crew to follow him, and they all filed through the narrow opening in the patched-together partition.

"You," said the Clerk.

Vijay stopped. "What?" he asked.

The Clerk peered up at him. She had green eyes and golden skin.

"She one of the Marshal-Steward's cousins?" muttered Took from the back of Vijay's mind.

That'd be too weird for words.

"You are identified as Edison Ray, registered and attached to the Pax Solaris."

"Yeah?" Meek was eyeing him. He had to make it good. "I'm on loan for humanitarian purposes. We've got a load of water to shift." Vijay flexed his arms. Around him, the crew grinned.

The Clerk did not even seem to see. "I have no authority for your addition to this work crew."

Vijay stuck his hand in his pants pocket and pulled out the faked manifest Meek had entrusted him with. "Right here, along with the cargo." He stabbed his finger at the appropriate line. "'One port assistant.' That's me."

The Clerk took the manifest and stared at it. Her eyes did not move back and forth like a person reading. She just stared.

And she blinked. "There is no specific identification code given."

Vijay groaned, but the other strongarms remained silent. Not only that, but they were starting to edge away from him.

Meek was the only one who moved in closer. "Is there a problem?"

The Clerk lifted her blank, unseeing eyes toward him. "I am uncertain." She tilted her face down toward the manifest again. Vijay's heart skipped a beat.

I can't miss this. This could answer everything. We could get out early, get Siri back home . . .

"Keep up the act, Vijay. You're just another bored bastard. Come on. No slips."

Vijay folded his arms and glowered at the Clerk. She brushed her fingers across the manifest one more time.

"It is allowable." She handed the sheet across to Meek. You may continue."

"Thank you, Seña." Meek bowed but gave Vijay a sour look as he did. Vijay shrugged and stuffed his hands in his pockets and tried to shoot a companionable eye roll to his fellow strongarms.

Not one of them showed the least sign of being on his side.

"Just walk, Vijay."

Yeah. Good idea.

A partition blocked off one of the loading elevators. Most of the space behind it was taken up by battered steel cylinders, about the size of a man's torso. They were piled there without any order, as if they had been hastily unloaded and left.

"All right," said Meek. "We need to get these"—he stabbed his finger at the canisters—"onto these"—he stabbed at a pile of empty cargo pallets—"and into there." The final stab was to the open doors of the air lock and the cargo elevator beyond. "Questions?"

No one said anything. Meek nodded. "Then go. And Papa Dare will be coming 'round to check the work, so I suggest you all get busy."

Vijay looked at the strongarms and they looked at him. Two peeled off and headed for the pallets. Each man pulled one off the stack and tossed it onto the port-yard stone with a rattle and a thud. The third stationed himself next to the canisters, and Vijay walked into place beside him, yanking his gloves out of his back pocket as he did.

"What'er those?" asked the wank next to the canisters.

"They're called gloves," grunted Vijay as he pulled them on. "I could spell that for you, if you could read."

"Ooo-ooo." The wank wiggled his fingers. "Our widdle saint might hurt his widdle finger. Maybe you get Mommy to kiss it all better . . ."

"Shut your hole," snapped Meek. "And get with the job."

The wank shut it, but the look he gave Vijay said they were not done with this little exchange of pleasantries. He grabbed up a canister and tossed it to Vijay. It landed awkwardly in his hands, and the contents sloshed hard.

"And here's one," remarked Took as Vijay heaved the can to the next man on the line.

One million to go.

Almost anywhere else, this would have been done by machines: forklifts, pallet handlers, driven by humans or remote control. On Dazzle, however, working machinery was rare, and expensive. People, on the other hand, were cheap, plentiful, and easily replaced if they failed to perform. Papa Dare believed in keeping his overhead low.

Vijay felt Meek and the Clerk watching him, but he had to keep his attention on the cargo, which the wank was heaving over as fast as he could.

Doesn't matter who's watching, as long as they don't take the gloves.

The real problem with the dependence on human labor was that the more people you needed for a job, the more people you must let near your secrets.

Like whatever was really sloshing around in the canisters.

The gloves on Vijay's hands were special, battered-looking versions of his uniform gloves. They were armored. They had a communication pad and a camera. They also had tiny scanning spectrometers in them. It was, after all, a very useful thing for a spy to be able to find out what was inside a box (or an envelope, or a can) without having to open it.

All the hardware meant the gloves were hot enough to ake his palms sweat, and the radiators in the spectrometers eren't doing his skin and bones any good at all. Vijay gritd his teeth as the Big Wank tossed him another can and he vung it to the next man in the line.

In fact, they were starting to hurt like hell.

"Just gotta get this one answer," said Took.

Get the answer, then we can blow this entire fuckless system and t Siri out of here.

"Wassamatter, Little Saint?" laughed the Big Wank. Maybe I should come over and kiss dat widdle fingee for o."

"Maybe you should suck my big dickee for me," mutred Vijay. He would have said it louder, but Meek was eyealling him, and now was not the time.

They filled one pallet. They filled two, three, four. Vijay st count. It was too hot in the yard, and the burn on his ands did not let up. The scanners had to get through the etal. They had to cross-check and verify the findings. That ok a lot of internal processing, and internal processing enerated heat, as did the scans themselves.

A dozen pallets. Two.

"Hang on, Vijay," said Took from the back of his mind.

Hanging. But remind me not to put the damn things on so early xt time.

"Experience is a bitch."

You got that right.

Three dozen pallets.

Took?

"Right here, Vijay."

If my fingers are blistered to the bone when I take these things off, 's going to look funny.

"It's not that bad."

You sure about that?

"It's the weight and the motion. And in case you hadn't noticed the Big Wank there has been trying to make you miss for the last hundred throws."

And here I thought I was a whiny little wimp.

"Not yet. I'll warn you if you get there."

Thanks.

"Anytime."

It took another hour, but at last, the final canister was strapped onto the final pallet. Vijay stripped off his gloves. Took, of course, was right. His hands were red, and they hurt like he'd been sunburned, but there was no obvious sign of the burning he'd felt.

There was, however, a faint readout on the palm of the right glove. Over by the ship, the toughs and the wanks slapped each other on the back and eyed Meek, who was tugging on pallet straps and looking for all the world like a genuine straw boss. Vijay smoothed out the glove, and glanced down to see what he'd been loading for the past three hours.

H_2O.

Vijay wiped his forehead and glanced up to make sure no one was paying any attention to him. He looked at the glove again.

H_2O.

A few trace chemicals—a little more salt than there should be—but no poison, no manufactured nanos. Habitat 3 was being stuffed to the gills with cans of water.

And Meek had even told him so. A floating ocean, he'd said.

Vijay stared, and the slick, sick sensation of failure slid across his skin.

"Decoy?" suggested Took.

Has to be. Shit. Well, okay, now we eliminate Papa Dare and his smuggling operation, and start looking for what's really going on. No big deal. False start.

"We've seen our share of those."

Oh, yeah. And ordinarily it wouldn't have bothered him, but this time . . . this time they needed to get Siri out of here, away from whatever was getting to her so badly.

"Preferably without your having to ask Terese to declare her unfit."

Yeah.

"Can't stand here, Vijay," said Took urgently. "Got to get this word home."

Right. He straightened up and stuffed the gloves in his back pocket as he walked toward the partition.

Vijay was absolutely unsurprised it was his friend and colleague the Big Wank who shouted, "Where you going, little Saint?"

Vijay jerked his thumb over his shoulder. "Gotta take a leak."

"Use the corner if you can't wait for launch," called Meek from his station by the pallets. "Nobody gets out of sight. Papa Dare's personal orders."

"Awww, come on!" Vijay threw up his hands. "I didn't sign up for this to turn into a pig," he said directly to the Big Wank, who did not miss it.

"You calling me a pig?" Big Wank straightened up. Which showed he had some kind of balls. Vijay had at least six inches on the guy and probably seventy-five pounds.

But the Big Wank had friends, and two of the other strongarms slouched into place behind him, their menacing eyes fastened on Vijay.

"Well, you started this," remarked Took.

Yeah. "Maybe I'm calling your *mother* a pig," he said to the Big Wank.

Wank swung straight for his throat, but Vijay was ready for it. He got his arm up in time to block the blow and drove his other fist hard into the Wank's solar plexus. Wank doubled over with a satisfying grunt, and Vijay kicked his ankles out from under him, laying him out on the stone.

"What the *fuckless* are you doing!" bellowed Meek, and Vijay took off running.

He stretched his long legs for all they were worth. In the light gravity and open space he practically flew. He forgot his pain, almost forgot he had four bad-ass, angry strongarms on his tail, and just ran.

"Whoooo-hooo!" shouted Took for him.

"Get that gate shut!" bellowed Meek. "He's robbing me!"

A shot whizzed past Vijay's head. The secops were hauling the gate closed. Another shot went off, and the gate stopped moving.

"What the hells!" shouted one of the secops. He yanked at the bars, but the gate didn't move. Vijay grabbed the secop by the shoulders and tossed him backward, right into Wank's little mob.

Vijay flew through the gate just in time to see Siri swing herself over the balcony and drop down onto the bridge underneath.

Siri? What's she doing here?

"Saving your ass."

She had her gun on her back, and now he knew what held the gate open for him.

"She always was a *wicked* good shot."

Oh, yeah!

Grinning fiercely, Vijay dove over the rail and landed on e balcony underneath. Wincing at the pain in his palms, he ung off the rail like a kid on the monkey bars and dropped wn another level. The bystanders screamed and ducked, d there was cursing and shouting, but it quickly grew dist. Siri led him on, hopping from bridge to bridge until e finally ducked into a sagging doorway.

She can't be too far gone. She's still with the program and Terese her out armed . . .

"Run now. Think later."

Pumped full of hope and adrenaline, Vijay darted into e warrenlike building and tore down the corridor, follow- g Siri to the back stairs.

le's coming, Siri."

I hear him.

Siri crouched in the blackness of the unused subway nnel.

She hadn't meant to save the construct. She'd just meant shadow it and find a place where she could meet it, like e would have done if it really had been Vijay, then work it a way to lure it down here.

But this was even better than she had planned. This way, followed her without asking any questions.

Just like Vijay would have done. Siri swallowed around e lump in her throat.

A shadow blocked the entranceway above. Siri lifted her ad. The construct didn't bother with the stairs. It hung er the rail and dropped, landing lightly on his toes.

Oh, very good.

"You can't talk to it, Siri. You can't give it a chance to t to you."

I know.

The construct looked around, but she was hidden in the darkness of the tunnel mouth and its eyes hadn't adjusted yet. It moved out of the light, into the space under the stairs, putting its back against the wall.

Doesn't want anything sneaking up behind it.

Siri drew a bead on the construct and fired. The epoxy hit it square on the left shoulder, jerking it backward and sealing it to the wall.

"What the hell!" it cried out. Her second shot got its right hand before it could twist out of the way. One more shot, and its boots were sealed to the floor.

Siri slung the gun over her shoulder and stepped forward, into the light.

"Siri?" it said, and a good imitation of Vijay's confusion creased its scarred face. "Siri, what's going on?"

She didn't answer. Shawn was right. She mustn't talk to it.

"Come on, Siri, you're scaring me. What's going on?"

It still had one hand free and it grabbed for her as she approached, but she caught its arm. With one twist, its elbow popped. She dropped the arm, which flopped and dangled uselessly, as the construct gasped in pain.

She cocked her head, listening carefully. There. She heard a buzzing in its throat. Of course. In its throat, behind its ear. That was where the container would be.

She pulled out the knife she'd brought for the purpose.

"I'll get you out, Vijay. Don't worry, lover."

She brought up the blade and the construct screamed.

"Siri!"

Siri jerked around. Another shadow emerged, from the other end of the tunnel. Siri crouched into a ready stance, but she couldn't get the gun up without dropping the knife. The shadow raised empty hands.

"It's Terese!"

"Field Commander." Siri straightened to attention, then suspicion hit her. "How did you know where I'd be?"

"I didn't. I had to guess where you'd bring something you needed to keep safe, since you abandoned your post without notice." Terese's voice grew sharp. "You want to explain to me why I shouldn't chew you out for going AWOL?"

Stupid, stupid, stupid . . . "I was going to tell you, as soon as I got Vijay out. I know you need proof . . ."

Behind her, the construct panted through clenched teeth. Terese gave it a quick glance. "You're right, I do," she said. "But I do see how important this is."

Siri sagged with relief. "You understand what's really going on, then?"

"Most of it. Some of it's not so clear."

"That's okay. I can explain the rest, just as soon as I get Vijay out." She raised the knife again and turned toward the construct.

"Siri, wait. I want to get Dr. Gwin to take care of the surgery. It's what we brought her for, after all. If we do this too quickly, we risk hurting Vijay."

Siri froze. Her gaze darted from the knife to the construct. It cringed back.

"You're right, you're right. I should have thought." Siri pressed the heel of her hand against her forehead. "It's been so hard these past few days. It's been just me and Shawn."

Terese laid a hand on Siri's shoulder. "You're lucky you have Shawn."

"Yeah." Siri looked up at her commander and smiled. "I shouldn't complain, I guess. Sorry."

"It's okay." Terese slapped her back. "Listen, I've got Gwin and her team up top. Let me bring them down to help secure this." She nodded toward the construct. "And we'll all get back to base."

Siri could not believe her ears. "You've got to get Vijay out of there now! I'm not sure how much longer he'll last!"

"We've got to get him into a sterilized space for the surgery," Terese reminded her. "We don't know what kind of infection an organic container could transmit down here."

"She has a point."

I know, but I don't like it. "We need to hurry. Vijay's voice is getting weaker."

"I know. Believe me." Terese stepped into the spotlight. "We're clear!" she called up the stairs.

Dr. Gwin was the first one down. The spiral skeleton of the stairway swayed under the force of her pounding footsteps. Two assistants followed, carrying a padded stretcher between them. Terese handed Gwin a set of release capsules, then she turned back to Siri.

"We're going to find out what happened here, Siri. I swear we are."

"We know what happened," Siri answered. "At least most of it. Once we get Vijay out, there's just one or two things I need to con . . ."

The drug finally hit, melting the world into a blur of color, and the last thing Siri saw was Terese leaning over her, the needle still in her hand and tears welling up in her eyes.

THIRTY-TWO

AMERAND

The yard and lobby of Common Cause house were as busy as ever when I walked in, and as usual, Liang was in the thick of it with Orry Batumbe. The saints stood shoulder to shoulder, both reading from a thick pile of sheets Liang held.

I waited for Liang to glance up. His gaze slid over me at first. Then he stopped and looked again, taking in the fact that I was in uniform, and alone. Beside him Orry Batumbe drew back, clearly far less certain about what he was seeing than his superior.

"If you're looking for Field Commander Drajeske, she left a couple of hours ago," said Liang. "I don't know where." He did not bother to disguise his anger at this fact.

I ignored that. "You're the one I'd like to speak with, Seño Chen."

Liang frowned but handed off the sheets to Batumbe. We walked down to his office. I followed, as silent as a Clerk, until he'd closed and latched his door behind us. I'd always wondered about that latch. It looked like it wouldn't stop a determined child, but I had a distinct feeling it knew exactly who came and went from this place.

"Are you all right, Amerand?" Liang asked me, and I think he really wanted to know.

I nodded. "More or less. But I need a favor."

He leaned back against his desk and folded his arms. "Now is not a good time. Things are kind of on the boil around here."

He knew about Hamahd at the very least. I was not surprised. He was wondering what I was doing here. I shouldn't have put the uniform back on.

"Liang," I said softly. "This is important—and it's personal."

"Why aren't you asking Terese?" His implication was clear. When I had sent my father to get a message to the saints, I'd sent him to Terese and not Liang, who had been helping me for years. In Liang's eyes, I'd switched sides somehow.

Who the hell knew saints had these kinds of arguments?

The truth was, I had thought about just going to Terese, but in the end I'd hesitated. Terese did not trust Emiliya. Could I really bring her a request to help someone she didn't trust?

"Terese hasn't got a terminal into the Security net, and you do," I said. "Please, Liang."

Liang sighed. He glanced at me again, then at the door. "All right. Once." He moved behind the desk.

"Thank you."

Liang touched his fingertips to the desktop and looked at me from under his furrowed brow. "Amerand?"

"Yes?"

"I'm trusting you. You've always been as up-front as you can with me, but the commander's brought you into whatever the Guardians are on. I'm not a Guardian. I've got no oath to keep, and I've got your people as well as mine depending on me."

I nodded. "I told you the truth, Liang. This is personal."

"Okay." Liang lit up the desktop, opening a single active pane with a letter board underneath it. He touched the black area to one side and a new panel opened. His hand moved across it, sketching some colored lines, then redirecting them. They all flashed green for a split second, and the pane was gone.

"You've got ten minutes." Liang marched out of the room and slammed the door shut behind him.

The latch snicked back into place without me touching it.

I swallowed hard and walked around the desk. I couldn't bring myself to sit in the comfortable chair. I laid my fingertips on the letters. They flashed blue as I touched them. I spelled out my commands and my passwords silently, without any tactile sensation but the smooth coolness of the desktop.

Liang's desk was the one terminal that the Common Cause saints had been permitted to connect into our system. It was meant to be our way to spy on their conversations with our people. I'd installed the taps myself. Since then, there'd been a lot of debate about whether we were actually catching everything that went through it. Personally, I had never believed we were, but I'd never bothered to fix it either. It suited me just fine to give Liang some privacy.

My ears strained. A dull humming filled my mind under my thoughts, and I realized my imagination was supplying the sound of a cleaning drone somewhere behind me.

Slowly, I worked my way into the Security's network, and from there through Fortress. From there, I leapt across to Hospital.

Sweat trickled down my brow even though my hands had gone ice-cold. They were watching me. They had to be watching me. They could see through walls. They could hear thoughts. They were waiting in their silence for me to come out. When I did, it would finally be over.

But at least I'd know what had really happened to Emiliya's family. I'd be able to help her, if only a little. It was this thought that kept me going. For once I'd be who I thought I was, who I wanted to be. One child of Oblivion being loyal to another.

The networks were not connected except by the thinnest of threads. Another way of keeping us apart from each other. But as I inched cautiously forward, the basic functions looked mostly the same. I called for a search. I entered the ID codes I had for Emiliya from carrying her as a passenger on my shuttle.

The screen cleared. It flashed yellow.

The droning was all my imagination. They couldn't really see me, couldn't really read my mind.

Numbers and code flashed past, stilled and cleared, and I could read:

```
B4291—SUBJECT 94AOB21D
Known living direct offspring: Child, Male, Am-
erand Laos Jireu 571BG000912AB24
```

I stared at my name. I read it again to be sure. My throat swelled and constricted. Child, Male, Amerand Laos Jireu.

This report was about my mother. My mother. How did Emiliya's codes get me to my mother? Why did they have a report about her on Hospital? She was out on a work detail. Had she been hurt? Was she sick? My mouth went completely dry. My vision twitched so violently, I could barely string the words together. Had I wasted all this time asking Liang to keep an ear out for word of my mother when I should have been asking Emiliya?

I forced my eyes to focus. I made myself read.

I read the data Emiliya had so carefully strung together for me. I read until I could not stand and I fell backward into Liang's comfortable chair.

She was dead.

I had known, on some level, but I hadn't believed. I'd been able to find my father and pull him out. I had believed I could do the same for my mother, someday, somehow. They had risked everything for me, how could I do anything less for them? I was all they had left.

But she was dead. Killed on Hospital.

We all suspected they used us in experiments. We whispered it to ourselves in the dark, but they'd denied it and we'd never seen it, because those sections of Hospital were off-limits to the likes of us. So it had remained on the level of other tunnel rumors, and we let it be.

Except Emiliya must have known. Emiliya had left this information for me.

Where is Emiliya?

My hands moved across the keys. I didn't even bother to cover my tracks. I used my open ID. I used my real name. I was past caring. I already knew the answer anyway. I was just looking for confirmation. No one could possibly call me out for looking for confirmation of a friend's death.

A friend who had died at 12:30:34:14:09, local date and time.

She found out at the last minute. They killed her because she knew. She always said she was just scan-and-stitch. They kept her away from the laboratory wings. That had to be it. It could not be anything else. I couldn't survive if it was anything else.

I looked at the screen again, at the date and time of Emiliya's death. No cause was listed. I had no right to know so much.

Of course not. After all, she didn't belong to me. She belonged to them. She was theirs, like I was theirs, as my parents and Kapa were theirs, to be used up as required, and there was nothing any one of us could do. Oblivion's children were born to be forgotten.

The whole desktop flashed bright red, then went black. My ten minutes must have been up. I got to my feet and walked out, closing the door behind me. Liang's clever lock would surely take care of the rest. I walked out through the lobby. Out of the corner of my eye, I saw Terese standing with a scarred, bald man beside the white clinic door. She didn't see me and I didn't stop. She and I were finished. There was nothing the saints could do for any of us anymore.

I was halfway across the courtyard when my father stepped out of the shadows.

Ever mindful of his role as my servant, my father bowed. "I thought you might require . . . something," he said softly.

I closed my eyes briefly. My guts twisted hard. "No, nothing." I couldn't draw him into this. I didn't want to tell him he was about to lose his last son.

"Amerand," he whispered. "Please."

My resistance shattered in an instant. I nodded, and we moved out into the middle of the yard, to where we were surrounded by voices. It was one of the paradoxes of an observed life. The place you had the most privacy was in the middle of a crowd.

I kept my gaze on the shifting mass of people, the tattered strangers who were as much my family as my blood kin had ever been. We'd all walked from prison to a trap. We'd all tried to escape, or to free those dearest to us.

We'd all failed.

Softly, I told my father what had happened and what I'd found.

He swayed on his feet, and I put my hand on his shoulder. He didn't look at me. His face remained still as stone, except for the single tear that traced its way down his cheek.

"I should have known," he croaked. "Really. I should have known."

"There was no way to know," I murmured.

"She was the one who got us onto the ship, the one that took us from Oblivion," he said. He still didn't look at me. It was as if he had lost the ability to move. "I never asked her how she did it, but she saved all our lives. After that, it was her idea to get you into the secops. She couldn't save your brothers, but she was going to save you even if it meant . . . if it meant . . ." His voice trailed away.

I tried to conjure up a memory of my mother, anything, but there was nothing. Nothing but the blackness of an empty tunnel. All the past had been stripped away from me.

"Go to the saints," I said to my father. "Ask for asylum. They'll get you out of here."

He turned his head, lifting his face toward me. "Why?"

"Because I'm going to make the Blood pay for what they have done to us," I said.

We stood there for a moment, my father and I, looking at each other, each of us finally seeing into the depths of the other, seeing the tunnel darkness, seeing past and future vanish into shadow.

My father shook his head slowly. "You do what you must," he said. "I will not be used against you."

I nodded. He would choose his ending now, as I had chosen mine, and we would both finally be free.

I clasped his shoulder once and turned away, wading into the crowd.

THIRTY-THREE

TERESE

What have they done to her, Terese?" Vijay demanded.

I was standing against the wall beside the quarantine room. Dr. Gwin's team had carried Siri inside and barred the door in my face. Vijay had refused to let anyone do anything more than put a field dressing on him to stabilize his broken elbow, then he'd run the whole way back at my side. Once we reached the base house, I had to order him to go with the nurse and get it set. Now he was back, his face white with all kinds of pain and his arm in a stabilization cast.

"What in all the hells have they done to her?" he asked again, looming over me.

"Gwin will find out." My mind still reeled. I wanted nothing so much as to lean against the wall and vomit, but I couldn't. As it was, everybody was staring at us, Solaran and Erasman.

"Vijay," I said to bring his attention down to me and away from the quarantine door. "What did you find out at the yard?"

He blinked like he didn't understand the question, then ran his palm across his scalp. "It's a dead end, Terese. They weren't loading anything but water."

"Are you sure?"

He plucked his gloves out of his pocket and held them out to me. "You can check it if you don't believe me."

Another time I might have reprimanded him, but I saw

the anguish in his battered face. He turned toward the quarantine door again. "She's got to be all right, Terese."

"She will be. If Gwin can't do anything for her here, we'll pull her out back to Earth. Misao will make sure she gets whatever she needs."

He nodded dully. "Can I stay here awhile? Just, you know, for when there's word?"

His cover was totally blown anyway. I nodded and he slumped against the wall. I twisted his gloves in my hands. I tried not to think. I tried to just wait. The answer to so much was inside the quarantine room, inside Siri.

Siri had gotten far more of this horrible riddle right than I'd been able to comprehend.

Time stretched out. I don't know how long. My feet ached. My stomach rumbled. Vijay said nothing. All I could do was sit there with one thought rubbing a sore spot in my mind.

Siri had been right about so much of this. She'd been right even about what had sounded so insane.

What else was she right about?

"Vijay?" I said quietly.

He turned his ravaged face toward me.

"How did Bianca find me?"

"What?"

"When I was . . . being held by the Redeemers. How did she find me? Siri . . . Siri said I had no idea what she did for me."

He was getting ready to lie. I could see it even though all the surgical alterations had stiffened his face.

I could also tell when, at the last second, he changed his mind.

"She had one of the inner circle picked up. She got a short-haul ship and she took him to it.

"She tortured him, Terese. And when he gave her the answer, she killed him."

No.

"But it didn't work. It was the wrong answer. He'd told er what he thought she wanted to hear, to get her to stop."

No. No. It isn't possible.

"Misao never found out," said Vijay. "I knew. Siri knew. Ve didn't tell you. You'd been through enough, and you hought—*you believed*—that she'd saved you. Siri covered or her. She said . . . she said Bianca knew it was a mistake. aid she'd been too outraged, too frightened. Said we all nake mistakes and she'd done it for a good reason—to save our life—and we found you in the end and that was all that nattered . . ."

I squeezed my eyes shut. "Stop," I whispered. "Please top."

Vijay turned his face toward the quarantine door. "I new you'd ask," he said. "Siri didn't think you would, but ou were always as bad as Bianca. Neither one of you could eave well enough alone."

"How long?" I asked. "Between what . . . what she did and vhen you really found me?"

"A few weeks."

I leaned my head back against the wall. Those last few veeks, that was when they'd found Dylan. Bianca had not •nly broken the first precept, she'd given them time to ut Dylan out of me.

I should have known. I should have known from the vay she let me go, from the way no one on my old team ver came and talked to me. I hadn't wanted contact, but hey didn't either. Siri didn't come because she was covering for Bianca. Vijay didn't come because he was covering for Siri.

Bianca didn't come because she knew I wouldn't be able to forgive her for committing a murder that did nothing more than get Dylan killed.

Had that murder, that guilt, driven her to attempt the takedown? This time she was going to break the rules and get it right? This time would make up for that other? Save all these lives to make up for the one she'd taken in my name?

You have no idea what she did for you.

Oh, Siri, you were right.

Finally, the quarantine door opened and Dr. Gwin stepped out. Vijay straightened up at once, and I was back at his side almost before I'd realized I'd moved.

"I need you in here, Field Commander. Not you." She added to Vijay, "You stay put."

She ushered me inside, through the clean lock, and shut the inner door behind us. The sound shuddered all the way through me.

The quarantine room was white and sterile. Screens had been mounted onto the walls and a whole spiderweb of cables connected them to junction boxes, gloves, and glasses. Siri lay on the table in the center, a pale sheet pulled up to her chin. Blue cuffs circled her wrists, pumping sedatives into her system.

"What can you tell me?" I said, forcing my voice into a brisk tone.

"I can tell you we are all in serious trouble."

"What?"

Gwin laid her hand on one of the screens and lit up a video: blood vessels, brain, and bone, all alive for me to see. I recognized the veinlike thread of the Companion implant aid against the shimmering grey matter. "Since you said Siri's instability was manifesting as voices, I scanned her Companion to make sure the nodes were solid and the output levels were what they should be.

"This is Siri's implant after we got her out of the peeled core. See these branches here and here?" She pointed at two threads.

I nodded.

"They weren't there when she left Earth. I did a close-up." Gwin touched the pane again. The video zoomed in farther, until the threads turned into neat lines of black squares laid over with white threads. "They're artificial, and they were probably tracked in there by a nano injection."

An injection? Like the pressure spray I had permitted Emiliya Varus to administer to Siri for her pain.

"I haven't had time to fully analyze this yet, but we've seen some of the resulting instability. And I'll tell you something else." Her voice was matter-of-fact, but she wasn't looking at me. Her face had flushed darkly. "These were clones."

"Clones?" I said blankly. "But they're chips."

"Term of art." She opened a second pane, to display a second set of little black squares, with the same pattern of threads as the ones in Siri's node. "These"—she tapped the second set—"are from Bianca Fayette's implant, back when it was whole."

Pain filled the empty space in my skull. Sick, hard, relentless pain. The idea of Bianca's body spread out for the slaves and vultures of Hospital, of her blood measured and microscopically analyzed, of Jerimiah laid bare for their analysts . . .

Jerimiah had been damaged. Oh, yes, he'd been damaged. I saw them taking the lace filigree of his network from Bianca's vivisected skull. I saw them laying it on a pure white table and gathering around it, bent over it, whispering and wondering at what they'd found, recording, measuring, analyzing.

Some of Jerimiah's nodes had been "disconnected."

Bianca hadn't sold out to the Erasmus System. She hadn't gotten Jerimiah cut out to keep him from informing on her. She'd been dismembered. She'd been an experiment. They'd taken her apart to see what her body could teach them, and it had showed them the defense and protection of every single field officer in the Guardians.

Hospital the size of a planet, Siri's voice whispered in my ear. *We don't know what they can do.*

The Erasmans were creating a network of human voices that were being implanted in the Clerks, Siri said. It sounded insane. Unless you substituted a couple of words.

The Erasmans were creating a network of Companions that were being implanted in the Clerks.

"Can you neutralize this?"

Dr. Gwin shook her head. "Not in these facilities. I'd have to wake her up and scan the interactions while she's in communication with it, and I can't wake her up because I can't disable her off switch here either."

Unstable as she was, if Siri woke up and saw that she was in the hospital, there was a very real chance she'd hit the switch and be gone.

Pain swam slowly upstream to my consciousness and I realized my hands had curled into fists. I opened them and saw the neat lines of red crescent moons on my palms.

"Can you keep her out and safe?" I asked.

Dr. Gwin nodded.

"Do it. I'll have your orders shortly."

She nodded again, and I left her there. I walked through the clean lock and out into the battered foyer.

Vijay was there. "What is it?"

I looked up at him. "I found the war."

THIRTY-FOUR

TERESE

Vijay grabbed me by the shoulders, whirled me around, and slammed me up against the wall. *"What have they done to her!"*

"You will stand down, Captain!" I bellowed.

Vijay stared at me, wide-eyed with panic. I watched the realization of what he was doing dawn on him. He lifted his hands away and snapped to attention.

"At ease." I was oddly grateful he'd pushed me to the wall. Without the support, I was afraid I wouldn't be able to stand. "And upstairs now."

I led him up to the third floor and into Siri's room. I bolted the door behind us. Probably the illusion of Siri was still on the other side. At this moment, I couldn't afford to care.

I faced Vijay. I felt hard as steel and sick to my soul. There, in the middle of Siri's listening room, I told him what had been done to her—to all of us.

When I finished, Vijay was white as a sheet. Anger rolled off him in tsunami waves. His hands clenched and unclenched and his eyes had gone distant. He was elsewhere. He was with the ones who had taken Siri's mind from her, and no service oath could reach that place.

"We've got to get you out," I said.

His eyes snapped back into immediate focus. "They don't know about me."

"This is not a request, Captain. You are at risk, and you're now putting the mission at risk. We have no counter for this attack, and we do not know how many ways they have to deliver it."

He swallowed, and licked his lips. "I want them dead, Terese," he croaked. "I want them all dead."

"I know." I laid my hand on his shoulder. "Believe me, I know." *Bianca, are you listening? Are you laughing at me?* "We're going to take the place down, and the one responsible is going to get to watch."

"We've got no orders."

I almost smiled. "We've got the ultimate order. The war's already started. Listen to me, Vijay, I am trusting you to get every last one of our people off this rock before I make it all hit the fan. Get through to the embassy and try for the flight permissions, but if they can't pull it out, you leave anyway."

"They'll try to shoot us down."

"I don't think so."

He stared at me, almost as if he were trying to figure out the punch line for my joke. "You don't *think* so."

I shook my head. "As long as it looks like we're turning tail and running, they're not going to care." He frowned at me, disbelieving. I swallowed my impatience. "They wanted us to find out about this, Vijay. They worked a massive illusion to make it look like this place was an active hot spot to draw us in." In my mind's eye I saw the black-and-white figure of Natio Bloom as Siri had shown him to me, bowing elaborately. "They wanted agents with Companions in their system. They wanted to alter us, and they wanted us to know who had done it. Now they want us to run away and pull every active field agent in the diaspora in behind us."

"But we can't . . ."

"They cloned Bianca's Companion nodes. They figured out how to use our ultimate protection to drive us insane."

I had to bite my lips for a moment before I could go on. "How much do you think they could sell this secret to the other hot spots for?"

The implications settled in, and Vijay's jaw dropped.

"*Go.*" I sat down at Siri's desk and pulled out my glasses.

"What are you doing?"

"I'm going to report to Misao, then find Amerand." I slipped my glasses on.

"*What?* Why?"

I hauled on every nerve I had to keep from shouting at him. "Because this has been so tightly planned from the beginning, I cannot believe he was brought in by accident. He's supposed to be in for the big finish."

"What big finish?"

"I hope to all the gods we don't have to find out." I grabbed Vijay's hand. "They do not get away with this. I swear it."

Revenge gleamed coldly in the depths of his eyes. "No, ma'am."

I released him and he marched out into the corridor, letting the door slam shut behind him. I faced Siri's box. I unplugged some cables, rearranged others, pulled on my gloves, and clipped my set to my ear.

"Field Commander Drajeske to Marshal-Steward Misao Smith," I said. "Priority One, ears only from Erasmus System. We are live and running. Repeat. We are live and we are running."

THIRTY-FIVE

AMERAND

The port yard looked perfectly normal when I reached it. The guards at the gate slouched. The Clerks prowled around the lower air-lock entrances. I even saw the infamous Papa Dare dressing down his subordinate Meek near one of the partitioned areas.

You wouldn't have thought it was the end of the world at all.

I walked up to the lower air lock for Bay 6. The Clerk there was a little brown man with copper-red hair and a datapad clutched in his delicate hand.

"I am here under the authority of the Grand Sentinel," I told him. "I am supposed to document the changes I made to the access codes for the engine compartment."

The Clerk looked at me and punched in a note on his datapad. "Captain Amerand Jireu?" he asked.

"Yes."

"I have you down here. You're to have supervised access only."

"It makes no difference to me." It didn't. I had assumed I would have at least one Clerk looking over my shoulders.

We rode the elevator up to the air lock and waited while it cycled. The Clerk thumbed his datapad restlessly, as if searching for something. I wondered what it was. He seemed different from some of the others I had seen lately. His eyes lacked the hard, concentrated glitter. But I didn't have thought to spare about that. I had my own plans to put into motion.

The upper air lock hissed open and we stepped into the peeled core. It had not improved in my absence. The air smelled stale, and the webbing in the emergency cradles dangled loose. So did the oxygen masks. The cradle caps had been left open. The internal drive squatted in the middle of the chamber, silent and solid, its silver branches inserting themselves into deck and ceiling like a giant's fingers.

I stepped carefully around to the control pad. I had caught the Clerk, or someone, in midinspection. Lines of code filled the screen. I read it, identifying which control quarter I was in more quickly than I would have expected. But it was not the place I needed. I touched the controls, scrolling down.

"You will report what you are doing as you proceed," said the Clerk fussily.

"No."

I had it now, the timing and targeting codes. These were dense and complicated, and this was done on purpose. You did not want someone casually altering this segment. These were the codes that kept your ship from jumping where there was known to be a planet, or a star, or some other physical object.

And they had been butchered, like the rest of the safety codes had been.

"You will report to me what you are doing," ordered the Clerk.

"No."

I could hear his harsh breathing behind me. He had never been defied before. He was a Clerk. Which of us would even think to argue with him? I kept my attention focused on the codes in front of me: matching broken commands, inserting new ones, reconnecting fragmented loops and feedbacks, smoothing over rough holes.

"You are removed!"

I turned and I stood. "Then go find a secops to remove me. Or will you be trying to do that yourself?"

I was unarmed, but so was he. I was taller than this little man. I was a tunnel runner and a secop, and I knew how to fight in small spaces. I was at the end of my resources and the end of my life. He was not. Not yet.

The Clerk opened and closed his mouth, gasping for air and words. Behind him, the air lock cycled, and we both jerked our heads up.

Terese Drajeske stepped across the bulkhead. She met my gaze, reading my expression, and my stance.

"You'd better get out of here," she said to the Clerk.

The Clerk swallowed. His thumb moved reflexively across his datapad, but he didn't seem able to connect to any other node. "You . . . you're not authorized to be here."

"No," she agreed. "But I'm telling you, if you want to live, you'd better get out of here."

It was too much. The Clerk had probably never needed courage, and surely had seldom needed to make a real decision. He darted out the air lock, and we heard his feet slamming against the decking as he ran for the elevator.

At another time, I would have been afraid. Right then, I could have laughed. One of our omniscient omnipresent Clerks had just run away from a saint.

As it was, neither of us spared him a glance.

"How did you find me?" I asked.

Her mouth twitched and she reached up, touching me on the temple, just as she had before down in the tunnel. "You're carrying my camera," she said, and she held out her gloved hand to show me the near-invisible silver speck. "Sorry."

I had no outrage left for the saints and their machinations. I plucked the speck from her finger, dropped it onto the deck, and ground my heel down on it. Terese made no move to stop me.

I turned back to the control pad and my work.

"What are you doing, Amerand?" she asked.

"You don't want to know." I scrolled down farther to check an identity, then copied it over into a broken code line, plugging a hole.

"Is this going to Fortress?"

"I said you don't want to know." I shoved two code lines that did not belong together into one statement and changed the acceptable inputs, one number at a time.

"Do you want to at least tell me why?"

"They killed my mother."

She stood silent for a long time. I kept working. I didn't have much time. That Clerk was reporting to somebody. Secops would be on their way soon. I had to get this finished.

"How'd you find out about your mother?"

"Emiliya left me a message."

More silence. Stretching out long enough for me to knit up and alter three more codes.

"And where's Emiliya?"

"She's dead too." I said it flatly, factually. I knew some part of me was shouting out my grief, but it was distant. I had tried to keep us alive. I had tried so hard. All I had wanted was for her, for me—even for Kapa—to survive. It was more important than love or friendship or anything else. We, I, had to stay alive. That was why my parents had brought me here, that was why they had put me into the academy—to keep me alive after they had failed my brothers. So many dead so I could live.

But we had all failed, and the only ones who would stay ive were the Blood Family.

"Amerand Jireu, I want you to listen to me."

"I don't have time to listen to you." *Don't make me fight you, rese. I do not want to hurt you, but I will not let you stop me.*

"Hamahd was right, Amerand. They're using you."

I swung around. She was still standing just in front of ιe threshold. Her hands were out a little from her sides, here I could see them. She was unarmed and her hands ere empty.

She knew I was ready to use force against her. She was ady for it. For me.

"They're using you," she said again. "This is a setup."

"You don't know what you're talking about."

"I don't?" The corner of her mouth twitched. "Then an- ver me this, Amerand: Why is this still here?" She threw her ands out, turning in a circle to encompass the disheveled ιamber. "Why the hell hasn't this great big security threat ιen towed out to the shipyard and put under lock and ·y?"

I waved her words away. "Favor Barclay was going to sell off."

"I've been to see Favor Barclay," she answered. "He says his mily is gone, but he's still here. He says he's covering their ·treat, but he's not acting like a man doing something he's roud of. He was in really sad shape. I think he's traded his mily's freedom in return for providing the cover for leaving iis where you could get at it."

She moved forward one step. Her gaze remained locked ɔn mine. Her hands stayed low and open. "Amerand, we ave been shown a gigantic illusion. We've been given ɔubles and toys and obvious paths from the beginning and we've taken them all. This is just one more. Somebody left this here for you."

"You can't know that."

"Then I ask you again: What is this still doing here?"

My breath heaved in my chest. I had to end this. "Field Commander Drajeske, do you know what the Blood Family have been doing with their time and their Hospital? They've given themselves immortality. Real immortality that doesn't need to be checked or renewed and can be passed on to their children. They dug it out of your Bianca Fayette. They killed hundreds of us to perfect it. If we don't stop them here and now, they go on forever!"

I watched with a kind of perverse satisfaction as the blood drained from her face. "Emiliya found the records. She got them to me before she . . . before she . . ." I couldn't finish. The grief and the anger moved closer. It crowded up against my rational thought. I needed to get this woman away from me. I needed to get back to my work. Even if my fellow secops weren't on their way up the elevator, I wasn't going to be able to hold on much longer.

I turned back to the access pad. I had four commands yet to repair. Just four. I could do this.

"You'll wipe the whole of Fortress out," she said.

"Good," I whispered.

"You'll kill thousands, Amerand, and you're not even going to get the ones you're aiming at."

"How can you be so sure?"

"Because it's a *setup*. It has been from the beginning. You have been *driven* to this." She spoke slowly, as if she were still fitting the pieces together in her head. "They killed your whole fucking world, *and* your best friend, then they let you find out they'd killed your *mother*. They let you find out they re going to become immortal! Then they left a loaded gun lying around so you could pick it up and pull the trigger! Amerand, they want this done!" She was speaking more strongly now, as if it had all suddenly begun to make perfect sense. "Where are they, Amerand?" Terese gestured back toward the open air lock. Where're the Clerks and the cameras? Where's secops? They let you in here and they're letting you set off the biggest bomb in the history of humanity."

"Why? Why would they want Fortress wiped out?"

"To cull the family. What you've told me about the immortality—it fits into everything else we've found. Those that are not worthy are not going to go into the future with the rest.

"But the murder of so many Blood relations has got to be done by you, or somebody like you. Somebody who's been driven crazy by loss and grief. The survivors will see you and they won't look for your puppet master. You'll take the blame for killing their relatives, the children, the hostages, the Clerks. Maybe especially the Clerks. They're the ones who could identify how the decisions were made."

Terese took one step closer to me. "Amerand, I've alerted my people. They'll be here soon. In force. I know that sounds strange coming from us, but you've seen only a part of what we can do if we absolutely have to."

But I turned away again. I stared at the access pad with its tidy black lines of code on the shimmering grey background. I thought about the tear I'd seen on my father's face. I thought about how I couldn't draw up any memories of my mother or my brothers.

"You'll let them live," I whispered hoarsely. "They've slaughtered and tortured and enslaved us, and you'll just let them live."

"No," she answered quietly. "I'll *make* them live."

"And what's the difference?" I sneered.

"Terms and conditions," she answered. "I told you I was tortured? The man who ordered that is still alive, and he's going to stay that way. In fact, he's immortal now. He's living in a comfortable pair of rooms in the middle of his home city, and he'll live there forever, nice and cozy. He can't go outside. He can't talk with another human being face-to-face. He can't even go comfortably insane. He's alive and stable, and we're going to keep him that way. He never gets away from what he's done, never gets to have a better life or another life. He never meets his Maker or sees his Heaven. He gets to watch while the kingdom he built fades from the historical record and the city he ruined is rebuilt by his enemies and opened up wide, because all the people he tried to lead to his brutal salvation like his enemy's way better.

"He's ours. He's *mine*, in his two-room cell, forever and ever.

"Do you want revenge for you and yours? Help me make the Blood Family live with what they've done."

My hand was shaking, making the fingers drum against my thigh. "It's not enough."

"And it's never going to be," she agreed. "But you can kill them all and it still won't be enough. It just gets you the wrong answers and prolongs the horror you're trying to end." She took one more step closer. "Have you remembered the hostages, Amerand? Those are Oblivion's children over there. You make the wrong move here and you're killing them all."

"Maybe they're better off dead." The words opened a kind of gate inside me, a flood of emotion so close to relief I couldn't even be afraid of it. I had held that thought in the

epths of me for longer than I knew. The fight for survival
xacted too high a toll. We were all better off dead.

"Do you really want to be the one who makes that deci-
on? Do you want to be like the Erasmus family, deciding
ho gets to count as a human being and who's just fodder
r your disappointment?"

"You don't understand," I whispered. "You don't under-
and!" I shouted.

"They've taken people from me, too. They used them
nd they murdered them. What else do I have to under-
and?" She reached out and gripped my hand hard, as if at-
mpting to squeeze her conviction into me. "I am not
oing to let Erasmus win, Amerand. I will *not* leave this sys-
m standing. But I need your help."

I was trembling. I had come here in the certainty that this
as the last thing I would ever do. There was no future for
e. There was nothing beyond this chamber. Terese was try-
g to rewrite the hastily constructed code of my last mo-
ents and force a future onto me.

I moved my lips, but there was no sound. *How?*

Terese understood me. "You were going to send this thing
to the middle of Fortress, right? Crack the city apart? I need
ou to pick us a new destination."

My mind sputtered, trying to force itself into some kind
f position that could take into account the possibility that
was not going to die. "Where?"

"Oblivion."

I heard the word, but my mind which had been so sharp
p until now could only absorb it slowly. "Oblivion is dead."

I watched compassion wash over her. I didn't want it, not
en, not ever. I didn't want anyone to understand what I

felt, or what I was going through. I wanted to hoard all the pain for myself.

"They've turned it into a bolt-hole," she told me. "They're going to hide there until after you've destroyed Fortress and the Pax Solaris has cleaned up. They think we'll just take away the refugees and abandon the system." The gleam of discovery lit her eyes. "This place is too far off the beaten path now, and takes too much effort to maintain. No one else would colonize it. The surviving Blood Family can wait until they're good and forgotten. They'll have all the time there is."

Anger, red and alive, burned in me. The gall was incredible. They'd allowed a whole world of people to die, and they were going to plunder the corpse.

I was breathing hard. I was dizzy. My whole mind was turning over, and I didn't know where to look, what to think. "What do we do?"

"Exactly what they want you to do. You're going to set this thing off. Only you're going to miss. Instead of jumping to the inside of Fortress, you're going to drop us as close as you can to Oblivion."

I considered this as best I could. I was going to Oblivion in a peeled core. I was going to my dead home. My first reaction was born of my time in the Security. "They'll shoot us down."

"It'll take seven hours for a missile to get there. I checked, as far as I could. My people will be here before then."

My second reaction came from my pilot's training. "We could end up inside Oblivion." And die. I had come expecting to die, so I wasn't quite sure why I suddenly cared.

"We could," she admitted. "This is on the face of it radically stupid."

"Then why are you doing it?"

"Because I want them focused on me. If they get their ands on me, I can make them think I'm just trying to cover ay people's escape." Her smile was thin and bitter. "They'll robably think I'm spying, but that's okay too."

"What are you really doing?"

"Spying and covering my people's escape," she answered o promptly that I knew she was lying.

"And if you die?" I asked.

Her voice was absolutely calm. "Then I die trying."

Die trying. I was so tired. I didn't know if I could. I wanted o just die. But maybe I had strength enough left for this. I ould have just killed myself after all, as Hamahd had done, s my father was going to do, but I'd wanted to accomplish omething first. Taking out Fortress in all its foul glory had een my something.

Perhaps I could change my plans. I had wanted to help ae Solarans. I'd wanted to help Terese. Perhaps I could die ying, too. Maybe then it wouldn't hurt so badly.

"I'll take you," I said, and I was able to meet her gaze again, nd her gaze was absolutely grim.

"Understand, if you come with me, you will be acting nder the laws and constraints of the Solaris Guardians. *All* f them."

All of them. "Yes."

"Will you swear it?" Part of me couldn't believe she was aking the time to do this. Another part of me understood erfectly.

"I swear on my mother's life and my father's. I swear on ae memory of Oblivion, I will abide by your commands nd follow your orders."

She nodded. "I accept your oath on behalf of the Solaris

Guardians." Then, suddenly, like a burst of starlight, a smile spread out across her face. She reached up and touched my cheek as she had once before. "Welcome to the fight, Amerand Jireu."

Then she stepped back until she moved into the nearest emergency cradle.

I turned to the access panel. I moved two codes. I changed three input parameters. I set the timer.

I slipped into the cradle next to Terese's. I secured my restraints and my webbing, and I looked across at her. She smiled at me from behind her oxygen mask.

I pulled my mask down. I closed the cap on my cradle.

I watched the access pad flicker over from silver to green to red.

The explosion went off right next to my ears. A world of weight slammed against my chest. I would have screamed, but I had no air in my lungs.

Darkness.

THIRTY-SIX

TERESE

I watched the access pad flash from silver, to green, to red. I tried to breathe deeply, calmly. Tried to get ready for whatever was to come. I glanced down at the message on the back of my glove—I'd left it up there. My last message, the one I'd sent to David at the same time I'd sent out the SOS to Misao. I kept it there, along with the red marker indicating it had gone through. Whatever happened next, I would not disappear without a word.

It was real to me, David, I'd said. It was always real.

The explosion tore the world apart.

My next awareness was pain. Pain in my head, in my rib cage, in my guts. Slowly, it trickled through to my conscious mind that if I was feeling pain, I was alive.

My eyelids felt heavy as concrete. I forced them open.

I saw nothing.

I tasted blood in the darkness. Panic screamed through my brain. I was in the cell, they were coming for me, there would be more pain, I couldn't stand any more pain . . .

I dragged in a breath that tasted of blood and tried to find my right hand. I thought I could feel my fingers, my palm, my wrist. I twisted my wrist, my numbing fingers searching for the release.

My arm fell forward and slapped against something. I hissed as fresh pain tore through my elbow joint. I flexed my index finger and felt the brush of my glove against the tip. I bent my wrist up and scrabbled against my cuff until I found the switch for my handlight and pressed it. A burst of white blotted out the world and I had to screw my eyes shut until that particular pain faded.

When I was able to open my eyes again, I was staring at a wall of salt-and-pepper stone, coated with a white powder that was all that was left of my cradle cap. I hung tight against the webbing. If it gave way, I would fall, full length against the pulverized silicate and stone.

I knew what it meant, and my breath started coming short and fast. It meant we'd missed. Instead of landing near the surface, we'd jumped inside Oblivion.

With some difficulty, I turned my head, my heart banging against my aching ribs. The sides of the compartment were curved. If I was this close to the stone, how close was Amerand? I gritted my teeth and raised my light, angling it to my right.

Amerand was also still in his straps, but he was wedged firmly between the wall of the compartment and the broken stone.

I took a deep, useless breath and pulled my arm back up, trying not to scream, but I got my oxygen mask off. There was air pressure, or I would have been bleeding out my pores by then. The atmosphere had to be breathable, at least in the short term, because there was no way anything in this shattered eggshell of an engine core was still functioning, including the O_2.

"Amerand!" I croaked. "Amerand!"

He blinked, slowly, groggily.

"Amerand, talk to me!"

His tongue pushed itself out of his mouth several times. I couldn't see any blood, but that meant nothing.

"Come on, Amerand, try!"

He turned his head back and forth. The mask grated against the stone, and dragged off over his cheek.

"A little more to the left next time," he whispered.

Relief washed through me. A smile flickered on his face, but rapidly turned into a grimace. "I'm stuck."

"Yeah. Hold on."

"Yes."

After some pained struggling and a lot of cursing, I managed to free my left arm so I could sort of brace myself against the stone underneath me while I undid my webbing. The gravity was light enough that I easily caught myself on both my hands, though the pain in my wrists made me gasp. I pulled my boots free from the ankle braces and let my feet drop.

For a moment, I just stayed there on hands and toes, as if I meant to start doing push-ups, breathing in the gritty, hot, stale air.

Stale air, repeated the part of my brain that still remembered the more usual hazards of spaceflight.

"Right," I whispered. "No time for this." I lowered myself onto my belly and twisted around. Slowly, I started wriggling toward Amerand.

"You noticed the air, too?" he said.

"I was hoping you hadn't." I stripped off a glove and shoved my hand into the narrow crack between his ribs and the webbing.

"I grew up in pressurized tunnels," he reminded me, and made an effort to suck in his gut. "Believe me, you learn that a smell like this means there's no new air coming in."

Stone tore my skin. I prodded cloth and skin and Amerand grunted. "Sorry."

Finally, my fumbling fingers found the webbing catch. The sharp edges of the stone dug deeper into my knuckles as I pressed and wriggled. At last I heard the blessed click and the security webbing drifted slowly down against my arm.

I edged my hand down. There was enough room to undo his right-hand cuff, but I couldn't slide my arm between his body and the stone to get to the other.

"How about your left hand?" I asked. "Have you got any room at all?"

"Give me a minute." He closed his eyes and bared his teeth. I waited, listening to the rustling as his fingers searched and strained. I tried to breathe shallowly. I tried not to think what it meant if we had come to rest in a pocket of stone deep in the core of Oblivion.

Click.

"Got it." Amerand opened his eyes. "I think."

"We'll find out in a minute." I scrunched backward, and he reached out, stretching and wincing and wriggling, until his fingers curled around the ragged stone ledge. One centimeter at a time, he eased himself out until he was crouched on hands and knees beside me.

It was noticeably warmer. Sweat coated my forehead.

"Now what?" he said.

I did not have the strength to sugarcoat the situation. "Now we find out if we're dead or not."

If we were only partway buried in stone, we might be able to break out through the damaged hull. If we were deep inside the moon's core, we had until this little pocket of air ran out.

"Up?" he suggested.

"Up," I agreed. I shined my light around the curve of the hull that had become our very low ceiling.

"Here." Amerand grimaced but reached out, tracing a thin black crack that had appeared between the stone and the hull.

I swallowed and pressed my hand experimentally against the hull where it curved overhead. "We've still got at least a couple of hundred pounds over us."

"If it's clear of the stone," he said. "Can you see anything we can use as a wedge?"

I held up my gloved hands. He stared at them, then at me.

"They're armored. Our materials scientists are very good," I said.

"All right."

I shifted. Every part of me hurt, but I managed to get my feet under me with no more undignified gasps of pain than strictly necessary. Amerand pulled one leg into place, then the other, and braced himself on the cradle's edge so he could crouch flat-footed on the stone with his shoulder pressed against the hull.

"Ready?" he asked.

I placed the very tips of my fingers against the thread-fine fissure. "Ready."

Amerand strained. He screamed and heaved upward. A thunderous cracking like the sound of a great tree falling surrounded us. Slowly, the hull separated from the stone.

Air. Sweet cool air rushed in on us, along with rich yellow light. I jammed my fingers into the space, and I prayed. Amerand shouted and the space widened and I turned both hands sideways and shoved them in farther.

Amerand panted beside me and when I turned my head a little, I could see that his face was streaked with dirt, sweat, and blood.

I held a couple of hundred pounds of broken ship's hull

supported on my hands. If our tech people were not as good as they were supposed to be, I was in for a whole world of hurt.

Amerand braced himself again, but before he could press up, the crash of rending metal sounded all around us. The hull peeled back and toppled sideways, and we stood blinking in the light and warmth of Oblivion's port yard.

Half a dozen men stood in front of us. They were Clerks. They wore the high-necked black jackets, but these had been shortened so they were more like tunics than coats. They had black gloves on their hands and their eyes glittered hard and distant as they silently lowered their black guns to take aim at us.

The Clerks said nothing. The guns clattered as they worked the actions.

I lifted my throbbing hands in surrender.

"Who are you?" demanded Amerand hoarsely.

They did not answer. One of them pointed to the floor beside him. Moving slowly, I put my knee on the ragged edge of the hole we'd made and pushed myself out. Amerand, not taking his gaze off these strange, militarized Clerks, did the same.

Five of them held their weapons leveled at us. The sixth strode across the floor made of the salt-and-pepper stone but polished to a high gloss. He laid his hands on a pair of gilded doors that would have been at home in the palaces of Fortress. They opened for him. He stood aside and nodded to us.

The message was plain, and there was nothing we could do. I laced my hands behind my neck. My shoulders cried out in protest, but I gritted my teeth. Amerand, after a moment's hesitation, copied my gesture.

I was glad. I did not want him giving these silent Clerks any excuse to shoot.

They surrounded us: two in front, two behind, and one on either side. They moved with eerie precision, and with no sound but the slap of soft-soled boots against stone. They did not look at one another. They barely looked at us. They didn't have to. They were listening to the voices in their heads.

The Clerks marched forward and we had no choice but to move with them.

I had seen blueprints and photos of the old Oblivion. It was a mass of narrow tunnels lined by single-person cells. What open yards there were had been built with secured guardhouses in the center so that the inmates were never without supervision. That was, of course, not counting the screens, the drones, and the guards in their mechanical armor.

That was all gone now. Swept away. What opened around us was another palace.

We walked along a granite thoroughfare. At our left hand there was a low wall carved from the same salt-and-pepper stone. A garden of blooming plants and miniature trees spread out below us. A stream bubbled over rounded stones and trickled down the middle of a lawn of grass and wildflowers. I smelled lemons and roses.

Mai Erasmus sat on a blanket in the middle of that garden, a perfect picture of pastoral bliss out enjoying the summer sun with her baby on her lap. She looked up as we passed and her eyes widened. She poked at the infant in her arms, trying to make the baby look up where she pointed and waved.

She grinned at me and waved once more, but they marched us around a corner.

I glanced up at Amerand. He kept his eyes rigidly ahead. His face had gone pale beneath the dirt and blood, and his knuckles were white behind his head. I could not begin to imagine what he was feeling.

This must have taken years. It must have taken dozens of flights back and forth. Now I knew what had been erased from the records I'd sent to Misao.

The military Clerks led us through cavern after cavern of parks and gardens. The chosen of the Blood Family laughed and ran through their exquisitely designed playland, exploring their new domain. There weren't a lot of them. I counted about thirty. Assuming that was somewhat accurate, the murder Amerand was supposed to have carried out on Fortress would have taken down at least seven hundred and fifty people. That was if you didn't count the Clerks and the servants, which I was fairly sure they hadn't.

I had thought the people of the Erasmus System were being exploited as labor to bring their masters profit. They weren't. They were being used to dig out the new city of Oblivion and serve in immortality experiments.

And to act as distractions for the stupid saints who came to try to help the thirsty population.

The natives of Dazzle hadn't seen it because they were willing to put up with anything as long as the OBs were kept away from the farm caverns. The natives of Oblivion hadn't seen it because the only form of government they had ever lived under was slavery and confinement.

We Solarans hadn't seen it because they'd showed us what we feared and we went tearing off after it.

There were no servants here, at least none that I saw. There were only Clerks. Some wore the short black tunics like the ones marching us forward. Some wore the more

ditional long coats. Whenever we passed them they
opped and turned, standing like statues, letting our little
rade go past.

The Clerks walked us about a mile. My knees and shoul-
rs were on fire by the time the thoroughfare ended at an-
her pair of the gilded doors. The lead Clerks laid their
lms on panels embossed with the eternal Erasmus family
e, and the doors swung outward.

The room was blank white and shining, like the holding
y on the habitat had been. A white-haired man sat at a
ack desk in the middle. He wore a gold-and-ruby collar of
nk around his bony shoulders, and he had a Clerk's glitter-
g eyes. A straight row of white chairs was arrayed in front
the desk. They were all high-backed, padded, and sealed
the floor. They all had restraints bolted to the arms.

"Good evening, Grand Sentinel," said Amerand.

The Grand Sentinel Torian Erasmus steepled his fingers
d smiled.

I rallied. I was going to have to talk fast if I wanted to sur-
ve long enough for the cavalry to come.

I had no chance.

The Clerk grabbed me from behind. I kicked back hard,
t he didn't even flinch.

"Stop this!" shouted Amerand. The nearest Clerk leveled
e gun at him. I stopped struggling and swallowed. The
asmus System was still firmly in place. If I fought, they
uld shoot Amerand.

Amerand and I stared wildly at each other and he under-
od why I had stopped struggling. He threw back his head
d shouted wordlessly at the ceiling. He was a hostage
ain.

Still.

"Don't, Amerand," I said. "Do not give them any excuse. You are my witness." *Not hostage. Witness. I have no Companion. I have no one else.* "If you're gone, nobody sees what happens here."

Torian smiled, frozen in place, fingertips pressed together.

I made myself look at him. *It doesn't matter,* I told him silently. *You're already finished. You just don't know it yet.*

The door opened and a slender, freckle-faced young man wearing medical whites entered the room. I was not surprised to see the Clerk's distant glitter in his tarnished gold eyes, or the pressure spray in his hands.

You're already finished, I repeated in my head. *You just don't know it yet.*

They slammed me into the chair. They closed the restraints on my wrists. I struggled. I couldn't help it. They caught my head and I tried to bite and I heard Amerand shouting and cursing and the pressure spray dug into the hollow behind my ear.

It hurt.

It hurt.

It *hurt.*

THIRTY-SEVEN

TERESE

Hello, Terese."

Dylan?

My eyes flew open. I was in the curving white room, but was alone. The desk and chairs were empty. My hands were free. But none of that mattered.

Dylan?

He was there. Black leather jacket and stupid tattoo and shit-eating grin. All of him.

"Yes."

I lurched to my feet. Warm, strong arms wrapped around me in a bear hug. I couldn't breathe, I could only feel. Dylan. I'd never known he would be so strong. We spun each other round.

Dylan . . . but they cut you out of me. You're gone.

He chuckled, setting me down again. "Not anymore."

I stepped back, just a little, just enough so I could look him over. *God and all the Prophets, it's good to see you!*

"You too, Terese. I've missed you."

But how . . .

"Ah-ah." Dylan laid a finger on my mouth. "Don't ask. If you ask, it'll spoil things." He took both my hands. "I don't ever want to have to leave you again, Terese."

No. Please, no.

"Okay then. Just enjoy. It's been a tough time. Catch me up, would you?"

I'd like to say I didn't talk. It would sort of be true. I didn't talk. I babbled.

Thirty years' worth of life, of names and places and things, of my contacts with the Guardians, such as they were, all sprinkled with "You remember who . . ." and "You remember how . . ." And when he didn't remember, I filled him in.

I didn't think about what I was saying. I didn't care. This was Dylan, back in my mind, safe and whole. The pain was gone, the black hole was gone, and I wasn't alone anymore. For the first time in three decades, I wasn't alone.

I told him about Dazzle. I told him about Vijay and about Siri, and finally about Bianca. I cried while he held me.

"Will they really do an open intervention?"

They're on their way, Dylan.

He pulled away. He walked away, taking his warmth away from me.

What's the matter?

"There's a problem, Terese."

What?

"Terese, if they come here . . . Misao and the others. They're going to take me away."

No. I shook my head. *Never happen. You have no idea what I had to do to make them let me come out here without you in the first place. They'll be thrilled you're back.*

"No, they really won't, Terese, and you know it as well as I do."

I did know it. They'd do it. I couldn't seem to think how it was Dylan was back, but I knew it wasn't an official act. They'd take him away, take him out. They'd leave me alone in the dark. All closed in the dark. They'd broken me into pieces before, they'd do it again.

No, Dylan. Not again.

He spread his hands. "I wouldn't want to, Terese. But I wouldn't be able to stop them."

What do we do?

"It's up to you." He walked over to me and laid his hands in mine. I felt the weight of them, and they were as broad and callused as I had always imagined they would be. "You're the one who brought them in. You've got to call it off. Stall them until we can figure out what to do."

How come I can touch you? I curled my fingers around his. *I could never touch you before.*

He smiled. "Absence makes the heart grow fonder," he said, lifting our hands. "It also brings technological improvements."

Technological improvements. Improvements from experiments carried out on Bianca, on Siri. Cold flooded me, knotting my stomach, forcing me to back away. How could I have forgotten even for a moment?

Who are you?

Dylan's face fell and he shook his head. "I'm Dylan, Terese. You know me."

No. You're not. You can't be.

"Look at me. Who else is there?"

I looked. I strained my eyes. There was nothing—the blank whiteness of the empty room, the chairs, the desk, and Dylan.

But this wasn't right. My hand flew to the curve behind my ear and found the hot welt there.

Those are clones, said Dr. Gwin's voice from memory. I saw again the black-and-white blocks of the chips that had been laid into Siri's network.

They must have laid down a whole new network for me. *Was it easier or harder that way?*

"I wouldn't know, Terese," said Dylan quietly.

Easier. It had to be easier. There would be no interference, no second voice of sanity to be counteracted. Just my permanently mourning mind, all primed and ready to believe in the miraculous return of the lost.

You're a ghost! You're nothing!

"You don't believe that, Terese," he said softly. "You can't believe that."

I slumped and I sagged. I fell back into the white chair. They hadn't even bothered to keep me restrained. This was Dylan, and he was with me again and he was real—and I couldn't fight him.

Dylan crouched down in front of me. "It's okay, Terese. We're needed here. We've got a whole new world of people who depend on us. Just stall Misao for a few hours while we sort out what to do."

I lifted my head weakly. Dylan smiled at me, and I took his hand. They had me. They had me in a way the Redeemers never had. They had not taken anything from me.

They had given me what I'd wanted most in the world.

They. *Who are they?* I tried to make myself think. *I should know. I should be able to understand.* I knew the names. I knew who had planned this and brought me here. I knew who held Amerand hostage now and forever.

You're Torian Erasmus, I said to Dylan. *You're the Grand Sentinel of the Erasmus System.*

For a single heartbeat, it wasn't Dylan. It was the white-haired man in his bright collar. And Dylan's hand vanished from mine.

Then it was gone, and it was me and Dylan, and I was holding his callused hand again.

"Does the name really matter, Terese?" he murmured. "I'm here with you now."

I didn't answer at once, and he frowned, just a little, and sorrow flooded me. It was cold, it was loneliness, deep in my head and my heart.

It was too much. It was going to drag me under, it was so strong.

Too strong to be real. Too strong to be mine.

I grabbed his hand again and I squeezed, too hard.

"It matters," I said through gritted teeth. "It does matter, Torian Erasmus."

And I pictured the white-haired man in his collar of rank. I pictured the Clerks and their guns. I formed the thoughts and I held them hard.

I had been trained for this. I had worked with a Companion for years, and I knew how to picture him. I could picture a world to put him in when I needed to. I had been in a cell for months with only Dylan and that world for relief, and I had gotten very, very good at this kind of focus.

My eyes cleared and I could see. At least, it seemed as if I could see. Dylan was gone. My hands were empty. Torian Erasmus sat at his desk, his mouth fixed in his death's-head smile.

"I can give him back to you, Terese." It was still Dylan's voice in my head. I'd never heard Torian's voice. I didn't have any memory to work from. "Anytime. Just say his name and he is here."

No.

Torian frowned. I'd hurt him. I'd hurt him and the sorrow rushed through me. Despair, bleak and uncomprehending. How could I hurt this man? I was making him keep Dylan away from me.

Who are you?

Patience, deep and profound, radiated from him. "I'm Felice Erasmus's father."

Shock blanked my mind, and the patient warmth flowed into me unhindered. "I took immortality, I think about the same time your Bianca Fayette did. I was able to watch my daughter's plans come to fruition, then fail." His anger shook me, a parent's righteous, disappointed anger. His grandchildren, the unworthy heirs of his beloved daughter, they'd been given everything, and they'd lost it all.

But he was not going to permit his family—his daughter's family—to perish. He'd planned this across the decades, with the vision of centuries.

"I truly owe Bianca a debt. I thought I was going to have to let them take me apart. I started the Clerks' network to protect and stabilize my family in case I had to give what I had, what I was, over to them. But then Bianca came, and that was no longer an issue." His smile was beatific. "That she was conspiring with Bern to destroy my family only made it easier for her to vanish. Liang didn't care what happened to her, and Bern couldn't let the truth be found out."

And you took her to Hospital. You cut her open and you experimented on her. You were looking for immortality and in addition you found her Companion.

"Yes. The debt we owe her is truly incalculable."

I was on my knees. I didn't remember falling. My focus wavered enough that I saw Torian stand up slowly and walk around his desk. He held out one long, well-kept hand.

"Accept this, Terese. Let me help you."

I stared at that hand. Hand. Hands.

Hands.

I saw Siri's hand holding the knife to Vijay's throat.

I saw filthy hands covered with my blood, reaching out, making me kneel like this. Voices whispered lovingly in my ears, swearing they were doing the work of God Almighty, and black despair overtook me, because I believed them.

I knew this. I *knew* this.

I looked up again and I clenched my teeth. One fiber at a time, I pulled myself to my feet. And there was Torian Erasmus sitting immobile at his desk.

No.

Despair again, a flooding black wave. I stood and let it wash through me. I did not resist. There was nothing to fight. It was pure feeling. It would come. It would go. I would still be here.

This was illusion. This was drugs and nanos and Dazzle. I reached inside myself and I found my voice, my real, physical voice.

"Amerand!" I shouted.

"Terese!"

"Amerand, I'm blind! What's Torian doing?"

"He's just sitting there, Terese, he's not moving."

And Amerand screamed and there was the sound of metal against flesh, and I whirled around, but I saw nothing.

"There's only you and me here, Terese," said Torian. "I see no one else. This is our place, and it will be from now on."

Warmth flooded me now, the pure primal security that comes with being with your best friend, your lover. This was the safest place. There could be no pain here, no worry, and no end.

I stood. I don't know how, but I stood. I let it rise in me, sweet and false and a thousand times more terrible than the despair had been.

"You can't move, can you?" I moved my mouth, I worked my throat. I would not speak to him as I spoke to Dylan. He was not Dylan. "You can't move because you've got to focus on holding me here and creating this illusion."

Torian shrugged. "It hardly matters. You cannot maintain your resistance for long. This takes a great deal more strength for you than it does for me."

Oh, it felt so good to be here with him. Better than it had ever been with Dylan. Only with David had I ever been this safe.

David. Memory bright as daylight flashed over me. David in the rooftop garden looking out over the winter city. David sad and struggling with what I had done. David fighting with my old ghosts and losing. Ghosts, after all, couldn't fail to comprehend. Ghosts couldn't disappoint you.

Except wasn't that what Bianca had done?

"Very pretty," murmured Torian. "I always did like Chicago."

And David and Chicago were gone, and we were in the white room again, and all the worry was gone. I was tired and I was safe. I could sleep now, and it would be all right.

You saw that. You saw my memory.

"I see everything, Terese. It's those little technological improvements—and the fact that I am a living being. We are connected now, you and I."

Lassitude, warmth, and safety. Connected through a wireless transmission, a buzzing in the background, right behind my ear where my Companion used to be. The place Siri had tried to cut Vijay.

"You're very close to accepting it. Rest now. You've earned it."

Sleep. I was so tired.

"When you wake, Dylan will be here with you, and nothing else will matter."

I wanted to lie down at his feet and sleep. It would feel so good just to stretch out on the floor.

"Go to sleep now, and Dylan will wake you when it's time. Nothing else matters."

I swayed on my feet. The edges of my vision blurred and dimmed, moving slowly inward, blotting out light with warm darkness.

Darkness.

Darkness from my cell. Darkness from the space under the stairs. Darkness can see you. Darkness creeps under your skin and into your head. Daylight thinks it sees, but darkness knows. Darkness is what you carry in a hole in your head.

I could hold on to darkness. I could grab hold of it as I never could the daylight. I could shape the darkness because I remembered it so well.

I knew what the stone would feel like under my hands, I knew the exact temperature of the air, the way the dust would grate against my throat. And I knew to the depths of my soul there was no way out.

And there in the darkness of my mind, I closed the door. I knew the sound, I knew the feeling. I felt the breeze of it against my skin. The hollow thud reverberated down into my bones.

"What are you doing? Where is this?"

Torian Erasmus groped through the blackness I'd brought down. I could feel him blundering through my nightmare, searching for the door with blind fingers.

It's locked, Torian. There's no handle. Nothing.

It was then I knew Bianca had foxed them. In the end, she'd foxed them all.

She'd been their test case. They had manipulated her Companion, trying to see how far they could make her go, but they couldn't keep her alive and she'd called for me at the very end. This was why. She knew they'd pull me in here, into this space of illusion and manipulation. She was betting on what I'd bring with me.

She'd broken the rules and cost me my Companion, and she had found a way to save us all.

And I thought Misao was the stone-cold manipulator among us.

I could be in this place forever. Waking or sleeping, this was where my mind went. I wore this darkness like I wore my skin. I had never been able to escape it. I wouldn't lose it now.

"What have you done?"

"I've closed the door, Torian, and I've locked you in here with me."

And he believed me. He had to believe me. This memory was stronger and more clear than anything he knew how to bring up. I was trained. He was only practiced. This was my final reality and I had pushed it into his mind.

I was his Companion. I was the voice in his head and the vision in his mind's eye.

I smiled into the darkness and listened to the sound of Torian Erasmus banging on the locked cell door.

THIRTY-EIGHT

AMERAND

After the Clerk poleaxed me, I couldn't do anything but crouch on the floor, curled around myself, fighting for breath. Slowly, I was able to open my eyes again.

Terese knelt in the middle of the floor. She was smiling up at Torian, a satisfied, almost beatific smile. My guts flipped over and if I'd had anything left in my stomach, it would have spilled. Torian sat where he was, his fingers steepled, smiling down at her.

The Clerks stood still and staring. Not moving. I pushed myself up onto my knees. They still didn't move.

"Terese!" I shouted. "Terese!"

She did not move. The Clerks did not move. Torian did not move.

I climbed to my feet. I walked to the front of one of the Clerks. I didn't waste time with tests or pranks. I lifted the gun out of his hands. I turned it on him. I discarded the oath I'd sworn her.

I worked the action, and I shot him. Simple as that. Bone splintered, blood spattered, and he fell.

I took aim again, and I shot the second Clerk. And there was more blood and the smell of burning, and he toppled next to the first. The gun bounced out of his hands and clattered onto the white floor.

I picked it up out of the rivulets of blood and slung it across my back.

I walked over to Torian. I rested the muzzle of my gun on his forehead.

"Let her go," I said.

He did not move. He did not blink.

"Let her go, Sentinel."

He did not move. He did not blink.

I shot him as well, and he fell across his desk, spilling blood across the black stone.

Then I crossed the floor. I sat down beside Terese, cradling the gun across my thighs. I took her limp hand, and held it tightly.

"You can wake up now, Terese. It's over."

She didn't look at me. She stared at Torian Erasmus, dead at his desk, the top of his head blown clean off by my shot. She smiled like it was a good thing.

Outside the door I heard screaming. I heard shouts and wails of despair. Then I heard the unmistakable keening of alarms.

The woman beside me did not move.

"Terese? Terese, please."

She didn't move. I took her gloved hand. There were words shining on the back of it.

It was real to me, David. It was always real.

I covered up those words with my palm. I held her hand and waited for her breath to stop.

Waited for the end of the world.

I don't know how long it was before the saints sliced open the locks and pulled back the doors. I only know the doors opened. I raised my gun at a bald, scarred man in a blue tunic, and there was a sharp pain in my chest and everything faded away.

When I woke again, I was in a comfortable bed with soft sheets over me. The room around me was done in pleasant shades of yellow and beige. The curving walls made me guess I was on a ship before I even turned my head and saw the scene through the window.

Out there was the black sky, and a ship the size of the building I'd used to live in, shining silver in the light of the distant sun. Two missiles flashed toward it, making orange-and-white arcs against the black sky.

Before they reached the ship, they burst apart in silent showers of sparks.

"How's your head?" asked a familiar voice.

I jerked around. My vision sloshed a little at the abrupt movement. In that moment, I saw Liang getting up out of a chair and realized I was in no way restrained.

"I've never had a tranq shot from a Guardian, but I hear the stuff is pretty intense." There was a basin of some sort near the bed. He turned a knob and water poured down. He caught some in a cup and held the cup out to me.

"Here. There's plenty more if you want it."

I pushed myself up and I drank. It was sweet and clean and tasted like light.

"Thank you." I handed him back the cup. My hands had been cleaned of blood. I wore a soft blue shirt.

"No problem." He set the cup on the edge of the basin and leaned against it, folding his arms. "You might be interested to know you're aboard the Guardian ship *Himalaya*, and you've been out for about six hours."

Light and motion caught my eye. Three more missiles streaked toward the ship outside. Three more bursts of fireworks made burning white blossoms against the black.

"Yeah, that's been going on for about six hours too." He actually sounded bored.

You've seen only a part of what we can do if we absolutely have to, Terese had said.

"They're just going to sit there and be shot at?" I croaked.

"Pretty much, yes. Real waste of missiles, but nobody seems to be able to give the order to stop." Liang shook his head. "Of course the Guardians may be interfering with communication. They kind of like it when whoever's shooting at them has to use up all their ammunition."

"Liang. What happened to Terese?"

He glanced at the door. "I think they're going to be in to talk with you about that."

He was right. The archway around the cabin's door blinked green and the door slid back. A shortish man with bright green eyes strode in, followed closely by the scarred, tattooed man who'd shot me full of tranqs. He wore the Guardian's blue uniform tunic, and I was grateful, because the look in his blue eyes spoke strongly of the desire to work cold-blooded murder. Behind him came a tall, blond woman I recognized as Dr. Gwin.

I swung my legs over the edge of the bed. My vision sloshed again, but I found my feet and my balance and was able to stand, though barely. I'd thought my weakness was due to exhaustion, but now I could tell it was because the gravity in this place was far heavier than I was used to.

"I am Captain Amerand Jireu of Erasmus Security Operations," I said. "And I surrender."

The man with green eyes nodded seriously. "I am Marshal-Steward Misao Smith," he said. "Tell me what happened."

And I did. In disjointed, rambling bits, I told them all

out the Grand Sentinel, about how I had been used, and
w Terese had saved me. How we'd managed to get to
livion. How they'd taken her.

How I'd tried to save her and done nothing at all.

It took hours. The Marshal-Steward had dozens of quick,
cise questions and Dr. Gwin had dozens more. When I
ged, they gave me water to drink. Food was delivered.
amed fish, fresh vegetables, flat bread, and something I'd
rd of but never tasted: tomato soup.

Liang just sat by the window. He watched my interro-
ion some of the time. Some of the time he watched the
works, which were growing less and less frequent.

Finally, even Dr. Gwin ran out of questions. The Marshal-
ward stood up and bowed. "Thank you for your assis-
ce, Captain Jireu."

"Can you tell me how Field Commander Drajeske is?" I
ed.

"She's stable," said Dr. Gwin. "Your information might
p us do better."

d that was more or less it. I was left in my well-appointed
in for a week. I was fed and comfortable. And God-
ne knew how much water I was given. There was water
drinking and for cleaning, and even for pissing in, avail-
e at any moment of the day. Liang came to visit me on
:asion, to give me the news and to make sure I was all
ht. Other saints came at other times, mostly in medical
r to supervise me in my exercises so I could stand up to
rigors of their too-strong gravity. They were chatty, but
nehow never managed to tell me much. The leadership
the Blood Family had collapsed and there was anarchy
Fortress. At first the Solarans didn't leave because, they

said, there was no one official to tell them to leave, since *Saeo* Mai and *Saeo* Esteban had abandoned their offices and no one could manage to organize a vote to replace them. Then they didn't leave because, they said, there was a refugee crisis, which Liang said had increased to amazing proportions since the Guardians had put the word out that anybody who wanted to be taken off the moons would be.

Then they couldn't leave, they said, because they had to make sure nobody on Fortress denied freedom of movement to people who were actively seeking asylum inside the Pax Solaris.

It was sometime into the eighth day when my door opened again and Vijay Kochinski entered. They'd removed his scars and tattoos, and his hair was a brushlike stubble sticking up from his tanned scalp.

"They're going to try to bring Terese around," he said. "You can watch if you want."

"Thank you." I got up out of my chair, and in a flash, his hand caught my arm, squeezing with an iron grip. He bent close to my ear so I could feel his hot breath on my skin.

"They're keeping Siri Baijahn in a drugged coma until they can work out how best to save her mind. They don't know if they *can* save her, or Terese," he whispered. "If this doesn't work, you had better get yourself elsewhere in a hurry, because I am not losing anyone else to your fuckless system, do you hear me?"

"It's not my system," I whispered back, but I knew that was a lie.

Without letting go, Vijay Kochinski walked me down the ship's corridors. The padded walls were all shaded in pleasant colors and the screens set at regular intervals showed

·nes from other worlds: natural settings mostly, but here
d there was a window onto some glittering city.

He took me into a small room. The back wall was a sin-
silver screen. He touched it and it seemed to clear. A few
t from me, Terese lay on a metal bed. She had tubes in
r arms and in her nose. The satisfied smile was still on her
e. People in medical whites swarmed around her, talking
fast in such deep technical language, I could barely rec-
nize one word in three. To one side stood the Marshal-
ward in his blue uniform coat. Next to him stood a tall,
n man with greying hair and dark rings under his eyes.

"We're ready," said Dr. Gwin.

The Marshal-Steward and the lean man came forward.
sao Smith pulled out a flat box from the pack he had
ng over his shoulder and handed it to Dr. Gwin. She and
r assistants laid sprays and patches against Terese. They
led out codes and levels. Misao Smith looked down at
r, and I recognized the stillness that came over his face.
did not want anyone to see what he was thinking.

"David." He spoke the name as a quiet order.

David. It was real to me, David. It was always real.

The lean man stepped up. "What do I do?"

"As soon as they've isolated the moment inside Jerimiah,
u hold her."

"What if it doesn't work? What then?"

The Marshal-Steward just looked at him. The other
an, David, gripped the bed rail until his knuckles turned
ite.

Dr. Gwin turned from her conference with a pair of the
edical technicians. Her hands were covered with white
oves. Words and codes flickered across them as she
uched Terese's forehead and her throat.

"What are they doing?" I whispered. I reached out, but I touched nothing but the smooth screen.

"They think she's trapped in a hallucination," said Vijay. "They think she's convinced herself she's back in her cell with the Redeemers. But they believe they've found a way to convince her she's being rescued."

"Now," Dr. Gwin said.

David licked his lips and slipped his arms around Terese, cradling her close. "Easy, Terese. Easy. I've got you."

And Terese stirred. She twisted and she struggled, shrinking away.

"Easy, Terese. Easy," said David. "I've got you."

"Bianca?" whispered Terese.

"It's me, Terese," he said, although his voice cracked. "I've got you."

But she twisted away from him again. "You're dead. You killed him. I can't die. I can't open the door."

"Terese, come on out. Jo is looking for you."

Misao grabbed the lean man's arm, digging his fingers in hard. "Stay with the script."

David turned on him. "You did not bring me here to just play Bianca. Any one of you could have done that. You wanted it to be me because I'm the one who can bring her back. So you shut up and let me talk to my wife!"

It was real to me. I laid my hand on the screen as if it were window glass.

David turned back to Terese again. He reached out a trembling hand and ran his fingers through her curling hair. "Terese? Did you hear me? Jo's looking for you. You promised you'd talk to Jo, and if you don't, she's not going to forgive either one of us."

"Jo?" whispered Terese. Dr. Gwin ran a cloth over her mouth. More water, I guessed.

"She's out here," David was saying. "And Allie and Dale."

"Who are they?" I murmured, not even turning to glance the man beside me.

"Her children," Vijay said. "That's her husband with her."

Inside me something crumbled into ash.

"Bianca," Terese said. "You don't . . ."

"It's not Bianca, Terese. It's me." His voice was strained. I could feel how close he was to breaking. "Won't you come out?"

"Dylan?"

Tears glittered in her husband's eyes. "No, Terese. Open your eyes. You'll see."

"Amerand?"

My heart stopped. But David just wrapped his hand around hers. He pressed a kiss against her forehead. She stirred, and she turned her face toward him.

"David."

And Terese Drajeske opened her eyes.

ABOUT THE AUTHOR

C. L. ANDERSON has been known to tell people she lives in a stately Victorian home on a windswept island in Lake Superior with her three sisters and their pet wolf, Manfred. She has also been known to tell people she is a science-fiction writer living near Ann Arbor, Michigan, with her husband, son, and cat. What is known is that this is her first novel for Spectra, and more of her work can be found at *www.bookviewcafe.com.*